D0953122

THE
SHAPE
OF
WATER

GUILLERMO DEL TORO
AND
DANIEL KRAUS

FEIWEL AND FRIENDS
NEW YORK

To love,

in its many forms and shapes

A FEIWEL AND FRIENDS BOOK
An imprint of Macmillan Publishing Group, LLC
175 Fifth Avenue, New York, NY 10010

THE SHAPE OF WATER. Text copyright © 2018 by Necropolis, Inc.
Illustrations copyright © 2018 by James Jean. All rights reserved.
Printed in the United States of America.

Our books may be purchased in bulk for promotional, educational, or business use.
Please contact your local bookseller or the Macmillan Corporate and Premium Sales Department at
(800) 221-7945 ext. 5442 or by e-mail at MacmillanSpecialMarkets@macmillan.com.

Library of Congress Control Number: 2017939959
ISBN 978-1-250-16534-3 (trade hardcover)
ISBN 978-1-250-30258-8 (international edition)

Book design by Patrick Collins
Feiwel and Friends logo designed by Filomena Tuosto
First edition, 2018

1 3 5 7 9 10 8 6 4 2

fiercereads.com

For brief as water falling will be death,
and brief as flower falling, or leaf,
brief as the taking, and the giving, breath;
thus natural, thus brief, my love, is grief.
—CONRAD AIKEN

It doesn't matter if the water is cold or warm
if you're going to have to wade through it anyway.
—PIERRE TEILHARD DE CHARDIN

PRIMORDIUM

1

RICHARD STRICKLAND READS the brief from General Hoyt. He's at eleven thousand feet. The twin-prop taking hits as hard as a boxer's fists. The last leg of Orlando to Caracas to Bogotá to Pijuayal, the knuckles of the Peru-Colombia-Brazil crotch. The brief is indeed brief and punctuated with black redactions. It explains, in staccato army poetry, the legend of a jungle god. The Brazilians call it Deus Brânquia. Hoyt wants Strickland to escort the hired hunters. Help them capture the thing, whatever it is, and haul it to America.

Strickland's eager to get it done. It'll be his last mission for General Hoyt. He's certain of it. The things he did in Korea under Hoyt have shackled him to the general for twelve years. It's a form of blackmail, their relationship, and Strickland wants washed clean of it. He pulls off this job, the biggest yet, and he'll have the capital to recuse himself from Hoyt's service. Then he can travel home to Orlando, to Lainie, to the kids, Timmy and Tammy. He can be the husband and father Hoyt's dirty work has never permitted him to be. He can be a whole new man. He can be free.

He turns his attention back to the brief. Adopts the callous military mind-set. Those sorry fucks down in South America. It's not subnormal farming practices to blame for their poverty. Of course not. It's a Gill-god displeased with their stewardship of the jungle. The brief is smudged because the twin-prop is leaking. He blots it on his pants. US military, it reads, believes Deus Brânquia has properties of significant military application. His job will be to look out for "US interests" and keep the crew, as Hoyt puts it, "motivated." Strickland knows firsthand Hoyt's theories on motivation.

Think of Lainie. Better yet, given what he might have to do, don't think of her.

The pilot's Portuguese profanities are justified. Landing is a terror. The runway is hacked from pure jungle. Strickland staggers from the plane to find the heat is visible, a floating bruise. A Colombian in a Brooklyn Dodgers T-shirt and Hawaiian shorts waves him toward a pickup. A little girl in the truck bed throws a banana at Strickland's head, and he's too nauseated from the flight to react. The Colombian drives him to town, three square blocks of clacking, wood-wheeled fruit carts and shoeless, potbellied children. Strickland wanders the shops and purchases on instinct: a cigarette lighter, bug juice, sealable plastic bags, foot talc. The countertops across which he pushes pesos seep tears from the humidity.

He studied a phrase book on the plane. "Você viu Deus Brânquia?"

Merchants chuckle and flutter their hands over their necks. Strickland hasn't the faintest fucking clue. These people smell sharp and steely, like freshly slaughtered livestock. He walks away on a blacktop road that is melting beneath his shoes and sees a spiny rat threshing in the black muck. It is dying, and slowly. Its bones will blanch, sink into the tar. It is the nicest road Strickland will see for a year and a half.

2

THE ALARM SHAKES the bedside table. Without opening her eyes, Elisa feels for the clock's ice-cold stopper. She'd been in a deep, soft, warm dream and wants it back, one more tantalizing minute. But the dream eludes wakeful pursuit; it always does. There was water, dark water—that much she remembers. Tons of it, pressing at her, only she didn't drown. She breathed inside it better, in fact, than she does here, in waking life, in drafty rooms, in cheap food, in sputtering electricity.

Tubas blare from downstairs and a woman screams. Elisa sighs into her pillow. It's Friday, and a new movie has opened at the Arcade Cinema Marquee, the around-the-clock theater directly below, and that means new dialogue, sound effects, and music cues she'll need to integrate into her wake-up rituals if she wishes to ward off continual, heart-stopping frights. Now it's trumpets; now it's masses of men hollering. She opens her eyes, first to the 10:30 p.m. of the clock and then to the blades of film-projector light finning through the floor-boards, imbuing dust bunnies with Technicolor hues.

She sits up and arches her shoulders against the cold. Why does the air smell like cocoa? The strange scent is joined by an unpleasant noise: a fire engine northeast of Patterson Park. Elisa lowers her feet to the chilled floor and watches the projector light shift and flicker. This new film, at least, is brighter than the last one, a black-and-white picture called *Carnival of Souls*, and the rich colors pouring across her feet allow her to slide back into dreamy make-believe: She's got money, plenty of it, and groveling salesmen are slipping onto her feet an array of colorful shoes. You look ravishing, miss. In a pair of shoes like this, why, you'll conquer the world.

Instead, the world has conquered her. No amount of gewgaws picked up for pennies at garage sales and pinned to the walls can hide the termite-gnawed wood or distract from the bugs that scatter the second she turns on the light. She chooses not to notice; it's her only hope to get through the night, the following day, the subsequent life. She crosses to the kitchenette, sets the egg timer, drops three eggs into a pot of water, and continues to the bathroom.

Elisa takes baths exclusively. She peels off her flannel as the water pours. Women at work leave behind ladies' magazines on the cafeteria tables, and countless articles have informed Elisa of the precise inches of her body she should fixate on. But hips and breasts can't compare to the puffy pink keloid scars on either side of her neck. She leans in until her naked shoulder bumps the glass. Each scar is three inches long and drawn from jugular to larynx. In the distance, the siren advances; she's lived her whole life in Baltimore, thirty-three years, and can track the fire engine down Broadway. Her neck scars are a road map, too, aren't they? Places she's been best not to remember.

Dipping her ears under bathwater amplifies the cinema's sounds. *To die for Chemosh*, cries a girl in the movie, *is to live forever!* Elisa has no idea if she's heard this right. She slides a sliver of soap between her hands, enjoying the feeling of being wetter than water, so slippery she can cut through liquid like a fish. Impressions of her pleasant dream press against her, heavy as a man's body. It is abruptly, over-whelmingly erotic; she skates her soapy fingers between her thighs. She's gone on dates, had sex, all that. But it's been years. Men meet a woman who's mute, they take advantage of her. Never once on a date did a man ever try to communicate, not really. They just grabbed, and took, as if she, voiceless as an animal, *was* an animal. This is better. The man from the dream, hazy as he is, is better.

But the timer, that infernal pip-squeak, ding-a-ling-a-ling-a-lings. Elisa splutters, embarrassed even though she's alone, and stands, her limbs shiny and draining. She wraps in a bathrobe and pads shivering back to the kitchen, where she kills the stovetop and accepts the clock's bad news: 11:07 p.m. Where did she lose so much time? She shrugs into a random bra, buttons a random blouse, smooths a random skirt. She'd felt ragingly alive in the dream, but now she's as inert as the eggs cooling on a plate. There's a mirror here in the bedroom, too, but she chooses not to look at it, just in case her hunch is true and she's invisible.

3

ONCE STRICKLAND FINDS the fifty-foot riverboat in its appointed place, he uses his new lighter to burn Hoyt's brief, SOP. Now the whole thing is black, he thinks, the whole thing is redacted. Like everything down here, the boat offends his military standards. It's garbage nailed to garbage. The smokestack is patched with hammered tin. The tires atop the gunwales look deflated. A sheet stretched between four poles offers the only shade on the vessel. It'll be hot. That's good. Burn away torturous thoughts of Lainie; their cool, clean home; the whisper of the Florida palms. Boil his brain into the kind of fury a mission like this requires.

Dirty brown water squirts between dock slats. Some of the crew are white, some tan, some red-brown. Some are painted and pierced. All lug wet crates across a plank that dramatically dips with the weight. Strickland follows and reaches a hull stenciled *Josefina*. Small portholes suggest the most perfunctory of lower decks, just big enough for a captain. The very word *captain* rankles him. Hoyt's the only captain here, and Strickland is Hoyt's proxy. He's in no mood for fatuous ship-steerers who think they're in charge.

He finds the captain, a bespectacled Mexican with a white beard, white shirt, white pants, and white straw hat signing manifests with excessive flourishes. He shouts "Mr. Strickland!" and Strickland feels like he's been transported inside one of his son's *Looney Tunes*: *Meester Streekland!* He'd committed the captain's name to memory somewhere above Haiti: Raúl Romo Zavala Henríquez. It fits, starting off well enough before ballooning into pomposity.

"Look! Escoces and puros cubanos, my friend, all for you." Henríquez hands over a cigar, fires up one of his own, and pours two glasses. Strickland was trained not to drink on the job but permits Henríquez his toast. "¡To la aventura magnífico!" They drink, and Strickland admits to himself that it feels good. Anything to ignore, just for a while, the looming shadow of General Hoyt, what it might mean for Strickland's future if he fails to properly "motivate" Henríquez. For the duration of the scotch, the heat of his innards equalizes with that of the jungle.

Henríquez is a man who has spent too much time blowing smoke rings: They are perfect.

"Smoke, drink, enjoy! It is all you will know of luxury for much time. It is good you came no later, Mr. Strickland. *Josefina* is impatient to depart. Like Amazonia, it waits for no man." Strickland doesn't like the implication. He sets down his glass and stares. Henríquez laughs, claps his hands. "Quite right. Men like us, pioneers of the Sertão, it is not necessary we express excitement. Los brasileños honor us with a word: *sertanista*. It has a fine sound, sí? It stirs the blood?"

Henríquez recounts in dull detail his trip to an outpost of the Instituto de Biologia Maritima. He claims that he has handled—with his own dos manos!—limestone fossils said to resemble descriptions of Deus Brânquia. Scientists date the fossils to the Devonian Period, which, did you know, Meester Streekland, is part of the Paleozoic Era? This, Henríquez intones, is what attracts men like them to Amazonia. Where primitive life yet thrives. Where man might page back the calendar and touch the untouchable.

Strickland holds his question for an hour. "Did you get the charter?"

Henríquez stubs his cigar and frowns out the porthole. There he finds something to grin about and gestures imperiously.

"You see the face tattoos? The nose dowels? These are not Indians like your Tonto. These are índios bravos. Every kilometer of the Amazon, from Negro-Branco to Xingu, they know in their blood. From four different tribes they come. And I have secured them as guides! It is impossible, Mr. Strickland, for our expedition to become lost."

Strickland repeats: "Did you get the charter?"

Henríquez fans himself with his hat. "Your Americans mailed me mimeographs. Very well. Our expedição científica will follow their wiggly lines for as long as we can. Then, Mr. Strickland, we move on foot! We locate the vestigios, the remains of original tribes. These people have suffered from industry more than you can imagine. The jungle swallows their screams. We, however, will come in peace. We will offer gifts. If Deus Brânquia exists, they will be the ones to tell us where to find it."

In General Hoyt's parlance, the captain is motivated. Strickland gives him that. But there are warning signs, too. If Strickland knows anything about untamed territory, it is that it stains you, inside and out. You do not wear white clothing unless you do not know what the hell you are doing.

4

ELISA AVOIDS THE western wall of her bedroom until the last moment, so that the sight might strike with inspiration. It isn't a big room, so it is not a big wall: eight feet by eight feet, and every inch covered in shoes bought over the years in budget or secondhand stores. Feather-lite spectator pumps in cherry and spice. Two-tone Customcraft with toes like garden spades. Champagne satin peep-toe heels, like a pile of fallen wedding chiffon. Three-inch Town & Countrys, brilliant red: wearing them looks like your feet are softly layered with rose petals. Relegated to the margins are the dirtied strapless mules, sling-back sandals, plastic penny loafers, and ugly nubucks of nostalgic value only.

Each shoe hangs upon a tiny nail that she, common renter, had no right to insert. Time is against her, but she takes some of it anyway, carefully selecting Daisy-brand pumps with a blue leather flower on a clear plastic throat, as if the choice is of utmost importance. And it is. The Daisys will be the only insurgency she brings off tonight, and every night. Feet are what connect you to the ground, and when you are poor, none of that ground belongs to you.

She sits on the bed to put them on. It is like a knight shoving his hands into a pair of steel gauntlets. As she wiggles the toe for fit, she lets her eyes stray across the slag heap of old LPs. Most of them were bought used years ago, and nearly all carry memories of joy pressed, right along with the music, into the polymer plastic.

The Voice of Frank Sinatra: the morning she helped a school crossing guard free downy brown chicks from under a sewage grate. Count Basie's *One O'Clock Jump*: the day she saw a clobbered baseball, rare as a red-footed falcon, pop out of Memorial Stadium and ricochet off a fire hydrant. Bing Crosby's *Stardust*: the afternoon she and Giles saw Stanwyck and MacMurray in *Remember the Night* at the theater below, and Elisa lay on her bed the rest of the day, dropping the needle on Bing and wondering if she, like Stanwyck's good-hearted thief, was serving a sentence in this harsh life, and if anyone, like MacMurray, would be waiting for her the day she was freed.

Enough: It's pointless. No one's waiting for her and no one ever has, least of all the punch clock at work. She puts on her coat, grabs the plate of eggs. The curious smell of cocoa is undeniable as she exits into a short hallway cluttered with dusty film cans holding who knows what celluloid treasures. To the right, the sole other apartment. She knuckles it twice before entering.

5

WITHIN THE HOUR, they depart. Delight, say the guides, is the dry season; it is called verão. Tragedy is the wet season; no one will even tell Strickland what it's called. The legacy of the previous wet season are furos, flooded shortcuts across the river's bends, and *Josefina* takes them while she can. These oxbow switchbacks transform the Amazon into an animal. It dashes. It hides. It pounces. Henríquez hoots with joy and throttles the engine, and the green, peaty jungle fills with toxic black smoke. Strickland grips the rail, gazes into the water. It is milk-chocolate brown with marshmallow froth. Fifteen-foot elephant grass bristles along the banks like the back of a colossal, wakening bear.

Henríquez likes to hand the controls to the first mate so he can take notes in his logbook. He boasts that he writes for publication and fame. Everyone will know the name of the great explorer Raúl Romo Zavala Henríquez. He caresses the logbook's leather, likely dreaming of an author photo of appropriate smugness. Strickland smothers his hate, disgust, and fear. All three get in the way. All three *give* you away. Hoyt taught him that in Korea. Just do your job. The most advantageous feeling is to feel nothing at all.

Monotony, though, might be the jungle's stealthiest killer. Day after day, *Josefina* traces an endless ribbon of water beneath expanding spirals of mist. One day Strickland glances upward to find a large black bird like a greasy smear across the blue sky. A vulture. Now that he's noticed it, he finds it every day, making lazy loops, anticipating his demise. Strickland is well armed, a Stoner M63 assault rifle in the hold and a Model 70 Beretta in his holster, and he itches to shoot the bird down. The bird is Hoyt, watching. The bird is Lainie, saying good-bye. He doesn't know which.

Sailing is treacherous at night, so the boat anchors. Usually Strickland chooses to stand alone at the bow. Let the crew whisper. Let the índios bravos stare like he's some kind of American monster. The moon this particular evening is a great hole carved through nightflesh to reveal pale, luminescent bone, and he does not notice Henríquez creep up on him.

"Do you see? The frolicking pink?"

Strickland is furious, not at the captain, but himself. What sort of soldier leaves his back exposed? Plus, he's caught gazing at the moon. It's feminine, something Lainie would do while asking him to hold her hand. He shrugs, hoping Henríquez will go away. Instead, the captain gestures with his logbook. Strickland looks into the distance and sees a sinuous leap and silver spray.

"Boto," Henríquez says. "River dolphin. What do you think? Two meters? Two and a half? Only the males are so pink. We are lucky to see one. Very solitary, the male boto. Keeps to himself."

Strickland wonders if Henríquez is playing games, mocking his offish proclivities. The captain takes off his straw hat, and his white hair glows in the moonlight.

"Do you know the legend of the boto? I suppose not. They teach you more about guns and bullets, eh? Many of the indigenous believe the pink river dolphin is an encantado, a shape-shifter. On nights like this, he transforms himself into a man of irresistible good looks and walks to the nearest village. You can tell him by the hat he wears to hide his blowhole. In this disguise, he seduces the village's most beautiful women and leads them back to his home beneath the river. Wait and see. We will find very few women along the river at night, so afraid are they of encantado kidnap. But I think it is a hopeful story. Is not some underwater paradise preferable to a life of poverty and incest and violence?"

"It's coming closer." Strickland didn't mean to say it aloud.

"Ah! Then we should definitely rejoin the others. They say looking into the eyes of an encantado curses you with nightmares until you are driven insane."

Henríquez pats Strickland on the back like the friend he isn't and ambles away, whistling. Strickland kneels beside the rail. The dolphin dives like a knitting needle. It probably knows what boats are. It probably wants fish scraps. Strickland unholsters the Beretta and takes aim where he estimates the dolphin will emerge. Fanciful fables don't deserve to live. Harsh reality, that's what Hoyt seeks and what Strickland must find if he hopes to get out of here alive. The dolphin's shape becomes visible beneath the water. Strickland waits. He wants to look it in the eyes. He'll be the one to deliver nightmares. He'll be the one to drive the jungle insane.

6

INSIDE THE SECOND apartment, a happy horde greets her: beaming housewives, smirking husbands, ecstatic children, cocksure teenagers. But they're no realer than the roles being played at the Arcade Cinema. They're characters in advertisements, and though these original paintings are executed with terrific skill, not a single one is mounted. *Easy-to-Remove Waterproof Lashes* is being used to block a cold-air crack. *Soft-Glo Face Powder* props open a drafty door. *The Hosiery Woes of 9 Out of 10 Women* has been repurposed as a table to hold paint tins for works in progress. This lack of pride depresses Elisa, though all five cats disagree. The strewn canvases make fabulous plateaus atop which they scout for mice.

One cat preens her whiskers against a toupee, spinning it upon a human skull named, for reasons Elisa can't recall, Andrzej. The artist, Giles Gunderson, hisses and the cat bounds away, mewling of litter-box revenge. Giles leans into his easel and squints through tortoiseshell glasses dappled in paint. A second pair of glasses is propped above his overgrown eyebrows, and a third is perched on the bald peak of his head.

Elisa rises to the toes of her Daisys to look over his shoulder at the painting: a family of disembodied heads hovering over a cupola of red gelatin, the two children jawing like hungry apelings, the father pinching his chin in admiration, and the mother looking satisfied about her rhapsodic brood. Giles is struggling with the father's lips; Elisa knows that men's expressions bedevil him. She leans farther and sees him shape his own lips into the smile he's trying to paint and it's so adorable that Elisa can't resist: She swoops down and gives the old man a kiss on the cheek.

He looks up in surprise, and chuckles.

"I didn't hear you come in! What time is it? Did the sirens wake you? Gird yourself, dearest, for new heights in pathos. The radio says the chocolate factory is on fire. Could anything be more dreadful? I wager children everywhere are tossing in their sleep."

Giles smiles beneath a fastidious pencil mustache and holds up, in each hand, a paintbrush, one red, one green.

"Tragedy and delight," he says, "hand in hand."

Behind Giles, a shoe-box-sized black-and-white television on a wheeled cart pulses static through the guts of a late-night movie. It's Bojangles tap-dancing backward up a staircase. Elisa knows it will cheer up her friend. Quick, before Bojangles has to slow down for Shirley Temple, Elisa makes the two-fingered sign for "look."

Giles does, and he claps his hands together, mashing red paint with green. It is beyond belief what Bojangles does, which is why Elisa is ashamed to feel a burst of ego: She could have kept pace with him better than Shirley Temple, if only the world into which she'd been born had been wholly different. She's always wanted to dance. That's why all the shoes: They are potential energy, just waiting for use. She squints at the television and counts off the beats, ignoring the competing music from the cinema below, and launches into a tap dance in time with Bojangles. It's not bad—whenever Bojangles kicks the face of a step, Elisa kicks the nearest thing, Giles's stool, which makes him laugh.

"You know who else could hotfoot down a staircase? James Cagney! Did we watch *Yankee Doodle Dandy*? Oh, we should. Cagney's coming down a staircase. He feels like a million bucks. And he starts flinging his legs around like his ass is on fire. Complete improvisation, and talk about dangerous! But that's true art, my dear—dangerous."

Elisa holds out the plate of eggs and signs, "Eat, please." He grins sadly and takes the plate.

"I believe without you, I would be a starving artist in the least figurative of senses. Wake me when you get home, won't you? I'll do the buying: breakfast for me, supper for you."

Elisa nods but points sternly at the Murphy bed locked in its upright position.

"When viscous fruit molds call to Giles Gunderson, he answers! Then, I promise: dreamland for me."

He cracks an eggshell against *The Hosiery Woes of 9 Out of 10 Women* and slides one pair of glasses past two others. His face resumes mimicking the smile he's trying to paint: that smile is a little bigger now, and Elisa is glad. Only the crashing fanfare of the downstairs movie's final frame jars her back into action. She knows what happens next: The words *The End* materialize on the screen, the list of featured players rolls, the houselights rise, and there is no more hiding who you really are.

7

THE NATIVES ARE mutants, unslowed by the swelter. They hike, they climb, they hack. Strickland has never seen so many machetes. They call them falcóns. Call them whatever you want. He'll take his M63, thank you. The inland trek begins on a penetration road some forgotten hero plowed straight into the rain forest. By 1100 hours, they find the plow strangled by creepers, the seat sprouting philodendron. Fine—he won't shoot his way through the jungle after all. He takes a machete.

Strickland considers himself strong, but his muscles are liquid by afternoon. The jungle, like the vulture, detects weakness. Vines rip hats from heads. Spiked bamboos stab outstretched limbs. Wasps with finger-length stingers seethe atop papery nests, waiting for a reason to swarm, and everyone who tiptoes past shudders in relief. One man leans against a tree. The bark squishes. It is not bark. The tree is layered with termites, and now they're thronging up his sleeve, looking to burrow. The guides have no maps but keep pointing, keep pointing, keep pointing.

Weeks pass. Maybe months. Nights are worse than days. They strip off trousers rock-heavy with dried mud, pour liters of sweat from their boots, and lay in mosquito-net hammocks, helpless as babies, listening to the frog croaks and the malarial moan of mosquitoes. How can so much space feel so claustrophobic? He sees Hoyt's face everywhere, in the burls of tree fungus, the patterns of tracaja turtle shells, the flight formations of blue macaws. Lainie he doesn't see anywhere. He can barely feel her, like a dying pulse. It alarms him, but there is so much that alarms him, second by second.

Days into the hike, they reach a village of vestigios. A small clearing. Thatched malocas. Animal hides stretched between trees. Henríquez darts about, telling the crew to stow their machetes. Strickland complies, but only to better grip his rifle. Being armed, isn't that his job? Minutes later, three faces surface from the maloca dark. Strickland shivers, a queasy sensation in such heat. Soon bodies follow the faces, picking their way across the clearing like spiders.

Strickland feels diseased on sight. His rifle twitches. Wipe them out. He's shocked at the thought. It's a Hoyt thought. But it's attractive, isn't it? Get this mission done, fast. Go home, see if he's the same man who left Orlando. While Henríquez carefully unveils his gifts of cooking pots and one of the guides tries to establish a shared pidgin, a dozen more vestigios bleed from the shadows to stare at his guns, his machete, his ghostly white skin. He feels flayed and finds no pleasure in the following festivities. Sour wildfowl eggs cooked over a fire. Some half-ass ritual involving the daubing of paint upon the crew's necks and faces. Strickland waits it out. Henríquez will get around to asking them about Deus Brânquia. He better do it soon. There are only so many insect bites Strickland will accept before he starts doing things his way.

When Henríquez leaves the fire to hang his hammock, Strickland puts himself in the way.

"You gave up."

"There are other vestigios. We will find them."

"Months down the river and you're just going to walk away."

"They think speaking about Deus Brânquia robs it of its power."

"That could be a sign it's close. That they're protecting it."

"Oh, you have come to believe?"

"It doesn't matter what I believe. I'm here to get it and go home."

"It is not so simple as one protecting the other. The jungle is more, how do you say it? Back and forth? Existing together? These people believe all natural things are connected. To introduce invaders such as we, it is setting a fire. Everything burns." Henríquez's eyes trail down to the M63. "You are holding your gun very tightly, Mr. Strickland."

"I've got a family. You want to be out here a whole year? Two years? You think your crew will stick around that long?"

Strickland lets his glare do its work. Henríquez is no longer strong enough to resist such a look. Beneath his filthy white suit, he's a skeleton. A rash of tick bites on his neck suppurates and bleeds from scratching. Strickland has seen him wander off the trail to throw up out of sight of his men. He grips his logbook to stop his hands from trembling. Strickland wants to hurl the worthless pile of papers to the ground and fill it with lead. Maybe that would keep the captain motivated.

"The young tribesmen," Henríquez sighs. "Gather them after the elders are asleep. We have ax heads and whetstones to trade. They might still talk."

Talk they do. The adolescents are greedy for loot and describe Deus Brânquia in such detail that Strickland finds himself convinced. This is no legend like the pink river dolphin. This is a living organism, some sort of fish-man that swims and eats and breathes. The boys, beguiled by Henríquez's map, tap the Tapajós tributary region in recognition. Deus Brânquias's seasonal migrations stretch back generations, the guide translates. Strickland says that doesn't make sense. Are there more than one of them? The guide asks. Long ago, the boys say. Now there is but one. Some of the boys begin to cry. Strickland's interpretation is that they are worried their greed has put their Gill-god in danger. It has.

8

Two stores stand opposite Elisa's bus stop. Thousands of times Elisa has stared at them; zero times has she visited either during business hours, sensing that to do so would be akin to shattering a dream. The first is Kosciuszko Electronics. Today's deal is Big Screen Rectangular Color TVs With Walnut Grained Finish, and several models, each with legs like Sputnik's antenna, are broadcasting the night's final images. An American flag cedes to a "Seal of Good Practice" screen before signing off, a sight that confirms Elisa's lateness. She prays for the bus to come. Who did the girl in the movie pray to tonight? Chemosh? Maybe Chemosh works faster than God.

She shifts her eyes to the second store, Julia's Fine Shoes. She does not know who this Julia is, but tonight she envies her so much she is pinpricked by tears, this bold, independent woman with a business all her own, inevitably beautiful with bouncy hair and a bounce in her step, so confident in her store's value to the Fells Point neighborhood that instead of turning the lights off at night, she leaves a spotlight upon a single pair of shoes placed upon an ivory column.

The gambit works. My, how it works. On nights when she isn't running behind, Elisa crosses the road and rests her forehead against the glass to get a better look. These shoes don't belong in Baltimore; she's not sure they belong outside of Parisian runways. They are her size, square-toed, and so low slung they'd slip off the foot if not for the snug, inward-leaning heel. They look like hooves in the best way: of unicorns, of nymphs, of sylphs. Every inch of lamé is encrusted with glittering silver, and the inserts are as shiny as mirrors— she can literally see herself in them. The shoes stir in Elisa feelings she thought that the orphanage had beaten out of her as a youth. That she could go places. That she could be something. That all was within the realm of the possible.

Chemosh answers her call: The bus hisses down the hill. The driver, per usual, is too old, too tired, too spiritless to drive safely. The bus makes its hard right on Eastern, hard right on Broadway, and barrels north past the heartbeat of fire-engine lights and the blood spill of the melting chocolate factory. The leaping, licking destruction is, at least, a kind of life, and Elisa contorts herself to watch it, feeling for a minute that she isn't rumbling through civilization's scabwork, but rather darting through some vicious, vital jungle.

All of it shrinks from the long, sulfur-lit driveway of Occam Aerospace Research Center. Elisa presses her cold face to the colder window to make out the illuminated clock on the sign: 11:55. Her shoes touch a single stair on her bound from the bus. The changeover from the busy swing shift to the tiny graveyard shift is chaotic, and it allows Elisa to move quickly, gazelling from the bus and deering up the service sidewalk. Beneath the merciless outdoor floodlights—every light at Occam is merciless—her shoes are blue blurs.

It's a single-floor elevator ride down, but some of the labs are more like hangars and the trip takes half a minute. The car opens into a two-story staging area, where stanchions direct staff along a narrowing path. Ten feet above the floor, in a Plexiglased observation chamber, stands David Fleming. Born with a clipboard instead of a left hand, he lowers it to review his subjects. It was Fleming who interviewed her for her job over a decade ago, and he's still here, his hyena scrutiny pushing him up the throat of command year after year. Now he runs the whole building yet still can't help meddling with bottom-rung employees. Over the equal period of time, Elisa has gone where janitors go: nowhere.

Elisa curses her Daisys. They stand out, which is the point, but there's a double edge. Her fellow graveyarders are up ahead: Antonio, Duane, Lucille, Yolanda, and Zelda, the first three disappearing down the hall while Zelda searches for her punch card as if choosing from a menu. The cards go into the same slots every day; Zelda is stalling for Elisa's sake, because Yolanda is behind Zelda and if Yolanda gets a shot, she'll dawdle at the punch clock to make Elisa one crucial minute late.

It shouldn't be this cutthroat. Zelda is black and fat. Yolanda is Mexican and homely. Antonio is a cross-eyed Dominican. Duane is of mixed race and has no teeth. Lucille is albino. Elisa is mute. To Fleming, they are all the same: unfit for other work and therefore easy to trust. It humiliates Elisa that he might be right. She wishes she could talk so she might stand on the locker-room bench and stir her coworkers with a speech about how they need to look out for one another. But that's not how Occam is set up. As far as she can tell, it's not how America is set up, either.

Except Zelda, who has always been protective of Elisa. Zelda is digging through her purse for glasses everyone knows she doesn't wear, waving off Yolanda's gripes about the ticking clock. Elisa decides that Zelda's boldness must be matched by her own. She thinks of Bojangles and darts off, mamboing through yawners, fox-trotting past coat-buttoners. Fleming will spot her speeding blue shoes, and her behavior will be noted upon a checklist; at Occam, anything beyond a tired slump earns suspicion. Yet in the seconds it takes Elisa to reach Zelda, her dancing frees her from all of it. She rises above the underground and floats as if she'd never left that lovely, warm bath.

9

FOOD RUNS OUT southwest of Santarém. The crew is weak, starving, light-headed. Happy, chattering monkeys are everywhere, mocking them. So Strickland starts firing. Monkeys fall like aguaje fruit, and men gasp in horror. This annoys Strickland. He advances against a gut-shot monkey, machete raised. The soft-furred animal curls into a woeful ball, its hands pressed over its sobbing face. It is like a child. Like Timmy or Tammy. This is like slaughtering children. He flashes back to Korea. The children, the women. Is this what he's become? The surviving monkeys scream in sorrow, and the sound pins into his skull. He turns away and attacks a tree with the machete until it spits white wood.

Other men gather the bodies and drop them in boiling water. Don't they hear the monkeys screaming? Strickland scoops up moss, plugs his ears with it. It doesn't help. The screaming, the screaming. Dinner is rubbery gray balls of monkey gristle. He doesn't deserve to eat but does anyway. The screaming, the screaming.

The wet season, whatever the fuck they call it, sniffs them out. The cloudburst is hot, like offal splatter. Henríquez quits trying to wipe steam from his glasses. He walks blind. He *is* blind, thinks Strickland. Blind to believe he could head up this expedition. Henríquez, who's never fought a war. Henríquez, who can't hear the monkeys' screams. The screams, Strickland realizes, are just like those of the villagers in Korea. As terrible as these sounds are, they tell Strickland what to do.

There's no need to incite a coup. Attrition does the job. A candirú spine fish, agitated by driving rain, darts up the first mate's urethra while he's pissing into the river. Three men take him to the nearest town and are never seen again. The next day, the Peruvian engineer wakes up spotted with purple punctures. A vampire bat. He and a friend are superstitious. They're gone. Weeks later, a torn mosquito net leads to one of the índios bravos being bitten to death, blanketed in tracuá ants. Finally, the Mexican bosun, best pal to Henríquez, is struck in the throat by a bright green papagaio viper. Seconds later, blood spurts from every pore of his body. There's no hope for him. General Hoyt taught Strickland just where to put the Beretta, right at the base of the bosun's skull, so that death comes quick.

Then they are five. With guides, seven. Henríquez hides below-decks, filling his logbook with daymare transcripts. His straw hat, once so crisp, has collapsed into its new role as bedpan. Strickland visits and chuckles at the captain's erratic mumbling.

"Are you motivated?" Strickland asks him. "Are you motivated?"

No one asks Richard Strickland about *his* motivation. Until now, he didn't have an answer. Never gave a shit about Deus Brânquia, that's for sure. Now there's nothing in the world he wants more. Deus Brânquia has done something to him, changed him in ways he suspects can't be reversed. He'll capture it with what's left of the *Josefina* crew—aren't they vestigios now, too? Then it's home, finally home, for whatever it's still worth. He masturbates under a torrid rain, above a nest of baby snakes, picturing silent, tidy sex with Lainie. Two dry bodies shifting like blocks of wood on a boundless veldt of tight, white sheets. He'll make it back there. He will. He'll do what the monkeys say, and then it will all be over.

ELISA USED TO exchange her fancy shoes for sneakers in the locker room. But it'd felt like a chopping, her hand the hatchet. You can't clean in heels—that was among Fleming's maxims the day she'd been hired. *We can't have any slipping and falling. No black heels, either, because there are scientific markings on some of the laboratory floors, and we can't have them marred.* Fleming had a thousand such bromides. These days, though, his attention is mostly elsewhere, and the discomfort of Elisa's heels has become comfort; it keeps her awake, alive to sensation, if barely.

A long-defunct shower room serves as the janitorial closet. Zelda takes her traditional cart, and Elisa hers, which they stock from shelves they're expected to keep in three-month supply. Then their eight cart wheels, plus eight more for the mop buckets, reverberate down Occam's long white hallways like a slow-moving train to nowhere.

They have to be professional at all times; some white-coated men linger about the labs until two or three in the morning. Occam scientists are a strange subspecies of male whose jobs drive them to absolute distraction. Fleming teaches his janitors to promptly exit any lab they find occupied, and it happens periodically. When two scientists finally leave together, they squint in disbelief at each other's watches, chuckling about the hell they're going to catch from their wives, sighing at how they'd rather crash-land at their girlfriends' pads.

They don't censor these comments when they pass Elisa and Zelda. Just as the janitors are trained only to see Occam's dirt and trash, the scientists are trained only to see the manifestations of their brilliance. Long ago, Elisa had indulged fantasies of workplace romance, of meeting that man who danced through the darks of her dreams. It was the notion of a silly young girl. That's the thing about being a janitor, or maid, any type of custodian. You glide unseen, like a fish underwater.

THE VULTURE CIRCLES no more. Strickland had one of the remaining two índios bravos catch it. No idea how the man did it. He doesn't really care. He leashes the bird to a spike he drives into *Josefina's* stern and eats his dinner of dried piranha in front of the bird. Lots of bones in piranha. He spits them, none close enough for the vulture to peck. Its face is purple, its beak red, its neck bassooned. It displays its wingspan but can do nothing but shuffle.

"Watch you starve now," he says. "See how you like it."

Back into the jungle with Henríquez left behind to occupy the boat. Strickland's terms now. No gifts. Lots of guns. Strickland pursues the natives as if General Hoyt himself is standing there giving the order. He teaches the men military hand signals. They learn fast. Their circle contracts around a village, beautiful synchronicity. Strickland shoots the first villager he sees to make a point. The vestigios flop to the mud, blubber secrets. Their last sighting of Deus Brânquia, its exact trajectory.

The translator tells Strickland that the villagers believe him to be the embodiment of a gringo myth—a corta cabeza, a head cutter. This appeals to Strickland. Not some foreign despoiler like Pizarro or Soto, but something born of the jungle itself. His white skin is piranha. His hair is greasy paca. His teeth are fer-de-lance fangs. His limbs are anacondas. He's as much a Jungle-god as Deus Brânquia is a Gill-god, and he doesn't even hear the final order when he gives it, can't hear shit past the screaming monkeys. But the crew hears it. They sever every head in the village.

He can smell Deus Brânquia. Smells like milky silt from the river bottom. Maracuya fruit. Crusted brine. If only he didn't have to sleep. Why don't the índios bravos ever get tired? By moonlight he stalks them and witnesses a ritual. Bark shavings pulverized into a globby pale paste atop a frond. One of them kneels, holds his eyelids open. The other rolls the frond and coaxes from it a single drop of liquid onto each eyeball. The kneeling one pummels the mud with his fists. Strickland is drawn by the suffering. He steps into the open, kneels before the standing man, and holds open his own eyelids. The man hesitates. He calls it buchité, makes gestures of caution. Strickland does not budge. Finally, the man squeezes the frond. A bulb of white buchité fills the world.

The pain is indescribable. Strickland writhes, kicks, howls. But he survives. The burning subsides. He sits up. Wipes the tears. Squints up into the guides' blank faces. He sees them. More than that, he sees *into* them. Along the crooked canals of their wrinkles. Deep inside the forest of their hair. The sun rises, and Strickland discovers an Amazon of infinite depth and color. His body sings with vitality. His legs are cashapona trees, sinewed with roots like fifty extra feet. He peels off his clothes. He doesn't need them. Rain bounces off his naked skin as if from rock.

The Gill-god knows it can't hold back the Jungle-god, not as the latter guns *Josefina* so hard hunks of its hull fall into the river. Deus Brânquia backs itself into a boggy bayou. There the boat breaks down. The bilge pump is clotted and the captain's cabin is filling with water and still Henríquez refuses to move. The Bolivian gets out the tools. The Brazilian hauls forth the harpoon gun, Aqua Lung, and net. The Ecuadorian rolls out a barrel of rotenone, fish pesticide from the jicama vine he claims will force Deus Brânquia to the surface. "Fine," Strickland says. He stands at the bow, naked, arms outstretched, electric with rain, and calls to it. There is no telling for how long. Days, maybe. Maybe weeks.

Deus Brânquia, at last, rises from the shoal, the blood sun carving the Serengeti, the ancient eye of eclipse, the ocean scalping open the new world, the insatiable glacier, the sea-spray spew, the bacterial bite, the single-cell seethe, the species spit, the rivers the vessels to a heart, the mountain's hard erection, the sunflower's swaying thighs, the gray-fur mortification, the pink-flesh fester, the umbilical vine cording us back to the origin. It is all this and more.

The índios bravos drop to their knees, beg forgiveness, cut their own throats with their machetes. The savage, uncontrolled beauty of the creature—Strickland shatters, too. He loses bladder, bowels, stomach. Bible verses from Lainie's pastor drone from a forgotten, squeaky-clean purgatory. The thing that hath been is that which shall be. There is no new thing under the sun. This century is a blink. Everyone is dead. Only the Gill-god and the Jungle-god live.

Strickland's crash is brief and happens but once. He will try to forget it ever happened. When he reaches the city of Belém a week later in a *Josefina* listing forty degrees and half-sunk, he is wearing the translator's clothes. Knowing too much, the man had to be killed. By now, Henríquez is recovered, clinging to the king post and blinking at the vaporous spring, throat bobbing as he works to swallow the fantasy Strickland has fed him. Henríquez was a good captain. Henríquez caught the creature. Everything went as expected. Henríquez looks to his logbook for corroboration, but he can't find it. Strickland fed it to the vulture, watched it choke, watched it seizure and die.

He confirms all of this on a phone call to General Hoyt. Strickland survives the call only with the distraction of green hard candies. Generic label, synthetic taste, but the flavor is achingly concentrated, almost voltaic. He cleaned out every market in Belém, harvesting nearly a hundred bags before making the call. The crunch of the candy is loud. Despite thousands of miles of wire, Hoyt's voice is even louder. As if he'd always been there in the jungle, observing Strickland from behind sticky fronds or veils of mosquitoes.

Strickland can think of nothing that worries him more than lying to General Hoyt, but the actual details of Deus Brânquia's capture, when he tries to recall them, make no sense. He believes the rotenone was, at some point, poured into the water. He recalls the sizzling effervescence. He remembers the M63, the stock a block of ice against his feverish shoulder. Everything else is a dream. The creature's balletic gliding through the depths. Its hidden cave. How it waited there for Strickland. How it did not fight. How monkey screams resounded off the rock. How before Strickland aimed the harpoon, the creature reached out to him. Gill-god, Jungle-god. They could be the same. They could be free.

He squeezes his eyes shut, kills the memory. Hoyt either buys his version of the capture or doesn't care. Hope trembles through Strickland's hands, rattling the receiver. Send me home, he prays. Even though home is a place he can no longer picture. But General Hoyt isn't a man who answers prayers. He requests that Strickland see the mission through to the end. Escort the asset to Occam Aerospace Research Center. Keep it safe and secret while the scientists there do their thing. Strickland swallows shards of candy, tastes blood, hears himself comply. One last leg of the journey. That's all it is. He'll have to relocate to Baltimore. Maybe it won't be so bad. Move the family up north, sit behind a tidy desk in a clean, quiet office. It's a chance, Strickland knows, to start over, if only he can find his way back.

UNEDUCATED WOMEN

1

"I'M GOING TO strangle him. Last week he swears to me he'll get the toilet to stop gurgling so I can get a single decent day's sleep, but when I get home it's like there's someone in there taking an eight-hour tinkle. He says I'm the janitor, why don't I fix it? That's not the point. That is not the point. You think I want to come home, dead on my feet, toes swollen up like gum balls, and just for fun stick my hand into the ice-cold water of the toilet tank? I'll stick his *head* in the tank."

Zelda is carrying on about Brewster. Brewster is Zelda's husband. Brewster is no good. Elisa has lost track of the odd jobs Brewster has held, the multitude of colorful ways he's been fired, the depressive dives he takes into his Barcalounger for weeks at a time. The details don't matter. Elisa is grateful for them however they come and signs appropriate interjections. Zelda began learning sign language the day Elisa arrived, an effort Elisa doesn't believe she can ever repay.

"And like I told you, the kitchen sink's been running, too. Brewster says it's the coupling nut. Whatever you say, Albert Einstein. If you're finished with your theory of relativity, how about you go to a hardware store? And you know what he says? He says I should just sneak a coupling nut from work. Does he even *know* where I work? All the security cameras here? I'm going to be honest with you, hon, about my future plans. I am going to strangle that man and chop him into little pieces and flush those pieces down the toilet so at least when the toilet's keeping me awake I can think about all those Brewster bits zooming off to the sewer where they belong."

Elisa smiles through a yawn, signing back that this is one of Zelda's better murder plots.

"So tonight I get up for work, because somebody in this family needs to afford luxury items like coupling nuts, and the kitchen is the Chesapeake Bay. I march right back to the bedroom, and because I haven't bought my strangling rope yet, I wake up Brewster and say we've got us a Noah's ark situation developing. And he says good. Baltimore hasn't had rain in forever. The man thinks I'm talking about rain."

Elisa studies her copy of the Quality Control Checklist. Fleming doesn't warn them when he changes it; it's how he keeps his workers on their toes. The three-sheet carbon form enumerates the labs, lobbies, restrooms, vestibules, corridors, and stairwells assigned to each janitor, each location tied to a numbered list of correlated tasks. Fixtures, water fountains, baseboards. Elisa yawns again. Landings, partitions, railings. Her eyes keep slipping.

"So I drag him into the kitchen where his socks get all soggy, and you know what he says? He starts talking about Australia. How he heard on the news Australia's drifting two inches a year, and maybe that's the reason everyone's pipes keep coming loose. All the continents, he tells me, used to be shoved together. He says if the whole world is drifting like that, then *all* the pipes are going to bust one day and there's no sense getting upset about it."

Elisa hears the wobble in Zelda's voice and knows where this is headed.

"Now, look, hon. I could have taken that man's head, drowned him in two inches of water, and still made it here by midnight. But you ever known a man who could wake up from a deep sleep and talk like that? He mixes me up so bad. Some weeks we can't put food on the table. Then this man of mine says 'Australia' and suddenly I get emotional? Brewster Fuller will be the death of me, but I'm telling you, the man sees things. Then, for a second, I see them, too. Past Occam, that's for sure. Way past Old West Baltimore. The Chesapeake Bay in my kitchen? This too shall pass."

From the lab to the left, a ruckus. They halt their carts; toilet scrubbers swing from pegs. For weeks, they've heard rumbles of construction behind this door, but that's unexceptional. A room isn't on your list, you ignore it. But tonight the door, previously unadorned, has been given a plate: F-1. Elisa and Zelda have never encountered an F. They always clean together the first half of every night, and together they frown and consult their matching QCCs. There it is, F-1, planted on their lists like a bomb.

The women angle their ears at the door. Voices, footsteps, a crackling noise. Zelda looks worriedly at Elisa; it pains Elisa to see her friend's yakkity mood so easily snuffed. It's her turn, Elisa tells herself, to be the bold one. She falsifies a confident smile and makes the sign for "go ahead." Zelda exhales, gathers her key card, and inserts it into the lock. The gears bite down and Zelda pulls open the door, and in the outrush of chilly air, Elisa has a swift intuition, from out of nowhere, that she has just made a disastrous mistake.

2

LAINIE STRICKLAND SMILES at her brand-new Westinghouse Spray 'N Steam iron. Westinghouse built the atomic engine that fueled the first Polaris submarine. That says something, doesn't it? Not just about a product, mind you, but a *company*. She'd been sitting at the back of Freddie's, her beehive inserted into the pink plastic of the flip-top dryer hood, when she paused, right in the middle of an interesting and, she thought, *important* story about a place called the Mekong Delta, where a group called the Viet Cong had shot down five US helicopters, killing thirty Americans, soldiers just like her Richard, so that she could instead linger upon the full-page advertisement. It depicted a submarine unzipping the white ocean on its dive down.

All those brave boys. The intrinsic danger of water. Would they die, too? Their lives depended on Westinghouse.

The image had resonated enough that she'd resolved to ask Richard what sort of brand of submarine a "Polaris" was. An army man since age nineteen, Richard's reflex to any question about his job is to clam up, so she'd waited until he was well fed and pacified by the popcorn gunfire of *The Rifleman* before asking. Without breaking his appraising gaze of Chuck Connors's ambidextrous gunmanship, he'd shrugged.

"Polaris isn't a brand. It's not like one of your breakfast cereals."

The word *cereal* snapped Timmy from his television stupor. Electricity crackled between the shag carpet and his corduroyed knees as he turned to resume a two-day-old conversation. "Mom, could we please get some Sugar Pops?"

"Froot Loops!" Tammy added. "Oh, Mommy, please?"

Richard has always been gruff. It's just his way. Before the Amazon, though, Richard didn't let her dangle from the cliff of her own ignorance like this, watching her flail without offering a hand. Lainie had yet to figure out the right reaction and chose to laugh at herself. Then Chuck Connors had been replaced by a Hoover Dial-a-Matic with variable Suction Control, operated by an actress who looked a bit like Lainie. Richard chewed his lip and looked down at his lap in what might have been remorse.

"Polaris is a missile," he said. "Nuclear-armed ballistic missile."

"Oh!" She'd wanted to soothe him. "That sounds dangerous."

"Better range, I guess. More accurate, too, is what they say."

"I saw it in a magazine and I thought, 'I bet Richard knows all about this,' and I was right."

"Not really. It's Navy shit. I avoid those bastards the best I can."

"That's true. You do. You've told me many times."

"Submarines. You wouldn't catch me on one of those death traps, I'll tell you what."

He'd looked at her then and smiled, and Richard, that poor, powerful man, hadn't any idea the pain his smile conveyed. Lainie senses that he's seen too much, in Korea, in the Amazon. There are things he'll never share. This is a sort of mercy toward her, she tells herself, even as it makes her feel as if she's all alone and floating away like a helium balloon.

No man who's spent seventeen months in the South American jungle can reacclimate to civilian life just like that. Lainie knows this and tries to be patient. But it's challenging. Those seventeen months changed her, too. Overnight, Richard had been stolen away by the ghastly General Hoyt and dropped into a world without telephones or mailboxes. Household decisions had to be made, all the time, and they'd hit her like a spray of buckshot. Where to take the car when it broke down. What to do with that skunk carcass in the backyard. How to stand up to plumbers, bankers, other men who thought a lady alone was ripe to be rooked. All while herding two kids bewildered and hurt by an abruptly vacated father.

And she'd been good at it. Yes, she'd spent the bulk of the first two months envisioning her new life from behind a gloss of tears: a widowed mother of two terrors who'd grow up shredding drapes and crayoning walls as she gulped down cooking sherry. Soon, though, her evening collapse had begun to feel like satisfied exhaustion. Gradually, tentatively, in private nooks of her mind, she began to shape a plan for when Richard was declared missing in action and the army ceased sending her checks. She scribbled figures on matchbooks, Timmy's school reports, the back of her hand, calculating estimated wages versus concrete expenses. She knew she could handle a job. It even sounded exciting. It also made her feel like the world's worst wife to find any spark of enthusiasm at all in the vanishing of her husband. But there would be a sort of peace without Richard, wouldn't there? Hadn't he always been a little hard? A little cold?

It's fruitless to rehash. After all, Richard did come home, didn't he? A full week now they've been back together, and doesn't he deserve the same wife he left behind? Lainie works up a smile until she believes in it. If those submariners trusted Westinghouse's nuclear whatsits, why, she should be proud to stand in her living room and use the Spray 'N Steam, the very first item she'd bought in Baltimore. Richard needs to look sharp for his new job, a place called Occam, and that makes ironing a priority. With so much wardrobe still boxed up, the children's clothes need ironing, too. Timmy looks feral in his ragged playwear, and Tammy's favorite velveteen jumper is dishrag thin. A housewife, she insists to herself, has plenty of interesting, important jobs to do.

3

TOUPEES ARE MADE from human hair. That Giles Gunderson's hairpiece doesn't altogether match the tussocks sprouting above his ears galls him. His real hair is brown, but get close enough and you'll see strands of blond and orange. Not that anyone has gotten close in years. Had he known he'd be shiny-domed by age thirty, he would have begun stockpiling hair decades ago. Every young man should do so; they should teach it in health classes. He pictures bulging trash bags of hair crowding his childhood closets, lugging them from his parents' house to his first apartment and beyond. He chuckles. No, sir, nothing strange about that.

Giles pockets one pair of his glasses, moves a second pair down from his forehead, tugs shut his suede coat, and steps from the cream-colored Bedford van that Mr. Arzounian, the Arcade's owner, lets him park behind the theater, that of the rusted sliding door and water-stained upholstery, dubbed by Elisa as "the Pug" for its buggy headlights and flat snout. Baltimore hasn't had a drop of moisture in months, but the wind is a cat-o'-nine-tails. Giles feels his toupee begin to lift from his scalp. He mashes his palms to his skull to restick the double-sided tape and rounds the Pug, head lowered against the wind.

It's the posture of a bruiser, but he feels the opposite, feeble and overweening. He fights the van's side door and removes his redleather, brass-buckled portfolio case. Carrying it makes him feel important. He scrimped for a full year in his thirties to buy it, and it remains the single piece of professional gear he'd set right alongside anything owned by Manhattan hotshots. He heads up the sidewalk, the gale giving him a brisk shove. Negotiating a door with a portfolio case is a sophisticated procedure; by the time he's through, everyone inside should be buzzing about the debonair gent with the giant leather bag.

Giles feels a familiar jab of doubt. His need to cushion his ego is pathetic, especially at a joint like this. Look around. Not a single soul has noticed his arrival. Giles stands taller in his own defense. Can these diners be blamed for their distraction? Dixie Doug's Pies is a fun house of colored lights and reflective surfaces, from the pedestals atop which plastic pies revolve to the refrigerated display cases backlit with jukebox plastic and piped with chrome.

Giles mazes into the queue. It's a weekday midafternoon, a peculiar time for pie, and he's second in line. He likes being here, he tells himself. It's cozy and warm and smells of cinnamon and sugar. He doesn't look at the cashier, not yet; he's too old to feel this nervous. Instead, he studies a five-foot glass tower, each level presenting a different dessert. Double-decker pies like department-store hat boxes. Sculpted pies like the bout of a cello. Pie puffs like a woman's breast. There is room for all kinds, all kinds.

4

F-1 is six times larger than Elisa's apartment, modest for an Occam lab. The walls are white and resplendent above clean concrete floors. Silver ranks of tables wait against the walls while caster-wheel chairs in packing plastic huddle like homeless people around a trash-can fire. Braided cables dangle from the ceiling and hospital lamps on jointed arms ogle down at nothing. Along the eastern side is a bank of beige machinery, the type Elisa has heard called a "computer." Janitors are forbidden to touch these imposing agglomerations of switches and dials, though they are expected to use compressed-air sprayers to blast away dust the final Friday of every month.

What is unique about F-1, and what beckons Elisa past the balking Zelda, is the pool. The crackling they'd heard was water expelling from an industrial hose into what resembles a giant stainless-steel sink built into the floor and enclosed by a knee-high ledge upon which three laborers have planted their boots. They are blue-collar Baltimoreans plainly uncomfortable with the job's confidentiality; they watch their foreman hold out a pen and clipboard to a man of receding brown hair and spectacles—an Occam scientist, for sure, but one she's never seen. He's late-forties but squats on the ledge like a hyperactive boy, ignoring the foreman so as to compare his notes to three gauges extending from the pool.

"Too hot!" he cries. "Much too hot! Do you want to boil it?"

The man has an accent. Elisa doesn't recognize it, and this wakes her up: She recognizes none of these people. Six workers, five scientists; she's never seen so many people at Occam this late. Zelda pulls on Elisa's elbow, and Elisa lets herself be backpedaled before a voice both of them know in their marrow speaks up.

"Attention, everyone, please! The asset is off the loading dock. Repeat: The asset is off the loading dock and is on the approach. Respectfully, I need the construction crew to stop where you are and exit the lab via the door to your right—"

David Fleming's white shirt and neutral slacks had camouflaged him against the computer. Elisa sees him now, his arm forked in a gesture toward the very door in front of which she and Zelda stand like scolded children. Every head in the room turns their way. All these men, staring at them, these infringing females. Elisa's cheeks burn, and she feels every ugly inch of her trash-spattered Occam grays.

"I apologize, everyone, our lady visitors are not supposed to be here." Fleming lowers his voice to that of a chiding husband. "Zelda. Elisa. How many times do you have to be told? When there are men working inside—"

Zelda shrinks like one accustomed to absorbing blows, and Elisa sidesteps in front of her, an instinctive shielding that puts her, to her shock, directly in the path of a man hurrying straight at her. Elisa snatches a breath, squares her shoulders. Corporal punishment was habitual during her youth, and though that was fifteen years ago, hands have been laid upon her before at Occam. Fleming manhandling her from an unsteady office chair from atop which she cleared cobwebs; a biologist slapping her hand from a paper cup that contained not old coffee but some kind of sample; a security guard giving her a hard spank on her way to the elevator.

"Don't leave." He is the man with the accent. The hem of his white lab coat is soaked gray from the pool and his half-laced wingtips make dog-tongue splashes. His dripping hand is held palm-up in appeal, and he turns to Fleming. "These girls are cleared, yes?"

"They're janitorial. They're cleared, yes, for janitorial services."

"If they are cleared, should they not hear?"

"With all due respect, doctor. You're new. Occam has protocols."

"But will they not clean this laboratory from time to time?"

"Yes, but only at my direct request."

Fleming's eyes snap from the scientist to Elisa, and she witnesses his recognition that he'd prematurely added F-1 to the QCC. Elisa jerks her head down at her cart, all those safe, crusty bottles and jugs, but it's too late to retract the stinger: Fleming's dignity is stung, and extra work for her and Zelda will be the punishment. The accented scientist sees none of this; he's still smiling, convinced of his benevolence. Like most of the well-intentioned privileged Elisa has met, he has no grasp of the priorities of the servile, how all they want is to get through a shift without trouble.

"Very good," the scientist says. "Everyone should understand the importance of the asset so that there are no mistakes."

Fleming mashes his lips and waits for the construction crew to exit. Elisa and Zelda shrink from the burly men's appraising looks. The scientist, blind to Elisa's discomfort, holds out his hand to shake. Elisa gapes in horror at the man's neatly clipped nails, clean palm, and starched shirt cuff. What will Fleming make of *this* etiquette breach? Worse than to take the hand is to ignore it, so she offers hers as listlessly as possible. The man's palm is damp, but his grip is genuine.

"Dr. Bob Hoffstetler." He smiles. "How do you work in those shoes?"

Elisa shuffles backward several inches so that her cart separates her shoes from Fleming's line of sight. Fleming can't be allowed to notice her shoes for the second time. She couldn't bear it if he robbed her of that revolt. Hoffstetler misses nothing; he observes her small retreat and angles his head curiously. He appears to be waiting on a reply, so Elisa pushes a smile onto her blushing face and taps her name tag. Hoffstetler's eyebrows settle in sympathetic understanding.

"The most intelligent of creatures," he offers softly, "often make the fewest sounds."

He smiles again and steps to the right to make similar introductions to Zelda, and though Elisa is mortified by the attention and curls her shoulders inward to make herself smaller, she notes with a somber sting that, in all her years at Occam, Dr. Hoffstetler's smile is the warmest she's ever received.

5

IT'S A FINE iron, no doubt about it. Forget fiddly demineralizer kits; it takes tap water straight, and it's so agreeable to have all the settings on one dial. And it comes with a wall mount; that'll be handy once her ironing board has a permanent place. For now, she's set up in the living room in front of the TV. This is how her army-wife friends in Orlando did their housework. Lainie had always resisted. Once during Richard's Amazon mission, she'd tried listening to *Young Doctor Malone* and *Perry Mason* on the radio while ironing and the distraction had been too potent. She got through a whole laundry basket without memory of having done so, and it bothered her. That's how unchallenging your daily tasks are, Lainie. That's how repetitive.

But last night in bed, insomnia had hatched an obvious but invigorating thought. The channel dial: She can change it. She doesn't have to watch *I Love Lucy*, *Guiding Light*, and *Password* like the other wives; she can watch *Today*, *NBC News*, and *ABC Early Afternoon Report*. It's a fresh idea, and it inspires her. So far, everything about Baltimore inspires her.

Getting dressed this morning—why, it'd felt like she'd been dressing for a cocktail party of intellectuals! She'd set her beehive before unfolding the ironing board, and by the tight ache at her temples, she knows it's holding. What unravels, however, is her attention, ten minutes into the first newscast. Khrushchev is visiting the Berlin Wall. Just the word *Khrushchev* makes her blush; she mispronounced it three years ago at a function packed with Washington bigwigs, and Richard's jaw had throbbed in embarrassment. And the Berlin Wall. Why does she know the name of every single character on *Captain Kangaroo* but not a thing about the Berlin Wall?

Lainie toggles the iron's selector, unable to decide which setting will best eradicate wrinkles. Is it possible Westinghouse has given her, and every other woman in America, too many choices? She examines the face of the iron, counts seventeen vents, one for every month Richard spent in the Amazon. She blasts the steam, dips her face into the draft, and imagines that it's the jungle's heat.

This must be how the world felt to Richard when he'd called her from Brazil. It had been like hearing a ghost. One second, she'd been cutting crusts off peanut-butter sandwiches and reaching for the ringing phone. The next, she'd dropped the knife and let loose a shriek. She'd wept, insisting to him that it was a miracle. She'd had to force the tears, though, hadn't she? Well, who could blame her? She'd been in shock. Richard had replied that he'd missed her, too, but his deadness of voice persisted; he sounded slow and mealy, as if he'd forgotten English. There was a crunching sound, too, like he was chewing something. Why would he be eating while talking to his wife for the first time in seventeen months?

It was easy to excuse. Maybe he'd been starving out in that jungle. He'd told her that they'd be moving to Baltimore, and before she could ask questions, he gave her his flight number to Orlando and gotten off the phone, still crunching. Lainie sat down, gazed at the home that, for a year and a half, had seemed so comforting and functional. Now it looked like a bachelor's disaster. Nothing shone from spray or scrub. The iron that had died eight months ago she hadn't even replaced. Oh, how she'd cleaned for the next two days, her scrubbing fists bursting through dishwashing gloves, her mopping hands weeping with blisters, her grouting knuckles trailing blood. A phone call from Washington rescued her, if not her marriage: Richard was being rerouted by sea to Baltimore. He'd meet her there in two weeks at a house of government choosing.

Lainie replays, almost hourly, the sight of Richard first walking through the door of the Baltimore house. The crisp, buttoned dress shirt he wore bagged about him like a druidic cloak. He'd lost weight and was pure, knotty muscle. His posture was wary and vulpine. He was shaven to a rubbery gleam, his cheeks milky white from being hidden by a jungle beard while the rest of his face had cooked bronze. For a long moment, they'd stared at each other. He squinted as if he didn't recognize her; her fingertips flew to her beehive, her lipstick, her fingernails. Was it too much? Too dazzling after he'd seen nothing but raw, filthy men for so long?

Then Richard had gently lowered his bag to the ground and a single quake had rolled through his shoulders. Two small tears, one from each eye, rolled down his smooth cheeks. Lainie had never seen her husband cry, had even suspected he didn't have the capacity, and to her surprise, it frightened her. She knew, though, that it was proof that she meant something, that *they* meant something, and she ran to him, bound her arms about him, pressed her own crying eyes into the stiff folds of his shirt. Several seconds later, she felt his hands on her back, but cautiously, as if his instinct had become to hurl off creatures that attached themselves to him.

"I'm . . . sorry," he'd said.

Lainie still wonders about this. Sorry for being gone? Sorry for crying? Sorry for his inability to embrace her like a normal man?

"Don't be sorry," she said. "You're here. You're here. Everything's going to be okay."

"You look . . . you feel . . ."

She wonders about this, too. Did she look as strange to him now as South American fauna did seventeen months ago? Was her softness the softness of sucking mud, of boar carcasses, of other sorts of jungle rot she couldn't begin to imagine? So she'd shushed him, told him not to speak, just to hold her. It's something she regrets. Whatever lost well of emotion his two tears had indicated was crusted shut by the following day, impervious to her gentle prods. It was Richard's protective instinct, perhaps, against the disorienting assaults of the city.

It was only when Timmy and Tammy rollicked down the stairs to greet their father did Lainie break from Richard, turn around, and consider the empty, unfurnished house behind her. Her knees wobbled with a terrible suspicion. What if she'd had nothing to do with Richard's tears? What if it had been the perfectly clean, virtually silent rooms behind her that had moved him?

She wrangles the same dress shirt Richard had worn home around the ironing board's nose. It's best not to think such thoughts. It's best to concentrate on what she can do now to be a better wife. Maybe it's not *Today*-worthy, but Richard's Occam job is important. Imagine what would happen if she left a burn mark on his shirt. It would hint at problems at home. And there aren't any. Her job is to help Richard by taking the mess of warfare, however it hits him, and to scrub away the dirt, the grease, the oil, the gunpowder, the sweat, the lipstick if it comes to that, and to iron it tidy again, for her husband and family, of course, but also for her country.

6

THE NAME ON his tag reads BRAD, but Giles has seen him wear JOHN on occasion, and once even LORETTA. Giles presumes the second was by mistake and the third a joke, but the misnomers have introduced enough uncertainty that Giles is reticent to use any of them. He definitely looks like a Brad: six-foot-one, six-foot-two if he'd quit slouching, a face of forthright symmetry, straight teeth bordering on horsey, and a whipped-cream dollop of blond hair. His eyes, as melted-brown as the chocolate from the burned-down chocolate factory, brighten when they see him. Giles swears they do.

"Hey, there, partner! Where you been?"

Brad's voice is broadly, unspecifically southern, and Giles becomes mired in its syrup. Hair worries engulf him: the gradient of his toupee, the crop of his mustache, the hazards of ear and eyebrow stragglers. Giles puffs his chest and snaps off a nod.

"Well, good afternoon to you." Too professorial; he unscrews it. "Hey yourself, partner." Who does he think he is, a schoolboy? "Very nice to see you, indeed." Three redundant greetings. Just perfect.

Brad stilts a hand to the counter and leans onto it.

"Now what might be your pleasure?"

"It's so difficult to say," Giles gushes. "What, if I may ask, would be your personal recommendation?"

Brad drums his fingers. His knuckles are scuffed. Giles pictures him pitching firewood in a forested backyard, wood flakes alighting upon moist, minor abrasions like golden butterflies.

"How you feel about key lime? We've got a key lime that'll knock you back to Newark. It's that one there, top floor of the tower."

"My, that is a vivid green."

"Ain't it? I'll fix you up with a nice, hefty slice, what do you say?"

"How can I spurn such a tantalizing hue?"

Brad scribbles the order and chuckles. "You always got the best words."

Giles feels a blush rise up his neck. He battles it back with the first thing that pops into his brain.

"*Tantalizing* comes from the Greek. Tantalus, one of Zeus's sons. A troubled boy, to be sure. Rather famously, he sacrificed his son and served him up to the other gods. Not unlike carving up a pie. But it's his punishment we commemorate. He was cursed to stand in a pool, hungry for fruit that was pulled away each time he reached up, and thirsty for water that ran away each time he kneeled."

"He chopped up his kid, you said?"

"Yes, though the point, I think, is that Tantalus was not permitted the escape of death. His fate was to suffer knowing that everything he wanted was right there in reach, but he could partake in none of it."

Brad chews over this, and Giles feels his blush resume its northerly creep. He's often marveled at how a single painting can say so much to so many people, and yet the more words one uses, the more likely it is for them to turn on their tellers and expose them. Brad, he is relieved to see, chooses to abandon classical analysis. He spikes the order on a spindle.

"I see you got your paint bag there," he says. "Working on anything good?"

Giles knows it's an old man's poppycock to make-believe that this or that cordial question throbs with furtive significance. He's sixty-four. Brad can't be older than thirty-five. Well, what of it? Does that mean Giles can't enjoy the spar of good conversation? That he can't feel good about himself as he has so rarely in life? He lifts his portfolio as if only now noticing it.

"Oh, this! It's not much. The launch of a new food product is all. It seems I have been entrusted with captaining an ad campaign. I'm en route to a meeting at the agency, as it happens."

"No kidding! What kind of food product?"

Giles opens his mouth, but the word *gelatin* feels flaccid.

"I probably shouldn't say. Confidentiality agreements, you know."

"Is that right? Lord, that sounds exciting. Drawing art, secret projects. Lot more exciting than slinging pies, I tell you."

"But food is the original art! I've always meant to ask. Are you Dixie Doug himself?"

Brad's guffaw is explosive; it tussles the bangs of Giles's toupee.

"I wish I was. Then I'd be sitting on top a whole hill of cash. Let me tell you. This here ain't the only Dixie Doug's. There's twelve of them. It's called 'franchising.' They send you this brochure, see. Lays out the whole shebang. Paint color, decorations. Dixie Dog, our mascot. The whole menu, even. They do studies. Find out what people like, scientifically. They truck it across the country, and we serve it up."

"Intriguing," Giles says.

Brad looks about, then leans closer. "You want to know a secret?"

There is nothing Giles wants more. He's harbored enough of them to know that receiving a secret from someone else magically lightens both parties' loads.

"This voice? It isn't even real. I'm from Ottawa. I've never heard a southern accent in my life, besides movies."

Feelings settle inside Giles, ice into a glass. He may have failed to confirm Brad's name, but he'll come away today with a superior prize. One day, he is certain, Brad will share his real voice, some exotic Canadian lilt, and then—well, that will have to mean something, won't it? Carrying his portfolio bag proudly, waiting on bright green pie, Giles feels more a part of the world than he's felt in ages.

7

"I DON'T NEED to reiterate to most of you the great lengths some of our best men went to make this possible, and how not all of those men came back to be able to share in the achievement," Fleming says. "What I do feel a responsibility to address—and I'm glad, frankly, that my janitorial girls are here to hear this—is that this is, without question, the most sensitive asset ever brought to Occam Aerospace, and it needs to be treated that way. I know you've all signed the forms, but let me say it again. Top-secret data is not for wives. Not for children. Not for the best buddy you've known since you were a kid. This is national security. This is the fate of the free world. The president himself knows your names, and I sincerely hope that's enough to keep you—"

Elisa's tensed body seizes at the crunch of a code key into a lock, and it's not even the lock behind her. Ten-foot double doors on the other side of F-1, which connect with the hallway that feeds to the loading dock, swing open. A helmeted man in military drabs rushes in from either side to secure the doors. They are armed, as are all Occam guards, but not with enigmatic handguns in unemphatic holsters. Large black bayonet rifles are slung across their backs.

A car-length, rubber-wheeled pallet is guided into the lab by a third and fourth soldier. It carries what Elisa, in the first seconds, believes to be an iron lung. Polio was the orphanage's unexorcisable boogeyman; any child forced to sit through overlong sermons and dry lectures could fathom the horror of being trapped forever in a neck-down casket. This object is similarly podlike but several orders larger, with riveted steel, compression seals, rubberized joints, and pressure meters. Whoever is inside, Elisa thinks, must be gravely ill for even his head to be kept inside the tank. Fleming is on the move, directing the pallet to a cleared space alongside the pool, before Elisa recognizes her own naïveté. Sick little boys do not earn four armed escorts.

The final man through the double doors is buzz cut with gorilla arms and the hulking gait of one suspicious of indoor spaces. He wears a denim coat over roughshod gray twills, and even these garments seem to constrain him. He circles the pod, muttering directions and indicating wheels to be locked, knobs to be adjusted. He doesn't point at these with a finger. Looped around his wrist is the rawhide strap of a scuffed orange baton ending into two metal prongs. Elisa isn't sure, but thinks it's an electric cattle prod.

Both Fleming and Dr. Bob Hoffstetler advance upon the man with right hands outstretched, but the man's furrowed eyes glare past them, across the length of the lab, directly at Elisa and Zelda. Dual veins fatten his forehead like subcutaneous horns.

"What are they doing here?"

In direct reply, the tank rattles violently upon its trailer and a high-pitched roar typhoons from within, sloshing water and frightening soldiers who expel curse words and bring about their rifles. What looks like a hand, but can't be, for it's far too large, slaps against one of the tank's porthole windows and Elisa can't believe the glass doesn't crack, but it doesn't, and the tank is rocking, and the soldiers are fanning into formation, and Fleming is rushing at the janitors and shouting, and Hoffstetler is wincing at his failure to protect them, and Zelda has two handfuls of Elisa's uniform, dragging her into the hallway along with their carts, and the man with the cattle prod holds his furious glare for a second longer before dropping his head between his shoulders and turning to face the screaming, captured thing.

8

THE BOXES FROM Florida are a problem. She knows it and promises herself to unpack them, first chance she gets, and that's an order! She recalls a treasured moment with Richard, years ago now, when she, emboldened by his orgasm, had dared make a sex joke, an allusion to "standing at attention." In later years, such lewdness from her would repulse him. But that one time, he'd chuckled and checked off the basics of military formation. Heels together. Suck the stomach. Arms along seams. No smiling. That's the efficiency she needs to emulate. She's got a utility knife for opening boxes. She's got Brillo Soap Pads, Ajax with Instant Chlorine Bleach, Bruce Cleaning

Wax, Tide Laundry Detergent, and Comet with Chlorinol, all locked and loaded and ready for duty.

She could unpack the boxes in two days if she buckled down. But she can't. Each time she slits packing tape, it's like knifing open the belly of a doe. Inside these boxes are seventeen months of a different life. One that had knocked her off the well-trod path she'd been on since she was a little girl: dating, marriage, children, homemaking. Pulling items from those boxes—it's like ripping organs from that other version of herself, that woman of ambition and energy and promise. The whole thing is silly, she knows that. She'll get to it. She will.

Only it's hard with Baltimore *right there*, right outside the window. After she gets the kids off to school, there's no resisting. Each time, it happens the same. She puts on her heels for Richard, as seeing her barefoot irritates him—Lainie blames this, too, on the Amazon, perhaps some shoeless tribe that disgusted him. When Richard leaves for Occam, off fly the shoes so that Lainie can scrunch her toes deep into the carpet. Not much grit, not really. A modicum of crumbs, that's all. Clean enough for now, surely. She gets dressed, goes out, boards a bus.

At first, she'd pretended that she was looking for a church. It wasn't a lie, not entirely. A family needs a house of worship. Her church in Orlando had been a literal godsend those months without Richard before she'd found her footing. Footing: She needs, again, to find it. Problem is, Baltimore has a church on every block. Is she a Baptist? They'd attended a Baptist church in Virginia. Episcopal, perhaps? She's not sure what the word means. Lutheran, Methodist, Presbyterian: Those all sound safe, untheatrical. She takes a seat on the bus, prim of posture, hands folded on her purse, and rolls specific church names over her lipsticked lips. All Saints, Holy Trinity, New Life. She laughs; it fogs the bus window, and she briefly loses sight of the city. How could she choose anything besides New Life?

9

WORKING WOMEN DON'T get to scurry home and bury their faces in pillows when they've been yelled at. You settle your trembling hands by wrapping them around your tools and returning to work. Elisa had wanted to talk about what she'd seen and heard—the giant hand slapping the tank window, the animalistic roar. From Elisa's first startled signs, though, it became clear that Zelda hadn't seen the hand and had taken the roar for yet another distasteful animal experiment that would only sicken her to consider in detail. So Elisa keeps her thoughts to herself, wondering if it's possible that Zelda is right and she mistook the whole thing.

The best thing for tonight is to scrub the images from her mind, and scrubbing is something Elisa is good at. She's in and out of toilet stalls in the northeast men's room, stabbing her swab under rims. Zelda, done mopping the floor, wets a pumice stone in the sink and frowns at the piss-crusted urinal partition she's squared off against for years, searching for a fresh complaint to lift their spirits. Elisa believes in Zelda as she believes in few others: She will find that complaint, and it will be funny, and they will begin to crawl from under this sticky film of debasement left by all those judging men.

"Finest minds in the country, they tell us, gathered right here at Occam—and there are pee freckles on the *ceiling*. You know Brewster's not the crispiest chip in the bag, but even he hits the target seventy-five percent of the time. I don't know if I ought to be depressed about this or go get the Guinness Records folks on the line. Maybe they'll give me a finder's fee."

Elisa nods and signs "Get on the telephone," opting for an old-fashioned, two-piece model to evoke visions of a herd of New York City correspondents with PRESS badges tucked into their fedoras. Zelda gets the reference and grins—a bursting relief of a sight—and

Elisa presses the joke, wiggling her fingers in the sign for "teletype," then signing a suggestion to send a letter via pigeon. Zelda laughs and gestures at the ceiling.

"I can't even figure out the angle of the—you know what I mean? I don't want to be indecent here. But if you think about the physics and all that? The angle of the garden hose, the direction of the spray?"

Elisa giggles soundlessly, scandalized and so very grateful.

"Only thing I can figure is it's a competition. Kind of like the Olympics? Points for height and distance. Points for style if you waggle it really good. And to think, all these years, we thought these science types didn't have any physical skills."

Elisa is in full silent guffaw, rocking back against the stall, the night's events bleaching away under Zelda's off-color scenario.

"Hey, there's two urinals here," Zelda chuckles. "I don't think synchronized peeing is out of the question—"

A man walks in. Elisa turns from the toilet, Zelda from the urinal. He wasn't there; now he is. It's so incredible, the women forget to react. A plastic sign reading CLOSED FOR CLEANING is all that defends female janitors from the threat of male incursion, but it's always been sufficient. Zelda starts to point at the sign, but her arm dies midway; it's not a janitor's place to assert the existence of physical objects to a man of higher station, and besides, her gibes about men's bathroom practices are still ringing from every pipe, locknut, and escutcheon of the undersink. Elisa feels shame, then shame for feeling shame. Thousands of times she and Zelda have cleaned this room, and it takes one single man to make *them* feel like the obscene ones.

The man paces coolly to the middle of the room.

He holds in his right hand an orange cattle prod.

10

THE REVOLVING DOOR of Klein & Saunders works its sleight of hand. On the street side, among briefcasers juking toward their next meeting, Giles is adrift, ancient, useless. The rotating chamber is where the metamorphosis happens, the glass turnstile reflecting an infinitude of possible, better selves. When Giles is ejected onto the lobby's chessboard marble, he's a new man. Art in hand, and with a place to take it, he's important.

It's been like this since before he can recall, the producing of art a mere prelude to the delight of *having* it, a concrete object he'd willed into being. Everything else he has is like his derelict apartment—at the end of the day, only rented. The first objet d'art in his life was a human skull his father had won in a poker game, named Andrzej after the Pole from whom it'd been won. It was Giles's first study; he drew it hundreds of times, on the sides of envelopes, atop newspaper faces, on the back of his hand.

How he got from sketches of skulls to working at Klein & Saunders twenty years later he can barely recall. His first job was at the same Hampden-Woodberry cotton mill as his father, habituating himself to the tickle of cotton fibers in his nose, the callouses wrought by pitching bales, the soft second skin of red clay anytime he ran cotton from Mississippi. At night, sometimes all night, he painted on discarded paper he plundered from work, rampageous portraitures that sustained him better than food, and make no mistake—he was plenty hungry. He used the Mississippi clay on his arms to make his oranges pop. Decades later, it would still be his secret.

In two years, he'd left behind both the mill and his confused father to take an art department job at Hutzler's department store. A few years later, he moved to Klein & Saunders, and there spent most of his career. He'd been proud, but not satisfied. His nagging discontent had something to do with art. True art. He'd once defined himself by that word, hadn't he? All those abstracts of Andrzej, all those male nudes wild-lined from cotton-bale callouses and blood-orange with Biloxi mud. Giles slowly came to feel that each false smile of joy he painted for Klein & Saunders vampired real joy from those who gauged their own happiness against advertising's impossible standards. He knew the feeling. He felt it every day.

Klein & Saunders works with prestigious clients. Hence the waiting room stocked with cardinal-red chairs of au courant German design and the libations cart managed by Hazel, the redoubtable receptionist who outdates Giles. Today, though, Hazel is absent, and some ad man's fawn-legged secretary has been tossed before a dozen impatient execs, a smile bolted to her fearful face. Giles watches her accidentally sever an incoming call while fretting over a tray of half-made drinks. He assesses the room's mood by the cloud of cigarette smoke: not lounging like Michelangelo's Adam, but scattered in locomotive puffs.

He forgives her for taking a minute to notice him.

"Mr. Giles Gunderson, artist," he heralds. "I have a two-fifteen with Mr. Bernard Clay."

She pushes a button and garbles his name into the receiver. Giles isn't convinced the message has been transmitted but can't bear to ask the poor thing to try again. Giles faces the throng. It's incredible, he thinks, that twenty years later part of him still desires to run with this stalking, snarling pack.

He considers the secretary, the drink cart. He sighs and steps behind the latter, clapping his hands for attention.

"Good sirs," he calls out. "What say this afternoon we mix our own drinks?"

They sputter at this interference into their rightful disgruntlement; each man hoists one eyebrow high onto his forehead. Giles knows this feeling, how pique slides toward suspicion. After all this time, he doesn't know how people so quickly sniff out that's he different. He thinks he can feel his toupee tape begin to rip free.

Should this moment tip wrongly, his rug will be the least of his problems.

"The advantage being," Giles proceeds, "that we can make them as wet as Baltimore is dry. Who's for a martini?"

The gamble pays off. Midafternoon businessmen, at their core, are toddlers—dehydrated and cranky—and one man's *Hear, hear* is pursued by another's *Amen to that*, and in a snap Giles is tending bar, performing speed pours and carving lemon twists to fraternity-house hurrahs. In the midst of the debauch, he gestures everyone aside so he can shake to life a single Brandy Alexander and present it to the secretary like an Academy Award. Everyone applauds, the girl blushes, sunlight skims off the cocktail's frothy top like a Hawaiian horizon, and for a moment Giles feels as if his world is once more ripe with potential.

11

Zelda knows what to do. It's a variation she's done a thousand times before, at work, certainly, but also all throughout life when pressed by men. Get out of sight, and fast. She adopts the detached smile of a servant, takes hold of her cart, and wheels it about. But the floor is soapy and the carts rolls too widely, striking the trash can and upsetting it with a clatter that bangs about the room. Just emptied, thank heavens, but she scrambles to upright it. Dropping to her knees emphasizes her weight, invites ridicule. She tries to do it quickly. While kneeling, she hears a crinkling sound. She looks up. The man is holding the last thing Zelda expects, the dictionary opposite of his electric rod: a plastic bag of bright green hard candy.

"No, no. Don't leave. You ladies seem to be chatting enjoyably. Girl talk. Nothing in the world wrong with that. You go right on ahead, I won't be a second."

The inflection isn't southern but has a crocodile's swishing tail. The man continues forward and for a flash it looks to Zelda that the man is heading for Elisa's stall. Did Elisa see something in F-1 that

Zelda missed? Elisa's always sensitive to people shouting at her, but her behavior since fleeing F-1 feels different, almost like she's stunned. Is this man here to drag Elisa away? Zelda hoists herself to her feet, another graceless move, and slides her hand across her cart for a weapon—the kettle brush, the squeegee. She knows about fighting, too. Brewster has more battle scars than her, but she has her share. This man tries to harm Elisa, she'll do what needs to be done. Zelda's whole life will be ruined, but she'll have no choice.

Instead, the man deviates, placing the cattle prod and candy bag on the sink, and steps over to the urinal and begins to unzip.

Now it's Zelda who looks to Elisa for help. If Zelda's terrified eyes missed something in F-1, maybe she can't rely on her eyes here, either. A man, taking out his thing, right in front of them? Elisa, though, is hinging her head left and right and up and down in chase of a suitable reaction. One thing's for sure: Zelda can't look at the man. Looking at him, in here, doing this—she has no doubt it's a fireable offense. All the man has to do is report them, obscene janitors, to Fleming and they'll be history. Zelda stares at the floor so hard she waits for her gaze to crack the tile.

Urine hisses into the clean urinal.

"Name's Strickland." The voice resounds. "I'm heading up security."

Zelda swallows. "Uh-huh" is all she can manage.

She tells her eyes to stay put, but they stray and see a spurt of urine splash to the mopped floor. Strickland chuckles.

"Oops. Guess it's a good thing you got mops."

12

RICHARD WOULD MALIGN her secret sightseeing as a misuse of time, and he'd be right. Her own gasps distract her from her guilt. The linebacker high-rises, mountainous billboards, robot-shaped gas pumps, cheddar-colored streetcars! She feels a knot inside of her fray as if her box cutter is being dragged along it. The bus rushes past signs that stay lit through the daytime drear: WE INSTALL MUFFLERS, $1.00 VARIETY STORE, SPORTING GOODS, JOIN THE AIR FORCE. She rings the bell and gets off at a West 36th shopping district locals call "the Avenue" and lets stores begin jostling for her dollar.

She tries to chime hello to all she passes, especially women. Wouldn't it be grand to explore the city with a friend who knew its secrets? Who could parry sarcasms about outrageous markups, what the bay-wind does to your hair, all of that? Who could draw from Lainie, and appreciate the special, secret vitality she'd felt during those seventeen months on her own? But Baltimore women are startled by her greetings and barely muster smiles. After an hour, Lainie feels lonely, doomed to outsider status. She gets back on the bus. A man walks the aisle, mistakes her for a tourist, and tries to sell her a visitor's guide. Her chest reknots. Is it her hairdo? In Florida, beehives were the rage, but not here. She is suddenly, deeply unhappy. She probably needs a visitor's guide. She buys one.

Baltimore, the guide scolds her, has everything required to satisfy an American family. What exactly, then, is her problem? Tammy would adore the Museum of Art. Timmy would love the Historical Society. West of town is the Enchanted Forest, some kind of story-book attraction. Photos show castles and forests, princesses and witches. The kids could hold their birthday parties there this summer. It's perfect, except for the park's so-called Jungle Land. Even the word *jungle* makes Richard set down the newspaper or turn the channel. They'd just have to be careful where they walked, that's all.

One of her past strolls took her to the docks at Fells Point. She's tried to forget this walk, but each morning the Spray 'N Steam sweats the truth out of her; she wonders if the Amazon boiled Richard to his rawest root. It had been a slate afternoon, rhythmed with the whap of ships against docks. She'd toed the edge of the Patapsco River, lifting her collar to her jawline. To get there, she'd gotten off at a bus stop usurped by a rag-clad hobo and walked through the broken bottles of the ugliest neighborhood she'd ever seen. There'd been a movie theater, too, and she'd nearly bought a ticket just to evade the ogling. But the marquee had been missing a few too many bulbs for her comfort, and the movie hadn't sounded pleasant at all—a circus of souls, something like that.

It was a lonesome spot. No one would hear her if she spoke. So she'd told lies into the cold, lapping water until there were none left to tell: She was happy that her husband had returned. She was ful-filled. She was optimistic about the future. She believed every statistic in the City of Baltimore leaflet Richard had given her. Only twenty percent of Baltimore households, it had boasted, owned a car, and Richard swore to her that one day soon they'd own two. He was sick of his T-bird breaking down, he said, and he wouldn't have his wife taking public transport while he was off saving the world.

On her way back to the bus stop, in the neighborhood she didn't like, she'd skirted a city worker spraying off the sidewalk with a hose. How nice, she'd told herself, to see a municipality taking pride in its upkeep. She'd pretended that the washing didn't dredge up stenches of dog urine, spoiled fish, moldering leaves, congealing sew-age, saliferous puddles, scorched oil, bodily excretions. One last lie before heading home, one more wrinkle to iron out.

13

BERNIE LEADS GILES into what Giles hopes is a meeting room but is merely a vacant office inside which has been wedged a table and two chairs. Bernie doesn't sit, so Giles doesn't, either. It feels unconvivial after the smiles and handshakes of the waiting room, even as Giles reminds himself that, if he has a friend here, it is Bernie Clay, not those rich old men in the lobby slurping down his mixed drinks. Bernie was part of the vote that kicked Giles out of the firm twenty years ago, it's true, but his heart hadn't been in it, and Giles reminds himself of the futility of martyrs—Bernie's family had to eat, too, didn't they?

Memories of the inciting event deject Giles, mostly because of its pedestrian predictability; clichés are anathema to any artist. That certain bar in Mount Vernon, the police storming in with raised badges. During the night he spent in jail, he'd thought of one thing: how the police blotter had always been his father's favorite section of the paper. Giles hoped the old man's eyesight, like his own, had worsened to the point that he couldn't read the blotter's small type, and then, when Giles never heard from his father again, knew that it hadn't. Within a week of being fired, Giles adopted his first cat.

Finagling meetings with Bernie has become a large part of Giles's job. But how can he complain? No one else at the firm, Mr. Klein and Mr. Saunders included, approves of Giles's freelance involvement. Giles applies a big, red grin, just like the father in his newest painting. More advertising, he thinks, this time for himself.

"What in heavens happened to Hazel? I never knew her to miss a day."

Bernie tugs loose his tie. "You wouldn't believe it, Gilesy. The old broad made doe eyes at a beverage bottler and whoosh. They make off to Los Angeles. Took the account with them, too."

"No! Good for her, I suppose."

"Bad for us. That's why everything's haywire, so apologies for the room, we're backed up. You know a good girl, you let me know, all right?"

Giles does, in fact, know a good girl, one whose job at a totalitarian research facility has been going nowhere for years. If only answering phone calls was Elisa's forte. The few seconds Giles spends musing in silence make Bernie fidget and what's left of Giles's spirit sinks. Bernie is alone inside a closed room with a confirmed fruit. As eager as Giles is to jabber about the good old ad biz, he can't let himself be the cause of this man's distress.

"Well, here, let me show you the work—"

"I've really only got a few—"

Both are grateful for the distracting clank of the case's buckle and slap of opening leather. Giles sets the canvas upon the table and gestures proudly. But what he feels is panic. Is there something screwy with the overhead lights? The bone structure of the family he painted is too pronounced, like their skin has worn down to an Andrzej polish. And did he really draw four bodiless heads? Did he not see how ghoulish that was? Even the colors look off, except for the gelatin, which, due to his all-night mixing, is the magmatic apotheosis of red.

"The red," Bernie sighs.

"Too red," Giles says. "I concur wholeheartedly."

"It's not that. Although the father's lips do look a little . . . bloody. It's the color in general. Red's out. We're not doing red centerpieces for anything anymore. Didn't I tell you that? Maybe I didn't. Like I said, things are haywire. Red's being axed across the board. The new thing—are you ready? The new thing is *green*."

"Green?"

"Bicycles. Electric guitars. Breakfast cereal. Eye shadow. Green's the future all of a sudden. Even the new flavors coming in, wall-to-wall green. Apple, melon, green grape, pesto, pistachio, mint."

Giles tries to ignore the quartet of mocking skulls and scrutinizes the gelatin of their desire. He feels so stupid, so blind. It doesn't matter if Bernie mentioned the color before or not. If Giles had any judgment at all, he would have known better. What kind of ogre's appetite would be roused by gelatin so red it looked as if sliced from a beating heart?

"It's not me, Gilesy," Bernie says. "It's *photographs*. Every client who walks through that door today, they want photo shoots, pretty girls holding hamburgers or encyclopedia sets or what have you. They want to be invited to the casting calls to check out the goods. I'm the last guy at this firm selling the bosses on actual art. Great art is great art, that's what I tell them. And you, Gilesy, are a great artist. Hey, you making any time for your own stuff these days?"

The painting is like key-lime-pie leftovers seen apart from the brilliant lights of Dixie Doug's: untantalizing. Giles slips it back into his portfolio case. The weight of the case on the way home will bring him none of the comfort it gave on the trip here. His own stuff? No, Bernie. Not for years. Not when he's busy painting and repainting gelatin that nobody wants, no matter the color of the future.

14

STRICKLAND FEELS THE hot creep of shame. The urine crawling across the slanted floor, it's too much. He'd meant to spook the janitors. He plans on spooking everyone who laid eyes on the asset tonight. It's a trick he took from General Hoyt when they were stationed in Tokyo. First time you meet a lesser, show him how little he means to you. As soon as he saw the black janitor, the bent back of the white janitor, the urinal, it all snapped together. But it's disgusting. Peeing on the ground, it's what he did in the Amazon. Cleanliness is what he craves now, and here he is, literally pissing on it.

He checks over his shoulder and gets a good look at the little one. She's got an open face. Clear of all that glop Lainie layers on. This makes him feel worse. He urges his bladder to empty. He looks around for something else to say. Finds the cattle prod. No doubt both women are staring at it. He haggled it from a farmer before departing Brazil. Some peasant who barely spoke English and yet called it "the Alabama Howdy-do." Really helped him move the asset in or out of the pool when the asset needed encouragement. There's a fat, dark red drop of blood clinging to one of the two brass prongs. It elongates toward the white porcelain. Another mess about to be made.

He brightens his voice to distract himself from his self-disgust. "That right there is a heavy-duty 1954 Farm-Master 30 model. None of that newfangled fiberglass crap. Steel shaft, oak handle. Variable five-hundred to ten-thousand volts. Go ahead and look, ladies, but do not touch."

His face heats up. It sounds like he could be talking about his cock. Disgusting, disgusting. What if Timmy heard him talk like this? What if Tammy did? He loves the kids, even though he's afraid to touch them, afraid he'll hurt them. All they have to judge him by is what comes out of his mouth. He feels a bloom of anger toward these women for bearing witness to his ugliness. Not their fault for being in this room, of course. But it's their fault being in this job, isn't it? For putting themselves in this position? The last drop of urine falls. He thinks of the pregnant bulb of blood hanging from the Alabama Howdy-do.

Strickland hitches his pelvis, tucks, zips his pants with a startling yowl. The women look away. Are there urine spatters on his pants? He's not in the jungle anymore. He has to think of such things all the time now. He wants to run from this overbright room and the mess he's made. Wrap this up, he tells himself.

"You both heard what the man said in the lab. I hope I don't need to repeat it."

"We're cleared," the Negro says.

"I know you're cleared. I checked."

"Yes, sir."

"It's my job to check."

"I'm sorry, sir."

Why is this woman making this difficult? Why can't the other woman, so much prettier, so much gentler looking, why won't she say something? The air in the room feels swampy. His imagination, it's got to be. His heart pounds. He reaches for a machete that isn't there. The Howdy-do, though. It'll make a fine replacement. He longs to wrap his fingers around it. He pushes a laugh through clamped jaws.

"Look. I'm not one of them George Wallace folks. I think Negroes have a place. I do. At work, in schools, all the same rights as whites. But you people need to work on your vocabulary. You hear yourself? You keep repeating the same words. I fought right next to a Negro in Korea who ended up court-martialed for something he didn't do, because when the judge wanted his story he couldn't say anything but *yes, sir* and *no, sir*. That's why we've got so many of your kind in jail. I don't mean anything personal by it. I heard they're closing down Alcatraz next month and there's hardly a Negro in there, and those are the worst criminals this country's got. That's a credit to your race. You ought to be proud."

The hell is he talking about? Alcatraz? These janitors must think he's a nitwit. The second he's gone, this restroom is going to explode with their laughter. Sweat pours down his face. The chamber is closing in on him, and it must be three hundred degrees. He nods, sees the bag of hard candy, swipes it, fishes inside. He didn't wash his hands first. Janitors, of all people, will notice that. Disgusting, disgusting. He shoves a green ball into his mouth. Gives the staring women one last look.

"Either of you ladies care for a candy?"

But the green ball is like a horse's bit. He can't make out a word of his own question. Oh, they'll laugh, all right. Fucking janitors. Fucking everyone. He'll need to be tougher on the scientists, not flub it like he flubbed this. Occam's no different than the *Josefina*. He'll make sure everyone understands that it's Strickland in charge. Not David Fleming, the Pentagon's flunky. Not Dr. Bob Hoffstetler, the benign biologist. He turns on his heel. It's slick. He hopes it's soapy water, not urine. He bites down on the candy so he won't hear his own wet footsteps and grabs the Howdy-do off the sink. The bulb of blood, it probably falls. And the janitors will wipe it away. But they'll remember it. Remember him. Disgusting, disgusting.

15

STRICKLAND'S OFFER OF candy only adds a sick sweetness to the revolting scene. Elisa lost her taste for candy at the age when most children would murder for it. Even the sugary pies Giles forces upon her at Dixie Doug's scrape at her throat. She recalls the origin of her distaste from a cringer's perspective, gawking up at adult gorgons every bit as inscrutable as Strickland. In the eyes of these early caretakers, Elisa wasn't handicapped; she was stupid and recalcitrant. The orphanage had the darling name of the Baltimore Home for Wee

Wanderers, but those who lived there slashed it to "Home," ironic given the attributes that storybooks always associated with home. Security. Safety. Comfort. Joy. Swing sets. Sandboxes. Hugs.

The older kids could show you outbuildings where you could find equipment stenciled with Home's prior title: the Fenzler School for the Feeble-Minded and Idiotic. By the time of Elisa's arrival, children whose files would have once encumbered them as *mongoloids, lunatics,* or *defectives* were gathered under the wings of *retarded, slow,* or *derelict.* Unlike the Jewish and Catholic orphanages down the block, Home's mission was to keep you alive, if barely, so that when you hit the street at eighteen, you could find a menial job serving your superiors.

Home's children might have united, just as Occam's janitors might have united. Instead, the paucity of food and affection circulated cruelty like a cough, and each child knew her or his rivals' pressure points. You were sentenced to Home because your folks landed in the poorhouse? You're Breadless Betty. Your parents are dead? You're Graveyard Gilbert. You're an immigrant? You're Red Rosa, Harold the Hun. Elisa never knew the real names of some children until the day they were pushed out the door.

Elisa's own nickname was "Mum," though housemothers knew her better as "22." Numbers tidied matters in the untidy world of unwanted children, and each child had one. Every item assigned to you had your number on it, making it easy to ascribe fault when something of yours manifested where it didn't belong. Ostracized children like Mum were luckless. Adversaries had only to wad her blanket under their coat, toss it outside in the mud, and watch as the "22" on the tag was identified and Mum was assigned her discipline.

Punishment could be delegated to any housemother, but the Matron herself often liked to dole it out. She didn't own Home, but it was all she had. As early as age three, Elisa intuited that the Matron saw Home's unruly brood as reflections of her unstable mind, and to keep the children in order was to keep herself sane. It didn't work. She'd laugh hard enough to make the littlest ones cry, then break into raging sobs that would further alarm them. She carried a sapling switch for the backs of legs and arms, a ruler for knuckles, and a bottle of castor oil for forced swallowing.

Treacherously, the Matron also carried candy. Because she depended so much on the feedback of pleading and sniffling, she smited silent Mum above all others. An incorrigible little monster, she called her. Secretive, up to something. Even worse were the opposite days when the Matron, her gray hair ribboned into obscene pigtails, cornered Elisa to ask if she wanted to play dollies. Elisa would go through the motions, terrified as the Matron asked if any bad little girls were wetting their beds. That's when the candy came out. It was okay to tell her secrets, the Matron said. Just point out the kids, so I can fix them. It felt to Elisa like a trap. It *was* a trap. Same as Mr. Strickland, crinkling his cellophane bag. One way or the other, offered sweets, all of them, were poison.

Elisa got older. Twelve, thirteen, fourteen. She sat alone at soda fountains, apart from the other girls, and listened to them talk about drinking alcohol; her glass of water tasted like soap. She heard them talk about dance classes; she had to freeze her hands on her ice-cream bowl so she wouldn't pound her fists. She heard them talk about kissing. One girl said, "He makes me feel like somebody," and Elisa dwelled upon it for months. What would feeling like somebody *feel* like? To suddenly exist not only in your world, but someone else's as well?

One of the places to which she trailed other girls was the Arcade Cinema Marquee. She'd never been inside a theater. She bought a ticket and waited to be asked to leave. She spent five minutes choosing a seat, as if it might determine her whole life's path. Maybe it did: The movie was *The Yearling*, and though she and Giles would poke fun at its schmaltz years later on television, it was the religious experience she'd never had inside a pew. Here was a place where fantasy overwhelmed real life, where it was too dark to see scars and silence wasn't only accepted but enforced by flashlight-armed ushers. For two hours and eight minutes, she was whole.

Her second film was called *The Postman Always Rings Twice,* and it was a fleshly, fervid froth of sex and violence, a nihilism for which nothing in Home's library, nothing adults had told her, nothing girls gossiped about had prepared her. World War II was only lately finished, and Baltimore's streets bustled with clean-cut soldiers, and she looked differently at them on the way home, and they, she thought, looked differently at her. Her interactions, however, were failures. Young men had little patience for flirtations made from fingers.

By her own estimate, she sneaked into the Arcade roughly one hundred and fifty times over her last three years at Home. This was before the theater's downturn; before plaster began dropping from the ceiling; before Mr. Arzounian started running films 24-7 in desperation. It was her education—her real education. Cary Grant and Ingrid Bergman gasping for air inside each other in *Notorious.* Olivia de Havilland writhing away from the madwomen of *The Snake Pit.* Montgomery Clift wandering through curtains of dust in *Red River.* Elisa was finally nabbed by an usher while slinking into *Sorry, Wrong Number,* but by then it didn't matter. She was a fortnight from what Home had deemed as her eighteenth birthday. She'd be booted out and forced to find a place, and a way, to live. Terrifying but also sensational: She could buy her own tickets, look for people to gasp against, or writhe from, or just wander among.

The Matron conducted Elisa's exit interview while smoking and pacing the length of her office, infuriated at Elisa's survival. A local women's group supplied Home's graduates with a month's worth of rent money and a suitcase full of thrift-store outfits, and Elisa was wearing her favorite, a bottle-green wool dress with a pocketed skirt. All she needed was a scarf to hide her scars. She added it to her crowded mental checklist: *Buy scarf.*

"You'll be a whore by Christmas," the Matron vowed.

Elisa shivered, thrilled that the threat didn't scare her. Why would it? She'd seen enough Hollywood films to know all hookers had hearts of gold, and sooner or later, Clark Gable or Clive Brook or Leslie Howard noticed the glow. This musing might have been what led her, later that day, not to a women's home but her favorite place in the world, the Arcade Cinema Marquee. She couldn't afford to see *Joan of Arc* with Ingrid Bergman, yet wanted nothing more than to lose herself among what the poster promised was "a cast of thousands"—just like the wider Baltimore of which she was now a part, except safely constrained to the screen.

She felt so irresponsible fishing forty cents from her purse that she hung her head, and that's how she noticed the poorly placed sign: ROOM FOR RENT—INQUIRE WITHIN. There was never any doubt. Weeks later and one rent check from losing the place, she saw an ad for a janitorial position at Occam Aerospace Research Center. She composed her letter, achieved an appointment, and spent the morning of her interview ironing her bottle-green dress and studying a bus schedule. One hour before her planned departure, disaster: great silver scythes of rain, and she owned no umbrella. She panicked, tried not to cry, and became aware of rumblings from the Arcade's other apartment. She hadn't met the man who lived there, though he was always around, some sort of shut-in. She'd lost the luxury of guardedness. She knocked on his door.

She expected squat, hirsute, unshaven, and leering, but the fellow who answered had an aristocratic air, tucked like an envelope inside jacket, sweater, vest, and shirt, pushing fifty but with eyes sparkling behind spectacles. He blinked and absently touched his bald head as if he'd forgotten to put on a hat. Then he registered her distress and smiled gently.

"Why, hello, there. To whom do I owe the pleasure?"

Elisa touched her neck in apology, then made the sign for "umbrella," an intuitive one. The man's surprise at her muteness lasted only a few seconds.

"An umbrella! Of course! Come in, my dear, and I'll pull it from the pile like Excalibur from the stone."

He dove into the apartment. Elisa hesitated. She'd never been inside a home that wasn't Home; she leaned rightward and saw baroque, shadowy shapes rippling with skulking felines.

"Of course you're the new tenant. How inhospitable of me not to visit sooner with the ritual plate of cookies. I'm afraid the only excuse I have is a deadline which has had me nailed to the desk."

The desk in question didn't look like a desk. It was a tabletop hinged at an adjustable angle. This man was an artist of some sort, and Elisa felt a windblown tingle. The table had at its center a half-painted image of a woman from over her shoulder, the curls of her hair as the chief focus. Beneath her was painted the legend: *NO MORE DULL DRAB HAIR.*

"My neglectfulness notwithstanding, please let me know if you need anything at all, although I do recommend that you pick up your own umbrella. I notice you have a bus schedule there, and the station is a longer walk from here than is ideal. Many things, as you have no doubt noticed, are less than ideal about the Arcade Apartments. But carpe diem, and all that fine stuff. I trust you're getting along all right?"

He paused in his canvas rifling and looked to Elisa for a response. She expected this; once people started talking, they tended to forget the disability over which they'd chosen to discourse. This man, however, smiled, his slender brown mustache broadening like open arms.

"You know, I've always wanted to learn sign language. What a wonderful opportunity for me."

The worried tears Elisa had been tamping for weeks should have fallen in a grateful gush, but she forced them back; there was no time to redo makeup. It only got harder over the subsequent minutes, as the man, Giles Gunderson per his magniloquent introduction, located the umbrella, decided to drive her himself, and refused to accept her signed protests. Along the way, Giles distracted her with how the word *janitor* came from Janus, the god of entrances and exits, only stopping the lesson when an Occam guard established that Giles's name wasn't on a list. The guard motioned Elisa to climb out of the van and into the slashing rain.

"'And wheresoe'er thou move, good luck / Shall fling her old shoe after,'" Giles had called out after her. "Alfred Lord Tennyson!"

Shoe, she'd repeated to herself, keeping eyes on her ugly, inherited heels as they splatted along a rain-run sidewalk. *If I get this job, I'll buy myself a nice pair of shoes.*

16

THE MYSTERIOUS ADVENT of Strickland has supplanted Brewster stories as the favored topic of conversation. Elisa can't quit thinking of what she saw in the tank, yet keeps it private from Zelda—the memory feels more preposterous by the day. Instead, and to Elisa's gratitude, Zelda has defused tension by poking fun at everything else. Realizing, for instance, that Fleming kept calling Strickland's armed guards "MPs"—Military Police—and not "Empties," a label that was even more fitting, as the silent, stern soldiers showed no proclivity for independent action. Empties are, at least, easy for the women to avert, as they march in a buckle-jangling lockstep beyond the abilities of gawky scientists. Even now they hear a few, and Zelda and Elisa sidestep them, turning down a hall they usually save for later.

"Even when the Empties aren't on the warpath, I know just where they are," Zelda says. "They breathe together, you notice that? It's like air coming out of the vents, all at once. *Whoosh.* I'm telling you, all these extra men here, and it's just as quiet as before? It's not natural."

Before Elisa can sign a reply, the aforementioned quiet, a decade undisturbed, is cracked in half. In the neighborhood in which Elisa lives, such a sound might have her looking for a backfiring car before hedging toward cover, wary of local tales of organized crime. Inside Occam, the bang is so astonishing it might as well be a spaceship crash; Zelda ducks behind her cart, as if cheap plastic and corrosive liquids will be her salvation.

Then another bang, then another. The sounds aren't sloppy. They aren't objects being dropped. They are of mechanical issue, urged by a trigger, and Elisa has no choice but to assume that they are, in fact, gunshots. Shouting follows, as well as the rabbity heartbeat of running feet, both noises muffled behind the nearest door, which is, of course, F-1.

"Get down!" Zelda pleads.

Zelda signs the order, too, and Elisa suffers a wallop of love for the woman. She realizes she is, indeed, still standing. The door opens, striking the wall as loudly as a fourth gunshot. Zelda recoils as if she took the bullet, toppling to a hip and crossing her arms over her face. Elisa's entire body jerks once, and then she's frozen by the size, speed, and force of the humanity gushing out.

Fleming is out in front. His grimace is familiar to anyone who's seen him overreact to a clogged toilet or a hallway puddle, the difference being the bloody handprints tracked up both of his sleeves. Coming third is Bob Hoffstetler, and he's the most upset of any of them, spectacles akimbo and his thin net of hair in an upright thatch. He carries a red, soaking wad of cloth that could be anything—towel, smock, undershirt. His eyes, usually so kind, shoot like darts into Elisa.

"Call an ambulance!" The accent, usually so delicate, is husky under hardship.

Between these regular-sized humans is Strickland, his deep-valleyed eyes ablaze and his lips peeled back, gripping with tourniquet tightness the wrist of his left arm, which ends not in the expected hand but a bouquet of fingers arranged at hinky angles, baby-breathed with blood, and vased in loose peels of skin. Blood drops to the floor as loudly as ball bearings. Elisa gapes at them, the ruby beads; they will be hers to clean.

Empties burst outward, kicking the blood beads. The guards break off on either side of Strickland, coming at Elisa and Zelda with rifles thrust out like dancers' canes. This is crowd control. This is clearing the scene. Elisa grabs her cart, wheels it around, and knows by its yawing swerve that the back wheels have been fully slickened.

17

ANTONIO IS THE first to make it to the cafeteria to ask if everything's okay. His crossed eyes pose the question to both Elisa and Zelda, but Zelda knows full well she's the one who has to answer. All this time and the crew hasn't bothered to learn so much as the sign-language alphabet. Zelda's tired of it. She doesn't want to be in charge here, or at home, or anywhere. It's too hard. Look at her hands—they're shaking. She conceals it by turning to face the Automat, scanning the geometric sandwiches and gamy fruit like it's just another three-in-the-morning dinnertime.

Duane arrives next, toothless as a newt and just as squeaky. Yolanda makes up for their timidity, cycloning in and honking on about how it sounded like someone was shooting up the joint, she can't work like this, she has half a mind to blah, blah, blah. Zelda lets her eyesight blur until she can only make out the Automat's nickel-operated compartments, each one an itsy-bitsy *Alice in Wonderland* doorway. If she could become small, she might crawl through one and get the heck out of here.

Instead, she's trapped to relive F-1's gory eruption in her mind, over and over. She tries to generate sympathy for Mr. Strickland. The next time he visited a men's room, would he even be able to undo his zipper? This stab at sympathy is like trying to chop ice with her hand. There's no way that man couldn't guess how it might feel for a black woman to be cornered by a white man with a cattle prod. She looks up and notices Lucille; her albino coloring cloaks her against the cafeteria wall.

"Look, even Lucille's upset," Yolanda cries. "¿Qué pasa?"

Zelda turns around. She's been avoiding it. She doesn't want to look at Elisa right now. She loves the skinny little lady so much, yet can't shake the certainty that this is her fault. She's the one who insisted they follow the questionable QCC directive to enter F-1, which grounded them on Strickland's bad side, and Zelda can't help but think Elisa purposely lingered outside F-1 tonight, which put them in the worst spot imaginable when the gunfire began.

Elisa wilts in her chair, like Zelda is stomping her chest. Zelda feels terrible, then tells herself to *quit* feeling terrible. Elisa's a good person, but she'll never get it. How could she? Things go wrong at Occam, and it won't be the white woman who gets blamed. Hell, Elisa goes around pocketing loose change from labs like it's nothing. What if it's a trap? Elisa would never even think of such a thing. What if a scientist left it there to test the night janitors, and when it vanishes, and Fleming is told, guess whose neck is on the butcher block?

Elisa lives in a world of her own devising. That's obvious from the shoes. Zelda imagines Elisa's perception as one of those dioramas she saw in a museum, perfect little realms, breakable but not if you walk softly. This is not Zelda's world. She can't turn on a TV without seeing black people marching, stabbing signs into the anger-stirred air. Brewster sees footage like that, he changes the channel, and Zelda, in her heart, is grateful, even if it's spineless. Anything racial goes down anywhere in the USA, and the looks she gets at the punch clock the next day are murder. All over the country, men like David Fleming are looking for reasons to fire women like Zelda Fuller.

What other work could she do? She's lived in Old West Baltimore since birth, and the row houses haven't improved much since then. Today, the neighborhood is more crowded, more segregated. Zelda gets the concepts of blockbusting and white flight, but doesn't give a damn. She dreams of the suburbs. She can taste the air, like pine and marmalade, feel it flushing Occam's toxins from her body. She won't be working at Occam when she lives out there—it's too far away. She'll be running her own cleaning business. She's told Elisa about it a hundred times, how she'll bring Elisa with her, hire other smart ladies, pay them square like no man would. She's waiting for Elisa to take it seriously. She never does, and it's hard to blame her. How would Zelda make enough dough with Brewster only working at whim? What bank would cosign a business loan for a black woman?

Zelda imagines the cafeteria is a white man's paradise of horseplay and joviality during the day, but at night it's as bare and clangorous as a cave. Footsteps resound down an adjacent hall, coming closer. It's Fleming, every last one of his promotions evident in his unfaltering stride. Zelda looks at Elisa, her best friend, her potential ruiner, and feels her dreams of getting out of Old West Baltimore, and out of Occam, start to drip down like blood off the prongs of Strickland's cattle prod.

18

"WE HAVE OURSELVES a pickle, girls. A real pickle."

The scene of the crime still vibrates from the ordeal. Without being asked, Elisa dips her mop into soapy water, wrings it in the vise, and swabs it at the tusk of blood. Fleming, meanwhile, issues the orders to Zelda. He always does. Zelda, at least, can verbally indicate comprehension.

"I need both of you inside F-1 right now," Fleming continues. "Emergency work. No questions, please. Just do the job. Do it well, but do it quickly. We don't have a lot of time."

"What do you want us to do?" Zelda asks.

"Zelda, this will go faster if you just listen. There's . . . biologic matter. On the floor. Maybe the tables. Check around. I don't need to explain this to you. You know how to do your job. Just make it all go away."

Elisa glances at the door. There's blood on the knob.

"But . . . will we be . . ."

"Zelda, what did I say? I wouldn't send you in there if you weren't perfectly safe. Just stay away from the tank. That's the big metal object you saw Mr. Strickland bring in. Do not go near the tank. There should be no reason at all for either of you to approach the tank. Is that understood? Zelda? Elisa?"

"Yes, sir," Zelda says, and Elisa nods.

Fleming starts to say more, then checks his watch. His terse part-ing words divulge a troubling loss of orating acumen.

"Fifteen minutes. Immaculate. Your complete discretion."

The lab is spare and orderly no longer. The concrete floor has sprouted a range of metal masts and stockades, each built with iron loops onto which an object, or a living thing, could be leashed. Carts of what look like medical devices extend from the beige computer bank like technological tumors. A table stands in the room's center, wheels pointed in four different directions. Surgical implements are scattered like punched-out teeth. Drawers are open, sinks are full, cigarettes still seep smoke. One smolders on the floor. The floor, as always, is where the hard work is.

Blood is all over. Gazing over it, Elisa thinks of magazine photos taken from airplanes of flooded lowlands. There's a hubcap-sized lake of blood congealing beneath the glaring lights. Smaller ponds, lochs, and lagoons trace Mr. Strickland's race to the door. Zelda pushes her cart through a lakelet and grimaces at the blood trailing behind the plastic wheels. Elisa has no choice but to mirror the movement, too astonished to hatch a cannier plan.

Fifteen minutes. Elisa pours water over the floor. It slithers, strikes blobs of blood, births pink pinwheels. This is how she was taught to do it at Home, in every arena of life. Thin out the mystery of life, the fascination, the lust, the horror, until you no longer question it. She lobs her mop head at the center of the gunk and drags it this way, and that, until the yarn-strands bloat and darken. This is normal. The sound, too, is normal—the wet swap, moist slurp—and she fix-ates on it. That soot scorch on the concrete could be from an Empty's fired gun; mop right over it. That's a cattle prod, one million pounds of menace, impossible to lift; mop around it.

Elisa tells herself not to look at the tank. Don't look at the tank, Elisa. Elisa looks at the tank. Even thirty feet away, next to the large pool, it's too big for the lab, a dinosaur crouching in wait. It has been bolted to four plinths, a wooden stairway providing access to a top hatch. Fleming was right about one thing: There's no blood anywhere near it. No reason to approach it. Elisa tells herself to look away. Look away, Elisa. Elisa cannot look away.

The moppers meet at the bloody area's vertex. Zelda checks her watch, swipes sweat from her nose, and steadies her bucket for a final pour, nodding for Elisa to gather the contraptions off the floor before the water floods them aside. Elisa kneels and collects them. A pair of forceps. A scalpel with a broken blade. A syringe with a bent needle. Dr. Hoffstetler's tools, for sure, though she can't make herself believe the man would hurt anyone or anything. He'd looked devastated charging from the lab. She stands and sets the items in a parallel arrangement on a table like a hotel maid. She hears water lap from Zelda's bucket and from peripheral vision sees its elongating tendrils. Zelda clucks.

"Will you look at that? Janitors have to sneak off to the loading dock to smoke. Meantime they're smoking cigars in here like this is some—"

Zelda is not a person typically given to gasps. Elisa spins around to see Zelda's mop timber forward. Her hands are cupped before her, holding two small objects the mop water washed back from under the table, objects she'd believed were cigars. Her hands shake and part, and the objects drop. One of them falls soundlessly. The other clinks, and from it pops a silver wedding band.

19

ZELDA HAS GONE for help. Elisa can hear her nurse flats firecracking down the hallway. She's left staring at Strickland's fingers. The pinky, the ring finger. Snaggy fingernails, poignant tufts of knuckle hair. The skin of the ring finger is pale on one end, blocked from sun for years by the wedding ring. Elisa's mind returns to the sight of Strickland bursting from the lab door. He'd been clutching his left hand. These are two of the fingers that had fished into the crinkling cellophane bag of green hard candy.

She can't just leave them there. Fingers can be reattached. She's read about it. Maybe Dr. Hoffstetler has the know-how to do it himself. She grimaces and looks around. F-1 is a lab. It must have containers, beakers. Occam labs, however, mock people like her; they're impossible to decode, provisioned with instruments of arcane utility. Her eyes fall in despair and she sees, next to a trash can, something more endemic to her field: a wadded brown paper bag. She goes for it, shakes it open, and sticks her hand inside the greasy paper to operate it like a puppet. Those nubs on the floor aren't human fingers. They're just pieces of trash needing to be picked up.

Elisa kneels and tries to collect them. They are like two chunks of chicken, too soft and small for her to get a grip. They fall once, twice, scattering blood like Giles's dropped brushes scatter paint. She holds her breath, locks her jaw, and picks up the fingers with her bare hand. They are as lukewarm as a limp handshake. She inserts them into the bag and crimps the top. She's wiping her hand on her uniform when she spies the wedding band. She can't leave that, either, but no way is she opening the bag again. She swipes the ring and drops it into her apron pocket. She stands, tries to restore normal breathing. The bag feels empty, as if the two fingers have wiggled away like worms.

Elisa is alone, in silence. But is it silence? She is aware of a soft wheeze, air being discharged through a vent. She looks across the lab, once again, at the tank. A second, more disturbing question poses itself. Is she, after all, alone? Fleming warned her and Zelda not to approach the tank. Sound advice. *Do not approach the tank*, Elisa reinforces to herself. She glances down. Her bright shoes are moving over mopped floor. She is approaching the tank.

Though she is encircled by advanced technology, Elisa feels like a cartoon caveman advancing upon a thicket despite the growls vibrating from within. What was foolhardy two million years ago is foolhardy now. Yet her pulse doesn't quicken as it did from Strickland's harmless fingers. It could be because Fleming promised her that she was safe. Or it could be because every night she dreams of the darkest water, and there it is, beyond the portholes of the cylindrical tank: darkness, water.

F-1 is too bright for her to adjust her eyes to the tank's interior blackness, so she sets down the paper bag and tunnels her hands against the porthole. Refracted light makes her feel as if she's spiraling until she realizes that the window is underwater. She squashes her nose to the glass to see upward. Here, at last, her pulse gallops, right along with the old iron-lung nightmares.

The dark water eddies with weak light. Elisa catches her breath: It's like distant fireflies. She presses her hands flat against the window, wanting closer, feeling a physical need. The substance turns, twists, dances like an arabesque veil. Between the points of light, a shape coalesces. Floating debris, Elisa tries to tell herself, that's all it is, and then a shaft of light hits a pair of photoreceptive eyes. They flash bright as gold through black water.

The glass explodes. At least, that is how it sounds. The crash is the lab door banging open, the shatter is the several sets of feet charging inside, and the scrunch is the paper bag being swiped up by her own hands. She's proving herself a caveman indeed, shrinking back from a bestial threat and rushing at civilization's centrum—Fleming, the Empties, Dr. Hoffstetler—hoisting the bag of fingers like a trophy, her trophy for having looked into the eyes of ravishing annihilation and lived to tell. She's giddy with survival, breathless, almost crying, almost laughing.

20

Various offices were offered to Strickland. First-floor berths with panoramic views of swooping lawns. He enjoyed spurning Fleming's largesse by instead insisting upon the windowless security-camera room. He had Fleming install a desk, cabinet, trash can, and two telephones. One white, one red. The room is small, neat, quiet, and perfect. He journeys his eyes across the four-by-four grid of black-and-white monitors. The interchangeable hallways. The sporadic twitch of a meandering night worker. After the occluded views of the rain forest, how relieving it is to see everything all at once.

He peruses the screens. The last time he saw the two janitors now seated right behind him was in the men's room, he burning with the mortification of runaway urine, they holding their laughter until he left. Different dynamic now, isn't it? An opportunity to reestablish a proper relationship. He lets his left hand dangle. Gives the janitors a chance to see the bandages, the shape of his reattached fingers. To imagine what they look like underneath. He could tell them. Pretty fucking bad is how they look. The fingers don't match his hand. They're putty-colored, stiff as plastic, attached by black thread the thickness of tarantula legs.

Strickland's only concern is that they can make out his fingers in the dim light. He unscrewed the overheads after moving in, preferring to let the sixteen screens fill the office with a ghostly gray. After the jungle's salacious blaze, bright lights are as bad as loud noises. F-1 is intolerable. Hoffstetler has begun dimming the lab at night for the creature's sake, but that's even worse. The idea that he and the asset share a light sensitivity enrages him. He's no animal. He left his animal self in the Amazon. He had to if he had any hope of being a good husband, a good father.

Just to make sure they see, he wiggles his stitched fingers. The blood screams, the monitors go hazy. Strickland blinks, tries not to faint. This pain, it's something else. The doctors gave him pills for it. The bottle's right there in the desk. Don't doctors know that suffering has a point? It grinds you harder, sharper. No thanks, doc. Hard candy will do.

Thinking of the sharp, stinging, distracting taste makes him finally turn around. Since Lainie refuses to unpack the boxes from the move, he'd had to dig out the Brazilian candy himself. It was worth it. The bag chuckles like a clean countryside creek when he picks it up. The glassy green ball billiards between his teeth. That's better. Much better. He exhales over a tongue being playfully stabbed by sugar and drops himself into his chair.

He's supposed to thank these two janitors. For finding his

fingers. That was Fleming's request. He would have told Fleming to stuff it, but he's bored. Sitting behind a desk all day. How do people stand it? Takes fifty signatures before he's authorized to blow his nose. A hundred signatures before he can wipe his ass. It's a shame not a single idiot MP landed a bullet in the asset during the attack. He's got half a mind to pick up the Alabama Howdy-do, march into F-1, and fix it so the asset has less life left to be studied. Once Deus Brânquia is gone, he'll be out from under General Hoyt, back into his wife's and kids' lives. He wants that. Doesn't he? He thinks he does.

Plus, he can't sleep. Not with this kind of pain. So, fine. He'll leak some gratitude upon the stupid janitors. But he'll do it his way, just to make sure they don't think he's some overgrown child incapable of not pissing all over the bathroom floor. Anyway, he's in no hurry to scurry home. The way Lainie looks at him, he can hardly stand it. Like the fingers don't compare to what the jungle ripped out of him and what he's tried to hastily sew back together. He's trying. Can't she see he's trying?

He picks up the first of two pulled files.

"Zelda D. Fuller."

"Yes, sir," she replies.

"Married, says here. But how is it your husband's got a different last name? If you're divorced or separated, that's supposed to be here."

"Brewster, that's his first name, sir."

"Sounds like a last name to me."

"Yes, sir. But no, sir."

"Yes, but no. Yes, but no." He screws his right thumb into a forehead beset by the pain crawling up his left arm. "Answers like that are going to make this last all night. It's twelve-thirty. In the a.m. I could've called you two here in the middle of the day, make it easy on myself, but I didn't. Best you can do is return the favor so I can get out of here, go to bed, have breakfast with my kids. That sound all right to you, Mrs. Brewster? I'm sure you have children."

"I don't, sir."

"No? Now why's that?"

"I don't know, sir. It just never . . . took."

"I'm sorry to hear that, Mrs. Brewster."

"It's Mrs. Fuller, sir. Brewster's my husband."

"Brewster. That's a last name or I'm a monkey's uncle. Well, I'm sure you have siblings. I expect you know how it goes with children."

"I don't have siblings, sir, I'm sorry."

"That surprises me a great deal. Isn't that unusual? For your people?"

"My mother died in childbirth."

"Oh." Strickland flips a page. "Here it is, page two. That's too bad. Although if she died in childbirth, I guess you can't miss her."

"I don't know, sir."

"Silver lining, is all I'm saying."

"Maybe, sir."

Maybe. It feels as if two balloons of acid are inflating inside his temples. *Maybe* they'll explode. *Maybe* his skin will fizzle from his face and these girls will get to see his shrieking skull. He presses a finger to the page and converges his wobbling eyes upon it. A dead mother. Implied miscarriages. Some kooky marriage. Doesn't mean shit. Words are useless. Take General Hoyt's brief about Deus Brânquia. Sure, it'd explained the mission. But had it imparted a thing about how the jungle gets inside you? How the vines penetrate your mosquito net while you sleep, slithering past your lips, boring through your esophagus, and strangling your heart?

Somewhere there's a government brief about the thing in F-1, and it's bullshit, too. What's inside that tank, you can't capture it in words. You need all your senses. His had been electric in the Amazon, fueled on rage and buchité. Returning to America had dulled him. Baltimore had put him into a coma. Maybe getting two fingers torn off can wake him back up. Because look at him. Here, in the dead of night, listening to low-paid night crawlers, hired precisely because they are slow, uneducated women, tell him, to his face, *maybe.*

21

"WHAT'S THE *D*?" he demands.

Zelda has been menaced by men in power all her life. A steel-worker following her to the playground to tell her that her daddy had stolen a white man's job at Bethlehem and was going to hang. Teachers at Douglass High who thought educating black girls would only make them covet things they'd never have. A Fort McHenry tour guide who tallied the number of Union soldiers killed in the Civil War and then asked Zelda if she didn't want to say thank you to her white classmates. At Occam, though, threats have only ever come from Fleming, and she's learned how to handle those. Know your QCC front and back. Know how to look forlorn. Know how to flatter.

Mr. Strickland is different. Zelda doesn't know him, and senses it wouldn't matter if she did. He's got lion eyes, like she saw once at the zoo, impossible to read to judge the degree of aggression. Forget divining any clues as to why she and Elisa have been called before this wall of security monitors, though it can't be good.

"*D*, sir?" she ventures.

"Zelda D. Fuller."

Here's a question with an answer. She rushes for it, heedlessly.

"Delilah. You know, the Bible."

"Delilah? The dead mother gave you that?"

She knows how to absorb a punch.

"That's what my father told me, sir. She had it planned out for a girl."

Strickland bites into his candy. He does this like a lion, too, jaws wide. Zelda knows cheap candy when she sees it, she practically grew up on it, but this is a new level of cheap. It cleaves badly; she sees splinters sliver into the man's cheek and gums. She sees blood, diluted by saliva, and can almost taste it, cold and edgeless, as opposite to hard candy as the color red is to green.

"Interesting lady, this dead mother," Strickland says. "You know what Delilah did, don't you?"

Zelda enters Fleming's scolding sessions prepared to deflect claims that janitors stole something that absentminded scientists only misplaced. Never before has she had to bone up on biblical characters.

"I . . . at church, they—"

"My wife's a churchgoer, so I'm up on most of the stories. What I recall is God gave Samson a bunch of strength. Slew a whole army with a donkey's jawbone, that kind of thing. Now Delilah, she was a temptress. Got old Samson to tell her his secret. So Delilah gets her servant to cut off Samson's hair and calls in her friends the Philistines, who poke out Samson's eyes and mutilate him till he's hardly a man anymore. He's just some thing they torture. That's Delilah. Real credit to females. Odd name, is all I'm saying."

The conversation shouldn't go like this; it isn't fair. Zelda knows the same Bible stories, but her body betrays her, turns her into the stooge Strickland expects—she can feel her eyes widen and her lips tremble. Strickland scans the file, and Zelda can hear his silent *tsk, tsk*. Zelda is ashamed to feel relief when Strickland shifts his gaze to Elisa. Zelda can still hear his thoughts, though. Laziness isn't strictly a Negro problem, no sir. The lower class is the lower class because they can't find their bootstraps. Take this white woman. All right face, nice enough figure. If she had an ounce of gumption, she'd be puttering about a tidy house taking care of kids, not working the graveyard shift like some sort of nocturnal beast.

Strickland crunches candy, picks up the second file.

"Elisa Esposito," Strickland says. "Es-po-si-to. You part Mexican or something?"

Zelda glances at Elisa. Her friend's face is taut with the particular anxiety she suffers when someone doesn't yet know she's mute. Zelda clears her throat and intercedes.

"It's Italian, sir. It's a name they give to orphans. She was found on the riverbank when she was a baby, and they gave her the name."

Strickland frowns at Zelda. She knows the look. He's getting sick of hearing her talk. Creating self-aggrandizing myths, he must believe, is yet another flaw of the common class. This girl here was found by the river. This boy here was birthed with a caul. Pathetic origin stories chanted as if proof of divinity.

"How long you two known each other?" he grunts.

"Whole time Elisa's been here, sir. Fourteen years?"

"That's good. Means both of you know how things run here. How things need to stay. I guess you're the two who found my fingers?" He rubs his head. He's sweating. He looks like he's in agony. "That's a question. You can reply."

"Yes, sir."

"I'm going to go ahead and thank you for that," he says. "We thought they ended up—it doesn't matter what we thought. Now I'm not real thrilled about the paper bag. Seems like there should have been something better than a bag. The doc says a wet rag would have been just as good as ice. He said they wasted a lot of time sterilizing the fingers before they could label the nerves and whatnot. I'm not trying to blame you here. But still. Right now, we don't know what's going to happen. It's like what Delilah here said about having children. The fingers will take or they won't. Well, there you have it. That's what I have to say about that."

"I'm sorry, sir," Zelda says. "We did our best."

An earnest apology delivered quick before you can feel bad about it—that's Zelda's method. Strickland nods, but then there's trouble. He looks to Elisa, expecting the same, and impatience darkens his tired, pained face. Elisa's silence comes off as rudeness. There's no hope in dodging this. Zelda sends a prayer up and steps into the lion cage once more.

"Elisa doesn't talk, sir."

22

MILITARY WORK INGRAINS certain assumptions into a fellow. A person who won't talk is suspect. They're choosing belligerence. They're hiding something. These two women don't seem sharp enough for subterfuge, but you never know. The lower classes, after all, are where you find your Communists, unionists, folks with nothing to lose.

"She can't talk?" Strickland asks. "Or chooses not to?"

"Can't, sir," Zelda says.

The throb in his arm fades to the background. This is interesting. It explains why this Elisa Esposito has kept this shit-hole job. Not obstinacy but limitation. Probably all explained on page two. He closes the folder, though, and gives her a long look. She can hear just fine, that's for sure. There's a raptness to her that is startling. Her eyes are locked onto his lips in a way most females would consider indelicate. He looks harder, wishing for buchité vision, and sees raised scar tissue in the shadow of her shirt collars.

"Some kind of operation?"

"They don't know," Zelda replies. "Either her parents did it to her, or someone at the orphanage."

"Now why would someone do that to a baby?"

"Babies cry," Zelda says. "Maybe that was enough."

Strickland thinks back to Timmy's and Tammy's infancies. How each time he'd returned from DC to Florida, he'd been stunned by the Lainie he found. Exhausted, floppy-limbed, fingers puckered from baths and diapers. Now suppose you worked at an orphanage. Suppose there wasn't one baby, or two, but dozens. He's read military studies on sleep deprivation. He knows the kind of dangerous ideas that begin to seem sane.

He wants to tell Elisa to stretch out her neck so he can watch the gray light of the monitors slide across the satiny extrusion of scars.

The ferocity of Elisa's eyes make her wild; the wounds indicate that she's tamed. It's an appealing combination. She fidgets under his stare and crosses her legs. Well, there you go. Just a regular girl after all. Except here's something else he wasn't expecting. She isn't sporting the rubber-soled shoes of every other janitor he's seen. These are coral pink. He saw shoes like this all the time in Japan. Painted on the sides of Air Force bombers. Worn by pinup models. In real life, though, hardly ever.

Elisa Esposito stares at her clasped hands, just like they all do, then appears to recall something. She digs into the pocket of her smock, withdraws a tiny, bright object, and holds it out. She looks somber, which makes the monkey motion of her other hand so strange. She's rotating a thumbs-up fist over her tits. She's a certifiable fruitcake, he thinks, until the Negro pipes up to remind him of sign language.

"That means she's sorry," Zelda says.

Elisa is holding his wedding ring. This, too, he'd assumed had tumbled down the asset's gullet. Lainie will be glad to see it. He, however, feels no emotion about it. He searches Elisa's face but can't find anything dishonest about the offer. She didn't steal the ring, nothing like that. Her expression is sincere. The circular pattern of her hand over her breast seems less simian, more sensual. He has a sudden, strange realization. His new aversion to light and loud noises— here's a woman built as if to those specifications. A woman who works in the dark of night. A woman who can't make a peep.

He makes a cup of his left hand and allows her to place the ring into it. It feels ceremonial, an inverted wedding.

"Can't put it on just yet," he says. "But thanks."

The girl shrugs and nods. Her eyes don't leave his. Damn, it's almost unnerving. He hates it. He kind of likes it. He looks away— that's unusual—to her pink shoes, bouncing in midair. Pain blurts up his arm for no reason at all. He grinds his teeth and reaches for the bag of candy and instead opens the desk drawer. The bottle of painkillers is right there, glowing white amid Eagle Black Warrior pencils. Sweat pops from his forehead pores, and he tries not to wipe it. Wiping sweat isn't a dominant gesture.

"That's the first thing," he says. "Second thing is, F-1."

The Negro opens her mouth. Strickland slashes his hand to shut her up.

"I know. You signed the papers. I know all that bullshit. I don't care. My job's to make sure you comprehend the *gravity* of that signature. You've been here fourteen years? That's nice. Maybe next year you get a cake. I hear fourteen years, you know what I think? Fourteen years is plenty of time to get lazy. Now, Mr. Fleming told you you don't clean F-1 unless he says. Here's what you don't know. You disobey, you don't deal with Mr. Fleming. You deal with me. And I represent who? The US government. We wouldn't have us a local problem. We'd have us a federal problem. Is that understood?"

Elisa's top leg slides off her lower. A positive, submissive sign, though he mourns losing sight of the shoe. Right then, one of the telephones begins to ring. The balloon of acid under his temple bursts from the noise and courses down his left arm, pooling under the wedding ring in his palm. A call this late? He flexes his bad hand, hoping to fight off the ache.

"Let me finish. You may have seen some things. So be it."

He's seeing things, too, streaks of red, tainted blood pumping directly into his eyeballs. Red—it's the red phone ringing. Washington. Maybe General Hoyt. He's got to get these girls the hell out of his office. Undaunted, his rivalry with Deus Brânquia rises from the swamp, the quicksand, the black depths of misery. The red phone, the red blood, the red Amazonian moon.

"Final words, now, listen, just listen. It doesn't take a genius to know we're dealing with a living specimen here. That doesn't matter. That doesn't matter at all. All you need to know is this. That thing in F-1? It might stand on two legs, but we're the ones made in God's image. We're the ones. Isn't that right, Delilah?"

The worthless woman can't muster but a whisper.

"I don't know what God looks like, sir."

The pain is absolute now. He is aware of individual nerve endings. It's as if the lights inside his body have been switched on. Fine, he'll take the painkillers. He's already gripping the bottle. He'll answer the red phone with cheeks full of half-chewed pills. Manufactured drugs, after all, are what civilized men ingest. And he is civilized. Or will be. Very soon. This phone call might even be the proving ground. Decisions are being made about the asset. And to advise about that he will need control. He thumbs off the lid of the pain-killers.

"God looks *human*, Delilah. He looks like me. Like you." He nods the women toward the door. "Though let's be honest. He looks a little bit more like me."

23

ELISA'S DREAMS HAVE begun to unmuddy. She's reclined at the bottom of a river. Everything is emerald. She springs her toes from mossy stones, glides through caressing grasses, pushes off from the velveted branches of sunken trees. Objects she recognizes appear gradually. Her egg timer in slow somersault. The eggs themselves, little moons in rotation. Shoes tumble past like a school of clumsy fish, and album covers descend like stingrays.

Two human fingers float into view, and Elisa wakes up.

A lot about Richard Strickland distresses Elisa, but his fingers are what haunt her. It takes several of these dreams before, one night, she bolts awake in understanding. She uses her own fingers to inter-act with the world. It's not ridiculous, she thinks, to be frightened by a man at risk of losing his own fingers. She imagines the equivalent in a speaking person and it's horrific: Strickland's teeth tumbling across riven lips, a man no longer capable, or inclined, to discuss what he does before he does it.

She, too, has things she won't discuss. It's the latter half of the night, when she and Zelda work separately. Elisa presses her ear to the ice-cold door of F-1. She holds her breath and listens. Voices tend to carry through lab walls, but tonight none do. She glances back at her cart, which she has parked in front of a different lab halfway down the hall, hopefully enough to hoodwink Zelda should she re-join Elisa earlier than expected. Elisa feels exposed while carrying so little—just a brown-paper lunch bag and her key card. She slots the card and wishes the lock's bite was softer.

Occam's constant is its uncompromising brightness. Lights do not turn off. Elisa has never been privy to so much as a single switch. F-1's dimness, then, is as outrageous as a fire. Once inside, Elisa presses her back to the closed door and panics that something has gone wrong. But this is clearly by plan: A perimeter of lights, in-stalled along the walls for this purpose, radiate a honey glow off the ceiling.

Plenty enough light to see by, but there are noises, too, keeping Elisa sealed to the door. Reek-reek, chuk-a-kuk, zuh-zuh-zuh, thoonk, hee-hee-hee-hee-hee, thrub-thrub, curu-curu, zeee-eee-eee, hik-rik-hik-rik, lug-a-lug-a-lug, fyeeeeeew. Elisa has spent every day of her life in the city, yet recognizes these as natural sounds, none of which have any place in this concrete bunker. They over-whelm F-1's after-hours inertia, impregnating every table, chair, and cabinet with predator menace. There are monsters loose in the lab.

Elisa's reason wrests control from the fear. The bird arias and frog dirges come from a single source, off to the right. They are record-ings, and this isn't so different than a movie at the Arcade—the lowered lights, the speaker sound track. Some Occam scientist has designed what Giles might call a mise-en-scène, an atmosphere in-side which unfolds the currently screening fantasy. Her guess is Bob Hoffstetler. If anyone at this facility has the empathy required for this artistic endeavor, it's him.

She crosses over the spot where she plucked Strickland's fingers from the floor. Her footsteps are loud, and she curses her forgetful-ness. She'd meant to wear rubber-soled sneakers. Or had she kept on her purple heels as subconscious inspiration? There's a hissing to her right. An anaconda attracted by the jungle's incantations? No—it's the roll of a reel-to-reel player. The stainless steel surface shimmers like a moonlit river; Elisa approaches until she is close enough to see the jumping VU meters. Canisters are piled about. MARAÑON FIELD #5. TOCANTINS FIELD #3. XINGU/UNKNOWN FIELD #1. Gathered also is a hill of other audio gear, none of which she can identify except for a standard record player.

Elisa steps away, circles the tank. One more foreboding sign: The top hatch is open. She expects the hair on her neck and arms to razor in dread, but it doesn't. She continues toward the pool. It is the pool, after all, that has monopolized her mind. Every bath she takes, she takes in this pool, or so she pretends. This make-believe persists throughout her whole routine: Eggs bobbing into water, the creak of the timer, the hope of shoes, the disappointment of LPs, Giles pausing his paintbrush to bid her good night, having no idea of the strange thoughts in her head.

A red line is painted on the floor a foot from the pool. It is unsafe to go any farther. So why is she considering it? Because she can't get it out of her head, this thing that Mr. Strickland has dragged here, that Empties guard with guns, that Dr. Hoffstetler endeavors to study. She knows that she's been the thing in the water before. She's been the voiceless one from whom men have taken without ever asking what she wanted. She can be kinder than that. She can balance the scales of life. She can do what no man ever tries to do with her: communicate.

She proceeds until the two-foot ledge pinches her thighs. The surface of the water is still. But not perfectly still. You only need to look, really look, to see the water breathe. Elisa inhales, exhales, and sets her lunch bag on the ledge. It crunches, as loud as driving a shovel into dirt. She watches the water's surface for reaction. Nothing. She reaches into the bag and winces at the rustling. Nothing. She finds what she wants, withdraws it; it glows in the soft light. A single boiled egg.

For days, she's dared herself to add this egg to the three she

makes each night for Giles. Now she peels it. Her fingers are shaking. It's the ugliest egg peeling of her life. White fragments drop to the ledge. The egg, at last, is revealed, and what is more coherent and elemental than an egg? Elisa holds it in the palm of her hand like the magical object it is.

And the water responds.

24

THERE IS A dark, underwater twitch, like the leg-jerk of a dozing dog, and a plip of water leaps a foot from the center of the pool. It lands and echoes outward in delicate concentric circles—and then the lab's soft babbles are overwhelmed by a ripsaw of ratcheting metal. The water is torn into an X-shape as four fifteen-foot chains, each bolted to a corner of the pool, pull tight and shark-fin to the surface, sizzling foam and slobbering water, all of them attached to a single rising shape.

The knifing water, the rainbow refractions, the bat-wing shadows: Elisa can't understand what she's seeing. There: the gold-coin eye reflections she first saw in the tank, sun and moon. The angle alters and the eyeshine winks out. She sees its real eyes. They are blue. No—green, brown. No—gray, red, yellow, so many implausible shades. It is moving closer. The water does the thing's bidding, barely rippling. Its nose is slight, reptilian. Its lower jaw is multijointed but rests in a noble straight line. It is moving closer. Upright, as if no longer swimming, but walking. It is the God-image Strickland referenced: It moves like a man. Why, then, does Elisa feel that it is every animal that ever existed? It is moving closer. Gills on either side of the neck tremble like butterflies. Its neck is brutalized by a metal collar that binds the four chains. It is moving closer. It has a swimmer's physique, with shoulders like clenched fists, but the torso of a ballerino. Tiny scales cover it, scintillating like diamonds, lucent as silk. Grooves run over its whole body in elaborate, swirling, symmetrical patterns. It is no longer moving. It is five feet away. Even the water streaming from its body makes no sound.

It looks from the egg to her. Its eyes flash.

Elisa crashes back to earth, her heart thwacking. She sets the peeled egg on the ledge, grabs the lunch bag, and hops behind the red line. Her stance is defensive and the creature responds, lowering itself until only the smooth crown of its head is visible. Its eyes bore into hers for an unsettling moment before shifting back to the egg; the eyes, at this angle, go blue. It skims leftward as if expecting the egg to match the move.

He trusts nothing, Elisa thinks, and then verifies to herself, with surprise, that the creature is male. She's somehow certain. It's in the bluntness of his bearing, the forthrightness of his stare. Elisa has a queasy thought: If she knows he's male, he must know she's female. She orders herself to hold steady. This creature might be the first man-thing she's known who is more powerless than herself. She nods for him to go ahead, take the egg.

He advances as far as the chains allow, two feet from the ledge. Elisa is postulating that the red line was painted at too cautious of a distance when the creature's lower jaw drops and a secondary mandible punches out like a bone fist. A fraction of a second later, the egg is vanished, the pharyngeal jaw is retracted, and the water is as still as if none of it had happened. Elisa hasn't the time to even gasp; she pictures Strickland's fingers toppling to the floor.

The surface of the pool shivers, a billion pinpricks Elisa interprets as pleasure. The creature looks at her with eyes so bright they're white. She takes a stabilizing breath through her puny, single-jawed mouth and directs herself to keep going, keep going, keep going. She reaches her shaking hand into the bag again. Chain links clang as he lifts a shoulder to shield himself from what might be a weapon. This, she sees, is what he has come to expect from Occam.

But it is simply another egg, the last one. She holds it up so that he can see, then cracks it against her opposite knuckle and peels off a bit of the shell. Carefully, now, carefully—she extends her arm, the egg upright in her palm, her proffering posture like that of a mythical goddess. The creature doesn't trust it. He dolphins his upper body from the water and hisses. His gills fluff, flashing a blood-red warning. Elisa lowers her face to show meekness; it is no mere show. She waits. His jaws gnash but his gills subside. Elisa seals her lips and resumes extending her arm. She shifts the egg so that she holds it atop her fingers, a ball on a tee.

Elisa is out of range of his jaw and, she hopes, his arm. She lifts her other hand until it mirrors the egg. She can't sign "egg" without letting the egg drop from sight so instead she uses the letters: E-G-G. He does not react. She signs again, the dog paw of the E, the fingerpoint of the G, and wonders what the signs might remind him off. Wolf? Arrow? Cattle prod? She asserts the egg, then the signs. She is desperate that he understand. Unless he does, this creature who seems to have materialized straight from her dreams can't fully exist inside her reality. The egg, the signs. Egg, signs, egg, signs.

Her hand is beginning to cramp when the creature at last reacts. Once resolved upon action, he shows no hesitation, gliding as near to the ledge as the chains allow and raising his arm from water without splash or sound. Spines sprout from the arm like dorsal fins, and his fingers are bound by translucent webbing and tipped with curled claws. This makes the hand look huge, and when the fingers flex, it's difficult to imagine them doing so for any reason other than crushing prey.

His fingers bend at the second knuckles. His thumb curls across pale palm scales. The webbing folds like diaphanous leather. It's an E, a clumsy one, but Elisa believes this creature is accustomed to much larger gestures: full-body tumbles within seething seas; darting attacks; unfolding to full height beneath a tropical sun. Elisa feels as if she's the one underwater. The creature dips its gills into the pool as if to remind her to breathe.

His palm releases the E and his fingers open into a hesitant fan. Elisa nods support and signs G, pointing off to her left. This is considered good signing, but the creature is a novice. His three smallest fingers pinwheel to touch the heel of his hand and he points his index finger directly at Elisa. Her vision spins. Her chest throbs joyfully, almost painfully. He *sees* her. He doesn't look through her like Occam's men or past her like Baltimore's women. This beautiful being, however he might have hurt those who hurt him first, is pointing at her and only her.

She drops her signing hand and moves forward, her purple heels fearlessly disobeying the red line. The creature paddles in wait, his eyes, blue now, watching her body so closely that she feels naked. She holds the egg over the ledge, into the zone of hazard, no longer afraid of what happened to Strickland. The creature rises, all portents of caution gone, gills ruffling, chest expanding, water slipping from the splendor of his gemlike scales. He is what the jungle field recordings only hinted at: a pure thing.

She grieves the bulky steel locked to his neck and chest before noticing a second perversion down his left side. Four metal sutures clamp shut a gash spanning lower ribs to external oblique. Blood corkscrews into the water like drowned carnations. It's while she frowns at the grisly wound that the creature strikes with viper speed. The egg is swiped—Elisa feels only a breeze from his webbed fingers and a coolness of scales—and then he is submerged, swimming upside down back to the pool's center. She closes her empty hand. It's shaking. The creature resurfaces, a hundred lonely miles away, trailing his nose across the egg's shell. He picks at it with a claw, as if wondering how the human had managed to husk it.

Finally, he attacks the egg with claw and tooth. Scraps of shell catch the low light like shards of broken mirror. Elisa can't help it: A silent laugh jets from her lungs. If there's any chewing at all, it's brief, and then the creature turns toward her, coin eyes twirling with the recognition that she is capable of wonders. Elisa has never been the recipient of such a look. She is light-headed with it, even as her purple heels feel nailed to the floor.

The jungle clangor is beheaded. A deafening pop slaps the lab like a sonic boom, and the creature dives, gone without a ripple. Elisa seizes, thinking she's been discovered, until a soft flapping sound tells her that the reel-to-reel tape has run out and the take-up spool is spinning. It can't be good for the machine; someone will be along to shut it off or restart it; she needs to get out of F-1 and be happy with what she's achieved, which she is, so much so that her chest will surely be bruised tomorrow from the ferocious hammer of her heart.

25

Eggs are bad enough. An omelet is worse. Omelets require fork and knife. Lainie should have thought of that. What kind of wife doesn't think of that? Strickland takes the fork in his right hand. The knife, though, is not so simple, not with these fingers. He glances up at her. She's unmindful of him. There's no other way to put it. A year and a half spent fighting in the Amazon while she did what? Wipe up juice spills? A wife is supposed to anticipate her husband's needs. Keep things spic-and-span, in all realms of his life.

Look at this place. Weeks have passed since their Baltimore arrival and still the house is backcountry, something from the Tapajós region. Wet bras and stockings loop from the shower rod like rattan vines. The heat's cranked to verão levels. The television makes insect roars while Timmy and Tammy charge like tusked peccaries. And those fucking unpacked boxes. When he does manage to relax, the boxes surge upward like the Andes, and he's back there again, his feet caught in the sucking mud (shag carpet), breathless in the fever mist (air freshener), paralyzed before the stalking jaguar (vacuum cleaner).

A man doesn't like to feel like prey in his own home. More often he stays late at Occam, despite having nothing to do. How can a home television set compare with sixteen security monitors? "You're never home," Lainie sulks. He has shrinking sympathy. She finds the upheaval of the move invigorating, and he has begun to hate her for it. Because he can't share in it, not until the asset is finished and his ass doesn't belong to Hoyt. Maybe if she'd clean the place his heart would stop pounding and he could stand being here.

Family breakfast, the whole reason he's awake after only four hours of sleep. How come he's the only one at the table? Lainie's calling the kids, but they don't listen. She's laughing, like their behavior is permissible. She's chasing them. She's barefoot again. Is this some kind of bohemian fad? Poor people go barefoot. They're not poor. He pictures Elisa Esposito's coral-pink shoes, her exposed toes, even pinker. That's how all women should be. In fact, Elisa strikes him as the natural evolution of the female species: clean, colorful, silent. Strickland looks away from his wife's feet in disgust, back to his plate, the uneatable omelet.

The last time he changed his bandages, he pushed his wedding ring back onto his swollen, discolored ring finger. He figured Lainie would appreciate it. But it'd been a mistake. Now he can't get the ring off. He tries to get the fingers to grip the knife. The pain is like twine being dragged through his arteries. His face is pouring sweat. The house, it's so goddamn hot. He looks for something cold. The bottle of milk. He picks it up, slurps from it, and gasps when finished. He spots Lainie in the kitchen, frowning at him. Because he drank from the bottle? Last year he ate raw puma butchered on the jungle floor. Still he feels guilt. He sets down the bottle and feels lost, a stranger. He's a decaying finger, and Baltimore is the body rejecting his reattachment.

He picks up the fork, manages to squeeze the knife in his left palm.

The knife catches on cheese, the handle clanking against the wedding ring. Pain flares. He mutters bad words only to find Tammy sitting across from him, staring. The girl is getting used to seeing her father struggle. It makes him feel weak, and he can't afford that, not with General Hoyt getting daily updates from Occam. He'll need to betray no sign of frailty if he hopes to convince Hoyt that his quick, brutal path, not Hoffstetler's lenient, winding one, is the right route to take in regard to the asset. Before Hoyt rang his red office telephone in the dead of night, Belém had been the last time he'd heard the general's voice. And it had rattled him. He'd preferred pretending that Hoyt had been left behind with the broken-down *Josefina*.

Tammy's cereal is untouched and bloating.

"Eat," he says, and she does.

Hoyt's voice did what it always did to Strickland. It's like he's one of those old metal soldiers, and Hoyt wound him. He'll snap his heels. He'll redouble efforts to enforce army doctrine upon Occam. Distantly he feels a melancholy. What little progress he's made at home will continue to move slowly. The lumbering inroads he's made with the children. The interest he's made himself take in Lainie's chronicles of shopping and childcare. It occurs to him that Hoyt isn't altogether different than the asset. Both are unknowable, somehow larger than their physical forms. Strickland is merely the secondary jaw that lashes from Hoyt's skull, and he'll have to keep biting, just a few weeks longer.

The knife catches and falls, its handle thudding past his bandaged fingers. It feels like they've been twisted in their sockets. Strickland slams the table with his right fist. Silverware jumps. Tammy drops her spoon into her bowl. He feels tears, that unacceptable expression of vulnerability, rush to his eyes. No, not in front of his daughter. He fumbles from his pocket the bottle of painkillers. He bites off the lid, taps the bottle too hard. White pellets dance across the tabletop until stickiness grabs them. Why is the table sticky? What kind of household is this? He nabs two, then three, then what the hell, four, and pushes them into his mouth. Grabs the milk bottle and swigs—fuck germs. The pills and milk form a paste. He slurps it down. Bitter, bitter. This house, this neighborhood, this city, this life.

26

LAINIE KNOWS THE kind of man she married. Once, after slashing himself building Tammy's crib, he'd wrapped his palm in duct tape and kept going. Another time he'd returned from a military exercise in Virginia sporting a forehead gash sealed shut with superglue. Finger reattachment is a different scale of injury, she understands that, yet still a dread rumbles her stomach each time she sees him gobble those painkillers.

Even before the Amazon, Richard had scared her a little. She figured that wasn't so rare; she'd noticed an arm bruise now and then on her Orlando friends. Now it's a different kind of fear. It's unpredictability, the scariest thing of all. There's nothing to panic about. It's only that the idea of drugs dulling Richard's investment in normal, everyday reality—well, it *concerns* her. A few pills down his hatch, and he starts looking like a stone-hearted hunter willing to destroy anything. Tammy's Thirstee Cry-Baby doll: Its mewl is suspicious. The Kem-Tone wall-finish samples she'd brought home from the hardware store: Stratford Green is too much like jungle, Cameo Rose too much like blood.

Lainie trots up the stairs. It's not to escape Richard's opaque glower. It's to find Timmy, the one person around who doesn't show proper fear—*respect*, she corrects herself—to the head of the family. This is troubling, though not as troubling as Richard's indulgence of it. Some days it seems like Richard is encouraging his son to denigrate his sister and challenge his mother, as if Timmy, at eight years old, is already superior to the household's females.

"Timmy," she sings. "It's breakfast time, young man."

A good wife doesn't think such thoughts, not about her son and not about her husband. She understands the use of pharmaceuticals. Six weeks after Richard disappeared into the Amazon, she'd been a disaster, face puffy from lack of sleep, throat raw from weeping. At the urging of a Washington secretary forced to listen to her sob over the phone, she'd gone to the family practitioner and, staring at her lap, asked him if it was true there was a drug that could make lonely wives stop crying. The doctor, made fidgety by her sniffling, dropped his just-lit cigarette in his rush to prescribe her Miltown—"mother's little helper," he called it, penicillin for your thoughts. He'd patted her hand and reassured her. All feminine minds were fragile.

The Miltown had worked. Oh, how it had worked! The snowballing panic of her every dire day smoothed into a drowsy disquiet, nudged even closer to calmness by an afternoon cocktail or two. She had an inkling she might be overdoing it, but when she saw fellow army wives at the mailboxes or grocery store, they too were slurring and butterfingered. But then Lainie had pulled herself together and tossed the tranquilizers into the toilet. On her way to Timmy's room, she catches carnivalesque reflections of herself in doorknobs, vases, picture frames. Is the independent Orlando Lainie entirely gone?

Lainie's relieved to find Timmy sitting with his back to the door at his table, a darling replica, she likes to imagine, of his father's workplace desk. She lingers at the door frame, chiding herself for having any misgivings about this cherub. He's his father's son, but he's also his mother's baby, a bright child with a voracious thirst for life, and she is lucky to have him.

"Knock-knock," she says.

He doesn't hear and she can't help but smile. Timmy is as focused as his father. Lainie comes forward, her bare feet silent on the carpet, feeling like an angel floating down to check on one of the world's saints, until she's directly above him and can see the lizard pinned through its four legs to the tabletop, still twitching, its abdomen an open slit that Timmy explores with a knife.

27

THE GASH IN the creature's side is healing. Each time Elisa visits, in the deadest of hours, she sees a lesser moil of blood following his glide across the pool. Only his eyes are visible, lighthouse beacons casting searchlights across a black sea. He swims right in front of her, and this is progress; no more hiding underwater. Her pulse rabbits. She needed this. She needed him to remember her, trust her. She shifts the heavy garbage bag she carries to the opposite hand. Not a surprising thing for a janitor to carry, though this bag carries anything but garbage.

To die for Chemosh is to live forever! The movie's muffled cry has become a second wakeup alarm she doesn't need. She's awake long before needed, thinking of him, the magnificence no thickness of chain can diminish. Julia's silver shoes are the only thing to distract her. She's never late for the bus these days and has plenty of time to cross the street and put her palms to the window glass. She used to feel glass on all other sides of her, too, invisible walls of the maze in which she was trapped. No more: She believes she sees a path out of that maze, and it leads through F-1.

The jungle field recordings aren't rolling tonight, and she's done enough tabulating of the lab's activity, in tiny hash marks at the bottom of her QCCs, to know this means no scientists have stayed late to reset the tapes. Occam is empty, Zelda is busy across the facility, and Elisa toes the red line and holds up the evening's first egg.

The creature sharpens his arc to drift closer, and Elisa has to resist smiling—that's giving him what he wants before he earns it. She stands firm, holding the egg upright. The creature floats in place by magic; if he's kicking to tread water, she can't see it. Slowly his large hand rises from the pool, water fluming between his forearm spines and through his chest's etched patterns. The small flexings of his five fingers are like five arms wrapping her in a tight embrace: E-G-G.

She's breathless behind her grin. She places the egg on the ledge and watches him take it, not with last week's savage swat, but with a grocer's discernment. She'd like to watch him peel it, see if he's improved at that task, but the weight of the garbage bag makes her impatient. Holding as much eye contact as possible, she walks backward until her hip knocks the table of audio equipment. She slides the reel-to-reel player back, moves aside the radio, and opens the lid of the record player.

Elisa is certain the player's presence is incidental. The gear likely came from a single scientist's closet, all of it knotted together by tangled wires. She withdraws from the bag the dusty relics of a forgotten young life that she's kept stashed inside her locker for days: record albums, the ones she quit playing around the time she quit believing she had any reasons left to hear them. She's brought too many, ten or fifteen, but how was she supposed to know in advance what kind of music this moment would demand?

Ella Fitzgerald's *Songs in a Mellow Mood*—would he find the low rumble distressing? *Chet Baker Sings*—is the beat too sharklike? *The Chordettes Sing Your Requests*—might he think the room had suddenly filled with other women? Lyrics suddenly seem like a bad idea. She selects the first instrumental album she finds, Glenn Miller's *Lover's Serenade*, and slides it from its sleeve onto the player. She looks back at the creature and makes the sign for "record." Then she turns on the player, drops the needle, and only then realizes it's unplugged. She finds both cord and outlet, brings them together—

—and the band swings to life in blasting brass syncopation, knocking Elisa to her heels. Piano, drums, strings, and horns dive down and soar up, catching the rhythm before a trumpet is let loose above it all like a tossed dove. She looks at the pool, certain that the creature will think she's betrayed him with an ambush. Instead, he is as still as if the water itself has frozen. The shells of his half-peeled egg float outward, a physical expression of his widening awe.

Elisa lurches to the table, takes the needle from the spinning circle. The trumpet dissevers with a squelch. She musters a smile to convince the creature that everything is fine. But everything *is* fine. It's beyond fine: The grooves in his scaled skin are glowing. She recalls a fragment of a news article regarding bioluminescence, a chemical light emitted by certain fish, but she'd imagined it like lightning bugs, soft bulbs in a distant night, not this dulcet simmer that seems to boil from the creature's center and steep the entire pool from ink black to a radiant summer-sky blue. He is hearing the music, yes, but he's also feeling it, reflecting it, and from that reflection Elisa can hear and feel the music as she never has before. Glenn Miller has colors, shapes, textures—how has she never noticed?

His lights are fading, though, and she can't imagine the water without them. She grabs the record player arm and drops the needle—

—and a saxophone solo wiggles atop the orchestra's snappy chugging. This time she's got her eyes on the creature, and his light doesn't only brighten this water, it electrifies it, imbues it with a turquoise glow that shines off the lab walls like liquid fire. The physical objects of table and records slide from Elisa's awareness as she is reeled toward the pool, her skin blue by reflection, her blood blue, too, she just knows it. Wherever the creature has come from, he's never heard music like this, a multitude of separate songs so meshed in joyful unison. The water directly around him begins changing— yellow, pink, green, purple. He's looking into the air, habituated to sounds having a source, reaching up with a hand as if to cradle one of the invisible instruments into his hand and inspect it, sniff it for magic, taste it for miracles, before tossing it back into the sky to fly again.

28

THE BOY ARRIVES at the table. He's not like his sister. He doesn't sneak up on you. He dumps himself onto a chair, coughs without covering his mouth, clashes his silverware. Stares right at you like a man. Between throbs of pain, Strickland feels pride. Raising kids, that's a mother's job. Being a model of behavior, though, that's something he can do. He smiles at Timmy. It's the smallest movement of muscle, but one that tightens his face, which tightens his neck, which tightens his arm, which tightens his hand, which tightens his fingers. His smile flounders.

"Does it hurt, Dad?" Timmy asks.

The boy's hands are soapy. He wouldn't wash up unless Lainie forced him. That means Timmy was up to something his mother found repugnant. That's good. Testing limits is important. He's given up trying to explain this to Lainie. She'll never understand that germs are the same as injuries. Both are required to build scar tissue.

"A little." The pills are starting to dull the blades of pain.

Lainie joins them. Instead of food, she lights a cigarette. Strickland gives her a cursory review. He's always liked her hair. A beehive, she calls it, a gravity-defying pod of swoops and tucks that must take some skill to maintain. But recently, coming home late from Occam tired or drugged and seeing the hairdo upon Lainie's bed pillow, it looks like something from the jungle. A spider's egg sac, bulging to expel a whorling fury of spiderlings. They had a solution for this in the Amazon. Gasoline and a match, unless you wanted infestation. It's a horrific image. He loves his wife. Right now is a hard time. These visions will fade.

Strickland picks up his knife and fork, but keeps his eyes on Lainie as she mulls her insurgent son. Will she show her fear at what the boy is becoming? Or will she try to take control over him? He finds the struggle interesting the same way he finds the asset's survival under laboratory conditions interesting. In other words, both are futile. In the case of boy versus mother, the boy eventually will win. Boys always do.

Lainie blows smoke from the side of her mouth and selects a tactic Strickland knows from interrogation procedure as "sidestepping."

"Why don't you tell your father what you told me?"

"Oh yeah," Timmy says. "Guess what? We're making a time capsule! Miss Waters says we have to put in guesses for the future."

"Time capsule," Strickland repeats. "That's a box, right? You bury it. Then dig it up."

"Timmy," Lainie prods. "Ask your father what you asked me."

"Mom said you do future stuff at work so I should ask you what to put in there. PJ says we'll have rocket packs. I told him we'll have octopus boats. But I don't want PJ to be right and me to be wrong. What do you think, Dad? You think we'll have rocket packs or octopus boats?"

Strickland feels all six eyes upon him. Any army man worth his bars knows the feeling. He suspends Operation Omelet, sighs through his nostrils, and looks from face, to face, to face. Timmy's antsy expectation. Tammy's pie-faced slackness. Lainie's restless lip-chewing. He moves to fold his hands, thinks of the pain that will cause, and instead sets them flat on the table.

"There will be jet packs. Yes, there will. It's only a matter of engineering. How to maximize the propulsion. Keep the heat down. Ten years, fifteen tops. By the time you're my age, you'll have one. A better one than PJ has, I'll see to it. Now, an octopus boat, I'm not sure what that is. If you mean a submersible we can explore the ocean floor with, then yes to that as well. We're making big strides in pressure resistance and water mobility. Right now, at work, we're doing experiments on amphibious survival."

"Really, Dad? Wait till I tell PJ."

It might be the drugs. Warm tendrils rope around his muscles, scrunching the pain like snakes scrunch field mice. It feels good to see this look of veneration on the boy's face. To see blind admiration in the face of his little girl. Even Lainie suddenly looks good to him. She still has a fine figure. Wrapped so tightly in that apron, so crisply ironed with that expensive Westinghouse iron. He pictures the garment's straps, knotted into a hard, tight ball at the small of her back. She deciphers his look, and he worries that her lips will twist, repulsed at him the same as she'd been at Timmy. But she doesn't. She half-closes her eyes, what she used to do when she was feeling sexy. He takes a deep, satisfied breath and, for once, there is no retaliatory shot of pain.

"You betcha, son. This isn't some Communist rat hole you live in. This is America and that's what Americans do. We do what we have to to keep our country great. That's what your daddy does at the office. It's what you'll do, too, someday. Believe in the future, son, and it'll come. Just wait and see."

29

LAINIE REFUSES TO keep track of how often she's returned to the Fells Point ports. She goes when life becomes too heavy to haul and thinks about tossing herself after it, but the water level is low from lack of rain and she'd probably just break her neck. Then where would she be? In a wheelchair, stuck in front of the television for good, shoving the Spray 'N Steam until she could stand it no longer and melted Richard's shirt, melted the ironing board, melted herself until the whole mess was a pastel-colored puddle Richard would have to get steam-cleaned by a pro.

She believes the lizard Timmy was torturing is called a skink. If she saw a skink on the porch, she'd broom that icky crawler into the shrubbery. If she saw one inside the house, well, she'd stomp it dead. She tries to convince herself what Timmy did is the same thing. But it's not. Most kids are curious about death, but most kids also feel reflex shame when adults catch them poking carcasses. Timmy, though, had looked at her in irritation, like Richard does when she presses him about work. She'd had to collect her courage, and quick, before insisting that he flush that thing down the toilet, scrub his hands, and get to breakfast.

After he'd finished, she stepped into the bathroom to make sure the skink wasn't clawing its way back up the bowl. Then she took a minute to appraise her mirror reflection. She patted down springy hair. Pinkied her lipstick. Pulled her pearls so the largest ones rested in the hollow of her throat. Richard didn't look closely at her these days, but if he did, would he see the secret she kept? Even Timmy, she thought, had gotten close.

It had been after one of her dockside trances that Lainie had plodded along the anchorage before going north past Patterson Park and east on Baltimore Street. She found herself dwarfed by tall buildings, coasting between them as if by canoe. She stopped outside one of the largest buildings in sight, a black-and-gold citadel with 1920s stylings. The revolving door turned and turned, blowing in a gust that smelled of leather and ink.

Lainie considers her morning news routine intellectual aerobics, and for that same reason she'd braved the whirling door. It spat her out onto a chessboard floor of a lobby carved from what looked like solid obsidian. Cutaway views of higher floors offered glimpses into what looked like an autonomous city. The workers here had their own post office, eateries, coffee carts, corner stores, newsstands, watch repair shops, security department. Modern women in smart outfits and men with briefcases crisscrossed the lobby, straight-backed with importance.

In this self-contained world, there was no Richard Strickland. No Timmy or Tammy Strickland. No Lainie Strickland, either. She was, rather, that woman she'd left in Orlando. She wished to bathe in the sensation so she took an elevator to a small bakery to pore over the display case. She decided on something she would enjoy herself, for once. When the clerk looked at her, she said, "Lemon Butter Ring, please." Except he hadn't been looking at her. A man, a building regular by the looks of his shirtsleeves, said, "Gimme a Lemon Butter Ring, Jerry," at the same time. She apologized, and the man chortled and told her to go ahead, and she insisted she oughtn't to eat an entire butter ring by herself anyway, and he said that yes, she should, Jerry makes them better than anyone.

The man was flirting but wasn't overbearing about it, and besides, in this midworld she was capable of anything, and when the man complimented her voice, she pretended to be inured to such fluffery and laughed it off.

"I'm serious," he said. "You've got a strong, soothing voice. You ooze patience."

Beneath her costume of calmness, her heart raced.

"Ooze," she said. "A word every woman wants to hear."

The man snorted. "Say, who do you work for in this joint?"

"Oh, no one."

"Ah, your husband, then. Whereabouts?"

"No, not that, either."

He snapped his fingers. "Mary Kay. The girls upstairs are wild about it."

"I'm sorry. I just came inside to—well, I just came inside."

"Is that right? Hey, this may be a little forward, but any chance you're looking for a job? I work at a little ad firm upstairs, and we're hunting for a new receptionist. The name's Bernie. Bernie Clay."

Bernie held out his hand. Before Lainie could transfer the Lemon Butter Ring so as to accept it, she understood that everything had changed. Over the following hour, she introduced herself as Elaine, not Lainie, rode alongside Bernie on a gleaming escalator, followed him through a waiting room of trendy red chairs, and sat in his office past which ambled dozens of jolly men and secretaries who threw looks her way. Not hostile, but not friendly, either, as if wondering if the woman in the beehive had what it took.

Lainie knows she did all of this, but recalls only snippets. What she remembers in full are the rapid calculations she made regarding the schedules of her kids and husband, all of which had to be gauged before countering Bernie's job offer, in a take-it-or-leave-it tone she couldn't believe came out of her mouth, with her own part-time proposal—the best she could do, she said.

She hears the thump of Timmy kicking his seat at the table, hears the tentative clink of Tammy's spoon against her bowl. Lainie rotates her head to see her reflection in the china-cabinet glass, wondering how beehives caught on in the first place. The secretaries at Klein & Saunders all have sleeker cuts, and though Lainie has only worked with them for a couple of days, she's begun to imagine what it would feel like if her hair, too, was styled that way.

30

ELISA SUSPECTS SHE'LL never again know nights of such marvel and delight. Encounters in F-1 are too wondrous to grasp undividedly. She relives them the best she can, in gasping instants, like movie scenes that belong on the Arcade's fifty-foot screen instead of being glimpsed on Giles's tiny TV. How the whole pool burns electric blue the instant she enters the lab. The V-shaped current of the creature gliding underwater to meet her. The eggs as smooth and warm as baby skin. The creature's head rising from the water, his eyes rarely gold now, but softer, human colors, and twinkling, not flashing. The safety lights' snug, orange glow, like morning in a manger. The massive, bladed weapon of the creature's hand, signing "egg" with motions gentle enough to stroke a gosling. Facial expressions she'd forgotten she could make: lip-biting excitement reflected in metal surgical tables, big-eyed anticipation reflected in pool water, heedless grins reflected in the creature's shining eyes. Even daily drudgeries, the frustrating preliminaries to visiting him, are bathed in his radiance. Morning eggs not plopping into her stovetop pot but capering. No more dragging her feet room to room upon waking: she's Bojangles in the kitchen, Cagney in the bedroom. Her choice of footwear getting showier by the day, sparkling down the Arcade's fire escape as if the railing is threaded with tinsel. Dancing across Occam's freshly mopped floors to watch the colors of her shoes gloss like a rising sun over a lake. Zelda giggling at her vivacious mood and remarking that Elisa's acting like she did when she met Brewster, a comment Elisa deflects while wondering, half-crazy, if that's exactly right. The scuffed, cat-fur cardboard of LP covers, the twelve-inch square revealed to be the precise dimension of joy. The creature signing "record" before she's halfway to the pool, standing near the ledge, torso revealed, his chest scales glittering like a drawer of jewelry. The pinching of dust from the record player needle like the wiping of a tear from her eye.

Miles or Frank or Hank or Billie or Patsy or Nina or Nat or Fats or Elvis or Roy or Ray or Buddy or Jerry Lee turned into angelic choirs, their every sung word gravid with a history the creature yearns to understand. His lights, his sensational lights, a symphonic reply to the purple glow of crooners, the blue pulse of rock and roll, the dusky yellow of country, the blinking orange of jazz. The touch of his hand, rare but thrilling, when he plucks eggs from her palm. The one time she dares hold nothing at all, and still he reaches out, draws his claws softly down her wrist, curling his hand into her palm as if enjoying the pretend-egg play, and letting her close her fingers around his, for that instant making the two of them not present and past, not human and beast, but woman and man.

31

SEX SIGNALS IN the rain forest were flagrant. Tortured ululations, fanned ruffles, engorged genitals, fulgent colors. Lainie's signals are just as obvious. The drop of her eyes, the pout of her lip, how she leads with her bosom. It's a wonder the children don't crumple their noses at the pheromones as she puts a coat atop her apron and herds them to the bus. She returns and lets the coat drop to the carpet like a movie star. She touches the banister of the stairs with a single arched finger and asks, "Do you have time?" His head is smothered in painkiller, roaring like a tornado heard from a storm cellar, and words are inaccessible. She pivots on her finger and climbs the stairs, hips swinging like the tail feathers of a sashaying macaw.

Strickland takes his plate to the sink and shakes the omelet into the drain. He flips the switch of the garbage disposal. It's the first they've owned. Blades whir like feasting piranhas. Specks of egg spatter the stainless steel. He turns it off and hears the floorboards overhead squeak and bedsprings creak. He's been given food, is being offered sex, is suffused in warm morning sun—what else could he want? Yet he disapproves of his wife's brazenness. He disapproves of himself, too, for the erection pressing against the sink. Seduction games belong in the Amazon, not here in this precise, planned American neighborhood. Why can't he control himself? Why can't he control anything?

He's upstairs. He can't say how he got here. Lainie is perched on the edge of the bed. He's sorry to see that the apron's coarse pragmatism has been replaced by a nightgown's sheerness. She sits with shoulders forward, knees together, one leg kicked out to the side. This pose, too, she's learned from movies. But is the sole of any starlet's foot so dirty? Strickland continues toward her, upbraiding himself with each step. Accepting a woman's lure is like taking an enemy's bait. Lainie's cunning: She waits, a shrewd shrug persuading a strap of the nightie to slip from her shoulder. He stands before her weak and worthless.

"I like it here," she says.

Discarded clothing hunches on the floor like vermin. Perfume bottles are scattered in insect chaos. The blinds are crooked as if cracked by earthquake. He does not, in fact, like it here, nor does he trust it. Everything in this city is an elaborate feint toward civilization, a bluff regarding the safe superiority of their species.

"Baltimore," she clarifies. "People are nice here. None of that phony southern stuff. The kids like their big backyard. They like the school. The stores are very impressive. And you like your job. I know you don't think about it in those terms. But a woman can tell. All those late hours. You're dedicated. I'm sure they appreciate you. You're going to do great there. Everything is going to be wonderful."

His bandaged left hand is in her hand. He can't say how this happened, either. He hopes it's the pills. Otherwise it's his traitorous body flooding with the intoxicants of prospective intercourse. She settles his fingers on the slope of her breast and inhales to expand it, stretching out her neck. He examines the flawless skin and in its place sees the two puffy scars of Elisa Esposito. Elisa, Elaine. The names are so close. He finds himself tracing the imagined scars with his fingers. Lainie kittens her neck into his hand. Strickland has a pang of sorrow for her. She has no idea of the things in his head. His current thought, for example, that he'd rather like to chew her to pieces, just like the hidden piranhas in their sink.

"Does that hurt?" She sinks his cold, sewn fingers into her hot breast, just above her heart. "Can you feel anything?"

32

LAINIE SEES WILDNESS in him and welcomes it. For too long now, his best energy has belonged to the jungle. But there's more at stake here in Baltimore than a military mission. She needs to remind him of that as often as she can. Timmy's time-capsule question had knocked Richard off his rails, and he'd responded excellently, doling advice like a father should. Lainie knows she just needs to give him time. Soon he'll be ready to talk to their son about what he did to the skink and how to be a good man. Because Richard is, despite his job, despite his fealty to General Hoyt, despite everything, *good*. She's almost sure of it.

Progressive women's magazines have instructed her not to offer her body as a reward, but what do they know? Have any of those writers and editors had a husband tossed into two different kinds of hell and come back alive? *This is how it could be*, is what she hopes their sex will tell him. *We could be happy, normal.* While she's at it, maybe she can convince herself of the same. Maybe her job at Klein & Saunders won't have to be a secret much longer. Maybe, if this goes well and he holds her tight afterward, drained and fuzzy-headed, she'll tell him right then. Maybe he'll even be proud of her.

His wildness, however, doesn't last. Richard is easily embarrassed when his own body feels ungainly, and between the lumpish shucking of his clothes and his awkward positioning atop her, he retreats into the brow-furrowed ogre he's been since the Amazon. She is purposely messy, her nightie half-open, one hand sunk into her tangled hair, the other gripping the coverlet, but he is flesh upon pistons, a tool for a task, and he enters her with syringe straightness. He thrusts without build, beginning at medium speed, not varying.

It is something, though, definitely something, and she crosses her ankles behind his back and digs her fingers into his biceps, and threshes her torso, not because it feels particularly good but to keep all of their parts in motion, for as long as she doesn't lie still there's a chance to see from fresh perspectives each moment, to believe that this act, as well as the larger act of their marriage, has yet to be resolved.

This takes energy and dedication, and it distracts her until she feels the warmth of Richard's hand on her neck. She takes care to open her eyes slowly so as not to startle him. His face is wet and red, and his eyes, also wet and red, are fixed upon her neck, where his thumb is tracing a diagonal line down each side of her throat. She can't interpret this but wants to encourage it.

"That's good," she whispers. "Rub me all over."

His hand slides upward, over her chin, and covers her mouth with a smooth ease she doesn't understand until she feels wetness roll down her neck. Against her lip, knuckle-hard, she can feel the wedding ring under a bandage. She tells herself to stay calm. He's not trying to hurt her. He's not trying to choke her. More wetness pools between her lips. She recognizes the taste. She refuses to believe it. She tastes it again and pushes her head sideways to break from his palm.

"Honey," she gasps. "Your hand's bleeding—"

But his wet hand slides over her mouth again. That's what he wants—he wants her mute. He's going faster now, the bedsprings shrilling and the headboard thunking in unexpected rhythms, and she presses her lips together to keep out the blood and breathes through her nose, and tells herself she can hold out until he's done, because here is that wildness she wanted, and at heightened levels. Some women like this. She's seen countless adventure magazine covers of helpless women in tattered dresses thrown about by Tarzanlike men. Maybe she can learn to like it, too.

His grip starts to slip as his body begins to hitch, and Lainie's able to force her head upright. Richard is no longer looking at the two lines he's been tracing in blood across her throat. His head is wrenched over his shoulder, neck muscles taut as he strains to see inside the closet. She feels his thighs shudder against hers and she lets her head drop back onto the pillow, feeling blood creep down both sides of her neck. It's too confusing to think about. There's nothing in the closet worth looking at, nothing at all. Just some crummy old high-heel shoes.

33

It's not every night that Elisa makes it into the lab, and on nights when she does, eggs in hand, and finds the creature inside the tank instead of the pool, her heart breaks. This rouses her from selfish exuberance, reminds her that there is no joy inside F-1, not really. Yes, the pool is preferable to the tank, but what would be preferable to the pool? Anything, everything. The world is full of ponds and lakes, streams and rivers, seas and oceans. She stands before the tank on these nights wondering if she is any better than the soldiers who captured the creature or the scientists who keep him contained.

What she knows for certain is that the creature can sense her state of mind, even through metal and glass. His body-lights fill the tank with colors so intense it looks as though he swims in lava or melted steel or yellow fire. Elisa worries about the severity of these emotions. Has she only made his life harder to live? Before peering into a porthole window, she swallows down thick tears and masks her trembling lips with the most serene smile she can manage.

He's waiting, circling just behind the portholes. He twists and rolls when he sees her, bubbles rising from his hands as they sign the words he likes best: "hello," "E-L-I-S-A," "record." She doubts he can hear anything from inside the locked tank, and this takes her broken heart and grinds it to dust. He wants her to put on a record he can't hear because it will make *her* happy, and that will make *him* happy.

So she goes to the audio table, relieved to be out of the creature's line of sight so he won't see the shudder of her sob or how she wipes tears with the crook of her arm. She puts on a record and takes bracing breaths before returning to the tank window, where he blinks perceptively, scanning her for authenticity before pushing off from one side of the tank to the other, back and forth, spinning and twirling, as if to impress her with a display of prowess.

Elisa laughs and gives him the show he wants, positioning one hand shoulder-high, the other waist-low, and waltzing to the music with the dance-partner substitute of an egg, sidestepping concrete pillars bolted with steel shackles and tables of sharp instruments as if neither are worse than bumbling fellow dancers. His pleasure is evident by the lavender that radiates from the tank, and after a time, she knows her dance floor well enough to close her eyes and imagine that it is his cool, clawed hand and strong, scaled waist that she holds.

34

THERE ARE PLENTY of reasons Elisa doesn't notice the man enter the lab. "Star Dust" is a song of bewitching rhythm, and during her earlier upset, she'd turned the volume dial further than usual. Mostly, though, it is that her ears have become attuned to specific kinds of late-night threats: The oafish rattle of a scientist turning out his pockets for his key card or the exacting snap of Empties marching down a hallway. This sound is one for which she isn't prepared, that of a man cognizant of the creature's heightened senses of vision and hearing. Elisa box steps and dips and waltzes, while the creature's luminescence dims to a worried matte black, a warning that Elisa, with her eyes so blissfully shut, has no chance to heed.

CREATIVE
TAXIDERMY

1

ONLY THE HEAT of the man's tears makes him aware of the pervading coldness: F-1's closed door against his back; the hall's catacomb draft; the corpse chill of his fingers clamped over his mouth. He'd laugh if he wasn't crying—of course the conduit of this epiphany is an egg. So much of his life has been dedicated to investigating what some call *evolution*, but he prefers to call *emergence*: the asexual replications of worm and jellyfish; the embryonic morphogeneses of fertilized ovum; the infinite other theoretical paths of life's progression that didn't end with mankind obliterating everything pure and good.

It's the same thing he used to tell his students. The universe folds itself along dull axial lines generation after generation, but what truly reshapes life are the foibled folds, the outright tears. Changes kick-started by emergences can last for millennia and affect us all. He'd flatter their young minds by telling them that, though he might be the only first-generation immigrant in the classroom, each one of them is quite exotic, a child of fantastic mutants.

Oh, he's awfully bold when on terra firma, snug behind a lectern, high on chalk dust. Now he's in the field, the real world. Why, then, does it feel more like fantasy every day? His mother used to call his daydream spells *leniviy mozg*. Translated: "lazy brain." They are, of course, the opposite; his hyperactive mind is what has driven him to be a scientist of repute. What those diplomas, ribbons, and honors are worth here in the real world, he's no longer certain. He could have pulled the janitor away from the tank, away from danger, and yet he, the ivory-tower coward, had simply raced from the room.

Frequently he returns to Occam late at night, unable to sleep until he's checked, a fourth or fifth time, the gauges of pool and tank. The asset, he has become certain, won't last much longer under such artificial conditions. One morning, they'll find it belly-up, dead as a goldfish, and Mr. Strickland will go around cheering and slapping backs, while he, on the other hand, will try to hold back a tide of tears. Only here, tonight, at last, does he understand the answer to the riddle of the asset's continued survival. This woman—this *janitor*—is keeping it alive, not through serums or solutions but through force of spirit. To drag her from the lab right now might be the same as dragging a dagger through the creature's travailing heart.

Other daggers are slicing into his soft, pink, pitiful human palm. It is a stiff manila folder, an object of outrageous import moments ago, now wadded to sharp-edged crumples. He relaxes his fist and smooths it out. He hadn't come to F-1 tonight to check gauges. He certainly hadn't come to have his bedrock beliefs fractured by a dancing janitor. Tonight's visit was to verify previously collected data. Inside the manila folder is an intel report he has compiled at great personal risk, a report that must be finished before tomorrow's rendezvous.

Faint strains of "Star Dust" rumble into his skull, still pressed against the lab door. He pushes off and staggers down the hall. He grips the folder tighter, no matter how it cuts into his flesh, to remind himself who he is, why he's here. He is Dr. Bob Hoffstetler, born Dmitri Hoffstetler in Minsk, Russia, and though one would be excused for inferring from his curriculum vitae that he is a scientist to his bones, his true occupation, the only real one he's ever had, goes by terms far more sincere than "the asset." He is a mole, an operative, an agent, an informer, a saboteur, a spy.

2

To SEE INSIDE Hoffstetler's rented house on Lexington Street would be to peg him as the sort of fanatic who arranges toenail clippings by length. The home is beyond spare. It's sparse. Cabinets and closets are kept empty and open. Nonperishable groceries remain in shopping bags on a folding table in the center of the kitchen. Perishable goods, too, remain in bags inside the refrigerator. There are no dressers in the bedroom; his spartan wardrobe is folded atop another table. He sleeps on a camping cot of steel frame and canvas. His medicine cabinet is bare, his pharmaceuticals holding military lines atop the toilet tank. The single trash can he keeps is emptied outside each night and scrubbed clean each week. All lights are bare bulbs; he has moved the fixtures to a box in the basement. The light, therefore, is harsh, and months after arrival, he still jumps at his own thrown shadows—some KGB operative, he always thinks, slinking close to cut short Hoffstetler's overlong mission.

Keeping a shipshape residence complicates the placing of wiretaps, bugs, other black-bag jobs. He has no reason to think the CIA is onto him, yet every Saturday, when other men crack open beers and watch sports, he runs a putty knife around drawers, windows, heat vents, doorjambs, and soffits, then makes a special event, like other men do of family cookouts, of disassembling and reassembling the telephone. Televisions and radios are burdens he doesn't need; he guts the phone in silence, pausing to read from library books that he returns, finished or not, every Sunday. It took the jarring sight of a janitor—identified by punch-card records as "Elisa Esposito"—dancing in front of an asset gone absolutely radiant for Hoffstetler to feel the full sadness of his lonely customs.

Today, though, his routine dislodging one of the hallway floorboards feels worse than dangerous. It feels wrong. It's a detestable feeling. *Wrong* is the bailiwick of parents, schoolmarms, men of the cloth. Scientists have no need of it. Yet caught in his throat like a fish bone is the certainty that what he saw last night changes everything. If the asset can feel that kind of joy, affection, and concern—he espied all three in its chromatic flux—no nation, for any reason, should toy with it like a specimen in a Bunsen burner. In hindsight, even his own experiments, done with doctorly care, feel wrong. Of the many emotions the asset has stirred in Washington, at Occam, and in his own heart, how is it, Hoffstetler wonders, that not a single one of those emotions has been shame?

The hollow beneath the floor holds a passport, an envelope of cash, and the crinkled manila folder. Hoffstetler picks up the folder, hears the toot of a taxi, and forces the plank back into place. It always happens the same. He receives a brusque phone call with a specific time and a code phrase; he drops all that he is doing; he formulates a lateness excuse for David Fleming. Then he stews in anxious acids until the time arrives, calls a cab, gets inside, and records the cabbie's name in a notebook to ensure no cabbie drives him to the meeting location more than once. Today's driver is named Robert Nathaniel De Castro. Hoffstetler wagers that his friends call him "Bob." What American name is more inoffensive or forgettable?

Past the airport, across Bear Creek Bridge, contiguous to the shipyards in the shadow of Bethlehem Steel, the industrial park is not a place men in suits are often dropped. Hoffstetler's wardrobe is limited to suits; blandness is his only disguise. He stows away his professorial peacock feathers and bores Robert Nathaniel De Castro with flavorless chatter and an unmemorable tip. He walks toward a warehouse until the cab is gone, then veers between container ships, past a transit shed, and over the tracks, doubling back around thirty-foot sand piles to make sure no one has followed.

He likes to sit atop a particular concrete block while waiting. He drums his heels on it like he's a bored little boy back in Minsk. Soon a Chinese dragon of dirt floats across the sky while tires crunch gravel like gnashed bones. A titanic Chrysler swings into view, black as a crevasse with chrome like liquid mercury, its tail fins slicing loaves of risen dust. Hoffstetler slides off the concrete block and stands before the purring beast in the swirling grit—his papa would call it *gryaz*. The driver's door opens and the same man as ever emerges, stretching a tailored suit across his bison breadth.

"The sparrow nests on the windowsill," Hoffstetler says.

"And the eagle—" The Russian accent is thick. "The eagle . . ."

Hoffstetler reaches for the silver door handle. "And the eagle takes the prey," he snaps. "What's the point of using a code phrase if you can't ever remember it?"

3

THE STYGIAN CHRYSLER wends him all the way back across the city. The Bison, as Hoffstetler has come to think of the driver, never takes the shortest path. Today, he scoops up west of Camp Holabird, circles the Baltimore City hospitals, and effects a stair-step pattern to the North Street cemeteries before dropping like an anvil into East Baltimore. Hoffstetler's leniviy mozg finds in Baltimore's grimy, gray street grid proof of the cosmological organization present in all matter, from the smallest corpuscles to most unfathomable galactic clusters. Thus he is but an insignificant pinprick playing a nugatory role in history. This, at least, is his prayer.

They park directly in front of the Black Sea Russian Restaurant. It never makes sense to him. Why the cryptic telephone calls, coded phrases, and loop-de-loop course if it ends every time at the highly conspicuous, mirror-plated, gold-inflected, red-sashed restaurant bedecked with filigreed nesting dolls atop malachite tabletops? The Bison holds the car door open and follows him inside.

It's still early. The Black Sea isn't open yet. There is clatter from the kitchen, but not much talk. Waitstaff sit smoking at a table, memorizing specials. Three violinists tune their strings to "Ochi Chernye." The sharp smell of red-wine vinegar mixes with the sweetness of fresh-baked gingerbread. Hoffstetler passes the restrooms, where hangs a poster issued by J. Edgar Hoover to inveigle immigrants to report *Espionage, Sabotage, and Subversive Activities*. It's an inside joke: There, in the last booth of the restaurant's farthest dogleg, backlit by the lunar glow of a giant tank crawling with lobsters, waits Leo Mihalkov.

"Bob," he greets.

Mihalkov prefers speaking to Hoffstetler in English to practice his conversation skills, but hearing his Americanized name from the agent's lips makes Hoffstetler feel strip-searched. It is no small thing that Mihalkov pronounces the name as *boob*. Hoffstetler wonders if this, like the FBI poster, is a backhand slap. On cue, musicians rush the booth like hatchet men, nod out a rhythm, and strike up. One point in the Black Sea's favor is its insusceptibility to wiretap, and the deafening strings further moot the point. Hoffstetler has to raise his voice.

"I ask once again, Leo: Please call me Dmitri."

Call it cowardice, but it is easier for Hoffstetler to keep his two personas separate. Mihalkov places a blini topped with smoked salmon, crème fraîche, and caviar onto his extended tongue, draws it in, and savors it. Hoffstetler finds himself smoothing the manila folder in his hands. How quickly this Russian brute, with a single belittling syllable, has muscled him into the position of timid supplicant.

Leo Mihalkov is the fourth intelligence contact he has had. Hoffstetler's reluctant embroilment in espionage began the day after his commencement at Lomonosov in Moscow, when agents of Stalin's NKVD came into view like shipwrecks from a draining lake. They fed him—a young, hungry scholar—a dinner of pickled tomatoes, zakuski, beef stroganoff, and vodka, followed by a dessert of government secrets: teams working to put satellites into space, advanced chemical warfare tests, Soviet infiltrators inside the US atomic program. It was as good as being fed poison. Hoffstetler was a dead man unless he obtained the antidote, and the antidote was, and always would be, strict allegiance to the Premier.

When the war was kaput, the agents said, America would sift Eurasia's rubble for gold, and who would they find? Dmitri Hoffstetler, that's who. His task was to willingly defect, become a good American. It wouldn't be so bad, they promised. His wouldn't be a life of pistol silencers and bitable suicide pills. He'd be free to follow his professional predilections, provided they were in fields ripe for top-secret harvesting whenever he was contacted by agents. Hoffstetler didn't bother asking what would happen if he refused. The men took care to mention his papa and dear mamochka with specificity enough that there was no doubting how easily the NKVD could tighten their fists around them.

Mihalkov shrugs at Hoffstetler's request. He's not a physically imposing man; in fact, he seems to enjoy making himself smaller by sitting in front of the lobster tank's blue vista. In this way, Mihalkov is a switchblade, compact and benign in snug suits, rose boutonnieres, and short-cut gray hair, until he's provoked and the sharp parts are sprung. He swallows the caviar and holds out a receiving hand while the crustaceans behind him appear to crawl out of his ears. Hoffstetler hands over the folder, fretting over the wrinkles like a mother over a child's unironed church clothes.

Mihalkov unravels the string tie, taps out the documents, shuffles through them.

"And this is what, Dmitri?"

"Blueprints. It's all there. Every door, window, and ventilation duct at Occam."

"Otlichno. Ah, English, English: good job. This will interest the directorate."

He pinches another blini before noticing Hoffstetler's tense expression.

"Drink this vodka, Dmitri. Four times it is distilled. Arrives in diplomatic valise from Minsk. Your homeland, da?"

This is the latest in a decade's worth of references to the knives held against his parents' jugulars. Unless Hoffstetler has become adrift in paranoiac seas. Unless he's fallen so deep undercover he can no longer see the outlines of the surface. He flaps a cloth napkin from its pinwheel fold and mops his sweat. The violinists can't hear anything beyond the vibrations passing directly into their chins, but still Hoffstetler leans forward and keeps his voice low.

"I stole those blueprints for a reason. I need you to authorize an extraction. We have to get the creature out of there."

4

MEMORIES OF HIS years teaching in Wisconsin are like the state's winter terrain: The bright sincerity of Midwestern living splotched by the ugly black slush of the reports he handed over to Leo Mihalkov, who would materialize behind snow whirlwinds in a sable overcoat and ushanka hat like Ded Moroz—Old Man Frost—of Mama's Christmas fables. Hoffstetler tried to sate Mihalkov with material thefts: electroscopes, ionization chambers, Geiger-Müller counters. It was never enough. Mihalkov squeezed and Hoffstetler, like a sponge, seeped litanies of top-secret atrocity. An American program involving abrading the scalps of retarded children with ringworm to study the effects. Mosquitoes bred with dengue, cholera, and yellow fever and loosed upon pacifist prisoners as part of an entomological weapons program. Most recently, a proposal to expose US servicemen to a new herbicidal dioxin called Agent Orange. Each test result Hoffstetler ferreted to the Soviet agent was itself a virus that putrefied the guts of his otherwise pleasant life.

He realized, with a heavying grief, that anyone too close to him might become future fodder for Soviet blackmail. He had no choice that he could see. He broke it off with the lovely woman he'd been seeing and quit hosting the university cocktail parties that had intoxicated him with amiable intellectualism. He christened the house the university gave him by removing most of the furniture and all of the light fixtures, emptying the drawers and closets, and sitting, that first night, alone in the center of the cleared floor, repeating "Ya

Russkiy," *I am a Russian*, until wet snow covered the windows and he began, in darkness, to believe it.

Suicide was the only exit. He knew too much about sedatives to rely upon them to do the job. Madison lacked a tall building from which to leap. Purchasing a gun with a Russian accent might draw undue attention. So he'd purchased a box of Gillette Blue Blades and placed them on the tub's rim, but no matter how hot he drew the bathwater, he couldn't dissolve Mama's warnings about Nečistaja sila—the Unclean Force—the demon legion into which all suicides were inducted. Hoffstetler cried in the tub, naked, middle-aged, balding, pasty-skinned, flabby, shuddering like a baby. How far he'd sunk. How very, very far.

The invite to be a part of an Occam Aerospace Research Center team analyzing a "newly discovered life-form" saved his life. This is no hyperbole. One day, the razor blades waited on the side of the tub; the next day, they were out with the trash. The news got better. Mihalkov got word to him that this would be the final mission required of him. Do his job at Occam and he'd be taken home, back to Minsk, back into the arms of parents he hadn't seen in eighteen years.

Hoffstetler could not begin quickly enough. He signed every release form he saw and started reading the partially redacted but plenty astonishing dispatches from DC. He quit his position at the college using the old chestnut of "personal issues" and arranged lodging in Baltimore. *Newly discovered life*: The term pumped his cold, withering body with warm jets of youthful hope. Inside himself, too, was newly discovered life, and for once he would use it not to ruin another being but to understand it.

Then he saw it. That's the wrong word. He *met* it. The creature looked at Hoffstetler through a tank window and acknowledged him in that distinctive way of humans and primates. In seconds, Hoffstetler was stripped of the scientific armor he'd constructed over twenty years; this was not some mutant fish upon which acts should be performed, but rather a being with whom thoughts, feelings, and impressions should be shared. The realization was freeing in the exact way that Hoffstetler, recently resigned to death, needed. Everything had prepared him for this. Nothing had prepared him for this.

The creature, too, was a contradiction, its own biology aligning with historical evidence from the Devonian Period. Hoffstetler began calling it "the Devonian," and of foremost interest was its profound relationship to water. Hoffstetler first theorized that the Devonian coerced the water around it, but that was too despotic. To the contrary, water seemed to work with the Devonian, reflecting the creature's disposition by kicking and frothing, or going as still as sand. Typically, insects were attracted to standing water, but those that made it inside F-1 were in thrall to the Devonian itself, zipping about in spectacular overhead patterns and pelting Hoffstetler whenever he made an aggressive-looking move.

His mind stormed with incredible hypotheses, but he hoarded them selfishly, limiting his first Occam report to digestible facts. The Devonian, he wrote, was a bilaterally symmetrical, amphibious biped showing clear vertebral evidence of a notochord, a hollow neural tube, and a closed blood system powered by a heart—four-chambered like humans or three-chambered like amphibians Hoffstetler did not yet know. Gill slits were evident, but so were the dilations of a rib cage atop vascularized lungs. This suggested that the Devonian could exist, to some extent, in two geospheres. What the scientific community might learn about subaquatic respiration, he typed frantically, was limitless.

The drawback to Hoffstetler's *newly discovered life* was a new naïveté. Occam had no interest in solving primordial mysteries. They wanted what Leo Mihalkov wanted: military and aerospace applications. Overnight, Hoffstetler found himself in the business of hindrance, fiddling knobs and adjusting valves, declaring equipment unsafe and data compromised, anything to buy more time to study the Devonian. This took creativity and audacity, as well as a third personal attribute he'd let atrophy under Mihalkov: empathy. Hence the special bulbs he'd installed to approximate natural light, hence the Amazonian field recordings.

Such efforts took time, and Richard Strickland had turned time into a species as endangered as the Devonian. Academia was rife with rivalry; Hoffstetler knew how to see the blade hidden behind a grinning glad-hander. Strickland was a different kind of rival. He didn't hide his antipathy toward scientists, cussing right to their faces in a way that made them flush and stammer. Strickland called out Hoffstetler's delays for the bullshit they were. You want to learn about the asset, Strickland said in so many ways, you don't tickle its chin. You cut it and watch how it bleeds.

Hoffstetler's instinct, too, was to shrink in fear. He couldn't, though, not this time. The stakes were too high, not only for the Devonian, but also for his own soul. F-1, he told himself, was the singularity of an untamed new universe, and to survive inside it, he'd need to create a third person. Not Dmitri. Not Bob. A hero. A hero who might redeem himself for saying nothing while innocents fell prey to the experiments of two heartless countries. To succeed, he'd need to live out the same basic lesson he'd taught his students: Universes form through collisions of escalating violence, and when a new habitat erupts, members of the local taxon will fight over the resources, often to the death.

5

"EXTRACTION," MIHALKOV MUSES. "This is the word Americans use for teeth. A messy procedure. Bone and blood all over your bib. No, extraction is not part of the plan."

Hoffstetler is unconvinced at the rationality of his own idea. Who is to say the USSR won't inflict baser tortures upon the Devonian than the US? But incertitude has matured into the better of two bad choices. Hoffstetler opens his mouth to speak, but the violinists hit a gap between songs and he snags hold of his breath. Their elbows swoop, and they're off again, the horse hair of their bows swaying like broken cobwebs. Shostakovich: lavish enough to blanket a conversation of any degree of danger.

"With these plans," Hoffstetler insists, "we can get it out of Occam in ten minutes. Two trained operatives is all I ask."

"This is your last mission, Dmitri. Why do you wish to complicate it? The happiest of homecomings awaits you. Listen, comrade, to the advice I give. You are no man of adventure. Do what you are good at doing. Sweep up after the Americans like a good maid and hand over to us your dustpan of dirt."

Hoffstetler knows he's being insulted, but the jab lands without muscle. Lately he's come to think that maids, specifically janitors, are more attuned to secrets than anyone on earth.

"It can communicate," he says. "I've seen it."

"So, too, can dogs. Did that stop us from shooting little Laika into space?"

"It doesn't only feel pain, it *understands* pain, the same as you or I."

"I am not surprised Americans are slow to acknowledge this. How long did they espouse that blacks do not feel the same pain as do whites?"

"It understands hand signals. It understands *music*."

Mihalkov takes a shot of vodka and sighs.

"Life should be like carving up red stag, Dmitri. You peel the skin, you strip the meat. Simple and clean. How I long for the 1930s. Meetings on trains. Microfilm hidden inside ladies' cosmetics. We transported objects we could touch and feel and know we were bringing home to the benefit of nashi lyudi. Vitamin D concentrates. Industrial solvents. Today our work is more like pulling bowels from a hole in the belly. We deal in untouchable things. Ideas, philosophies. No wonder you confuse them with emotion."

Emotion: Hoffstetler pictures Elisa's orchestration of the Devonian's lights.

"But what is wrong with emotion?" he asks. "Have you read Aldous Huxley?"

"First music, now literature? You are a Renaissance man, Dmitri. Da, I have read Mr. Huxley, but only because Stravinsky speaks so highly of his work. Did you know his newest composition is a tribute to Mr. Huxley?" He nods at the violinists. "If only these novices could learn it."

"Then you've read *Brave New World*. Huxley's warning of sterile baby hatcheries, mass conditioning. Is this not where we are headed if we are not guided by what we know is the innate goodness of human nature?"

"The path from Occam's fish to this future dystopia is a long and tiring one. You must not be so softhearted. If popular fiction is your hobby, may I suggest H. G. Wells? Let me tell you what Wells's Dr. Moreau said. 'The study of nature makes a man at last as remorseless as nature.'"

"Surely you are not defending Dr. Moreau."

"Civilized men like to pretend that Moreau is a monster. But this is the Black Sea, Dmitri. We are alone. We can be honest with each other. Moreau knew that you cannot have it two ways. If you believe the natural world is good, then you must also accept its brutality. This creature you hold in such high regard? It feels nothing for you. It is remorseless. And so should you be."

"Man should be better than monsters."

"Ah, but who are the monsters? The Nazis? Imperial Japan? Us? Do we not all do monstrous things to prevent the ultimate monstrous act? I like to visualize the world as a china plate held aloft by two sticks, one the US, the other the USSR. If one stick rises, so must the other, or else the plate goes smash. Once I knew a man by the name of Vandenberg. Embedded in America, like you. Cockeyed with ideals, like you. He did not make it, Dmitri. He sank into a body of water that I am not at liberty to specify."

Bubbles burp up from the lobster tank as if water, all water, had participated in swallowing Vandenberg. A subtle shift in the music's signature: the violinists moving aside to allow the arrival of a waiter who, with a diffident bow, slides a plate of lobster and steak before Mihalkov. The agent grins, tucks his napkin into his collar, and arms himself with cutlery. Hoffstetler is glad for the distraction; he is rattled, but given what happened to this Vandenberg fellow, doesn't believe it is wise to let Mihalkov know it.

"I serve at the pleasure of the Premier," Hoffstetler says. "I pursue the asset only so we alone will know its secrets."

Mihalkov cracks the lobster, dips white flesh in butter, chews in large, slow revolutions.

"For you, so loyal for so long," he says from behind the food, "I will do this favor. I will ask about extraction. I will see what is possible." He swallows, points his knife at Hoffstetler's empty place setting. "Do you have time to join me? Americans have an amusing name for this dish. They call it 'surf and turf.' Look behind me. Choose the lobster that suits you. If you would like, we can take it to the kitchen, and you can watch it boil. They squeak a little, it is true, but they are so soft, so sweet."

6

SPRING COMES. THE gray scrim lifts from the sky. Lumps of old snow, bundled in shadows like shivering rabbits, vanish. Where there was silence, solitary birds cheep and impatient boys crack baseballs across sandlots. The swells of dock water lose their sickle edges. Menus change—you can smell it through windows open for the first time in months. But all is not well. Still the rain abstains. The grass is as rumpled as morning hair and yellow as urine. Garden hoses unravel for an unslakable task. Tree limbs hold buds like fists. Drainage grates face their thirsty, stained teeth to the sun.

Elisa feels the same way. A torrent inside her is being held at bay. She hasn't been inside F-1 for three days—five days if you count the weekend, which she does, every minute of it, keeping a running sum in her head. The lab has been occupied. There are more Empties than before and their patrol is more vigorous; before a single mopped floor can dry, it is blotted by boot prints. When Elisa arrives at work, it isn't only Fleming lording over the shift change. It's Strickland. She looks away from him, hoping she didn't just see him smile at her.

The laundry room still smarts the eyes five years after the washing machines were removed. This happened after Elisa came upon Lucille passed out from bleach fumes. In a valorous feat Zelda likes to recount over Automat lunches, Elisa lifted Lucille into a four-wheeled laundry cart and rolled her into the cleaner air of the cafeteria before calling the hospital. Occam doesn't like attention; all laundry work was outsourced to Milicent Laundry, and Elisa and Lucille were lucky to keep their jobs.

Only sorting duties remain. Zelda and Elisa separate dirty towels, smocks, and lab coats onto large tables as Zelda runs through a fresh Brewster story. Zelda had wanted to watch *Walt Disney's Wonderful World of Color* last night, but Brewster had insisted upon *The Jetsons*, escalating a row until Zelda had shaken her husband off the Barcalounger like trash from a wastebasket, to which he'd retaliated by belting the theme to *The Jetsons* at top volume over her program's entire hour.

Elisa knows that Zelda tells the tale to lift Elisa from the doldrums she is unable to hide and declines to specify. She is grateful, and between pitching items into carts, she signs interjections with as much vigor as she can muster. They finish and push their carts into the hall. Elisa has the squeaky one; it caterwauls enough that an Empty pokes his helmeted head into the far end of the hall to evaluate the threat. Their route takes them right past F-1. Elisa strains to listen for telltale sounds while trying not to look like she's listening.

They turn left and head down a windowless corridor black but for the orange parking-lot lights eking through double doors being held open by a block of wood. Zelda pushes open a door, pulls her cart after her, and holds the door for Elisa to follow. They are met, as they often are, by the other graveyarders, standing like birds on a wire, puffing on cigarettes. Scientists dare flaunt Occam's smoking ban, but not janitors; several times per night they gather at the loading dock, their quarrels suspended for the duration of a smoke. It's a risk: Breaks are allowed in the main lobby, but not here, not this close to sterile labs.

"You need to oil those wheels," Yolanda says. "I heard you squealing a mile away."

"Don't listen to her, Elisa," Antonio says. "It gives me time to comb my hair nice for you."

"Is that hair?" Yolanda gibes. "I thought that was the clog you plunged from the bowl."

"Miss Elisa, Miss Zelda," Duane calls. "How come you two never smoke with us?"

Elisa shrugs and points to her neck scars. One puff of one cigarette in the work shed behind Home was all the experiment she'd needed; she'd coughed until blood had darkened the dirt. She wheels the squeaky cart down the ramp, waves at the Milicent Laundry driver in the van's side mirror, and begins chucking material through the open rear doors into waiting baskets. Zelda parks her cart alongside Elisa's but turns back to the others.

"Oh, hell," Zelda says. "I do kind of miss the taste. Give me that cigarette."

The others hurrah as Zelda joins them at the top of the ramp. She accepts a Lucky Strike from Lucille, lights up, takes a drag, and nestles the elbow of her smoking arm into the palm of the opposite hand. It's a pose that has Elisa fancying a younger, lither version of her friend being slung about a brass-blasted dance hall by a zoot-suited suitor, maybe Brewster. Elisa follows Zelda's exhaled smoke as it rises, catching the sodium light before drifting in front of a security camera.

"Don't worry, sugar."

She's startled into looking down at Antonio. He winks one of his crossed eyes and swipes an innocuous broom from where it rests against the wall. He lifts it, handle upward, until the end taps the bottom of the camera. An accumulated spot of dirt on the camera's bottom panel reveals how the janitors tilt the camera upward, the same way every night, before tapping it back down into place.

"Make us a little blind spot for a few minutes. Pretty smart, huh?"

It takes a minute for Elisa to realize that she has ceased loading laundry. The Milicent Laundry driver honks; she doesn't react. Duane tries to joke her awake, asking her how come she brings so many more boiled eggs for lunch than she can eat; she doesn't react. Zelda finally stubs her cigarette, gestures for the driver to relax, and hustles down the ramp to do her share of the loading.

"You all right, hon?" she asks.

Elisa hears her neck bones crackle in a nod, yet can't look away from the smokers as they toss their smoldering butts in capitulation to the clock and leave Antonio to nudge the security camera back into prosecutorial position. She barely hears Zelda shut the van doors and bang them to tell the driver he's free to go. *Blind spot*: Elisa nuzzles into the phrase, explores it, finds it familiar, almost cozy. Zelda and Giles aside, she lives her whole life in a blind spot, forgotten by the world, and wouldn't it be something, she thinks, if this invisibility were the thing that allowed her to shock them all?

7

DAYSHIFTERS FILTER INTO the locker room. Zelda makes eye contact with those she trained over the years. Funny how they got promoted and she didn't. They pretend to look at watches, busy themselves with purses. Well, Zelda doesn't forget a face. Some of these fancy-pants dayshifters had been the graveyard shift's worst rumormongers. Sandra once claimed to have seen, in B-5, flight plans used in gassing the populace with sedatives. Albert declared that the cabinets of A-12 hid human brains simmering in green goo— probably, he theorized, the brains of presidents. Rosemary swore she'd read a discarded file on a young man, code-named "Finch," who didn't age.

That's what rumor mills do: They grind. So Zelda puts little stock in the gossip swirling around F-1. Is there something strange in that tank? You bet there is—it bit off two of Mr. Strickland's fingers. But strange is Occam's racket. Anyone who's been here a spell knows not to get into a lather about it.

That ought to include Elisa. Lately her friend's behavior has Zelda at sixes and sevens. Oh, she saw how Elisa behaved when they pushed the laundry carts past F-1. That squeaky wheel might as well have been the girl's whine. Zelda figures it will pass; everyone takes her turn getting gung-ho about government conspiracy. Try as she might, though, she can't shrug it off. Elisa's the one person at Occam who sees Zelda for who she is: a good person and a darn hard worker. If Elisa gets herself fired, Zelda doesn't know if she can take it. Selfish, maybe, but also true. Her knuckles ache, not from gripping mops but because fingers are how Elisa talks, and the idea of losing that daily conversation, that daily affirmation that she, Zelda Fuller, matters— it hurts.

One true thing about F-1: It had top dogs pulling harder at service personnel than anything before. Elisa keeps lingering around that lab, she'll be playing with real fire. Zelda finishes dressing, sits on the bench, and sighs, enjoying the sharp smell of Lucky Strike. She unfolds a QCC from her pocket, gives it another look. Fleming keeps transposing details, trying to trip them up; if she were Elisa, she might suspect Fleming did this to keep them too busy to concoct theories. Zelda rubs her tired eyes and keeps checking, every row, every column, as the dressed dayshifters bang lockers. The QCC is full of empty, unfillable boxes, the same as her life. Things she'll never have, places she'll never go.

The locker room is crowding with women. Zelda looks around, past legs being hoisted, clothes hangers being untangled, bra straps being adjusted. The QCC isn't the only reason she has lingered here. She's been waiting for Elisa, so they can wait for the bus together—waiting to wait, the story of her life. Admitting it makes her feel pathetic. The last person Elisa's thinking about these days is Zelda. The QCC fades before her vision until the night's biggest unchecked box is revealed to be Elisa. Where is she? She hasn't changed out of her uniform. Which means she's still inside Occam. Zelda stands, the QCC gliding to the floor.

Oh, Lord. The girl was up to something.

8

THE MATRON'S VOICE rings through her skull. *Stupid little girl.* Elisa slows her gait to wait out two gabbing dayshifters ambling toward the end of the hall. *You never follow directions, no wonder all the girls hate you.* There: She's alone. She scoots to the F-1 door and slots the key card. *One day I'll catch you lying or stealing and throw you out in the cold.* The lock engages, and she throws open the door, an outrageous act at this hour. *You'll have no choice except selling your body, you shameful girl.* Elisa slides inside, shuts the door, presses her back against it, and listens for footsteps, her fearful mind conflating nightmare images of the Matron hurling little Mum down the steps only for David Fleming to catch her.

Occam is swelling with morning staff. It's a treacherous time for Elisa to make this visit, but she can't help it, she needs to see him, make sure he's all right. But it's difficult to see anything at all; F-1 is fully alight, as bright as it was the night the creature's tank was wheeled inside. Elisa squints and staggers, but also smiles, despite everything. Just a quick visit to let him know she hasn't forgotten him, to sign to him that she misses him, to radiate with warmth at his sign of E-L-I-S-A, to lift his spirits with an egg. She takes the egg from her pocket and dashes forward, her legs beginning to remember how to dance.

She hears him before she sees him. Like a whale moan, the high-frequency sound bypasses her ears to pull tight like wire around her chest. Elisa stops, completely: her body, her breathing, her heart. The egg slips from her hand, makes a soft landing on her foot, and wobbles through water puddles left behind by a struggle. The creature is neither in pool nor tank, but on his knees in the middle of the lab, his metal bindings chained to a concrete post. A medical lamp on an adjustable arm pounds him with wattage, and she can smell his salty dryness, like a fish left on a pier to fester. His twinkling scales have gone dull and gray. The grace of his water postures has been clobbered by the harsh bends of a forced kneel. His chest rattles like that of a phlegmy old man and his gills labor as if pushing against weights, each opening betraying raw redness.

The creature turns his head, saliva draining from his gasping mouth, and looks at her. His eyes, like his scales, are coated with a dull patina, and though this makes reading the color of his eyes difficult, there is no mistaking the gesture he makes with his hands, cinched though they are by chains. Two index fingers, pointing urgently toward the door. It's a sign Elisa knows well: "Go."

The sign also, by design or chance, draws her eyes to a stool next to the concrete post. She doesn't know how she missed it before, such a bright color in all this laboratory drabness. Upright on the seat rests an open bag of green hard candy.

9

NEVER, IN ALL of Zelda's years at Occam, has she passed through its halls in civilian clothing. Her work garb, it turns out, has been a magical cape; without it, she is *noticed*. Yawning scientists and arriving service staff see her in a way that gives her an unanticipated rush of warmth before it is punctured by an icicle of dread. Her flower-print dress, tasteful elsewhere, is indecent in this domain of white coats and gray uniforms. She covers as much of it as possible with her purse and charges forth. The shift-change chaos will last for a few minutes more, enough time to find Elisa and give her a forceful shaking.

She hustles around a corner to find Richard Strickland stepping from his security-camera office. He teeters as if stepping off of a boat. Zelda knows this kind of unstable weaving. She saw it in Brewster before he stopped drinking. In her father, during dementia's grip. In her uncle as his house burned down behind him. Strickland rights himself and rubs eyes that look crusted shut. Did he sleep here? He completes his lurch from the office, and Zelda recoils at the clang of metal upon the floor. It is the orange cattle prod. Strickland is dragging it behind him like a caveman's club.

He doesn't see her. She doubts he sees much of anything. He lumbers off in the other direction, a blessing except that Zelda knows where he's headed, and it's where she's headed, too. She rotates her mental map of Occam. The underground level is a square, so there is an opposite path to F-1. But it's twice as long; she'll never make it before him. Strickland wobbles, puts a hand to the wall to steady himself, and hisses at a pain in his fingers. He's slow. Maybe she *can* make it. If only she can cough up the fear clotting her lungs and get her feet to—

She's moving, arms swinging. She passes a cafeteria astir with smells, not reheated Automat eatables but actual cooked breakfasts. She clips a white woman putting on a hairnet and receives a hard *tsk* scolding. Secretaries, alerted by the clop of her shoes, poke their heads from the photocopy room. Then, trouble: a bottleneck at Occam's amphitheater, a room so rarely open at night she'd neglected to figure it into her calculations. Scientists file inside, maybe to view some sort of dissection, though Zelda feels it's just as likely they're screening a horror flick, maybe the one she's currently living, a coven of white-coated monsters leering at her large body and sheen of sweat.

They make things difficult for her. Haven't they always? She is forced to assert her shoulders against their suddenly inert bodies, pleading *I'm sorry* and *Excuse me* until she squeezes out the other side and barrels onward, trying to ignore the laughs aimed at her backside. She *is* sorry, she thinks, and there *is* no excuse. Her heart is pounding. She can't catch her breath. It is thanks only to momentum that she spills around the second corner and sees, at the far end, trudging her way, Strickland.

Zelda is spotted. To turn away now would be to admit wrong-doing. What else can she do? She walks straight toward him. It is the boldest thing she has ever done. Her heart lobs against her rib cage like a handball. Her breathing is a mystery, hijacked by mysterious muscles. He's eyeing her like an apparition and lifting the cattle prod, a bad sign, though at least it's no longer chortling along the tile.

Both stop directly in front of F-1. Between gasps, Zelda forces a greeting.

"Oh, hello, Mr. Strickland."

He's inspecting her with glazed eyes. No light of recognition, even though he's met her twice. His face is haggard and wan. A residue of a granulated powder coats his lower lip. He abandons his study of her face with a disdainful grunt.

"Where's your uniform?"

He's a man who knows how to cut: do it first, do it deep. With the inspiration of the desperate, Zelda holds up the only item she carries.

"I forgot my purse."

Strickland squints. "Mrs. Brewster."

"Yes, sir. Except it's Mrs. Fuller."

He nods but looks unconvinced. He looks, in fact, rather lost. Zelda has observed this before in white people new to being alone with black people; he doesn't know where to look at her, as if he finds her very existence embarrassing. It makes him mumble, a sound too low to be heard from inside F-1. If Zelda wants to warn Elisa, she needs to exploit Strickland's discomfiture and keep him occupied for as long, and as loudly, as possible.

"Say, Mr. Strickland." Zelda brightens her voice to hide its tremor. "How are those fingers of yours?"

He frowns, then considers the bandage on his left hand. "I don't know."

"Do they have you on any pain relievers? My Brewster broke his wrist once at Bethlehem Steel, and the doctor fixed him up pretty good."

Strickland grimaces, and for good reason: She's shouting. Zelda doesn't care about his reply, though the thirsty pass of his tongue over his lip's white powder tells her everything about his pain-killers. He dry-swallows, and whether by prescription or placebo, his stoop straightens and his glazed, glassy eyes snap into frighten-ing focus.

"Zelda D. Fuller," he rasps. "*D* for Delilah."

Zelda shudders. "How is your . . ." Suddenly, she can't think. "Your wife, Mr. Strickland." She's got no idea what she's saying. "How is your wife enjoying—"

"You're graveyard shift," he growls, as if this is the worst thing she could be, worse than the other things about her that are so self-evident. "You got your purse. Go home."

He slides a key card from his back pocket like a stiletto and stabs it into the lock. Zelda goads herself to finish her question, some happy babble about his wife, a courtesy even Richard Strickland will be forced to return, but he's retreated into his natural state of looking through her, a woman who barely exists, and he's through F-1's door, the cattle prod clanking off the knob, a final warning, or at least Zelda hopes, for Elisa, wherever she is.

10

FUCK, IT'S BRIGHT. It's sewing pins into his eyeballs. He'd like to rush back to his darkened office, shut his eyes beneath the soft gray blan-ket of the security-camera monitors. It's a chicken instinct. He's here for a reason. It's time to step in, face Deus Brânquia, force Hoff-stetler's experiments to completion. No, not Deus Brânquia. The *asset*, that's all it is. Why has he started thinking of it as Deus Brân-quia again? He's got to stop that. The good old Alabama Howdy-do, the heavy-duty Farm-Master 30 cattle prod, is long and straight in his palm, a handrail guiding him from an opiate haze back into the real world.

Only took two MPs to help him fish it from the tank and chain it to the post, not a single finger lost. The MPs won't say shit. He's their boss. He'd sent them packing after that, only to discover he'd left the Howdy-do in his office. His office—the desk drawer, the pills. A co-incidence. He didn't leave the cattle prod there on purpose. He didn't.

He thinks of Lainie's distraught report of how she'd caught Timmy cutting open a lizard. It hadn't bothered Strickland at all. Hell, he'd been proud. He ought to take a lesson from his own son. When was the last time Strickland has been alone with *this* lizard? He'd have to go way back, the Amazon, gripping the harpoon gun in a dim grotto echoing with monkey screams. Deus Brânquia—the asset—speckled with rotenone, reaching out to him with both arms. As if they were equals. The arrogance of it. The insult.

Now look at it. He's got a nice, clear view of its suffering. Quartered on bloody knees not capped to bear weight for this long. Bleeding from uprooted sutures. Sections of its abhorrent anatomy palpitating and pulsating for air. Strickland holds up the Howdy-do and waggles it. Deus Brânquia bristles its webbed spines.

"Oh," Strickland says. "You remember?"

He relishes the finicky click of his heels as he circles the post. The moments preceding torture are always sensuous. The tumescence of fear. The ache of two bodies being kept apart before inevitable impact. Acts more creative than Strickland has patience for flowering in the victim's imagination. Lainie would never understand this sort of foreplay, but any soldier who's felt the blood rush would. Lainie's blood-smeared neck slides into his mind. A fine, invigorating image. He takes a green candy from the bag, sucks it, pretends its sharp tang is that of blood.

When he bites down, the crunch shatters his eardrums. Elisa Esposito must be the only point of silence left in the world. His own is being eaten away by the monkeys, which have returned. Chattering from behind security monitors. Hooting from under his desk. And screaming. Of course, screaming. When he's trying to think. When he's trying to sleep. When he's trying to nod along to his family's tedious daily chronicles. The monkeys want him to resume the throne of Jungle-god. Until he does, they'll keep screaming.

So he gives in. Just a little. Just to see if they'll soften, just a notch. The Howdy-do? Why, it's not a cattle prod at all. It's one of the índios bravos' machetes. The monkeys giggle. They like it. Strickland finds that he likes it, too. He rocks the machete like a pendulum, imagining he's chopping through the buttress roots of a kapok tree. Deus Brânquia reacts violently, pulling against its chains, the paroxysm of a fish you'd thought was dead. Its gills fluff, widening its head to twice its size. A dumb animal trick. Doesn't work on humans. Not on gods, either.

Strickland flips a switch. The machete hums in his hand.

11

Limbs pretzeled into a hard metal box, hair snagged in a hinge, knee abraded and bleeding, and yet Elisa feels no pain. Only fear, that mighty dust storm swirling up from her insides, and anger, thundering her skull into a new shape of thick, broad forehead and long, curling horns. She'll ram her way out of this box and on her new animal hooves charge this horrible man, even if he kills her in the process—anything to save her beloved creature.

Elisa hadn't been able to identify the voices at first, but inside F-1, all human timbres mean trouble, and she'd tensed like a varmint and looked for a hole inside which to burrow. It wasn't Strickland she first saw through the opening door, but Zelda, her casual dress as gobsmacking as a bright red wedding gown. Zelda had been trying to warn Elisa, and Elisa had to honor that risk. She dove into a medical cabinet, cracking her knees hard enough to draw tears to her eyes. Like everything in F-1, the cabinet was wheeled and began to

roll. She stuck out a hand and pressed her palm to the floor as a brake.

Now there's Strickland, pacing ten feet away, too close for her to close the creaky cabinet door. She constricts herself, hidden only by shadow, and self-strangles her panting. Her chest and left ear are flattened to the cabinet floor and she can feel through the flimsy tin the thump of her heart. *Don't move*, she tells herself. *Run, attack*, she tells herself.

Strickland swings the prod with a ballplayer's ease. It makes a sidearm swoop and sticks the creature's armpit. Two gold lights flash and the creature's body clenches, scales rippling over seizing muscles, torso twisting as far from Strickland as he can get—mere inches. It's only because Elisa can't cry out that she doesn't. She covers her mouth anyway, fingertips digging into her cheeks. Everybody has felt electric shocks of some sort, but she can't imagine the creature ever has. He'd believe it black magic, a bolt shot from a vengeful god.

Strickland looks damaged and desperate. He lumbers behind the post. There, out of the creature's sight, he removes his blazer, folds it like a man who's never had to fold his own laundry, sets it beside the candy bag. It is a snakelike shedding of a skin that chokes Elisa with dread. The white shirt beneath is stained with what looks like old food. It doesn't look to have been ironed in some time.

"I got some shit to say to you," he mutters.

He slides the prod across his injured left hand like a pool player so that it aims at the nape of the creature's neck. Elisa can feel her hands signing into the darkness: "Stop, stop." Strickland takes his shot; sparks fly and the creature's head rockets into the concrete post. His head lolls back, his forehead scales crushed and shining with blood. To Elisa, they are still beautiful, silver coins dipped in red ink. His gills sinuate, confused from the shock, and he lets loose a dolphin whimper. Strickland shakes his head in disgust.

"Why'd you have to be so much trouble? Leading us to hell and back. You knew we were there. You could smell us, sure as we could smell you. *Seventeen months*. Hoffstetler says you're real old. Maybe to you, seventeen months is a drop in the bucket. Well, I'll tell you what. Those seventeen months—they ruined me. My own wife looks me in my face like she doesn't know me. I come home, my little girl runs the other way. I'm trying, I'm fucking trying but—"

He kicks a cabinet just like the one in which Elisa hides, denting the door right where her face would be. He flips the table to its side. Medical instruments catapult across the lab. Elisa draws more tightly into a ball. Strickland rubs his free hand over his face and the bandage unfurls, and in the underlayers Elisa sees concentric brown rings of blood as well as a splotch of yellow. There's a dark ring, too. The wedding band she returned to him. He's forced it back on, right over his reattached finger. Elisa, already sick, feels sicker.

"I dug you out of the jungle like I'd dig a stinger out of my arm. Now you get hot tubs and pools. And what do I get? A house no better than a jungle? A family no friendlier than all those native fucks in all their fucking villages? It's your fault. It's all your fucking fault."

Strickland thrusts the prod like a fencing blade, triggering fire against the creature's sutures, then back-swinging to strike them again. Elisa sees one of the sutures tear, scaled flesh peeling away from raw muscle. A stench of smoke and singed blood fills the lab, and Elisa buries her mouth into her elbow while her stomach convulses. She doesn't, then, see the second cabinet being kicked over, only hears its clatter like a full drum kit being tossed down a staircase. Her own cabinet, she realizes, is the next in Strickland's destructive path.

She peeks from the cabinet and finds, close enough to smell the insomniac stink, the back of Strickland's legs, the trousers wrinkled from being slept in and spattered with old coffee and fresh blood. If she had a knife, she thinks wildly, she could slice his Achilles tendon or go stabbing for a calf artery, terrifically vicious acts she's never before considered. What has happened to her? She thinks she knows, despite the dark irony: What has happened to her is love.

"You're going to pay for it," Strickland snarls. "All of it."

There is the hum of the Howdy-do and the malodor of hot metal, and he bucks away, the prod striking Elisa's cabinet with an incidental but deafening crash. She grinds her teeth, rigid with horror, and watches Strickland lift the prod like a jouster's lance and gallop straight for the creature's eyes, those former beacons of flashing gold turned flat, milky plashets. Though the cabinet vibrates, she envisions it clearly: The prod will pierce an eye, pump the creature's brain full of electricity, and end the miracle of his life while she, every bit as slow as the Matron accused, does nothing.

Strickland's foot glances against a small object. It twirls away in a mocking arc. He stutter-steps, nearly trips, and then halts to watch the object putter to a stop. He mutters, bends down, and picks it up. It is the boiled egg Elisa dropped upon seeing the chained creature, a fragile little thing of atomic potential.

12

It was Fleming who'd suggested they check F-1 for the truant Strickland. Hoffstetler had scoffed, opining that Strickland had no business in there, but seconds after he trails Fleming into the lab and sees Strickland's anthropoid shape pacing about in the center of the room, he feels as naive as he has since arriving in Baltimore, the epitome of the cloistered professor duped by a real world that discarded rules as it saw fit. The Devonian—it's on the floor. Hoffstetler hadn't been notified the creature was being removed from the tank; thus, a rule follower to his stupid core, he'd believed it an impossibility.

Even Fleming, still crossing the lab, is sharp enough to suspect misconduct.

"Good morning, Richard," he says. "I don't recall this procedure on the schedule . . . ?"

Strickland lets an object slip from his hand to the floor. Does Fleming not also see this? It's the cattle prod, this ruffian's armament of choice, and Hoffstetler's heartbeat quickens. He goes on tiptoes like a child, trying to ascertain that the creature is all right. Strickland has something in his injured hand, too, but it's small enough to palm. Hoffstetler was disturbed before; now he's frightened. He's never known a man like Strickland, so unpredictable in his acts of concentrated id.

"Standard," Strickland says. "Disciplinary matters."

Hoffstetler speeds up, passing Fleming, his cheeks flushing in the hot beam of Strickland's sneer. Disciplinary matters, perhaps—the man did lose two fingers—but standard? There is nothing standard about this. The Devonian's condition is appalling. The sutures over its original harpoon wound have ripped, and it's bleeding everywhere, from its armpit, the back of its neck, its forehead. From grayed lips hang gooey strands of saliva long enough to touch the slurry of blood, salt water, and scales in which it kneels. Hoffstetler drops to his knees beside the Devonian without fear; it is bound with chains and, furthermore, barely has strength enough for breathing, much less unleashing its secondary jaw. Hoffstetler palms its wounds. Blood flows thick and dark through his fingers. He needs gauze, he needs tape, he needs help—so much help.

Fleming clears his throat, and Hoffstetler thinks, *Yes, please, step in, stop this, he won't listen to me.* But what comes out of Fleming's mouth is as far from a rebuke as Hoffstetler could imagine.

"We didn't mean to interrupt breakfast."

Only an utterance this preposterous could get Hoffstetler to look away from the mutilated Devonian. Strickland looks down like a boy called out for stealing candy and opens his left hand to reveal a single white egg. He seems to consider it for a moment, its possible meaning, but in Hoffstetler's opinion, an egg is too fragile a thing for a beast like Strickland to understand, too gravid with purpose, too symbolic of the delicate perpetuation of life. Strickland shrugs, drops the egg into a wastebasket. The egg, to him, is of no consequence.

To Hoffstetler, it is the opposite. He hasn't forgotten, and will never forget, how the quiet janitor had held just such an egg in her hand when waltzing in front of the Devonian's tank. Slowly, Hoffstetler turns his head, as if he's making a casual inventory of F-1. His neck bones squeak, trying to reveal him. He shoots his eyes into every potential hiding place. Under desks. Behind the tank. Even inside the pool. It takes ten seconds to find Elisa Esposito, big-eyed and clench-jawed, clearly visible through a cabinet door her own body prevents from being shut.

Hoffstetler's throat feels choked by cords of rushing blood. He holds the eye contact with her, then closes his eyes once, the universal sign, or so he hopes, for *keep calm*, though he knows full well that panic is the pertinent emotion. There is no telling what might happen to this woman if caught. This isn't stealing company toilet paper. A graveyard-shift woman like her? Apprehended by a man like Richard Strickland? She might simply vanish into the mist.

Elisa has become critical to keeping the Devonian alive. Perhaps even more so following these injuries. Hoffstetler has to distract Strickland. He turns back to the Devonian. The damage to the janitor is theoretical; the damage to this singular organism is real, and gruesome, and might yet kill it if Hoffstetler can't get it back into the healing waters of tank or pool right away.

"You can't do this!" Hoffstetler shouts.

Both Strickland and Fleming had begun to speak, but now both cut off, leaving the lab silent but for the Devonian's gasping. Hoffstetler glares up at Strickland, who appears to relish the whippersnapper insurgence.

"It's an animal, isn't it?" Strickland mutters. "Just keeping it tame is all."

Hoffstetler knows true fear: each time he's accessed classified papers for Soviet agents. Never anger, though, not like this. Everything he's ever done, said, or felt about the Devonian feels superficial, even flippant. His haggling with Mihalkov over whether the creature was smarter than a dog, their debate over Wells and Huxley. In some ways, he suddenly feels, this creature in F-1 is an angel that, having deigned to grace our world, had been promptly shot down, pinned to corkboard, and mislabeled as a devil. And he was a part of it. His soul might never recover.

Hoffstetler bolts upright and stands face-to-face with Strickland, his glasses sliding down a face suddenly slicked with sweat, unable to stop from pooching his lip like a surly mal'čik defying his papa. He won't get anywhere with Strickland, he never has, but Fleming has come with news, and Hoffstetler has a hunch that it might be the tool he needs to keep Strickland at bay. He prays that Elisa can hold on, just for a few more minutes.

"Tell him, Mr. Fleming," Hoffstetler says. "Tell him about General Hoyt."

The mere word does it. It's a small satisfaction for Hoffstetler to see what he's never before seen, a crease of disorientation fold through the center of Strickland's face: forehead wrinkle, brow furrow, lip rumple. Strickland takes a step away from Hoffstetler. His heel lands upon a fallen object, and he looks down, seeming to notice the overturned tables and spilled implements for the first time—a mess he has, in fact, made and can't hide. Strickland clears his throat, gestures vaguely at the spill, and when he speaks, his voice makes a pubescent break.

"The . . . janitors. They need . . . to clean up better."

Fleming, too, clears his throat. "I don't want to be awkward about this, Mr. Strickland. But Dr. Hoffstetler is right. General Hoyt called me this morning. Direct from Washington. He asked me to prepare a document for him. Clarifying, you know, the two different philosophies you and Dr. Hoffstetler have regarding the asset."

"He . . ." Strickland's face has gone slack. ". . . called *you*?"

There is unease in Fleming's small, tight smile, but there is pride, too.

"An unbiased recorder," he says. "That's all he was looking for. I'm just to collect the information and present it to General Hoyt so he can make an educated decision about which course to take."

Strickland looks sick. His face is pale, his lips an ill violet, and his head tilts slowly downward, as if by rusty crank, until he is staring at

Fleming's clipboard like it's a saw blade about to start spinning. Hoffstetler doesn't understand what kind of hold Hoyt has over Strickland, and he doesn't care. It is an advantage, for him, for the Devonian, for Elisa, and he leaps at it.

"For starters, David, you can tell the general, that I, as a scientist, as a *humanist*, beg him to explicitly forbid behavior like this, unilateral decisions to harm the asset without reason. Our study has not yet left its crib! We've so much to learn from this creature, and here it is, beaten half to death, suffocating while we stand and watch. Let us move the creature back into the tank."

Fleming lifts his clipboard. His pen zags across a piece of paper, and just like that, Hoffstetler's objection is logged, down in permanent ink. His chest warms with victory, so much so that he finds Elisa again and flashes his eyes to say that it's all going to be okay, before looking back at Strickland. The soldier is staring at Fleming's ink squiggle, his jaw quivering, his eyes blinking in addled horror.

"Nn," Strickland blurts, an ejection of nonverbal upset.

Hoffstetler is energized, powered by the same rich fuel he used to burn during big university lectures. Quickly, before Strickland can achieve anything more intelligible, Hoffstetler kneels beside the creature and indicates the shivering gills and shuddering chest.

"David, if you will, take note of this. See how the creature alternates—perfectly, flawlessly—between two entirely separate breathing mechanisms? It is too much to hope that we can replicate, in the laboratory setting, all of its amphibious functions— lipid secretion, cutaneous drinking. But respiratory emulsions? Tell General Hoyt that I am confident that, given enough time, we can formulate oxygenated substitutes, fabricate some semblance of osmoregulation."

"A crock—" Strickland begins, but Fleming's doing what he does best, taking notes, giving Hoffstetler his full attention. "All this is a crock of—"

"Imagine, David, if we, too, could breathe as this creature breathes, within atmospheres of incredible pressure and density.

Space travel—it becomes so much simpler, does it not? Forget the single orbits toward which the Soviets work. Imagine weeks in orbit. Months. Years! And that's only the beginning. Radiocarbon dating indicates that this creature could be centuries old. It dazzles the mind."

Hoffstetler's chest, ballooned with confidence, is pinpricked by shame. He's telling the truth, but it's arsenic on his tongue. For two billion years, the world knew peace. Only with the invention of gender—specifically males, those tail-fanners, horn-lockers, chest-pounders—did Earth begin its slide toward self-extinction. Perhaps this explains Edwin Hubble's discovery that all known galaxies are moving away from Earth, as if we are a whole *planet* of arsenic. Hoffstetler comforts himself that, on this morning, all such self-contempt is worth it. Until Mihalkov can authorize the extraction, Occam's dogs need bones on which to chew.

". . . of *shit*." Strickland manages to complete his sentence. "Crock of *shit*. You can tell General Hoyt that Dr. Hoffstetler—*Bob*—sides with the Amazon savages. Treats this thing like some god. Maybe it's a Russian thing. Write *that* down, Fleming. Maybe in Russia they got different gods than we do."

Hoffstetler's throat clogs with alarm; he swallows it down, a hard bolus. Richard Strickland wouldn't be the first colleague to undermine him for his ancestry, but he might be the first with the means to uncover the full truth. Although Hoffstetler has never met General Hoyt, not even seen a photo, he feels he can see the man take shape against F-1's ceiling, a giant puppeteer who enjoys butting two marionettes against each other to see which one deserves sponsorship. Hoffstetler conceals his unease by looking back down at the wheezing creature. Hoffstetler's career path is marked by spikes of ego, it's true, but this is one kind of attention he'd never wanted.

It is also, however, a fight from which he can't withdraw, not if he wishes the Devonian to live, if he wishes Elisa Esposito to live, if he wishes to live with himself. Beneath the medical lamp, squatting in the dying creature's coagulating blood, Hoffstetler has the abrupt notion that the Devonian's melding with the natural world only begins with the Amazon, and that its death might mean the death of emergence, the cessation of progress, the end of everything and all of us.

"The keys." Boldly, he holds out a palm to Strickland. "We must return it to the water at once."

13

LATELY HE CAN'T sleep. Until he can, and then it's into the pitch. Three in the morning, he's gasping and choking, and Lainie's rubbing his back like he's a boy, but he's not a boy and those can't be tears on his cheeks, and he repels her hands, and still she goes on shushing, asking if it's his fingers and won't he let the doctor examine them again, but it's not his fingers, and she starts in about how it must be the war, then, she's read about it in magazines, how war can haunt a man, but what would this woman know about war, how it eats you, but also how you eat it, and what would she know about memory, for it doesn't seem possible that she, in her life of ironing boards and dirty dishes, has forged a single memory like those scorched onto Strickland's brain.

In the dreams, he's back on the *Josefina*, skating beneath cutlasses of fog, the blood of the crew drooling from the deck, the only sound the slavering suck of toothless mud. He steers the ship into a grotto as tightly curled as a conch, and a curtain of insects parts, and the being rises, except it's not Deus Brânquia, it's General Hoyt, naked and pink and shining like rubber, holding out the same Ka-Bar knife he'd held out to him in Korea and making the same grim bargain.

He can see Hoyt well enough. How he liked to stand with one hand dandling his medals and the other caressing his extended belly. His eyes half-closed but rarely blinking. A puckish grin wedging through his round cheeks. But he can't hear him. His memories of Hoyt, all the orders, all the compliments, all the slippery inducements, have been scrubbed of voice. Not mute, not like Elisa, but rather obscured, the same way the redacted words of Hoyt's Deus Brânquia brief had been obscured by black blocks. They sound like long, hard shrieking and look like redactions: ████████████ ████████

Even here, in this lab, he can't imagine how Fleming could have understood such senseless shrieking from Hoyt. Strickland feels a faintness he hasn't felt since the high heat of Korea, the even higher heat of the Amazon. Maybe Hoyt heard about the reattached fingers. Maybe Hoyt thinks Strickland has lost his ability to control a situation. And if Strickland loses Hoyt's confidence, what leverage will Strickland have to sever ties and be free? He blinks hard, looks about, thinks he sees green vines kinking through ventilation grates, green buds nosing from electrical outlets. Is it the painkillers? Or is it real? If he can't put an end to this experiment, Deus Brânquia will win and the whole city might become another Amazon. Strickland, his family, all of Baltimore will be strangled inside of it.

He makes a fist, knowing what will happen. Pain slurps like a thick, hot syrup from his infected fingers into his arm, then heart. His vision swims, then focuses with a buchité-like clarity. Hoffstetler's still got his palm upward, awaiting the keys. He's still talking, too, about the benefits of the specialized light fixtures, the reels of field recordings. He's promising to provide Fleming with graphs and data to send to General Hoyt, just as soon as they tuck this poor little creature back into its comfy tank. Strickland bears down. He's got to get tough, and now.

He laughs. It's harsh enough to interrupt Hoffstetler.

"Data," Strickland says. "That's when you type something on a page and all's a sudden it's true, right?"

Hoffstetler's throat, that reedy, crushable thing, bobs in midspeech. His palm drops and Strickland is glad to see it. Indeed, it fills him with warmth, with hope. Are those Hoyt's pleased redactions he hears? They seem to softly shriek from the vents of the computer: ██████████████████ Hoffstetler must hear it, too. He hurries to the tank to indicate one of its bothersome gauges.

"Twenty-eight minutes. This chronometer tracks the time since the tank is last breached. The asset's limit outside of water is tracked no further than thirty. We can discuss General Hoyt's report later. The keys, Mr. Strickland. Do not make me beg."

But begging is exactly what Strickland would like to hear. He hunkers down next to the asset, right where Hoffstetler had been. An enjoyable pose, even with Deus Brânquia convulsing so hard that scales speckle Strickland's shirt. He feels like a cowboy examining livestock that has dropped to the dirt, frothing at the mouth and requiring a shotgun mercy. He traces a finger along the contour of Deus Brânquia's expanding and collapsing chest.

"Now take this down for the general, Mr. Fleming. This here isn't data. This is something you can touch with your own hands. All along the ribs here, you see that? That's jointed cartilage. It's like knuckles laced together. The going theory is it separates the two sets of lungs, primary and secondary." He raises his voice. "Am I getting this right, Bob?"

"Twenty-nine minutes," Hoffstetler says. "Please."

"Now this cartilage is so thick we can't get a clean X-ray. Lord knows we've tried. I'm sure Bob can tell you how many times. But here's the bottom line General Hoyt needs to know. If we want to find out what makes this thing tick, there's no discussing it. We need to crack it open."

"For God's sake." Hoffstetler's voice is how it should be. Distant, thin.

"The Soviets could be down in South America right now, fishing another one of these things out of the river."

"Another one? There is not another one of these, not in the world! I promise you!"

"You weren't on that boat with me, were you, Bob? Reading a couple books about a river isn't the same as seeing with your own eyes the miles and miles of it. The millions of *things* in it. More than that computer of yours can count, I guarantee you."

Happy redactions shriek from the computer: ███████████

██████████ Strickland's surprised no one else can hear it. Then again, he's not. No one else has the military background. Strickland can't understand the finer points of the shriek, but he can feel them in his gut, in his heart. He was, once upon a time, like a son to Hoyt, wasn't he? Hoyt must be proud, seeing his boy grow into a man like this. Strickland has to fight not to feel proud, too. He swipes at his eyes, just to make sure they're dry. Maybe he'll accept Hoyt's help here, just a little. But he won't fall under Hoyt's spell, not again.

"Thirty minutes," Hoffstetler says. "I'm begging now. I'm begging."

Strickland swivels on one of his heels. Hearing Hoffstetler beg isn't enough. He wants to lock eyes with him, make him remember this moment. Hoffstetler, though, isn't looking at him. He's staring off across the lab, teeth bared and forehead twitching, almost as if signaling a fourth person in the room. Strickland recalls the egg. He doesn't know why he recalls it. There had been an egg on the floor, hadn't there? He begins to follow Hoffstetler's gaze across the lab.

A gurgling hack blasts from the creature. Strickland looks down, the egg forgotten. Deus Brânquia is seizuring. Scales are being shed by the dozens. An off-white slime bubbles from its mouth. It tenses all at once, as if poked by the Howdy-do, or the machete, whatever the tool might be. Then it passes out. Its full weight slumps into the harness. Urines pools from under it, turning the white slime and red blood a murky orange. Strickland has to stand up to get out of the way. He hears Fleming's pen and hopes he's not recording this. It's disgusting, disgusting, not fit for Hoyt's consumption. Just as inappropriate, though, would be to let Deus Brânquia die before Hoyt had his say. Strickland digs the keys from his pocket and backhands them at Hoffstetler. Scientists: no coordination. Beneath the shrieking, Strickland hears the keys hit the floor.

14

MORNING MIST, CIGARETTE smoke, his own tired eyes: Through such shrouds Giles spots her half a block away. No one walks like Elisa. He ashes onto the fire escape and folds his arms upon the railing. Clubbed by blasts of wind, Elisa doesn't make herself a blade, but rather a fist, hulking her upper body past phantom foes, arms linked with invisible rugby cohorts. Her feet, though, operate on a different plane, making long, deft, dancer's strides in shoes bright enough to bring shining life to the neighborhood's funereal gray. Shoes are to Elisa, Giles realizes, what his portfolio case is to him.

He stubs the cigarette, goes back inside. He's up early, showered, and fed for his crucial return trip to Klein & Saunders. He shoos a cat from Andrzej the skull and removes the hairpiece. He stands before the bathroom mirror and centers it, scooches it, combs it. It isn't as convincing as it once was. The toupee hasn't changed. He has. It no longer looks right for a man his age to have so thick a mane. But how can he drop the act now? It'd seem to the outside world as if he'd been scalped. On the other hand: What outside world? He stares at the gaunt fossil in the mirror and ponders how he happened into a snare of such contradiction: A man no one looks at worrying about his looks.

A knocking on the front door jars him. He hustles through the apartment, checking his watch. He warned Elisa yesterday that he had an appointment this morning, but she hadn't given a response. Lately she's been lost in thought; Giles, dispirited by his reflection, suddenly dreads that she's been hiding something awful, some untreatable cancer. The knocking is frantic.

Before he can reach the door, Elisa enters, pulling a stocking hat off her head, which fans propellers of staticky hair. Giles relaxes some. Barging in is a robust tradition of theirs, and despite Elisa's nocturnal calendar and the meager vittles of the underpaid, her cheeks are so red that he's struck by wistfulness. Under equal exertion, his face would be winding-sheet white.

"Bursting with brio this morning, aren't we?" he asks.

She's past him, all but ricocheting off the walls, signing recklessly enough to send columns of old paintings swaying. Giles holds up a finger for patience and closes the door to keep the chill out. When he turns back, she's still going. Her right hand wiggles—"fish," he thinks—and she pulls inward from both shoulders—"fireplace," he thinks; no, "skeleton"; no, "creature"—and then a similar motion, but rounded—"trap," he thinks, or something like it, though he's probably wrong, she's talking far too rapidly. He holds up both hands.

"A moment of silence, I beseech you."

Elisa sulks her shoulders, glares like a rebuked child, and opens two shaking fists: no specific sign, just the universal gesture for exasperation.

"First things first," he says. "Are you in trouble? Are you hurt?"

She signs the word like she's squashing a bug: "No."

"Wonderful. Can I interest you in Corn Flakes? I only ate half a bowl. Nerves, I'm afraid."

Elisa scowls. Frigidly, she signs "fish."

"Darling, I told you last night, I have a meeting. I'm practically out the door. Why the sudden craving for fish? Don't tell me you're pregnant."

Elisa plants her face into her hands, and Giles's chest tightens. Has his quip made this poor girl, single since the day he met her, cry? Her back convulses—but it's a hiccup of laughter. When she lifts her face, her eyes remain wild, but she's shaking her head as if in disbelief of an absurdity he has yet to comprehend. She exhales to calm herself, shakes her hands as if they're on fire, and gives Giles a steadfast look for the first time. After a second, her mouth tweaks to the right. Giles groans.

"Food in my teeth," he guesses. "No, it's the hair, isn't it? I've got it all cockeyed. Well, you took a battering ram to my door before I could—"

Elisa reaches out and plucks beech leaves from both suede coat and sweater, residue of a recent windstorm. Next she turns his bow tie one-hundred-and-eighty degrees. Finally, she pets his temple where real hair meets toupee, though this feels more like an act of affection than a corrective. She steps back and makes the sign for "handsome." Giles sighs. Here is a woman who can't be counted on to deliver the unvarnished truth.

"As much as I'd like to be a reciprocal monkey and pick your fur of lice, there is the aforementioned meeting. You wish to tell me something before I go?"

Elisa fixes him with a dour look and raises both hands to signal that she's about to begin signing. Giles straightens his spine, a student receiving an oral exam. He's got a hunch that Elisa wouldn't appreciate a grin right now, so he tucks it under his mustache. His pervading fear, expanding by the year, is that he, a washed-up, never-was, so-called artist and his broken battalion of debilitated cats, are to blame for inhibiting Elisa's potential. He could improve her life by simply moving out, finding some bland stable of old folks who'd have him in their bridge group. Elisa, then, would be forced to seek out those who might expand her world rather than restrict it. If only he could handle the grief of losing her.

Her signs are slow, deliberate, absent of affect. "Fish." "Man." "Cage." O-C-C-A-M.

"Remedial," Giles proclaims. "You can go faster than that."

What follows is as startling as a Miltonesque monologue delivered by a bashful kindergartener. Gone is Elisa's penchant for searching for the perfect words. Her hands take up the agility typically limited to her feet, and her narrative flows with symphonic clarity, even as it yaws with improvisational zeal. Mechanically, it is breathtaking, and like any well-told story a pleasure to read, even if every plot point pushes the story into a genre darker than Giles prefers. For a time, he thinks she is spinning fiction. Then the details become too unsparing, too mordant. Elisa, at least, believes every word.

A fish-man, locked up in Occam, tortured and dying, and in need of rescue.

15

IRONING: THIS TEDIOUS, humid, cramping drudgery has become the ideal cover for a double life. Richard's never ironed a shirt in his life. He has no concept of the scale of the task, if it takes half an hour or half a day. Lainie wakes up before dawn, speeds through as many chores as possible, hustles the kids off to school, and then watches the morning news through steam, stretching out the ironing until Richard leaves. The hours she'd bargained for with Bernie Clay run ten to three, allowing her plenty of time to get to work, and also plenty enough to return home and mask the exotic scent of fresh office paper with the pedestrian odors of perfume.

Richard drives away, the old Thunderbird clanging, and Lainie folds the ironing board she's been pretending to use for ten, or twenty, or thirty minutes. Lying to a husband is a virus in a marriage, she knows this, but she hasn't found the right way to tell him. She hasn't felt such thrill and promise since when? The days of being courted by Richard, maybe, that sharp-suited soldier fresh out of the Korean War? The early days of courting, anyhow; months into dating, at which point betrothal was inevitable, she'd already begun to feel loose gravel beneath her feet.

Lainie doesn't let herself dwell on the past. So many parts of her current days excite, interest, and satisfy her, none more than the quick change into the work ensembles she keeps ready in the back of her closet. It's a new kind of challenge, dressing for a job. She's taken written notes of the secretaries' wardrobes. She's made three separate trips to Sears. Formal, not casual. Handsome, not pretty. Flattering, not frilly. Contradictory objectives, but that's being a woman. She keeps skirts slim and flannel, collars petaled or bowed, bodices modest and belted.

The bus ride to work is just as gratifying. Mastering the bodily etiquette of public transport, claiming a seat all her own, snugging into her arms a handbag packed with paratrooper efficiency, and best of all, the cursory but fond eye contact between her and other employed women. They sat alone, but they were in this thing together.

The men at Klein & Saunders—well, they're men. For the first week, her rear end was pinched exactly once per day, each time by a different man acting with the smug entitlement of someone choosing the plumpest shrimp from a buffet. The first time, she'd squealed. The second, she'd clammed up. By the fifth, she'd learned the working woman's scowl enough to get the offender to offer a guilty shrug. She glared at this final pincher long enough to watch him join a group of chuckling backslappers. Her pinched butt burned. The whole week had been some sort of sophomoric contest.

So she'd set out to win it, to prove she was more than a grabbable ass. No doubt it was the same goal of the agency's typists and secretaries. Or the ladies on the bus. Or the women who scrubbed floors at Richard's lab. No matter her mood, Lainie held her head high. She drilled herself on the phone system over lunch. She projected her voice with a confidence that, day by day, she began to believe. The pinching dwindled. The men were kind to her. Then, even better, they quit being kind. They relied on her; they snapped at her when she messed up; they bought her cards and flowers when she saved their skins.

And at that, Lainie has become adept. It is both science and art, marshaling the parade of egos that crowded the lobby: tycoon execs, TV commercial playboys, yearling models. She learned to dial dead phone lines and improvise baloney to impress clients. "Hi, Larry. Pepsi-Cola had to reschedule to Thursday." Lainie intuited when to do this. It was like monitoring Richard's mood before asking for spending money. Of course, these days she didn't ask; she had money of her own. She was proud of it and longed to share that pride with her husband. But he wouldn't understand. He would take it as a personal affront.

Word reached Bernie that his impulse hire was paying off. Last week, he'd asked her to lunch. For the first half hour, he'd been like the rest of them. He'd pressured her to get an adult drink, and when she'd declined, ordered her a Gin Rickey anyway. She sipped at it once to appease him, and he'd taken that as a signal to reach across the table and place his hand atop hers. She could feel his wedding band. She slid her hand away, keeping her smile tight and cold.

It was like she'd passed a test neither had realized was being given. Bernie took a slug of his Manhattan, and the alcohol appeared to melt the salaciousness into an easy, uncomplicated affection. What must it feel like, Lainie wondered, to be a man and so blithely modify your intentions without fear of consequence?

"Look," he said. "I invited you to lunch to offer you employment."

"But I have a job."

"Yes, a job—a part-time job. What I'm talking about is a career. A full-time position. Eight hours a day, forty hours a week. Benefits. Retirement package. The whole ball of wax."

"Oh, Bernie. Thank you. But I told you—"

"I know what you're going to say. Kids, school. But you know Melinda in accounting? You know Chuck's girl, Barb? There's probably six or seven ladies we've got on this deal right now. There's a day care in the building. You bring them with you bright and early, and there's a bus that comes around delivers them to their schools like packages. Klein & Saunders picks up the tab."

"But why—" She held the Gin Rickey to settle her fidgeting fingers, even considered taking a gulp to settle her pulse. "Why would you do that for me?"

"Well, heck, Elaine. In this racket, you find someone good, you lock her down. Otherwise, she ends up at Arnold, Carson, and Adams spilling all our trade secrets." Bernie shrugged. "This is the sixties. A few years from now, it's going to be a woman's world. You'll have every single opportunity a man has. My advice is get ready, position yourself. Get in on the ground floor now. Receptionist today, but who knows? Office manager tomorrow? Down the road, future partner? You got the stuff, Elaine. You're sharper than half the boneheads in the building."

Had she drained the cocktail without realizing it? Her vision swam. To steady it, she looked past the bastion of ketchup, mustard, and steak sauce, and out the window, and saw a mother struggle with a grocery bag while pushing a wobbly baby carriage. Lainie looked in the opposite direction, into the restaurant's murk, and saw sharp-suited sharks flashing teeth at heartsick mistresses, who prayed the men's hungry looks meant something beyond their being devoured.

Lainie could guarantee them that the looks meant nothing. Just last night, Richard was saying that the asset he'd been hired to guard was nearing the end of its utility, and when it was gone, maybe the Stricklands would pull up stakes from Baltimore. He doesn't like it here; she's seen him with encyclopedia volumes on his lap, looking up Kansas City, Denver, Seattle. But Lainie *does* like it here. She thinks it's the greatest city in the world. To be uprooted from the one place where she feels useful capsulizes the danger of attaching yourself to a man in the first place. You're a parasite, and when your host begins to die—say, from an infection in his fingers—your blood-stream is poisoned, too.

She wanted to say yes to Bernie. She thought about it every day, every minute.

But would that be saying no to Richard?

"Tell you what, you think about it," Bernie said. "Offer's good for, let's say, a month. Then I guess I'll hire a second girl. Hey, let's eat. I could eat a horse. Two horses. And the chariot behind them."

16

FEAR DROPS ONTO Giles's back like a pterodactyl shot from the sky. Occam is Baltimore's own Bermuda Triangle, and he's heard the wild rumors, most of which end with the suspicious death or disappearance of a courageous investigator. He feels a nausea. What Elisa is suggesting is far beyond the abilities of two broke deadbeats living above a crumbling movie theater. The fish-man of Elisa's delusion must be a poor fellow born with physical deformities—and she wants to break him out?

Elisa is a good person, but her life experience is terrifically limited; she's incapable of appreciating how deep run the fault lines of America's Red Scare. Undesirables of all sorts risk their lives and livelihoods on a daily basis, and a homosexual painter? Why, that's as undesirable as they come! No, he doesn't have time for this rubbish. He has a meeting with Bernie, an advertisement over which he has slaved.

Giles turns away, knowing the gesture will hurt Elisa. It hurts him, too, to the point that he has trouble sliding his revised canvas into the portfolio case. He faces the wall before speaking, a cowardly tactic that prohibits a mute person's interruption.

"When I was a boy," he says, "a carnival pitched its tents out at Herring Run. They had a special exhibit, a whole tent full of natural oddities. One of them was a mermaid. I know because I paid five cents to see it. A sizable fortune for a boy in those days, I assure you. And do you know what this mermaid was? It was dead, first of all. All the paintings of some bare-breasted beauty didn't square with the old mummified thing in the glass case. What it was was a monkey's chest and head sewed to a fish tail. I knew that. Anyone could see that. But for years I told myself it'd been a mermaid, because I'd paid my money, hadn't I? I wanted to believe. People like you and me, we need belief more than others, don't we? Yet in the cold light of day, what was the mermaid? What was it really? Creative taxidermy. That's so much of life, Elisa. Things patched together, without meaning, from which we, in our needful minds, create myths to suit us. Does that make sense?"

He buckles the case, the smart clicks the very sound of wisdom. He's got to get going, after all; perhaps this will be the first of many small jiltings he delivers to Elisa like inoculations. He dons a placating grin and turns back around. His grin freezes solid. Elisa's cold stare brings the outdoor chill gusting back into the apartment, and he shields himself from the spitting frost. She's signing, bludgeon-hard and whip-fast, a tone he's never seen her take, certain repeated symbols engraving themselves onto the air like Fourth of July sparklers. He attempts to look away, but she lunges into his line of sight, her signs like punches, like shaking him by the lapels.

"No," he says. "We're not doing it."

Signs, signs.

"Because it's breaking the law, that's why! We're probably breaking the law even talking about it!"

Signs, signs.

"So what if it's alone? We're all alone!"

It's a truth too cruel to be spoken. Giles darts to the left. Elisa moves to block him. Their shoulders collide. He feels the impact in his teeth and stumbles; he has to slap a hand to the door to steady himself. It is, without question, the worst moment the two of them have ever shared, commensurate to a slap. His heart is pounding. His face is flushed. There's something wrong with his toupee. He pats his scalp to make sure it's in place; this only makes him blush more. Abruptly, he is near tears. How did things go so wrong so fast? He hears her panting and realizes he's panting, too. He doesn't want to look at her, but he does.

Elisa is crying, and still, the signs, the signs Giles can't help but read.

" 'It's the loneliest thing I've ever seen.' " He groans. "You see? You said it yourself. It's a thing. A freak."

Her signs slash and punch. He bleeds and bruises.

"'What am I, then? Am I a freak, too?' Oh, please, Elisa! No one is saying that! I'm sorry, dear, but I really have to go!"

There is more signing ("He doesn't care what I lack"), but Giles refuses to repeat it aloud. His shaking hand finds the knob and pulls open the door. Cold wind crystallizes the single unfallen tear at the corner of each eye. He steps into the drafty hall, catching another sentence ("I either save him or let him die"), but he reminds himself that somewhere in the city is a building, and inside that building is an appointment book, and in that book is his name. That isn't fantasy; those are facts. He takes a single step away before pausing and must raise his voice from a squeak.

"It's not even human," he insists.

They are the words of a quailing old man pleading to live out his days in peace. Before he can angle the portfolio case out of his own way and escape via the fire escape, just as he's turning away, he catches her signed reply and it feels as if those signs brand themselves into his back, right through his jacket, his sweater, his shirt, his muscle, his bone, deep enough that the words ache like a fresh wound all the way to Klein & Saunders, where they begin their itchy conversion into scars that he'll be forced to read for the rest of his life: "NEITHER ARE WE."

17

WORD FROM WASHINGTON is that the asset is to be put to sleep, chopped like a steak, shipped off in samples to labs around the country. Hoffstetler has one week to wrap up his research. Strickland leans back in his office chair and tries to smile. Mission's nearly finished. A better life waits on the other side. He should use this week to relax. Find a hobby. Get back to where he was before the Amazon. Maybe even visit the doctor like Lainie keeps nagging, get his fingers checked out. He strikes that idea. Looking at the fingers reminds him of jungle rot. Better keep them hid under bandages, just a while longer.

So he comes home early. He'll surprise Timmy and Tammy by being there when they get back. Strange thing is, Lainie's not there. He sits in front of the TV and waits. It's the opposite of what he planned. He waits and crunches painkillers. What's the point? He might as well be at work. Late afternoon, she finally returns. By that point, he doesn't know what's what. The pills smudge details until they are as unintelligible as General Hoyt's shrieked orders: ███████ ████████ Strickland doesn't see groceries in Lainie's arms. The dress she's got on, it doesn't look familiar. She's clearly startled to see him, then laughs and says she'll have to go back to the store tomorrow, she'd forgotten her pocketbook.

Observation is what Strickland does. He can tell you which scientists are left-handed, what color socks Fleming wore last Wednesday. Lainie is talking too much, and Strickland knows that's the truest tell of any liar. He thinks of Elisa Esposito, her soothing silence. She'd never lie to him. She hasn't the power, or inclination. Lainie is hiding something. Is it an affair? He hopes not. For her sake, and also his, because of what might happen to him, legally speaking, after he dealt with the adulterers.

He compresses his emotions for the night. Next morning, after the kids catch the bus, he kisses Lainie good-bye over the hot ironing board and drives the Thunderbird to the next block. He parks under a giant beech tree. Not the cover he'd prefer. The limbs are skeletal from lack of rain. But it'll do. He's had his four breakfast pills, but that's it. Needs to keep his observational ability sharp. He kills the engine. He silently prays that Lainie doesn't appear on the road in front of him. This is their marriage. This is their life. Please, just stay home, clean the kitchen, unpack the boxes, anything.

Fifteen minutes later, she appears on the cross street, suddenly done ironing. He feels a needle of shame. He'd once promised her that no wife of his would have to take public transportation. He forces the needle from his mind with a mental flex. They'd both made promises, hadn't they? He's the one who forced his wedding ring back on only for his finger to bloat around it. He fights the Thunderbird for a good minute to get it started, then rolls out, creeping a block behind his wife. He idles as she waits for the bus, and when it pulls out, he follows.

The bus lets people off in front of a grocery store. Lainie isn't among them. Strickland reminds himself that good surveillance requires an open mind. Maybe she doesn't like the prices at that store. When the bus leaves an entire downtown shopping center without expunging Lainie, Strickland's mind snaps shut. If his wife had some special errand today, she'd had all morning to tell him about it. Whatever she's doing, she's doing it behind his back. He grips the steering wheel so hard he feels a snap in one of his injured fingers. One of the big black stitches, perhaps, ripping from rotting flesh.

Then the car dies. No dramatic deathbed scene. It coughs weakly, one last time, and then Strickland is coasting. He throws it into neutral and tries to reignite it, but there isn't a wisp of life. The bus swerves back into traffic with a noise like the asset's squeal of pain, and there's not a thing he can do about it. Through engine smoke far thicker than Lainie's ironing steam, he muscles the Thunderbird to the curb. The only spot is in front of a fire hydrant. Just fucking perfect. He slams the gear into park. Shoves his way out of the car. Stares down the road. Vehicles swarming like wasps. People scurrying like roaches. The whole city a venomous nest.

He kicks the car door. It leaves a dent. His toes sing in pain and he hops in a circle, running every cuss word invented into a single, vulgar masterwork. He finds himself turned around, looking across the street. What he finds is a white-hot fireball. Beneath it are giant plates of liquid fire and smooth runners of lava. His head throbs from the overkill of light. He has to shield his eyes to make sense of it. Sunshine sizzles from the rotating-earth sign, floor-to-ceiling windows, and endless chrome trims of a Cadillac dealership.

Strickland doesn't recall crossing the street. But he's wandering the car lot. Under garlands of snapping flags. Beside an actual palm tree. Staring into headlight eyes turned angry by the V-shaped emblem between them. Trailing his fingers across the Cheshire grins of front grilles, those hundreds of slippery fangs. He pauses before one of the cars. Seals his hands to the scalding hood. Feels strong and smooth and sharp. Even his damaged fingers feel reinforced. He leans over the hood and inhales. He likes the hot-metal smell, like a gun after being fired.

"Cadillac Coupe de Ville. Most perfect machine mankind's ever made."

A salesman has joined Strickland. Strickland registers thin hair, razor burn, a flabby neck. Further details melt in the too-bright sun. The man is perfectly automatized, as metallic as the vehicles he sells. He sidles alongside the Caddy as if he, too, moves on hubcapped wheels, the creases of his suit and pants as sharp as tail fins. He strokes the hood, his watch and cuff links as bright as the chrome.

"Four-stroke spark-ignition V-8. Four-speed gearbox. Zero to sixty in ten-point-seven. Clocked at one-hundred-and-nineteen on the straightaway. Runs as crisp as a fresh dollar bill. AM/FM stereo sound. Have the whole London Philharmonic in your backseat. All deluxe interior. White leather. It's a presidential suite in there. Those aren't seats. Those are sofas. Davenports. Divans. Settees. Air-conditioning good enough to keep your drink cold, heater good enough to keep your little lady warm."

His little lady? She's trundled on down the road to who knows where. Leaving him behind with an Occam job that's nearly complete. Whether he chases Lainie or drives himself, all alone, out of this execrable burg, he'll need wheels to replace that heap illegally parked across the street. This man of metal is stronger than him. Is it any use fighting? He protests because that's what you do in car lots, but it's pitiful. "I'm just looking."

"Then look at this, my friend. Tip to tail, here to there: eighteen-and-a-half feet long. That's two basketball hoops, the second balanced atop the first. You think you could sink a basket that high? Look at the width. That'll fill a car lane, won't it? Look how low it sits, like a lion.

Two-point-three tons, it weighs. You drive this darling out of here, you rule the road, simple as that. Power windows. Power brakes. Power steering. Power seats. Power everything. Just plain power."

That sounds good. It's what any American man deserves. Power means respect. From your wife, your kids, flunkies who don't know anything harsher in life than a car breaking down on the road. He's better than that. All he needs is a way to tell everyone to steer the hell out of his way. He's starting to feel better. Not just better, but good, for the first time in a while. He manages one more demurral, though any good salesman can hear his capitulation, and this is the best salesman of all time.

"I'm not sure about the green," Strickland says.

The lot confirms that Cadillacs come in as many shades as Elisa Esposito's shoes. Stardust gray. Cotton-candy pink. Raspberry red. Oil black. This one is green, but not the solacing glass-green of his hard candy. It's silkier, like a creature that ought to have died centuries ago glimpsed through still waters as it trawls a riverbed.

"Green?" The salesman is offended. "Oh no. No, siree. I wouldn't sell you a green car. This, my friend, is *teal*."

Something shifts inside Strickland. The salesman has shown him the way. Power: He had it as the Jungle-god. He still has it now. He thinks back to one of Lainie's jabbering pastors. What was one of God's first displays of power? To name things. The Jungle-god can name things, too. They become what he wants them to become. Green becomes teal. Deus Brânquia becomes the asset. Lainie Strickland becomes nothing at all.

He leans down to peer inside. He'll be sitting inside it in a moment. But it feels good to tease himself. The dashboard has a hundred dials and knobs. It's F-1, packed into a single front seat. The steering wheel is whip-thin, the strap of a nightie. He imagines wrapping his fingers around it, how easily the red blood from his torn fingers will wipe from the white leather. The salesman has moved behind him. He whispers like a lover. The limited-edition color. Twelve coats of hand-polished paint. Four out of five successful men in America drive a

Caddy. Forget the rockets everyone's shooting into the sky. Sputnik's got nothing on the de Ville.

"That's the business I'm in." Even with the deed all but signed, Strickland feels the need to impress the man.

"That right? Now, how about you slide in there."

"National defense. New initiatives. Space applications."

"You don't say. You can adjust the seat—there you go."

"Space stuff. Rocket stuff. Stuff of the future."

"The future. That's good. You look like a man who's headed there."

Strickland draws a long inhale through his nose. He's not only headed into the future. He *is* the future. Or will be, once his job as Jungle-god is complete, the asset is gone, his family matters are resolved, and the pills are no longer required. He and this car will be joined together, a man of metal, same as the salesman. Fused on a factory assembly line of the future. A future where the world's jungles, and all of the creatures therein, are modernized by concrete and steel. A place void of nature's madness. A place of dotted lines, streetlights, turn signals. A place where Cadillacs just like this, just like him, can roam free, forever.

18

EVERYONE AT KLEIN & Saunders dresses to project style; it's part of their job to anticipate trends. This old fellow isn't wearing a suit of modern cut. He isn't even wearing a suit. His blazer and trousers are mismatched. Maybe his eyesight is to blame; he wears crooked glasses, thick-lensed and paint-flecked. There's paint on his mustache, too. His bow tie, at least, is clean, though she's never seen a bow tie in this office before. It has its charm, though, just as the toupee does, though she doubts it's the kind of charm he intended. Lainie wants to protect him, this grandfather figure, from the pack of wolves kept beyond the frosted glass door.

She recognizes him as Giles Gunderson right away.

"You must be Miss Strickland." He beams and strides forward.

On his phone calls, of which there have been many, it has always been "Miss Strickland"—not "honey," not "toots." For his polite, dogged pursuit of a single meeting with Bernie, Mr. Gunderson has become Lainie's favorite freelancer—and least favorite as well. Favorite because talking with him is like talking with the gentle grandfather she never knew. Least favorite because it is her job to pass along Bernie's hogwash excuses and hold back apologies when she hears, popping through the telephone, the cracks of Mr. Gunderson's pride.

He reaches to shake her hand, an unusual gesture. "Oh! You're married. All this time, I should've been saying, 'Mrs. Strickland.' How rude of me."

"Not at all." The truth is that she likes it, the same as how she likes that everyone here calls her Elaine. "And you have to be Mr. Gunderson."

"Giles, please. My royal processional must have tipped you off. The heraldic displays and tableaux vivants."

Desk work has taught Lainie to hold her smile regardless of confusion or embarrassment. Mr. Gunderson—Giles, what a suitable name—senses it straightaway and offers an apologetic chuckle.

"Forgive my obtuseness. I toddle around most days without a single person following a word of my nonsense. It makes me ever so popular."

He smiles, and it is so sincere, so patient, so absent of ulterior design, that she has to fold her hands or else risk reaching out to take his again. It makes her feel silly, and she looks at the appointment book to hide her blush.

"Let's see, I have you down for a 9:45 with Mr. Clay."

"Yes and I'm fifteen minutes early. Always be ready to go, that's my motto."

"Can I get you some coffee while you wait?"

"I wouldn't say no to some tea, if you have it."

"Oh! I don't think we have tea. It's coffee all the time here."

"That's too bad. They used to keep tea. Perhaps just for me.

Coffee—a barbaric drink. That poor, tortured bean. All that fermenting and husking and roasting and grinding. And what is tea? Tea is dried leaves rehydrated. Just add water, Mrs. Strickland. All living things need water."

"I never thought about it like that." An arch remark comes to mind; typically she would bottle it, but next to this man, she feels safe. She leans in. "Maybe I'll serve only tea from now on. Turn all these grabby apes into gentlemen."

Giles claps his hands together. "Capital idea! Why, the next time I come, I expect your ad men to be wearing cravats and discussing the finer points of cricket. And *we* will serve only tea, Mrs. Strickland. You must get used to using the royal *we*."

The telephone rings, then rings again, two lines at once, and Giles bows and sits, keeping his portfolio case at his feet like a dog. By the time Lainie is finished telling Bernie's secretary that Giles has arrived and routing the calls, a trio of execs from a detergent company has arrived at the desk, all of them clearing throats, and after them, a bald-headed duo she knows has been giving Klein & Saunders headaches about a kitty-litter campaign. A half hour of appeasement passes before Lainie has a moment to breathe, at which point she notices Giles Gunderson still sitting there.

The lobby, by strategy, has no clock, but Lainie keeps one on her desk. She makes a surreptitious study of Giles and decides that his unmovable smile is his way of bracing against inevitable affront. Lainie considers darting through the office to see if any of the secretaries have tea, the manna that might set Giles at ease. Instead she waits, and waits, until the insult of Bernie's lateness hangs in the room like oily exhaust from a backfiring bus. The brume thickens as thirty minutes becomes forty, and forty creeps, at the pace of a fraying rope, toward one hour.

Each passed second further instills Giles's profile with nobility. There is something familiar about his bearing. When Lainie recognizes it, she catches her breath. It is the same poise she saw reflected in the ladies' room mirror during her first week at Klein & Saunders as she'd adjusted hair and makeup and practiced her defenses against butt pinches. It had been part of the Elaine Strickland she'd developed apart from her husband—the Elaine Strickland she's *still* developing. She'd raised her chin so high she'd almost looked down her nose, and that's what Giles is doing, constructing, as grandly as necessary, a fantasy of his importance.

They have nothing in common—she the young wife and he the doddery gent—and yet for that instant seem to Lainie to be more alike than any two people on earth. It is too much for her to take. She places on her desk the placard she uses for bathroom breaks (SEAT YOURSELF, BE RIGHT BACK!) and, without allowing herself a chance to think better of it, plunges through the frosted-glass door and into the office.

19

"ALL HOPES FADE . . ."

"When spring . . . while the spring . . ."

"As the spring recedes. *As the spring recedes.* Is this Chekhov? Is this Dostoyevsky? Nyet. It is a sentence simple enough for a glupyy rebenok. This whole enterprise, it is bear claws, digging into my flesh!"

Hoffstetler is never calm when called to see Mihalkov. Now, though, he is frenetic, unable to restrain body or tongue. Today's cab driver had complained of him kicking the back of the seat, and while waiting in the industrial park, he'd pounded his shoe heels into his concrete block enough to carve out twin caves. His mood isn't lightened by the Bison, an oaf intelligent enough to pilot a Chrysler all around Baltimore but unable to memorize a remedial code phrase. Hours were being wasted at a time when there weren't seconds to spare.

The violinists, called to duty on the Black Sea's day off, are crusty eyed in disheveled suits. They raise untuned instruments when they see Hoffstetler, but he elbows past before they can hit the first note of Russian cliché. The effulgent blue of the lobster tank makes a brown murk of the booths below; the murkiest shape is Mihalkov himself in his usual seat. Hoffstetler bolts that way, striking a two-top with his hip. It smarts, and he sees in his mind the creature's ripped sutures.

"This foolishness must end! Hours I spend waiting in the park or being driven around by your pet beast!"

"Dobroye utro," Mihalkov says. "Such energy so early."

"Early? Do you not understand?" Hoffstetler hurries through a triumphal arch and stands over Mihalkov, his hands in fists. "Every minute I am not at Occam is a minute those savages might kill it!"

"The loudness, pozhaluysta." Mihalkov rubs his eyes. "I am with headache. Last night, Bob, I overindulged."

"Dmitri!" Hoffstetler's spittle disturbs Mihalkov's black tea. "Call me Dmitri, mudak!"

It speaks well of Hoffstetler's proficiency as an informant, he will think later, that he had never, before that moment, had to experience the full abilities of a man trained by the KGB. Mihalkov, eyes cast down with the misdirection of a headache, snatches Hoffstetler by the wrist and yanks downward, as if closing blinds. Hoffstetler is driven to his knees. His chin lands on the tabletop and he bites down on his tongue. Mihalkov twists Hoffstetler's arm behind his back and pulls upward. Hoffstetler's chin grinds into the table. The musicians, directly in Hoffstetler's eyeline, snap shut their jaws, nod out a rhythm, and start playing.

"Look at the lobsters." Mihalkov tidies his mouth with a napkin. "Go on, Dmitri."

Pivoting on his chin hurts. Blood from either his chin or tongue dampens the table. He looks up with his eyes. The tank looms, a tsunami caught behind glass. Even under duress, Hoffstetler can see what Mihalkov means. Usually the crustaceans are torpid, shrugging along the tank's bottom like barnacles. Today they are agitated, antenna swaying and claws pinching as they flex legs and carapace to scrabble up the walls, claws clacking against glass.

"They are like you, are they not?" Mihalkov asks. "They should relax. Accept their fate. And yet, left alone, they get big ideas. Climbing, escape. But it is wasted energy. They do not know the size of the world beyond their tank."

Mihalkov picks up a fork. Hoffstetler's eyes go to it. It's clean, silver, lustrous in the low light. Mihalkov presses the points against Hoffstetler's shoulder.

"A little twist and the arms come right off. Like butter." He drags the fork to the nape of Hoffstetler's neck. "The tail also. Very simple. Twist and pull, and off it comes." The fork moves again, the tines ticking across his shirt until they rest against his biceps. "The legs are easy. Wine bottle, pepper mill—roll the arms flat and the meat, it just squirts out." He licks his lips as if tasting the melted butter. "I can teach you how to do it, Dmitri. It is a good thing to know, how to take an animal apart."

He releases his hold and Hoffstetler slumps to the floor, cradling his wrenched arm. Though his eyesight is blurred by tears, he sees Mihalkov gesture and feels the Bison's huge hands lifting him into the air and depositing him in the booth. The comfort of the seat is somehow grotesque; writhing on the floor made more sense. He fumbles for a napkin, holds it against his chin. There is blood, but not a lot. Leo Mihalkov knows what he's doing.

"My superiors have told me that extraction is impossible." Mihalkov drowns two spoonfuls of sugar in his tea. "I made your case. A convincing one, I thought. The Soviet Union, I told them, does not lead the United States in many categories. But in space, we lead! The Occam asset, it would solidify this." He sips, shrugs. "But what does a brute like me know about such things? I am what you said: a pet beast. All of us, Dmitri, are the pet beast to someone."

Hoffstetler crumples the bloody napkin in his fist and gasps through panting.

"So it dies, then? We just let it die?"

Mihalkov smiles. "Russia does not leave its countrymen without recourse."

He wipes his hands clean and lifts from the seat cushion a box. It is small, black, made of industrial plastic. He undoes the box's fasteners and opens it to reveal three objects nestled into slotted protective foam. Mihalkov extracts the first item. Hoffstetler is familiar with many a gadget, but this is something new. It is the size of a baseball and constructed from a curled knuckle of metal pipe like a homemade grenade, except that the soldering is professional and the wiring held in place with tidy epoxy putty. A small green light, yet unlit, is taped next to a red button.

"We call this a popper," Mihalkov says. "It is one of the Israelis' new toys. Secure it within ten feet of Occam's central fuses, depress the button, and five minutes later it will release a surge strong enough to disable all electricity. Lights, cameras, everything. It is highly effective. But I warn you, Dmitri, the damage is temporary. The fuses are replaced, and the power will return. I do not expect you to have more than ten minutes to complete your task."

"My task," Hoffstetler repeats.

Mihalkov nestles the popper back into the foam and, with the gentleness of a farmer scooping up a baby chick, withdraws the second item. This Hoffstetler recognizes, for he has wielded so many in so many regretful ways. It is a fully assembled syringe. Mihalkov removes the final item, a small glass vial filled with a silver liquid. He holds these items with more care than he held the popper and gives Hoffstetler a sympathetic smile.

"If the Americans are exterminating the asset, as you say, then there is but one course of action. You must get to it first. Inject it with this solution. It will kill the asset. More important, it will eat away the asset's insides. When it is through, there will be nothing left to study but bones. Perhaps a little handful of scales."

Hoffstetler laughs, a snort that spatters the table in spit, blood, and tears.

"If we can't have it, neither can they. Is that the idea?"

"Mutually assured destruction," Mihalkov says. "You know the concept."

Hoffstetler braces one hand against the table and covers his face with the other.

"It didn't want to hurt anyone," he sobs. "It went centuries without hurting anyone. We did this to it. We dragged it up here. We tortured it. What's next, Leo? What species do we wipe out next? Is it us? I hope it is. We deserve it."

He feels Mihalkov's hand settle atop his, pat it gently.

"You told me it understands pain like we do." Mihalkov's voice is soft. "Then be better than the Americans. Be better than all of us. Go ahead, listen to your author Mr. Huxley. Think of the creature's feelings. Deliver it from its suffering. When you are finished, we wait, four or five days, just for appearances. Then I will take you, myself, to the embassy and put you on a ship to Minsk. Picture it, Dmitri. The blue skies like nothing they have here. The sun like the Christmas star through the snowy trees. So much has changed since you've seen it. You will see it again. You will see it with your family. Concentrate on that. All of it, it is nearly at the end."

20

EVERYONE KNOWS THE front-desk girl, and everyone is busy. But today they halt their activities to watch her pass, her unerring smile gone grim and her studied saunter supplanted by a step so swift it flutters the hem of her dress. Lainie comes at Bernie's secretary at such a march that the secretary, well-trained, responds defensively, "He's not in." Lainie presents roadblocks to clients all day; she knows how to dodge them, too. She swerves around the secretary, snatching the knob of Bernie's door and pulling it open.

Bernie Clay is kicked back in his leather chair, ankles crossed atop his desk, a highball in one hand, face stretched in a laugh. Relaxed on the sofa are the copy chief and lead media buyer, chuckling over look-alike drinks. Too late, but bound by protocol, the secretary buzzes Bernie to say that Elaine Strickland is entering. Bernie's smile fades to a look of perplexity. He gestures with his drink at the other men.

"This is called a meeting, Elaine."

She'll faint, she'll be fired, she's so stupid, what was she thinking?

"Mr. Gunderson . . . is waiting for you."

Bernie squints, as if hearing Chinese.

"Right. But I'm in an important meeting."

The copy chief snorts. Lainie looks at the sofa. Both men are smirking. A cold marble of sweat plummets down her backbone, even as she feels an angry roil at how these men just sit there, half-drunk and entitled. She holds tight to the resentment. If she must faint, let her do it from a respectable height. She plants her feet.

"He's been waiting for an hour."

Bernie rocks his chair to an upright position. Liquor slurps over the rim of his glass, hits the carpet. Not his concern, Lainie thinks: a janitor, one more of the overlooked, will take to her knees to do the scrubbing. Bernie sighs at the men and cricks his head at Lainie, as if to say, *Let me deal with this.* They stand up, buttoning jackets, not bothering to hide the collegial grins of watching a buddy butt heads with a strident female. The copy chief winks at Lainie as he passes. The media buyer brushes so close that Lainie is certain he can hear, if not feel, the crash of her heart.

"I know I offered you full-time employment," Bernie says, "but let's not let that go to our heads. Do your job, Elaine. And I'll do *my* job. I'll come and get Mr. Gunderson when I'm ready. I hope that's before closing time, but we'll see."

"He's a nice man." Lainie despises the tremor in her voice. "He waited two weeks to get an appointment—"

"This is what I'm saying. You don't really know what you're talking about, do you? Everyone who walks through that door has a history. Don't you? Let me tell you something about nice old

Mr. Gunderson. He used to work here. Until he got arrested for moral depravity. Surprise. So when you charge in here, with other people in my office, and say *Mr. Gunderson*, that's what they think of. It doesn't make my life easier. I'm the only one in town who'll work with Mr. Gunderson. I do it out of the goodness of my heart. Let me tell you something else. His work? It's useless. Sure, it's good. But it's antique. It doesn't sell. Two weeks ago, he brought me this big red monstrosity and I had him redo it green. I did it because I don't have the heart to tell him the truth. He's finished in this biz. At least my way he gets a kill fee. So, really, Elaine, who's the nice one now?"

Lainie no longer knows. Bernie exhales indulgently, gets up, puts his arm around her, and guides her to the door, where he instructs her, tolerantly, she has to admit, to tell Mr. Gunderson that Mr. Clay had an emergency, and that he's to leave his painting behind. That way the hard hearts in accounting can deliver the bad news later. Lainie feels like a child. She nods, a good girl, her forced smile crimping her face in a way she associates with home, the dinner table, pretending everything is all right.

When she returns to the lobby, Giles stands up, straightens his jacket, and strides forward, portfolio case swinging. Lainie scurries behind the desk as a soldier might into a foxhole, and selects from her inventory a tone of apology and the script that goes with it. Mr. Clay is busy handling an unforeseen event. I didn't know. It's my fault. I'm so sorry. Won't you leave your work with me? I'll make sure Mr. Clay sees it. She wonders if this is what it feels like to be Richard, to feel your heart harden to stone with every word. Giles shatters that stone by beginning to unbuckle the portfolio case without protest, accepting her blatant lie, not because he believes it, but because he doesn't wish to cause her further upset. Forget what Bernie said about moral depravity. Giles Gunderson is the kindest man Lainie has ever known.

"Stop."

It sounds like her voice. It feels like her voice, too; her lips feel the plosive pop. But how can such an insubordinate sound come from a woman blinded by Spray 'N Steam vapor, weighed down by a bee-hive hairdo, deafened by the repetitive thwack of a headboard against a wall? Still the voice continues, over the belligerent tele-phone and the harrumphs of the waiting room's latest arrivals, so that she, just this once, might prioritize a man who is no one else's priority.

"They don't want it," she says.

"They . . ." Giles adjusts his glasses. "I'm sorry?"

"They won't tell you. But they don't want it. They'll never want it."

"But it's . . . they asked for green and—"

"If you leave it with me, you'll get a kill fee. But that's all."

"—and it's as green as can be, it can't get any greener!"

"But I don't think you should."

"Miss Strickland?" Giles is blinking hard. "*Mrs.* Strickland, I mean—"

"You deserve better than this. You deserve people who value you. You deserve to go somewhere where you can be proud of who you are."

The voice, Lainie realizes, feels sovereign from her because it's not only speaking to Giles Gunderson—it's speaking to Elaine Strickland. She deserves better; she deserves to be valued; she deserves to live in a place where pride is not an exotic gift. Once more, the young wife and doddery gent are one and the same, stamped as deficient by people who haven't the higher ground to make the accusation. Klein & Saunders is a start but only that: a start.

He's fussing with his bow tie, searching the corner of the room for clues, but she keeps nodding, harder and harder, urging him to do the right thing, to walk out of the room. He exhales with a weak shiver and stares down at his portfolio case. Then he inhales sharply and looks right at her, his eyes sharp with tears and his mustache quivering with a brave smile. He holds out the case. Not the painting—the whole case.

"For you, my dear."

She can't accept it. Of course she can't. But Giles's arm shakes the very same way her voice had shaken; he's matching her impulsive heroism with that of his own, begging her to take the burdensome baggage of his life off his hands. Lainie takes the case, her fingers settling into grooves shaped by his fingers over the years into soft red leather. She sees the shifting of Giles's shadow as he moves away, but she doesn't look up. It would only make it harder for him, she senses, and besides, she's looking for a place to set down the case so that it, heavy with significance, doesn't crash through three floors of the building.

21

HOFFSTETLER IS CHECKING, for the final time, the barometers reporting temperature, volume, and pH from the F-1 pool, his assistants wheeling hand trucks of equipment from the lab for good, when he's struck by a staggering fact. He might never again be this close to the Devonian, at least while it still breaths. On Monday, a sickening three days off, he himself will dissolve it from the inside via Mihalkov's hypodermic solution.

Had it been the body armor of lab coats and battle shields of briefcases that had made him impervious for so long to others' pain? Well, today he wears no coat; he threw it to his office floor, disgusted by its invisible soaking of blood. And his briefcase? In mere days it has come to represent the collapse of his meticulously maintained life; it is filled with crumpled notes, cracker bags, cookie crumbs. For once, no modicum of professionalism separates death and deliverer in F-1.

Hoffstetler's victim—he won't permit himself to think of the Devonian by any gentler term—floats at the pool's center, the chains affixed to its harness as still as rods. Its sole show of life is the light spilling from its eyes like smelted gold across the water. Hoffstetler thinks of Elisa Esposito's dancing and the Devonian's delighted illuminations, and he's gripped by a fierce jealousy. It isn't fair that she got to love it, and it her, while he—he's saddled with a murder no god will forgive. He replaces the barometers, tries to shake off all feelings of tenderness. Those won't make it any easier to jam the killing needle through bony plates.

He has no reason to believe the Devonian feels anything toward him but hatred. None at all. And yet, as he hears the lab doors close behind his assistants, he finds himself raising his eyes imploringly. If Elisa did it, he could have done it as well: make contact, *real* contact, with the Devonian. He's managed to live with himself despite repeated trespasses of the humane. Can he forgive himself for this final trespass as well?

The lab is empty and still. Hoffstetler sets down his notebook, not caring if it gets wet, if all his carefully notated facts go blurry, for what good have facts done him at Occam? He crosses the red warning line and lowers himself to the pool's ledge, dampness soaking through his seat. His hands are used to being empty; they fumble for each other while his spine slumps. It is a melancholic pose, like hunching at the graveside of a loved one. Another fantasy of humanity. He has no loved ones. Not in this land. Even the Devonian, a being of another world, has him beat in that regard.

"Prosti menya, pozhaluysta," he whispers. "I am so sorry."

The gold-hued water undulates as softly as a field of wheat.

"You cannot understand me. I know this. I am used to it. My real voice, my beautiful Russian—no one here can understand it. In that way are we similar? Perhaps if I speak with enough feeling you will understand?" Hoffstetler taps his own chest. "I am the one who failed you. Who could not save you. Despite the diplomas I have packed away in boxes. Despite the honorifics they attach to my name. All of this to parade me about as *intelligent*. But what is intelligence? Is intelligence calculations and computations? Or must true intelligence contain a moral component? Each passing minute, I believe more that this is the case. And therefore believe that I am stupid, stupid, stupid. These chains, this tank—this is your repayment for saving my life. Do you know that you did? Can you smell it in my blood? I had the razor blades all picked out. And then they found you, as if from the pages of the Afanasyev fairy tales I read as a boy. Stories of magical beasts, strange monsters. It is you, my dear Devonian, who I have waited to meet my whole life. Our relationship—it should have been wondrous. I know my world is dry and cold. Yet there is so much in it that I could have shown you, that might have brought you joy. Instead, you and I have no relationship at all, do we? You do not even know my name."

Hoffstetler smiles into the vague shape of his dark reflection.

"My name is Dmitri. And I am so very, very pleased to meet you."

Sobs break out of him. Hot tears blast down his cheeks, a dozen at once, like he's the one injected with Mihalkov's serum, he's the one whose guts are melting. He braces himself against the ledge and watches the tears patter into the pool, a diminutive rainstorm, the first Baltimore has seen in months.

The water is cut in half. It is the Devonian's hand, slicing upward like a shark, its claws like five pearlescent fins. Hoffstetler recoils, totters from the ledge. But there is nothing to fear. The Devonian is three feet away, having swum close without a sound, and is already retracting its arm. Hoffstetler watches with held breath as the creature passes its fingers through its mouth, over its tongue. There is no question what is happening.

The Devonian is tasting his tears.

Hoffstetler knows that he is fortunate that none of his team enters F-1 at that moment. His mouth is open in a silent bawl, his face is slick and flushed, his whole body is shuddering. The Devonian's double jaws gnash over his salty tears, and its eyes soften from metallic gold to sky blue. The Devonian lifts himself upright in the pool, seeming to defy gravity, and bows to Hoffstetler. There is no other word for it. Then it quietly dives under, its webbed feet giving a final wiggle that, to Hoffstetler reads like a *thank-you* as well as a *good-bye*.

22

DRIVING IT OFF the lot is a dream. The de Ville's tires don't touch the pavement. They roll on cottony clouds. On the whorls of his cigarette smoke. On the bouncy curls of the girls giving him, and his car, lusty looks at every stoplight. All he'd have to do is open the door and they'd pile inside. Happily, willingly, and knowing their place: the backseat. The American Dream—he'd thought it was lost. Misplaced in the boxes from the move. But wouldn't you know it? Those clever boys in Detroit had managed to build it out of steel. All you had to do, mister, was pony up the cash, and it was yours.

Plenty of choicer parking spots exist at Occam, but Strickland picks the one on the end. Everyone who parks will see the Caddy. Even the buses ferrying service staff will have to pass it. He gets out, squats beside the teal beauty, inspects it. A blemish of dirt near the wheels. Some grit on the front fender. He takes a handkerchief and buffers the spots until they gleam. He feels better than he did this morning. Lainie's got a secret, and that's unacceptable. But the car helps. The car is a partial solution. He pulls out the bottle of pills and knocks a few into his mouth. There's another solution, an even better one, inside Occam.

His mood is optimistic enough that he doesn't bark at the janitors smoking on the loading dock instead of the upper lobby. They toss their butts and scatter. Strickland manages a grin. So what? Let the rank and file blow off a little steam. He even picks up the broom they left lying there and props it against the wall. He enters Occam via his key card and ambles down a bustling hall. Scientists, administrators, assistants, cleaners. Is everyone looking at him? He's pretty sure they are. And why not? He feels like the de Ville. Huge and shining. Gobbling up the road and everything on it.

The second solution is Elisa. She doesn't get in until midnight. Strickland keeps himself good and medicated until then. He'll cut back on the pills, he will. Just not today. Every task he selects is spiked with anticipation. He dusts the security monitors with the same gentle motions he used on the Caddy. He tracks down a puffy-eyed Hoffstetler just so he can boast about the coming vivisection. He finds a cardboard box and gets a head start on collecting personal items from his desk. He pictures Occam, and Baltimore, diminishing in the Caddy's rearview mirror. Washington, too. Is that Elisa in the seat beside him? If Lainie's going behind his back, why can't he do the same? He and Elisa will drive until General Hoyt can never find him.

Twelve fifteen, he taps the intercom.

"Could you find Miss Elisa Esposito and send her on over to Mr. Strickland's office? I made me a little spill."

A spill. He supposes he should make one. He looks about, sees the bag of hard candy. He doesn't need all that candy. Not until he gets off the pills anyway. He gives the bag a flap. Watches the balls race into dark corners like green mice. It's a little vigorous; they roll pretty far. What if she doesn't buy it? He laughs once and feels his stomach flip. He's nervous. He hasn't felt nervous about a woman in a while.

A single knock at the door. He puts on a big grin and looks up. There she is, prompt as a schoolgirl and decked out in janitorial grays. Mop held like a bō staff and chin tilted down in the classic posture of mistrust. He can feel cool air on his back molars. Is his grin too wolfish? He tries to shrink it. It's like relaxing a stretched rubber band. It still might fire off, shoot across the room if he's not careful. He's not used to handling grins.

"Hello, there, Miss Esposito. How are you tonight?"

The girl is as taut as a cat. After a moment, she touches her chest, then fins her hand outward. Strickland sits back in his chair. A scintillating rush passes through his head. It's hope. He's forgotten how it feels. He's made so many mistakes. Getting involved with Hoyt. Letting Lainie stray, possibly out of reach. Right now, though, right here under the monitors' soft, dim light, there's a chance. Elisa is everything he needs. Quiet. Controllable.

Elisa extends her neck into the room and looks about. This dings Strickland's serenity. She looks as if expecting a trap. Why would she think that? He went out of his way to wrap new bandages over his unsightly fingers and to stow the Howdy-do out of sight under the desk. He gestures at the floor.

"No need for the mop. I only spilled some candy. Rolled right out of the bag. Don't want it to attract bugs. Pretty easy little job. Guess I could've done it myself. Except I got a bunch of stuff to do. That's why I'm here so late. Paperwork."

There is no paper on his desk. He should have thought of that. While Elisa consults her cart, he extracts a random file from his desk. Elisa enters the room with dustpan and brush held like nunchucks. She's as observant as a cat, too. Her eyes are on the file he's suddenly holding. He doesn't like that, feels caught in a lie. But he does like her looking at him. She kneels in a corner to brush up a candy. Looks good doing it, too. Strickland feels a surge of power. Same as he did from the vibrations of the Caddy's V-8. Power windows. Power brakes. Power steering. Just plain power.

"I'm not real used to these late hours, I guess. Get tired and clumsy. I guess you're used to it, though, huh? It's morning for you. You're probably full of energy. Hey, you want some candy? Not from the floor, I mean. I still got some here in the bag."

She's in front of the desk now, crouched between the chairs. She looks up, holds his eyes for a few seconds. The gray monitor light flatters her. Her hair is storm clouds. Her face a lambent silver. The scars on her neck two glowing lines of nightsurf. He loves those scars. He wonders if there are other places on a woman's body where scars might look as pretty. Lots of them, probably. Elisa shakes her head. No candy, no thank you. She starts to look away, but Strickland doesn't want to lose sight of those scars.

"Hey, hold on. I've got a question." On cue, one comes to him. "When you say you're mute—well, I guess you didn't say it. The Negro woman said it. You can't say anything." He laughs. She doesn't. Why not? It's a harmless joke. "Anyway, I've been wondering. Is it a hundred percent? I mean, if you get hurt, do you make a noise? Not that I'm planning on hurting you." He laughs. Again, no reaction. Why won't she relax? "Some mutes, you know, they squawk a little. I was just wondering."

The words don't come out perfect. He's not given to pleasantries. He's no Dr. Bob Hoffstetler, rattling off all the reasons he's so damn brilliant. Still, the question deserves a nod, a gesture, something. Instead, Elisa turns away, gets back to her task. From the sound of it, as quickly as possible. Strickland takes a second to think. If anyone else ignored him, they'd regret it. This janitor, though, it only augments her blissful silence. He's left staring at her backside. Tough to get a sense of it under that uniform, but he figures it's good enough. Definitely good enough if she keeps wearing shoes like that. The shoes are leopard patterned. *Leopard patterned.* If she's not wearing them for his enjoyment, then whose?

Each candy cracks when it hits the dustpan. Like twigs cracking in the jungle, the approach of a predator. Strickland stands up, paces before the monitors to shake it off. Right away, Elisa rises to her feet. She's either done or done trying, and bolts for the door, but can't move very fast. Candy rolls all over the dustpan, a balancing act fit for a circus. Strickland blocks the door with his right arm. Elisa pulls up short, the green candies clacking like bronchitic lungs.

"I know how it sounds," he says. "Me, who I am. You being you. But we're not that different. I mean—who do you have? Your file says you don't have nobody. And me, I guess it's not the same for me, but it *feels*—what I'm trying to say is that I *feel* the way you do. I figure we both got things in our lives we'd change if we could. You know?"

Strickland can't believe it, but there it is. He's raising his left hand, touching one of the neck scars. Elisa's whole body stiffens. She swallows hard. A birdie pulse palpitates her jugular. He wishes he could feel its throb, but his fingers are bloated, bandaged, one of them pinched numb by a wedding ring. The ring Elisa presented to him right here in this office. He switches hands, traces a neck scar with his index finger, half-closes his eyes, gives into his senses. The scar is soft as silk. She smells so clean, like bleach. Her frightened breath purrs like the Caddy.

In the Amazon, his party found the cadaver of a marsh deer, its antlers tangled in the ribs of a jaguar. The índios bravos had supposed that the two beasts had been locked together for weeks prior to dying, a grotesque crossbreed. That's him and Elisa, Strickland thinks. Two opposites, trapped together. Either they find a way to work together to break free, or both of them wither to bones. Female brains, he knows, require time to think. He lets his arm slide down the door frame. Elisa doesn't wait. She plunges outside, unloads the dustpan into the trash, grabs and wheels her cart. She's leaving, she's leaving.

"Hey," he calls.

Elisa pauses. In the brighter lights of the hall, her cheeks are pink, the scars red. Strickland feels a swirl of panic, loss, and frustration. He forces a smile, tries to mean it.

"I don't mind you can't talk. That's what I want to say. I even kind of like it." A good-natured entendre pops into his mind. Is it a permissible one? Will she respond positively to it? His head is dizzy from pills, and he doesn't dare miss the opportunity. His rubber-band grin stretches again, close to snapping. "I bet *I* could make you squawk. Just a little?"

23

ZELDA SEES ELISA leaving Mr. Strickland's office. There's a bunch of possible valid reasons. Maybe Strickland, with his bulky bandaged hand, made some kind of mess. Or Elisa's QCC had a note from Fleming about cleaning the normally restricted room. But when in their Occam history have either Zelda or Elisa fielded a special directive from Fleming without sharing it to speculate on its meaning? Elisa has said nothing. These days, does she ever? Zelda tells Elisa a Brewster story, Elisa asks no questions. Zelda tries to ask what's wrong, Elisa pretends not to hear. Each snub is a poke to Zelda's ribs as hard as if from Strickland's cattle prod. She's building up bruises. She winces over them even at home. Brewster has noticed, and when Brewster notices, you know your signals are firing like flares.

"It's Elisa," she'd admitted.

"Your friend at work?"

"She's just been treating me . . . Oh, I don't know."

"Like the help?" Brewster snapped.

That's Brewster. You catch him anywhere but in front of the TV, he's switchblade sharp. Too sharp for Zelda; you don't nourish a friendship this long and let it go, a petal in the wind. Some outside force is in play, and it has to be F-1. Since the time Strickland nearly caught Elisa inside, Zelda has twice spotted Elisa pushing her cart from the direction of F-1. Zelda gives Elisa every chance to share details, from the open-ended *Did you see anything interesting tonight?* to the pointed *I sure wonder what's going on in F-1.* Elisa divulges nothing. Not even a shrug. More than out of character, it's rude, and Zelda's beginning to wonder if she should follow Brewster's advice, respect herself, and turn her back.

Is Elisa's friendship really so much to lose? Zelda figures she could integrate herself into the other graveyarders, no problem. A couple more cigarettes smoked on the loading dock, a chuckle shared at Elisa's expense, and wham—she'd be current with all the inside jokes. It would hurt, but work was work, and Occam, she reminds herself, is but one limb of her life. She has family. Aunts and uncles and their various snarls of offspring, not to mention Brewster's busted family tree of half-cousins, third cousins, and fringe clingers she'd never quite placed. She has neighbors, too, some of whom she's known for fifteen years, some who hurrah when she arrives at their cookouts. And there is church, which is family and neighbors both, where they get loud, where they embrace and cry, where there is always support, always love.

There it is: all the proof that Zelda doesn't need Elisa.

But Zelda *wants* Elisa. She's headstrong about it, like a teenager forbidden to see a friend. Except she's not a teenager. She's the one, not Brewster, not her family, not her church, who gets to say when her pride has taken too much stomping. If she wants to give one more chance to a friend who's out of chances, she will. Besides, a woman goes crazy when a man's involved—men, too, go just as crazy—and that's her working theory: Elisa Esposito is having herself an affair. If F-1 is the rendezvous point, then it has to be Dr. Hoffstetler, doesn't it? That man who's been so nice to them? Who so often works such late hours? Who doesn't wear a ring?

Zelda doesn't hold it against her. Heck, she's tempted to offer congratulations; Elisa hasn't had a man since Zelda's known her. True, the affair could get her fired, but also true is that, if it works out, maybe she and Dr. Hoffstetler could leave Occam together. Can you imagine it? Elisa married to a doctor?

Tonight, though, after seeing Elisa hurrying away from Strickland's office, Zelda isn't sure. No doubt Strickland also has a key card to F-1. What if that nasty man with his rusty Howdy-do, who, come to think of it, had gotten himself an eyeful of Elisa's legs when they met in his office, had made some sort of move? Elisa's smart, but she's got squat for experience when it comes to men. And if Zelda's ever met a man who'd take advantage of a woman like that, it's Mr. Strickland.

A metal rigidity screws into Zelda's jaw, fists, and feet, all parts that could get a meek janitor in trouble at a place like Occam. She makes a choice. She only has to skip two rooms, storage spaces rarely dirty to begin with, to trail Elisa for the final half hour of the grave-yard shift. Zelda feels like a creep. Worse, her detective work turns up nothing concrete. Neither Elisa's uniform or hair seem ruffled from a physical encounter. Something, though, happened in Strickland's office; Elisa fails to hang a feather duster upon its cart peg three straight times.

The shift bell rings. The janitors rebound to the locker room. Zelda keeps her watch on Elisa, speeding up her clothes change so she can make it to the punch cards right behind her. Only when they are outside, beneath the melon orange of a sunrise scar, waiting in the bus stop's calf-high gravel dust, does Zelda send up a prayer, snag the startled Elisa by the sleeve, and pull her over to the trash can, spooking a raid of squirrels. Elisa's eyes, red and tired at this hour, flash with caution.

"I know, hon. I know. You don't want to talk to me. You don't want to talk at all. Then don't. Just listen. Before the bus comes, just listen."

Elisa tries to dodge away, but Zelda exploits something she rarely does, her size and strength, and pulls Elisa back by the cuff hard enough that Elisa's hip gongs the trash can. Elisa begins to sign with an angry energy, and Zelda gets the gist of the points and slashes. They are excuses, justifications, pretexts. It's telling that not one of them is an apology. An apology would be admitting that she'd done something wrong.

Zelda brings both of her hands atop Elisa's, gentling them like tussling pigeons and bringing them into the comfort of her bosom.

"You're not signing anything worth my time, and we both know it." Elisa quits resisting, but her face stays hard. Not unkind, just hard, as if holding a wall before a secret too big to show. Zelda exhales. "Haven't I always tried to understand whatever bothered you? From the first day you came? I remember that poster Fleming hung up in the locker room when you first started. Picture of some Marilyn Monroe type with a mop, all these arrows pointing out her attributes. *Hands willing to help. Legs ready to run the extra mile.* Remember that? Remember how we laughed and laughed? That's when we became friends. Because you were so young and so shy and I wanted to help. That's still all I want."

Elisa's forehead ripples in turmoil. She starts at the crunch of gravel, a half-dozen workers adjusting their feet while digging out bus tokens. That means the bus is in sight. Zelda can't hold her friend here much longer. She constrains Elisa's hands as tightly as she can in the cage of her own hands; she can feel the rustles of Elisa's delicate pigeon wings.

"If you're in some trouble, don't be frightened. Don't be scared. I've seen all sorts of trouble in my life. And if it's a man—"

Elisa's eyes dart back toward Zelda's. Zelda nods, tries to encourage her, but Elisa's pulling away, and the snort and hiss of the bus can't be ignored. Zelda's eyes go bleary all at once, a sluice of tears that she despises; it's every emotion she doesn't want to show when trying to display strength. Elisa breaks away, but Zelda calls out. Elisa stops, half-turns. Zelda wipes her eyes with the back of her hand.

"I can't keep asking you, hon," she moans. "I've got my own problems. My own life. You know one of these days, I'm leaving this place and starting my own thing. And I always pictured you coming along. But I got to know—do we just clean together? When we take the uniforms off, are we still friends?"

The swelling sun brings glistening definition to the tears that, in perfect match to Zelda's, begin rolling down Elisa's cheeks. Elisa's face twists, as if she wants to speak, but she clenches her hands, her method of biting her tongue, and can only shake her head before breaking toward the bus. Zelda turns away, purposefully blinding herself with the sun, and wipes her wet face with a quaking arm, then leaves it there, cover against the glare, the grief, the loneliness, all of it.

24

TAKE YOUR PICK of the city's army of ad men, and after a tough day they'll have their bellies to a bar, washing down the hard luck, cursing the iniquities of their chosen racket. But what is Giles Gunderson doing? First off, he'd delayed mourning until the following day because he was old and tired. Second, it's not beer he's throwing back, it's milk. Third, he's alone.

He thought he'd never get out of bed again. No work, no money, no food, no friends if Elisa remains furious. Why elongate the inevitable? Then morning light had crystalled through his bedroom window, the resultant rainbows remindful of the chromed display cases at Dixie Doug's. If anything could extricate Giles from the briar patch of doom, it was the attentions of Brad—unless the alternate name tag was correct and he was actually JOHN. Giles had dressed in clothes that, for the first time, seemed not permeated with character but simply old and put on his toupee, an exercise in disgrace. Then he'd attempted to ignore the Pug's mortal chokes and tape together the shredded ribbons of his pride so that he might enter Dixie Doug's with a soupçon of his usual verve.

But Brad wasn't there, and the queue, a rattlesnake, had him coiled. Forced to order, and mindful of his destitution, he smiled wanly at a perky young woman name-tagged as LORETTA and or-dered the cheapest thing on the menu, a pitiful glass of milk. Now he sits at the counter, despite how stools play hell with his hip. Gulp down the milk, make a quick getaway, get on with the business of dying.

He swivels to the right so he might distract himself with the black-and-white TV lodged between tureens of plastic utensils. The reception is snarled, but ropes of static can't hide the familiar con-trasts of Negroes toting signs in circles. Milk goes sour on Giles's tongue. Oh, this is just what he needs! Giles considers calling for Loretta to turn the dial, but she's in high flirt, transmogrifying winks and wiggles into whole fleets of ordered pies. At least Dixie Doug's blares country-western music; he can make out only snatches of the news report. Something about William Levitt, the pioneer of "suburban" living. Something about how Levitt won't sell plots to Negroes. Giles aches at the file footage of Long Island's Levittown. He imagines himself in one of the pastel abodes, exiting each dewy morning in a snug house robe to water magnolias. It'll never happen; he'll serve a life sentence in that mice-ridden shoebox above the Arcade, and that's if he's lucky.

Elbows fold themselves onto the counter. Giles looks up and there he is, an angel floated in from short-order Elysium. Even Brad's

comfy hunch can't hide a height that must be taller than Giles's previous estimates. Six-foot-three. Six-foot-three at least! Brad leans
across the counter, smelling of sugar and dough. He loosens one big,
lazy finger from the knot of his arms to indicate a plate of bright
green pie that has manifested alongside the milk.

"Remembered how much you like that key lime."

Brad's fake Southern accent is back, and Giles melts. Fake accent,
fake hair, what's the difference? Are we not allowed our little vani-
ties, especially when they please someone about whom you care?

"Oh!" Giles pictures his emptied wallet. "I'm not sure I brought
enough cash to—"

Brad scoffs. "Forget it. It's on the house."

"That is far too kind. I won't hear of it. I'll bring by the money
later." An idea strikes him, a deranged one, but if this, his lowest
point, isn't the time for insane acts, what is? "Or . . . you could give
me your address, and I could swing it by?"

"Now who's being too kind? Shucks, working here, it's like tending bar. You get to know people. Hear their stories. And I can tell
you, mister, most people? They hold a conversation about as well as I
can hold a bag of cats. We don't get a lot of customers like you. Smart,
educated. All that stuff you told me about the big food launch what-
chamadoodle? You got a lot of real interesting things to say, and I'm
obliged. So eat up, partner."

Bernie must be right, Giles thinks. He's old, he's sentimental, he's
trapped in a different time. Why else is it that, at this meagerest gen-
erosity, tears have begun to gather along his eyelids.

"I can't tell you what it means to . . . I work alone, you know, and
conversation . . . I talk to my friend, of course, my best friend, but
she's . . ." Elisa's parting signs are still branded into the flesh of his
back. "Well, she's not much of a conversationalist. So . . . I thank
you. From the bottom of my heart. And you must call me Giles." He
forces a smile, and it feels brittle, his whole skull feels brittle, a thing
as shatterable as Andrzej. "You can't be bankrolling my key lime
habit and calling me 'partner.'"

Brad's laugh is sunshine, lemonade, mowed grass.

"Heck, I never knew a Giles before, if you want the truth."

Giles can see it in the purse of Brad's lips, his real name about to be divulged with the same easy affection with which he'd confessed his Canadian heritage. After this, thinks Giles, there will be no more prying for clues; there will be no more paging through phone books like a lovesick schoolboy; there will be no more humiliation in this life that has been filled with nothing else. On this worst morning of his life, all will be saved.

"I do want the truth," he says, and it sounds profound.

Here is Giles's truth. He has alienated his one confidant. The ad campaign he'd lied to Brad about "captaining" ended with a hack-job painting he'd given to a merciful receptionist. He has no future. He has no hope. All of this is why, he will postulate later, he succumbs to his long-delayed desire, as delirious as a child electrified by too much sugary pie. The last time he spoke to Brad, he'd explained the etymology of *tantalize*, how Tantalus had reached for fruit and water forever just out of range. Now Giles reaches, too.

He settles his hand atop Brad's wrist. It's as warm as fresh bread.

"I like talking to you, too," Giles says. "And I'd like to get to know you better. If you'd like it as well. Is the name really . . . Brad?"

The merry twinkles of Brad's eyes wink out, as quietly and completely as if he'd passed away. He stands up, not six-foot-three or six-foot-four, but ten feet, one hundred, one thousand, pulling away from the counter and into the stratosphere. Giles's hand slides off the warm skin and drops to the cold counter, a withered, blotched, veiny, wobbling thing. From the god lording above comes a voice leached of its butter-and-syrup accent.

"What are you doing, old man?"

"But I . . . you . . ." He is effete, adrift, isolated in bright lights like a specimen. "You bought me *pie*."

"I bought everyone pie," Brad says. "Because I got engaged last night. To that young lady right there."

Giles's throat clenches. The same thick, hairy finger of Brad's that had pointed at the suggestive free pie now points at Loretta, that smooth young thing, jiggling and giggling, the apogee of normalcy. Giles looks at Loretta, then Brad, then Loretta, back and forth, a helpless geriatric. Next in the queue is a black family—mother, father, and child—who stare at the overhanging menu, whispering to one another their pie-related plots. Brad's face, Giles observes, is bright red from the disgrace of Giles's touch, and such anger has to go somewhere.

"Hey!" Brad shouts. "Just takeout for you. No seats."

The family's chatter peters out. Their heads turn, as does every head in Dixie Doug's, to look at the fuming Brad. The mother in the queue gathers her child into her hands before she replies.

"There are plenty of seats . . ."

"All reserved," Brad snaps. "All day. All week."

The family's eager expressions curl away from Brad's fire. Giles is overcome with nausea. He grips the counter to halt his stool from spinning only to find that it isn't moving. Behind Brad, Giles sees the TV's blur, and Giles, because he deserves it, accepts its contempt. People see blacks protest on the news every day, probably while ironing laundry, and feel nothing. Giles, though, can't stand the sight. It's not due to some swell of compassion. It's out of self-preservation. He has the privilege—the *privilege*—of being able to hide his minority status, but if he had any pride at all, he wouldn't be making furtive touches across a diner counter. He'd be standing alongside those who are unafraid of getting their skulls cracked open by batons. Disgracing himself is one thing; letting it spill onto these innocents just trying to purchase saccharine, overpriced, so-called pie is unacceptable.

"Don't talk to them like that," he says.

Brad angles his sneer at Giles. "You better leave, too, mister. This is a family place." The doorbell dings, and Brad looks up. The father, likely familiar with the taste of a busted lip, is herding his family out of harm's way. Brad plants onto his face a radiant grin, one Giles used to think Brad baked up special just for him, and dollops the accent on thick: "Y'all come back now!"

Giles glares down at the key lime pie. The color is identical to that of his painted gelatin, a synthetic, otherworldly green. He runs his eyes across Dixie Doug's. Where have the pulsing colors and chrome liquescence gone? This is a graveyard of cheap plastic. He stands and finds himself firmer on his feet than expected. When Brad again looks his way, Giles is surprised to see that the object of his fantasies isn't so tall after all. Indeed, they are the same height. Giles adjusts his bow tie, straightens his glasses, brushes cat hair from his jacket.

"When you told me about your franchising," he says, "I was impressed, I admit it. The decorations, how they truck in the pies, everything."

Giles pauses, in awe of the inflexibility of his voice. Other diners, too, look on as if they feel the same. Vain though it might be, Giles wishes that the family of three was still there to hear him. He wishes his father was there to hear, too. He wishes Bernie Clay, Mr. Klein, and Mr. Saunders were there. He wishes everyone who'd ever dismissed him was there to witness this.

"But do you know, young man, what franchising really is?" Giles makes a sweeping gesture across the diner. "It is a crass, craven, vulgar, piggish attempt to falsify, package, and sell the unsellable magic of one person sitting across a table from another person. A person who *matters*. You cannot franchise the alchemy of greasy food and human affection. Perhaps you have never experienced it. Well, I have. There is a person who matters to me. And she, I assure you, is far too intelligent to be caught in here."

He pivots on a heel, Brad's face joining the TV's smear, and marches through the diner, silent now but for the country crooning. He's at the door before Brad can rally a retort.

"And it's not Brad. It's John, faggot."

The word has chased him home before, after he's offered some promising fellow the delicate bait of a double meaning, plus the failsafe of a third meaning should the double meaning be understood and rejected, except today the word does not chase so much as it does fuel, propelling him through Baltimore streets, into his parking space behind the Arcade, up the fire escape, past his own door, and inside Elisa's apartment after the alert of a quick knock. He sees the second he enters that she isn't asleep as she should be; he keels toward the beacon of the lit bathroom, where he finds her on hands and knees, partner to a sudsy bucket, paused from the perplexing activity of scrubbing the bathtub so vigorously that the surface gleams like marble, casting Elisa, the whole room, probably the whole theater below and the city's entire metropolitan grid in a new, bright, better light.

"Whatever this thing is doesn't matter," Giles says. "What matters is you need it. And so I will help you. Just tell me what to do."

25

ELISA GLANCES AT her friend as he fusses his paintbrush within the hand-cut stencil taped against the sliding door of the Pug. After dislodging plates of caked dirt, the two of them loosened decades of exhaust grit with citrus-based dish soap before scrubbing the van with clay—a janitor's trick. Giles has done all this wearing the same houndstooth vest he wears when vultured over his drafting table, and he's making the same squint. Seeing him released, however, into the sweet fresh air of spring is like seeing him released from dungeon shackles. The late Sunday sun warms the top of his bald scalp, and when was the last time he went outside without his toupee? It makes Elisa happy. Giles has been different this weekend; all hesitance has been cored from him. If this, Elisa thinks, is their final day together, before they enact her plan, before arrest, before sentencing, maybe before being shot dead, it has been a good day indeed.

She can't observe him for long. Her arms quake beneath another load of unreturned milk bottles, each cleaned and filled with water.

She climbs inside the van. Everything behind the front seats has been cleared to make room for a hodgepodge of boxes and baskets arranged atop a piece of carpet. Elisa lets the bottles roll from her arms and places them, one by one, into a box padded with a blanket. They clank and slosh; her stomach behaves in kind. She sits back against the inner wall, panting.

"Yes, do take a moment's rest." Giles flicks his smiling eyes from his stenciling. "You're working too hard. Worrying too hard as well. In a few hours, my dear, all of it will be over and done with, one way or the other. Focus on that. The only thing I'm certain of is that uncertainty is the hardest thing in life to endure."

Elisa smiles; she is surprised, but she does. She signs: "Did you finish your ID?"

Giles dabs paint, blows it dry, then sets his brush crosswise atop a tin of paint. He removes his wallet, withdraws a card with flourish, and presents it across his opposite wrist as he might a sword. Elisa takes it, examines it, and then digs her authentic Occam ID out for comparison. The texture and weight are wrong, though if anyone is handling the card that closely, it's likely the game will already be lost. Otherwise it is as convincing a piece of work as anything Giles has done. That it was a new medium for him, and completed over a single day, makes the effort all the more impressive.

She signs the name on the ID: "Michael Parker?"

"I thought it was a good, hearty, trustworthy name." Giles shrugs. "Naturally, my friends can call me Mike."

Elisa scans the details harder, and with a smile, signs: "Fifty-one years old?"

Giles looks crestfallen. "No? Not even with the hair? What about fifty-four? A single dab of paint, and I can add three years, just like that."

Elisa grimaces. Giles sighs and snaps his fingers for the card. He picks up the paintbrush, twists the bristles so that they taper into a point, and touches it softly to the ID.

"There. Fifty-seven. The absolute best I can do. Now stop being rude to poor old Mike Parker."

He gets back to work, scowling for show. Elisa is sick with sustained tension, so dizzy she feels as if swimming, and yet bundled in a peculiar warmness, the interior of the van somehow the most comfortable spot in the world. So much of her life she's felt alone, but at this second there is plentiful proof to the contrary. If they are caught in a few hours, her second-biggest regret is that she won't be able to thank Zelda for wanting, nearly begging to help. Elisa couldn't do it to her; if Elisa and Giles get caught, Zelda can't be involved. It's a terrible feeling, pushing Zelda away. Still, Elisa thinks, she must have done something right in her life to earn that kind of loyalty.

The sounds of Giles stowing his gear drag her back to harsh reality. A wind too dry to hold a drop of water buffets the inside of the Pug, and she feels from inside the theater the rumble of a sinister music cue. Elisa climbs out of the van, slits her eyes at the dusking sun.

"I'm proud of you."

Elisa looks down at Giles. He's on his haunches, rinsing his brush. The sinking sun backlights him, but she can make out the serene lines of fond contemplation.

"Whatever happens," he says, "I'm old. Even my alter ego, Mike Parker, is old. What does this kind of risk matter to us at the end of the day? But you're young. Your life sprawls out ahead of you like the Atlantic Ocean. And yet look at you. You're not afraid."

Elisa lets herself absorb the compliment, because she needs it, and then, to clear the air, simpers and signs with overblown motions. Giles frowns.

"Oh. You *are* afraid? *Very* afraid? Well, don't tell me that, dear. I'm terrified!"

His exaggeration of fright makes the real thing somehow governable. Elisa smiles, grateful for the buoy, and steps back to gaze at Giles's stenciled handiwork in the melodrama of an orange-purple sunset. She catches her breath. A doctored ID card slid into a pocket is one thing. A fraudulent sign painted onto a registered motor vehicle is another level of audacity:

MILICENT LAUNDRY

Behind the lettering, the Pug's cleaned door, luminous in the sun, becomes a pool into which Elisa slips and inside which she drowns until, in a great turnabout, she is graced with the creature's abilities and begins to swim, even to breathe, not merely bubbled to the top like boiling eggs, but darting through the currents of this impossible scheme. Awareness of the cramped, dirty alley, suffused in the stink of tossed popcorn, doesn't go away, and yet she believes she can feel an entire ocean's worth of creatures converging on one spot, looking to her for guidance. The time has come.

26

THE BOTTLE CAP blunders from sweaty fingers, bickers off floor tiles, squirrels behind the toilet. Hoffstetler wants to fall to his knees, scrabble after it like a junkie. One of the janitors will find it, one of the scientists will lift fingerprints from it, and Strickland, cattle prod crackling, will collar Hoffstetler before he can schedule to meet the Bison's Chrysler. But there's no time. Monday's graveyard-to-dayshift change, Occam's most turbulent thirty minutes, is near. He's got to steady his hands, his breathing, his mind, and do this. Not for himself. He'll do it for the children whose lives were ruined by the classified medical studies that he allowed to happen. The Devonian, in its own way, is one more child being abused. Hoffstetler can avert its misery, and in that end, find a snip of redemption.

He pries the stopper and rubber tip from the syringe, tosses both in the toilet, and flushes it; the roar matches the pulse in his ears. Toilet-water flecks his face and hangs on his skin like warts as he pushes the needle into the bottle and draws the plunger. The silver solution eddies gorgeously into the barrel. He knows the law of nature: A substance that beautiful can only be deadly. He places the syringe into the pocket of his lab coat, wipes his face with his sleeve, and exits the toilet stall, trying not to look at the changeling face in the mirror. The poised, aloof college professor has been replaced by a red-faced, curled-lip murderer.

27

ANTONIO TAKES TEN years to find his punch card. It's the crossed eyes, Zelda figures. Lord knows how he cleans a desk without knocking all contents to the floor. Hostile thoughts, but Zelda decides she deserves them. Elisa had a whole weekend to consider Zelda's question: *Are we friends?* The answer, it seems, is no. Here it is, the end of Monday's shift, and Elisa hasn't said a word to her. Won't even look at her. Zelda's had it. At least that's what she tells herself: She's had it. Maybe Brewster's right. A white friend is only a friend for as long as she needs you. What sticks in her head, though, is how fish-belly pale Elisa's face had been tonight, how she kept looking over her shoulder, how half the cleaning products she picked up tumbled from the uncontrollable shake of her hands.

Yolanda pokes Zelda in the back. The line has shuffled forward, and so she does the same, except when she reaches for her punch card, the most ordinary thing in the world, it takes longer than Antonio's ten years—it takes a lifetime. It's like she's reaching across a bottomless chasm. Humiliation and anger, it seems, no matter how much she deserves them and wants to own them, are slippery objects to Zelda, as slippery as this punch card. It flutters from her fingers, lazing down like a broken wing.

28

THE PUG JOUNCES up Falls Road. He's got to arrive per Elisa's schedule, one hour before the real laundry truck will show up—any earlier will raise suspicion. He barrels through pools of streetlight sodium, along the squiggled vein of the Jones Falls stream, past the black copses of Druid Hill Park, around the purple lawns of the Baltimore Country Club. Parts of the city he's never explored and never will. Giles goes heavy on the pedal when nervous and takes the left at South Avenue so fast he can feel the passenger-side wheels almost lose contact with the pavement. The Pug slams down on wasted shocks and a box in the back overturns to unleash water-bottle missiles like a Polaris submarine. Giles curses, wrestles the vehicle, slows before a dark complex called Happy Hills Convalescent Home for Children, the last landmark before Occam Road.

He hasn't been here since the day he drove eighteen-year-old Elisa to her interview. Nothing has changed. Thick woods on either side of the road still look to hide trolls, and the illuminated clock on Occam's sign still glows like a second moon. He's long regretted having had a role in Elisa taking this job. But not today. Today she has a purpose, and it is a beautiful thing to see. He tries to remember that as he follows the LOADING signs, passing through an empty parking lot. Well, not totally empty: He notices a giant green Cadillac Coupe de Ville before the Pug's headlights strike a checkpoint guard holding up a hand for Giles to stop, while his other hand comes to rest upon the handle of a holstered gun.

29

THE GRAY LIGHT of the security monitors are all the sunrise Strickland needs. He climbs from the floor, his bed on nights he can't bear to look at Lainie, and into his chair. His guts squelch, the sound of digesting painkillers. Must be hard work, because when he coughs there's blood. It dots the white envelope on his desk. He wipes it. It smears, but that's all right. Makes the envelope pulsate with importance. And it is important. It's the paperwork for today's dissection of the asset. He removes the document. It's clean, beautiful—not a word is redacted. He doesn't bother to read it, signs his name on a few dashes. He does linger over the diagrams. The autopsy looks pretty standard for a beast of such alleged scarcity. Y-shaped incision. Cracking the ribs in half. Scooping out the organs. The serrated-saw scalping. Brain plopped onto a pan. He can't fucking wait.

Footsteps outside his door. Strickland looks up from the schema. This early, he expects Mr. Clipboard. But it's not Fleming. It's Bob Hoffstetler. He looks like shit. Sweaty, pale, skittish. Looks like Raúl Romo Zavala Henríquez, way over his head. Strickland leans back in his chair. Laces his fingers behind the head. It hurts, but the posture is worth it. This should be fun.

30

ZELDA KNEELS TO pick up the punch card. Yolanda's going wild behind her. But all Zelda hears is Brewster carrying on about how she shouldn't trust anyone. He doesn't know Elisa, though, does he? Of course he doesn't. Despite their long years of friendship, Elisa's never been to Zelda's home, not once. But Zelda *knows* the girl. She *knows* she knows the girl. And this is not the Elisa she knows.

Elisa's card waits in its slot, unpunched despite Elisa's rapid exit from the locker room. A small detail, maybe, until you add it to every-thing that's been going on at Occam over the past several days. Equip-ment under dust covers being wheeled out of F-1. Scientists shaking hands at coffee-and-doughnut farewells. A mixed mood that feels like the last week of senior year: excited, but fearful, and sad, too. Zelda can feel the whole building clenching as if for impact. Something big is happening today, and Elisa, it seems abruptly clear, has gotten her-self entwined. And how does Zelda know this? It'd been right there in front of her all night, squeaking across the floors.

Elisa's shoes. She'd been wearing ugly, gray, rubber-soled sneak-ers, built for running.

Zelda swipes up her card, punches it, and then, in an act that makes Yolanda spit acid, finds Elisa's card and punches that, too. Punch cards, after all, are the first evidence to which Fleming will look to find out who is here and who's not if something goes wrong. Zelda wheels around, bumping past Yolanda without apology, and hustles back in the direction of the labs. Go wrong? Her hunch is that a lot is going to go wrong, a whole lot, and very quickly.

31

HOFFSTETLER TILTS TOWARD Strickland's desk. He's holding the syringe inside his pocket. Mihalkov will never find out. He'll never need to know. Half the solution for Strickland. Half for the Devonian. The first needs to be killed to ensure the second can be killed cleanly. Hoffstetler tells himself that the wicked, hateful mudak deserves it. The glass of the syringe is oily, slipping from his grip. He wipes his fingers on the inside of his pocket, takes a drier hold. He's nearly to the desk. Don't stop moving.

"Go back and knock first," Strickland says.

They are senseless words, and Hoffstetler, his brain hardwired for sense, rejects it like a computer fed defective data, and does the worst thing, he stops moving, right in front of a wall of monitors that blind him with sixteen screens of gray light. He raises a hand to shield his eyes, the hand that, one second ago, had held the syringe. It's empty now, a soft, flabby, harmless thing.

"Knock . . . ?"

"Protocol, Bob," Strickland says. "I know how you value protocol."

"I wanted . . . to give you one more chance . . ."

"*Me?* Give *me*? Bob, I don't follow. You're free to tell me about it, of course. Just go back to the door and knock first."

32

NOT A SENSITIVE vehicle, the Pug, but the naked tires feel part of Giles's flesh, and pulling away from the checkpoint, he feels every pebble that passes beneath. Sure, the guard had waved him through without checking ID, duped by the van's paint job. But the checkpoint was always going to be the easy part, wasn't it? Giles slows to a creep as he rounds the back of the facility. A figure leans on a wall, smoking between two lights. Giles wipes the fogged windshield. Yes, that has to be it: the loading dock. He tries to swallow his fear, but his throat is sandpaper.

He begins to pull in between painted yellow lines. The guard snaps awake, lifting both palms as one does to question an imbecile. He spins a finger, and Giles flinches at his error. He's supposed to back in. Of course he is. You don't load a van through the front. He wipes sweat from his face, shifts to reverse, and pulls back into the first leg of a three-point turn. This is bad. Oh, this is very bad. He'll go a mile out of his way to avoid the public debasement of parallel parking. Now here, in the predawn dark, he's got to back into a narrow slot while a wary guard observes? Giles checks the rearview mirror and sees the suspicious red eye of the guard's lit cigarette. Giles shifts into reverse, grasps the wheel, and prays to the General Motors gods for a vehicular miracle.

33

"Well, howdy, Bob. Come on in. What can I do for you this morning?"

Hoffstetler feels every inch the scolded child Strickland intended him to feel. Ten or twelve times he knocked on the door, while Strickland grinned, far too much time being lost. He lurches back before the strobing security screens. He's baffled with fear, off-kilter enough that, thrusting his hand into his pocket, his index finger grazes the tip of the needle. Too close—he hisses panic into the bared teeth of his artificial smile.

"I just . . . wanted to make sure you . . . wished to go through with this."

"These here are General Hoyt's orders." He lifts the topmost document, a superficial sketch of the asset perforated into butcher's portions. "And I just initialed them. That means two hours and forty-five minutes from now, you and me act like good Americans and go gut that fish. I know how you feel. But think of it this way. The Japs, the Huns, the Chinese. They're intelligent creatures, too, aren't they? But we sure as hell had no problem killing *them*."

Hoffstetler visualizes springing across the desk. He knew it might come to this. A graceless act, but so unlikely for a man his age that it might be all the surprise he needs. Strickland will raise an arm to defend himself, or turn his back—it doesn't matter. The needle will pierce any part. Hoffstetler's thighs are tensed for the vault when he notices the most minute of motions. Perhaps his eyes have become trained to detect anthropocentric detail of any size, down to the cilia of simple protocells and organelles. Just behind Strickland's head, in the seventh monitor, the security camera's perspective tilts upward, from a laundry van backing into a loading dock to the empty black sky above it.

Hoffstetler lets the syringe drop into his pocket. He replies that yes, of course, he'll see Strickland at the euthanasia, but the polite sounds are muffled by the singing of his heart, *"Slav'sya, Otechestvo nashe svobodnoye!"* the Soviet state anthem. Mihalkov—he came through. After eighteen years of letting Hoffstetler struggle alone, the Russians have arrived to help.

34

ELISA SPRINTS INTO the laundry room. It is happening: For a second, she'd glimpsed the Pug backing into the loading dock and making such a serpentine production of it that the guard had rushed forward, a troubling thing, even as it had allowed Elisa space enough to take the broom and nudge the security camera upward before scrambling away. Her waist strikes the industrial sink, and she plugs the drain, cranks both hot and cold knobs. She snatches towels from a bin and hurls them under the water. Elisa and Zelda have spent years ridiculing Fleming's QCCs, but now she's got to hand it to the man: The practices rutted into her brain keep her on task when she otherwise might collapse in terror.

She scoops the sopping towels from the sink and drops them, heavy as mud, into the closest empty laundry cart. She keeps going, her uniform getting wetter, until the cart is half-filled, then wrenches off the water and clenches the cart handle. She pushes; the cart doesn't budge. Her marrow turns to ice. She tries again, teeth bared, muscles tight, bearing down on her sneakers. The first inch is the toughest, but after that the cart slugs forward, one rotation, two. Her stopped heart picks up the beat, only to hiccup again: It's the squeaky cart, the one that yowls like a tomcat, and there is no time left for switching it out.

GILES RECOILS FROM the knuckles against his window. The guard makes a cranking motion with his hand. Giles doesn't know what to do but obey. He rolls down the window, and the guard's features come into sharp definition: sleepy brown eyes, unkempt mustache, hairy ears. He frowns as he runs the light over Giles's clothing, and Giles is jolted by memory: Twenty-two years ago, the night of the arrest at the gay bar that got him booted from Klein & Saunders, all those mustached cops and how their flashlight beams across his body felt like assault.

"You don't look like Laundry," the guard says.

"Thanks." This is how a driver would talk, Giles thinks, not *thank you, good sir.*

The guard doesn't appreciate the joke. "ID?"

Giles grins so hugely he believes teeth might start dropping from his jaws and pretends to search for his wallet, hoping the guard, cold and tired, will tell him to forget it. There is silence from the guard; Giles has no choice but to produce the ID. He holds it so the guard can read it without touching, but it doesn't work. With viperous speed, the guard, not so drowsy after all, plucks it. The flashlight turns the ID's papery stock translucent. Giles can see right through it as the guard scratches it with his thumbnail. The 7 Giles had inked to advance Michael Parker's age comes off.

"Oops," Giles says.

"Out of the van," the guard says.

Then all the lights at Occam Aerospace Research Center go out.

36

Zelda is in the laundry room when it happens. Six years ago, both halves of her duplex were robbed, and she'll never forget how quickly she'd known that something was wrong. She'd been barely out of the car, Brewster still behind the wheel. Nothing was missing from the front patch of grass; there was nothing to take. And yet, everything was wrong. The grass was wrong, bothered by shoes different than theirs. The door was wrong, the knob rotated in an odd way. Most of all, the air was wrong, half-sucked away by a stranger's panting, the rest stirred into wasplike agitation.

Staring at the drops of water on the floor, Zelda feels the same direful certainty. Nothing overt is wrong; water gets on floors. Why, then, does she edge around it like a detective around a pool of blood? Because, if she looks closely, the water drops themselves are evidence. They aren't round beads snug with surface tension. They are slashes, describing a tale of haste—Elisa's haste. These telltale patterns remain visible to her even after the overhead lights blink out and she is pitched into black.

It is the kind of event that has to be lived with for a minute before it can be believed. Occam is never dark. Even closet lights don't turn off. An exhausted groan comes from the walls and then silence descends, a true silence bled of white noise, leaving Zelda alone with the drub of her own bodily machinery. No—not entirely alone. Far down a dark hall, she can hear the shrill squeak of the laundry cart with the bad wheel.

37

IF SHE HADN'T already been reaching for F-1's door, Elisa doesn't know how long it would've taken her to find it in the deluge of darkness. She muscles her cart across the still, shushed lab, the bad wheel screaming in the quiet, her constant dreams of the room her only map until her eyes begin to adjust to the low level of light—the first rays of dawn, she has to assume, eking in from first-floor windows and curling like smoke through ventilation passages heretofore invisible.

The cart strikes nothing until the ledge of the pool. Gray flashes of rocking water wheel through the darkness like thrown knives. Can he see her? Into blackness, she signs with the fever of prayer, words she can only hope that he's learned. "Come." "Swim." "Move." She's sprawled across the ledge, leaning over the pool, signing. Water laps against her. She's still signing, signing. There's no knowing why the lights went out, but it will foster a panic, and panic will drive people to protect their most significant asset. There's no hope for the creature, or Elisa, if he doesn't come, swim, move, and now.

Two golden eyes crest like dual suns. Elisa goes wordless. Next thing, her shoes are off, her legs are in the water, her uniform is wrapping around her thighs like cold tentacles. She shivers and slogs toward him, arms outstretched. The golden eyes are wary, of course they are— he's been pursued before. Elisa takes another step and the pool bottom slopes dramatically; suddenly the water is at her chin and she's gasping, and the weight of her clothes drags her farther down the slope, and farther, and now she's sputtering, and the only signs her hands are making now are the desperate, empty grasps of a drowning woman.

38

THE MONITORS SNAP with static electricity. The screens not yet black. A fading gray, sixteen dying eyes. Nothing's being watched. Nothing's being taped. Control is all Strickland has wanted since boot camp, Korea, the Amazon—control over his family, control over his own fate, and now it's severed, machete into jungle root. He stands. His knee strikes his desk so hard he hears wood crack. He hobbles, tips against the monitor bank, steadies himself with dead fingers. That hurts, too, and he pushes away. It's black lunar terrain. His foot upsets a trash can. His shoulder rams a wall. He has to fight his way through the doorway, as if it's a tiny one built for a dog.

Footsteps, urgent but faltering, rise from the hall like a drip of rain. A beam of light scribbles across the black air.

"Strickland?" It's Fleming, civilian putz, never any help.

"What the fuck"—sudden pain, everything hurts—"is this?"

"I don't know. Fuses?"

"Well, call someone."

"The lines are down. I can't."

Strickland's instincts are always finest when it comes to contact. His fist shoots out as if by slingshot. Grabs Fleming by the collar. Their only instance of touching besides the first-day handshake. But it always loomed, didn't it? The threat a man of blood and soot poses over a pencil pusher, clipboard waver? Fine stitching in Fleming's collar rips as Strickland curls his biceps.

"Find someone. Now. We're being invaded."

AN OBJECT PRESSES against Elisa's back. Seems too big for a hand, but it flexes like one, with palm cradle and finger posts. Another presses to her chest, five claws pricking, just barely, her breasts and stomach. There is strength enough here to squash her, but instead she is lifted, as gently as if she were a butterfly, until her head is out of the water. She coughs against the rolling muscles of a large shoulder as she's floated backward to shallower depths. She can't form coherent thoughts: He is holding her, his scales under her hands both soft as silk and sharp as crystal, and though no words pass, everything, everything is being said.

Her body jerks. He's reached the limit of his chains. She snaps awake, establishes footing, and pulls from her sodden apron pockets the best tools she and Giles could scrounge: A bolt cutter and pair of pliers she'd smuggled in under her coat. The grooves across the creature's body glow red, but only for an instant. He stares at her, only inches separating their eyes, and then stands upright, his chest emerging so that she can access the chains locked to the harness. Removed from water, his gills begin to fluff, but there is no doubting any of this. He understands. He trusts. He, like she, has nothing left to lose.

She wedges the bolt cutter around a chain link. Instantly she perceives that she's made a fatal misjudgment. The link is too thick, and the cutter blades can't get a grip; it's like trying to bite a basketball. Elisa snugs the chain into the blades and tries to gnaw at it, but it has no effect beyond the flimsiest of scratches. She pockets the cutters and jams the needle nose of the pliers inside a link and tries to pull open the jaws to break it from within. This method gives her no leverage. Her hand slips, and the tool tumbles into the water. She doesn't try to save it. There's no point. She's as red-handed as possible, soaked inside the F-1 pool with Giles waiting outside, with no way at all of cutting the creature free. It feels like a mercy when a man's voice speaks from the darkness.

"Stop," he says.

40

GILES BELIEVES HE is turning in a bravura performance as The Man Who Can't Unlock His Seat Belt when the lights go out. Not only the two lights of the loading dock. All of them: Office windows, sidewalk path, lawns, awnings, parking lots, they all blink shut. The guard steps back from the van, scans the building, reaches for his radio.

"This is Gibson, loading dock. Everything all right in there? Over."

Elisa hadn't said anything about the lights going out. Giles takes the opportunity to peer into the side mirror at the loading-dock doors. He wants her to emerge. He also hopes she doesn't, not yet. This guard isn't going away. He will need, then, to be distracted. Giles leans out of the window and clears his throat.

"Sir?" He curses softly; that's not driver-speak. He tries again: "Buddy?"

The guard adjusts his transmitter. "This is Gibson, loading dock, over."

"Terribly sorry about the ID card," Giles says. "I'm afraid I'm a little sheepish about my age. See this? It's a hairpiece. I'm afraid I'm a vain man, though I assure you it does not interfere with my laundry-toting capabilities."

The guard turns on him, deftly unholstering his gun.

"I'm going to say this one more time, Mr. Parker. Get out of the van."

HOFFSTETLER SLIDES ACROSS the ledge, crashes into the water, grabs Elisa by the shoulder. The creature hisses, a sound like shaving ice, but, for once, death doesn't scare Hoffstetler.

"Who are you working with?"

He asks because he still can't believe that music and dancing, those vanguard tactics that kept the Devonian alive, could have been the brainchild of this nondescript janitor. But it takes one second of staring into her despairing eyes to affirm that she is that rarest of all things, a truly independent operative beholden to no principle beyond her sense of what is right.

"You moved the dock camera, didn't you?" he says. "You're taking it out of here, aren't you?"

She nods, and his mind whirls. There are no Russians. He just blew Occam's electrical grid with Mihalkov's popper, and the only person here to help him is a frail-boned woman who can't speak. It's a situation doomed enough to laugh at, but he thinks of what he used to tell his students. Imagine being a planet. Don't laugh, he'd tell them. Try to imagine it. Eons of loneliness, and then one day your ellipsis peaks toward that of another planet and there is a gasp of nearness. Wouldn't you try to make the most of it? Wouldn't you, too, combust and flare and explode if you had to? That is Elisa Esposito and Bob Hoffstetler: two lonely, unlikely bodies grasping at each other for just this precious instant.

"Tell it not to hurt me," Hoffstetler says. "I'm going to unlock it."

42

THE SECURITY-CAMERA screens are cold and lifeless when Strickland barges his way back into his tar-black office. He thunders about, knocking shit over. He feels blind. Handicapped. Like the creature, which can't hardly breathe regular air. Like Elisa, who can't talk. His swiping hand knocks the phone from the table. It lands with a pitiful little ring. He wonders if it was the red phone. General Hoyt. Jesus Fucking Christ. If Hoyt hears about this, Strickland will spend the rest of his life making up for it—

There. His good hand wraps around the smooth oak handle of the machete. No, the Alabama Howdy-do. It's more and more difficult to keep that straight. The steel shaft zings against the metal cabinet behind which he keeps it hidden. He thumbs the switch. The Howdy-do hums to life. He waves it before him as he heads in the direction of the door. This time he doesn't run into anything. It's like the office is afraid of him now.

The hallway is lit by the barest gloss of infiltrating dawn. Only a few footsteps and voices echo down the corridors. Whoever fried the fuses knew what they were doing. The shift change is the perfect time to strike. A bottleneck at the elevator. General confusion in the front office. But only a few early birds in the actual halls and laboratories. Who would know this? The same man who'd just been in his office. Bob Hoffstetler. The Russkie. Strickland moves down the hall as fast as the darkness allows, snorting the smoking ozone of the Howdy-do.

"The asset!" he shouts to anyone listening. *"Lock down the asset!"*

43

NEITHER ARE SUITED for physical labor, this slight woman and this gone-to-seed mid-forties biologist. The laundry cart might as well be filled with cinder blocks. Hoffstetler, though, trusts the properties of propulsion and momentum. They just have to get it moving. But Elisa abandons the handle and leans into the cart to arrange wet towels to better hide the creature inside. She does it with such affection that Hoffstetler hates to snap at her, but he does. This woman has set in motion a plot the Soviet government decided was too risky, and it deserves the reward of a real attempt. She scurries back, they push, the towels rustle with the creature's fear, and the wheels, weeping in protest, begin to turn.

It takes, by Hoffstetler's estimation, the length of an entire career to reach the lab door. In the hallway, darkness still reigns, but he knows it won't last; as Mihalkov said, the popper blows the fuses, but any homeowner with half a brain will be able to fix them. They bear down and push the cart in the direction of the loading dock. The only sounds are the squeaky wheel, their own grunts of strain, and the wheeze of the creature under the towels, until the serrated buzz of an angry voice reverberates from the next corridor:

"The asset! Lock down the asset!"

Hoffstetler knows, at once, what he must do. He takes a bottle of pills from his pocket and presses them into Elisa's hand. "Mix one of these in the water every three days. Do you understand me? Its water must be kept at seventy-five percent salinity." She stares in confusion. "Strict protein diet. Uncooked fish. Raw meat. Do you understand?" She's shaking her head even as he's handing her the syringe. "If you're not going to make it, use this. Don't let them cut it open. Please. It has secrets we're not supposed to know. None of us deserve to know." Except, perhaps, this janitor, he thinks. "It can only last thirty minutes out of water. Hurry. Hurry!"

She nods, but it's loose, as if her head might topple off her neck.

There is much more he needs to tell her, a lifetime's worth of information and caution, but he's down to mere seconds. He bolts into the darkness, following the bellow of Strickland's voice.

44

ELISA PUSHES, HER leg muscles shaking, her arm muscles ready to burst. The cart moves by inches, every speck of grit on the floor a massive speed bump she's forced to surmount. But she hears Hoffstetler calling for Strickland and this lights a fire under her feet as much as the hoarsening of the creature's breathing. She pushes, and it's hard, but what's harder is acting normal at the approach of a confused-looking man, some white coat who, in a detail of almost obscene normalcy, is still holding his cup of coffee. He only glances at Elisa, of course he does, because women like her are invisible. Never has she been so grateful.

She reaches the sharp left turn leading to the loading dock. She can see morning light between the doors. But the stubborn wheel won't budge. The cart won't turn. People are coming. She hears footsteps, more than before, and voices of increasing hysteria. She kicks the wheel, and her feet almost slide out from under her. The cart is leaking water, the whole area is slippery. She gets behind the handle again, determined to bulldoze left with sheer strength, but her feet can't get a grip in the puddle. Her knees hit the floor. She hangs from the cart like a child from a jungle-gym bar, afraid to drop.

Fingers curl around her arm.

45

ZELDA HOISTS ELISA to her feet. The girl is wild, trying to tear herself away, scrabbling for something in her pocket, but Zelda holds tight. Elisa isn't just shaking. She's convulsing, breath pounding, eyes blinkless and frenzied. Elisa's hand rises from her pocket, holding what looks like a hypodermic syringe. A drop of silver liquid hangs from the tip, jeweled in the barest smidge of dawn's blush. Zelda slowly draws her eyes from the needle's point to Elisa.

"Honey," she whispers. "Settle down."

Her voice creates an effect that her face hadn't. Elisa pushes the needle back into her pocket and collapses against Zelda, taking handholds of her uniform. Zelda has felt this kind of rageful hurt only at funerals and lets it happen, wrapping her arms around Elisa's throttling back. Her uniform is wet. It's soaking. Zelda looks over Elisa's shoulder into the pile of wet laundry. White towels, white lab coats, white sheets—

And a single golden eye.

"Oh my God," Zelda gasps. "Oh my God."

Elisa pulls apart, grasping Zelda by the forearms, pleading with every quiver. Maybe it's her ability to use those fingers to talk, but somehow through them everything is answered: why she's been so cold with Zelda, why she's tried to drive her friend away. It was because of *this*, because she didn't want Zelda to become culpable in *this*, and it is just this dedication to their friendship that makes Zelda damn all good sense and take her place at the cart's handle.

"You're crazy," Zelda says. "Now push."

46

STRICKLAND KNOWS THE shadow-shape of Hoffstetler as sure as he knows the Russian's flat-footed gait. He's got him. Strickland moves faster, charging up the center of the hall by a single window's worth of morning rays, ignoring an MP who salutes and asks for instruction. It takes a few steps for Strickland to pick up on a very unexpected thing. Hoffstetler isn't running away. Hoffstetler's coming straight at him. Strickland stops, thumbs the cattle prod, readies it at his side, opens his mouth to yell. But Hoffstetler speaks first.

"Strickland! It got free! I went inside to ready it, and it dragged me into the pool!"

"You expect me to believe—"

Hoffstetler grabs Strickland's coat. Strickland recoils, wants to jam him with the Howdy-do, but it's so sudden, so bewildering.

"It's not me, Richard! Somebody broke in! Got it out!"

"You're the dirty Red who came into my—"

"If it was me, would I be telling you this? We need to shut down the whole facility!"

Hoffstetler's face is so close their noses touch. Strickland glares, trying to make out the scientist's eyes. Truth is in the eyes. He's seen it in every man he's threatened. Every man he's killed. If only he could see it.

Then, a little favor: All the lights in the universe blast back to life.

47

GOING DARK HAD been a soft thing, a closing of one's eyes for sleep. When Occam's lights return, it's at stadium wattage, tungsten exploding from windows like backdraft fire, parking-lot lights pounding down like lava. The guard shields his eyes and spins, the building itself having become the ambusher. Giles has one leg out of the driver's door and hesitates, blinded, too, but somehow, between his pressed eyelids, he looks in the right direction and sees the double doors open and Elisa emerge with a cart, just as planned, except with a large black woman helping her push.

Giles knows he is not a man of action. It has hurt him, again and again. It has taken the life he should have had. Not today. The guard is still staring at the building when Giles has an idea, one he doesn't allow to reach the scale upon which notions so consequential are weighed. He grabs the door with both hands and slams it into the guard with all of his strength. The van sits high and the sound of the metal door against the man's skull is awful, and so is the bag-of-bones rattle of the body hitting the pavement, but it is done, the first violent act of his life, and though it does not make him feel good, he knows there is plenty of violence to share, especially here.

48

THE CART DESCENDS the ramp by itself, crashing into the back of the van. Elisa sprints after it while Zelda shuts the ramp doors to camouflage their exit. Elisa pulls open one of the van doors and starts pitching wet towels inside, just enough to uncover the creature. He is curled like a fetus, one of his great hands shielding his darting eyes from the brilliant overhead floods. She reaches in, takes him under the arm, tries to lift. He comes with her, but only a little. His gills are ballooning, his posture is wracked, he can barely stand.

Zelda is there—again, her friend is there. She takes the creature's other arm, her face scrunching in revulsion until she feels the cool, chain-mail texture of his body. She touches him for no more than ten seconds as they roll him into the back of the van, but in that time, Elisa glimpses the stunned comprehension on Zelda's face. This is no mere creature, no overgrown lizard. This is more like a man, but greater in every aspect, a higher grade of creature than they are, stranded in a cold, arid desert he was never meant to enter.

"Go," Zelda breathes. "Go!"

There is no time for grateful farewells. Elisa points at the security camera, signs "They can't see you," and scoots Zelda toward the doors, for they haven't seen her yet, she can still get back inside and plead ignorance. But Zelda is still standing there, slack and astonished, when Elisa slams the van's doors and the vehicle lurches from the dock, tires squealing louder than the laundry cart's bad wheel.

49

STRICKLAND RUNS. HE loathes it. Running in an office is the ultimate proof he's lost control. But there's no choice. He hurtles through the lobby, thumping people to the floor, and scrambles up the utility stairs and through the lobby, exploding out the front door and stopping to get his bearings. Two MPs are right behind Strickland, and Fleming behind them. Outside, morning has fully arrived. Scientists are treading up the walk for work, yawning. Secretaries pause to adjust their lipstick in compact mirrors. Everything is normal.

That sound, though. A vehicle, too close to be going that fast. Strickland springs to the right, across the lawn, rounding the corner of the building. There it is, like a giant snowball plowing down Everest, a white laundry van careening toward him.

"Shoot it!" Strickland cries, but the MPs are still catching up, and there's nothing a man with a cattle prod can do to a speeding behemoth. The checkpoint guard scrambles out of the way. Still the van swerves, an unexpected clue to the driver's unwillingness to cause casualties. There is only one vehicle in that part of the lot, and the van swipes it. The car's rear end crumples. It is a long, gorgeous teal Cadillac Coupe de Ville.

"No." Strickland's chest hurts like he's the object being struck. He hears his voice spiral upward, girl-pitched. *"No, no, no!"*

50

THE VAN JOLTS, the tires spin. Giles feels the punch of Elisa's body hitting the back of his seat. Burnt rubber wafts up. They're stopped. Feet from freedom, they're stuck. He looks over the Pug's hood and sees the van's front bumper locked with the bright green Caddy's. He hears a broken scream—he thinks it's a woman—but it's a hulk of a man barreling toward the van in a silverback lope, holding some sort of bat.

Giles curses, cranks the van into reverse, pounds the gas. The van slugs backward a yard. Metal screeches. Broken glass pops like fireworks. The running man is fast; he's halved the distance. Giles switches the gear to forward and stomps the pedal. Chrome crunches and the pinched bumpers whine. He looks up and sees armed men with raised guns calling for the running man to get out of the way so they can fire. The man, though, is crazed. He jumps a hedge, shouting nonsense. Giles rolls up his window, a pitiful defense.

And it's good he does. The man's bat strikes the window. A crack halves the glass. Giles cries out, twists the steering wheel right and guns the engine, then twists it left and guns it again. The man strikes the window again, creating a spiderweb. Then again and it shatters, hard little pellets raining against Giles's face. It is then that the van's bumper tears off and the man has to leap back to avoid being sideswiped. There are sparks as the Pug shears through the back of the Caddy, spitting green paint, a lot of it, multiple coats, it seems to Giles.

51

HIS GILLS OPEN wide, revealing dizzying layers of red lace, and hold there, the filaments fluttering like centipede legs in search of solid ground. His gasps are short, growing further apart. His arm rises from the wet laundry, draped in it like a child playing ghost, and his hand curls and continues upward, like the first part of him going to heaven.

Elisa grabs his wrist, brings it back to earth. It struggles back outward, and suddenly she sees it: the sign for water. She's been packing him in towels, deaf to bottles clanging all over the floor. They bank and spin with Giles's turns, but she snatches one, screws off the lid, and douses the creature's face, eyes, gills. He arches his back, leans into it. It seeps into his body through grooves that have gone a miserable brown, the liquid vanishing seconds after it hits, and still he's dry, still he's gasping.

"Is it all right? Is it alive?" Giles hollers.

Elisa kicks the wall with both feet, the closest she can get to signing "faster."

"It's morning! It's traffic! I'm doing my best!"

She kicks again. Hoffstetler had said thirty minutes was all the creature could take and fifteen must have passed by now, maybe twenty; time is lost. Her attention knifes back to the creature. He's making a choking noise, and Elisa, who knows only human consoling techniques—a pathetic limitation, she now realizes—slides an arm beneath him and hitches him up to a sitting position, while her other hand corrals another bottle and starts pouring it over his body.

He absorbs, he gulps; his freshly watered eyes, now at window level, go from gold to dandelion yellow; even nearly suffocated, he appears amazed at the world unfolding outside the van. Elisa looks, too, wondering if the city possesses a shred of a jungle's magic. Gray scaffolding of unlit neon lights daubed with orange sunlight. The surging yellow whale of a trolley. A Coca-Cola billboard of a man and woman, nestled as closely as Elisa and the creature, the woman holding a soda bottle as Elisa holds the next bottle of water. She thinks, just for a moment, that Baltimore isn't the futile anthill she's forced herself to accept, but its own tangle of tales, morass of myths, forest of fairies.

The Pug, swooping behind the Arcade, loses control, and though Giles brakes, the left front of the van, no longer protected by a bumper, smashes into the trash bins. No one has time to care. When Giles throws open the back doors, Elisa is ready, the creature draped in a wet lab coat and hooded in a wet sheet. The climb up the fire escape is a blundering, gawky, graceless slapstick, the sickening opposite of Shirley Temple and Bojangles.

Somehow they make it to the top, and also down the hall, and also through Elisa's door, and Giles lets go at the bathroom threshold because of the narrow clearance, and it's Elisa alone who has to guide the creature down, but they're both weak now and it's more like a fall, his useless legs buckling against the tub and dropping back-first into the waiting water. The splash hits Elisa's face like the van's bottled water had hit the creature's face: ablution, baptism. He dwarfs the apartment's tub, but so would most men, Elisa tells herself, and she cranks the hot-water knob because a full night has cooled what's there. The pipes squeal and shudder, then water unloads right next to the creature's head. The surface rises fast, covers his face. Elisa waits for bubbles of breath. There is nothing. She stirs the water with her hand to match the heat of F-1's pool.

"Who was that woman helping you?" Giles pants from behind. "Do you employ a whole nest of saboteurs?"

Yes, the pool: She thinks of how she slipped beneath the water, how her mouth flooded with salt. She reaches into her pocket, withdraws Hoffstetler's bottle of saline pills. Another object comes out, clatters to the floor.

"Good Lord," Giles says. "Is that a *syringe*?"

One pill every three days, is that what Hoffstetler had said? Or three pills every one? The creature is a sunken rock; there is no time to ponder. She shakes three pills directly into the water. They fizz, and she stirs again with her hand, slopping the salt toward the creature's face and neck. Then, terribly, there is nothing more to do. She takes the creature's hand. That massive, webbed thing, resplendent with rainbowed scales, striated with delicate spirals. She adds her other hand, folding his clawed fingers until she can squeeze their joint fist as a surgeon might squeeze a heart.

Giles's shadow falls over them.

"You were right," he breathes. "He's beautiful."

The creature's hand tightens around hers, swallowing it whole as a snake does a rodent. A death spasm, Elisa thinks with a jagging sob, until the bathwater begins to glow, a flicker of cobalt at first, a trick of the eye, then blossoming, then burning sapphire blue, transforming the cramped, dank, windowless chamber into an endless aquarium inside which they swim, too, effervescent, ethereal, and alive.

TROUBLE
YOUR HEART
NO MORE

1

On a tray, on his desk, are the blistered remains of a gadget. Strickland's been staring at it for hours. A section of metal pipe peeled open by some kind of explosion. A red blotch that looks like deep-fried plastic. Black, crusted veins that probably used to be wiring. Truth is, he doesn't have the first fucking clue. He's not even really trying. He's just staring.

Whatever sort of bomb it was, it melted everything. That's his life now, isn't it? Melted. His efforts to be a dad. The cardboard notions he'd had of domestic tranquility. Even his body. He glances at the bandages. He hasn't changed them for days. They're gray, damp. This is what happens to corpses in caskets. They melt to black sludge. And it won't stop at his fingers. He feels the decay worming up the arteries of his arm. Tendrils of it already gluing to his heart. The Amazon was replete with such rank fecundity. There might be no stopping it.

A knock on his door. He's been staring at the tray so long that it aches to roll his eyeballs. It's Fleming. Strickland dimly recalls requesting this visit. Fleming had gone home to sleep. To *sleep*. After this level of disaster? Strickland never considered leaving Occam. He convinced himself it had nothing to do with how, if he wanted to go home, he'd first have to assess the damage to the Caddy. The thought is disrupted by Fleming clearing his throat. The gray light of the security monitors is like an X-ray. Strickland can see Fleming's flabby organs. His twiggy bones. The pulsing electrodes of his fear.

"You making any progress with that?" Fleming asks.

Strickland doesn't glare. To glare requires an ounce of respect. Over the top of the clipboard behind which Fleming hides, Strickland can see a neck bruise from where he throttled Fleming during the blackout. The fucker's as tender as a fruit.

Fleming clears his throat again, consults his clipboard. "We have a lot of paint chips to work with. That should tell us a lot. Make, model. Best of all, we've got the whole front bumper. We can put out search parties right away to look for a white van without a bumper. It'd be easier if we could involve local police, but I understand why you don't want to do that. Right now we've got the whole lot roped off so we can measure tire treads."

"Tire treads," Strickland repeats. "Paint chips."

Fleming swallows. "We've also got surveillance tapes."

"Except from the camera that matters. Do I have that right?"

"We're still combing the footage."

"And not a single eyewitness who can tell us anything useful."

"We've really only just begun interviews."

Strickland drops his gaze back to the tray. Food belongs on a tray. He imagines eating the gadget. His teeth cleaving against the metal bits. The swallowed pieces sitting heavy and strong in his stomach. He could become the bomb. The question would be where he chose to place himself when he exploded.

"If you don't mind me saying so," Fleming continues, "I believe we're dealing with highly trained elites here. Well financed and well equipped. Infiltration took less than ten minutes. My opinion, Mr. Strickland, is that this is the work of Red Army Special Forces."

Strickland doesn't respond. Russian penetration? Could be. First satellite, first animal, and first man in space. Next to those feats, the theft of the century is nothing. Plus, there's Hoffstetler. Except Strickland can't find a feather of proof Hoffstetler did anything wrong last night. The whole attack, it doesn't *feel* Russian. It's too sloppy. The van he assaulted with the Howdy-do was a piece of junk. The driver some hysterical old man. Strickland needs time to think. That's why he called Fleming here. Now he remembers. He sits up straight. Grabs his painkillers. Tosses a few into his mouth and chews.

"What I wanted to say," he declares, "what I want to make absolutely clear, is that we confine knowledge of this situation to Occam until I give the say-so. Give me a chance to contain it. No one needs to know about this, not yet, you understand?"

"Except General Hoyt?" Fleming asks.

The rot threaded up Strickland's arm freezes like sap in winter.

"Except . . ." Strickland can't finish.

"I . . ." Fleming, needing a shield, brings the clipboard to his chest. "I called the general's office. Right away. I thought—"

The last of his melt is rapid. Strickland's ears seal off with his own liquefied flesh. The job he'd nearly completed at Occam, everything he'd achieved in the Amazon. All of it had been plenty enough to bargain away the binds roping him to Hoyt. What is it all worth now? Hoyt knows he's failed him. The career tower Strickland has climbed at Hoyt's goading is revealed to be a guillotine. Strickland falls from it in two halves and lands in something soft. It's the slime of a rice paddy. He's choked by the stench of excrement fertilizer. Deafened by the idiot chortle of passing oxcarts. Oh, God, God, God. He's back in Korea, where it all began.

Korea, where Hoyt's job was to guide the southward evacuation of tens of thousands of Koreans, with Strickland as his personal deputy. It was in Yeongdong, where General MacArthur ordered their group to make a stand, that Hoyt collared Strickland, pointed at a truck, and told him to drive. Drive he did, through steaming, silver rain, keeping pace with herons on their lazy, flapping hops from one paddy to the next.

They arrived at a former gold mine halfway filled with squalid clothes. Strickland figured he was to burn them, same as they'd burned so many villages so that the People's Army of the North couldn't nab the spoils. Only when Strickland got closer did he see they weren't clothes. They were bodies. Fifty of them, maybe a hundred. The inside of the mine was pocked with bullet holes. It was the worst of army rumors come true, a massacre of Korean innocents. Hoyt smiled, took gentle hold of Strickland's rain-slicked neck, and caressed it with his thumb.

████████████████████ he said.

When Strickland thinks back on it, Hoyt's words are but more shrieked redactions. The gist, though, he recalls well enough. A scout had brought word to Hoyt that not all of those dispatched inside of this mine were dead. That was bad for Hoyt. Bad for America. If survivors crawled out and told their story, the US would have a real mess on its hands, wouldn't it?

Never, ever would Strickland let himself blubber in front of Hoyt. He unslung his rifle. It felt like he was tearing off his own arm. But Hoyt held a finger to his lips, then waved it around in the rain. It was just the two of them out here. Not too wise to draw attention. Hoyt drew from his belt a black-bladed Ka-Bar knife. He held it out to Strickland and winked.

The leather handle squished like putrefied meat in the muggy rain. The bodies were muggy, too, piled five or six deep, the limbs bent and raveled. He rolled a woman out of the way. Brains spilled from a hole in her head. He dug a man from the heap. Intestines spooled out, bright blue. Ten bodies, twenty, thirty. He burrowed into the cold carnage, like tunneling into a corpse's womb. He was lost, slippery and stinking. Most were dead. But some were, in fact, alive, whispering, maybe begging, probably praying. He cut every throat he found, just to be safe. No one was alive here, he told himself, not even Richard Strickland.

He didn't trust the sound when he heard it. How do you trust anything in the bowels of hell? But it kept on, a reedy whine, and at the bottom of the pile he found a woman. Dead, but rigor mortis had turned her body into a protective cage for her baby. The baby was alive. Some miracle. Or the opposite of a miracle. Uncovered, the baby began to cry. It was loud, just what Hoyt didn't want. Strickland tried to wipe the Ka-Bar of hair and gristle so he'd get a clean cut. But he was shaking too much to trust himself. And wasn't that the point of all of this? To trust? In Hoyt? In violence? In war? That bad was good, that murder was compassion?

There was a puddle. Half rainwater, half blood. Strickland gently pressed the baby's face into the liquid. Maybe, he prayed, the baby *was* a miracle. Maybe it could breathe in water. But no such creature existed, not in the whole world. A few twitches and it was over. Strickland, too, wanted his life to be over. He rose to his knees, bodies rolling off his back. Hoyt came to him, cradling Strickland's head against his round belly and petting his bloody hair. Strickland gave himself over, held on tight. He tried to listen to what Hoyt was saying, but his ears had clogged with blood and tissue.

███████████

Then it was a whisper; now it is a shriek. What he'd done was an atrocity, a war crime that would be on the front page of every paper in the world if it ever got out, and it would fuse him to Hoyt until one of them was dead. Alone in his Occam office, all these years later, Strickland finally understands. The earsplitting wails of Hoyt's redactions—how had he missed the connection? They are the screams of the monkeys, one and the same. All his life, primal voices have pushed him to accept the mantle for which he's been groomed. It is why Deus Brânquia had to be captured. It is why the Jungle-god must destroy the Gill-god. No new deity fully ascends until the old deity is slain. He should have listened to Hoyt all along. The monkeys—don't be scared by their orders.

Follow them.

2

THE CHARCOAL IS a stick of dynamite in his hand. It's not a tool he uses much. You don't choose charcoal to depict Etiquette Antiseptic Deodorant Cream or Tangee Summer Rouge. It's untidy, the opposite of what such products demand, and black makes people wary, not in the mood to buy. Ah, but there was a time when he'd accepted nothing else! He'd used it for nudes, mostly, as charcoal was the rawest instrument and demanded rawness of its subject. Drawing with it was equivalent to witchcraft. Even patches of paper he ignored came to life as angled cheekbones, lifted foreheads, thrust clavicles, the slopes of buttocks, the sides of bellies. Finer features sank into cinder and rose reborn, the story of evolution played out in two dimensions.

He was so young then and unafraid of mistakes, eager to seize mistakes, in fact, as the catalyst of artistic surprise. Giles wonders if he still has it in him. Will his aching old hands impede him from modulating color from black to heather to smoke to fog? Will the tremble of his old fingers prevent him from smudging the texture from burlap to twill to silk to suede? It is one day since the heist; his ears are attuned for police sirens. The only thing to settle his mind, and his hands, is to work. He selects a pencil of medium thickness. It is gummy from decades in a cigar-box coffin. He chips at it with a thumbnail and lowers it to the paper, which lies on the easel, which rests on his lap, which sits on the closed toilet.

The creature watches from beneath bathwater. It is still learning how to breathe the water of the Arcade Apartments, and can do little but roll. This it does rather comfortably, like a young man not ready to leave bed. Giles smiles at it; he smiles at it a lot. First it was to assure the unknowable sphinx that he meant it no harm. Now Giles's smile is genuine, and he has to laugh. How flat and empty his cats' eyes now seem! There is so much to be read in the creature's ever-changing eyeshine. The interest it has in Giles and his colorful array of pencils, not a single one of them a scalpel or cattle prod. How it is coming to trust Giles, perhaps even like him.

No, not *it*—*he*. Elisa has been adamant about that, and Giles is happy to comply. It doesn't hurt that the creature is ravishing, a billion dazzling gems molded into the shape of a man by an artist orders of brilliance superior to Giles. He doesn't think they make oils or acrylics capable of reproducing such incandescence, nor watercolors or gouache capable of capturing the darker whispers. Hence the route of simplicity: charcoal. Giles says what he recalls of the Hail Mary and makes his first stroke, the S-curve of a dorsal fin.

"There," he gasps. Then, a chuckle of amazement. "There it is."

He can't see the sink mirror at this angle, but he feels he could be thirty-five again, even twenty-five—that bold, that brave. He makes another line, another. Not a work of art, he warns himself, just a sketch, something to get the old juices flowing. Still, he can't help but feel that these rough lines are the most vibrant he's made since the day he accepted the job at Hutzler's, the forerunner to Klein & Saunders, the forerunner to forgetting everything that mattered.

Miss Strickland—*Mrs.* Strickland—had she been some kind of lipsticked, beehived seer? She'd told Giles the truth. Not only the truth that Bernie didn't want what he'd come to sell, but that he shouldn't debase himself in the process. *You deserve to go somewhere where you can be proud of who you are*, she'd said, and that was here, right here, in the home of his best friend, within touching distance of the greatest living thing he'd ever seen.

Elisa had little information to give about the creature's origin, but that didn't matter. Giles senses the creature's divinity, and practice sketch or not, no artistic charge requires graver attention than that of depicting the sacred. Raphael, Botticelli, Caravaggio—as a young artist, he'd studied all of them in library books and knew the rewards and risks of portraying the sublime. It required personal sacrifice. How else did Michelangelo complete the Sistine Chapel fresco in four years? It's a joke, comparing himself to Michelangelo, but there is a similarity. Both had access to something the world at large had never seen. Even if the police sirens do come—by God, it has been worth it.

He starts to gesture for the creature to turn slightly, then laughs at the preposterous request. How quickly the portraitist's prerogative returns! But the creature responds, adjusting so that his left eye rises above the waterline, as if to get a sharper look at the signal. Giles holds his breath, decides to finish the gesture. The creature follows the spinning finger, as he might have followed a winged insect or bird in his native land, calmly appreciative, devoid of hostility. The creature blinks. His gills settle softly.

Then, a willing model, he turns.

3

WHEN DID DEPARTMENT stores replace their overhead lights with supernovas? For how long has the binned fruit wept at its own beauty? At what point did baked goods begin sighing sugary secrets into a cloud that beaded upon her face like happy tears? When did shoppers, those disapproving ladies with bulky purses and rude carts, transform into women who smiled at her, insisted she go first, complimented her on her choices? Perhaps they'd seen what Elisa saw reflected in butcher-counter glass: not a timid huncher hiding her throat scars, but a woman straight of back pointing out the cuts of fish and meat she wanted. Quite a lot of both, the butcher probably thought, but why not? Surely a woman like this had a hungry man waiting at home. And she did. Elisa laughs. She *did*.

Not just meat, either. Eggs, loads of them, cartons arranged in her cart in playful crisscross patterns that make other shoppers laugh at her moxie. Bags of salt, too—Hoffstetler's saline pills won't last forever. It takes her a while to find these items, but she doesn't mind. Shopping for someone else is wonderful. Giles had offered to do it, but she'd refused; she felt only she could intuit what the creature needed. She'd used public transit, ignoring uniformed police, reminding herself that they had no clue what she'd done, and gone all the way to Edmondson Village. Zelda has always raved about the shopping-center cornucopia, and she'd been right. Zelda: Elisa has a lot to say to her, and she will, on her next shift—it's critical she not miss a single shift if she hopes to evade suspicion. Thinking of Zelda, Elisa's heart, already full, presses at the limits of her rib cage.

She is surprised to find at the front of the store a section of plants and flowers. It draws her in; she lets the reaching fronds and dangling ivy toss across her cheeks. This is what the creature had needed to fill the lab's bareness and what he needs now to round the bathroom's sharp edges. She selects the leafiest plants she can find. Two thick, potted ferns; they'll hide a lot of porcelain and tile. A fan palm with leaves like the creature's hands; maybe he will feel less lonely? A dragon tree tall enough to reach the lights over the sink; perhaps it will tint the whole room green.

Piled inside the cart, the leaves tickle her nose, make her giggle. How is she going to get all of this home? She'll have to buy one of the handcarts she saw near the entrance. An unexpected expense, but what difference will a few more dollars make? Today is the first day of her life she hasn't counted pennies, and she's determined to revel in it. She's as conscious of her big smile as she would be a gaudy hat. She ought to try to temper it. Any cop in his right mind sees a woman this overjoyed about buying groceries, a red flag will rise.

It's difficult, and quite amusing, to navigate through the plants in her cart, and upon steering into the checkout aisle, the cart bumps into a standing display. A hundred cardboard air fresheners dance from their hooks. She idles a finger across them. They are shaped like little trees, each advertising a different scent. Pink cherry. Brown cinnamon. Red apple. Several are green. REAL PINE SCENT!, a cellophane package proclaims.

She doesn't think her smile can get bigger, but it does. She plucks one from the rack. No—she takes all the green ones off the peg. Six of them. Not much trees for a jungle, but a start.

4

EVEN WHEN HIS tears drop to the paper, Giles makes it work, smearing them with the side of his hand, imbuing harsh lines with a fluidic softness resembling that of the creature's scales. He smiles at this revelation, even as he expects that it is only the first of many to come. Tears, a drop of blood, the touch of saliva from a kiss: The creature would use his magic to turn these substances, too, into art, into grace.

Giles lifts a hand, spins a finger. The creature shifts to offer Giles yet another angle, stretching his resplendent neck, almost preening. Giles laughs, tastes salt, licks it away, and draws, draws, draws, a starving man at a banquet that he worries the waiters might whisk away. When he begins to speak, he doesn't notice it; his murmur is the rustle of charcoal over paper.

"Elisa says you're all alone. The last of your kind. Something like that." He chuckles. "Try as I might, I don't catch everything she says. Naturally I didn't believe her at all at first. Who would? Then I saw you and, if I may say so, you're very convincing in person. I hope you can forgive my early reticence. Perhaps even sympathize. What did you think when you first saw the inside of a naval ship or the tank they put you in? I can't imagine your thoughts were especially flattering to the human race. Things change."

The ridge over the creature's eyes: He draws it mist-gray, defenseless.

"But then Elisa finds you. And there again, yes? A change. In her, for sure. But also, I suspect, in you? Perhaps we humans are not all so bad? If such a thought has crossed your mind, I thank you, though I'd warn you that it's a charitable assessment."

The cascading plates of his chest, sleek as petals, each one drawn a darker silver.

"Now that I've properly met you, though—oh, I'm Giles, by the way. Giles Gunderson. The custom is to shake hands, but seeing how we're to the point of bathroom nudity, I think we can forgo that. You see, now that I've met you, I find myself circling back to where I began. I'm not certain that I agree with our Elisa. Are you all alone? Are you really? For if you are an anomaly, then so am I."

The diaphanous fins drawn ash-cloud gray, the bones black slashes.

"It's silly. But I feel as if I, too, were plucked from where I belonged. Or when—perhaps I was born too early. The things I felt as a boy . . . I was too young to understand them, too out of place or time to do anything about it. Now that I understand? Well, I'm old. Look at this thing. This body I'm stuck inside. My time is ending, even though it feels like I never *had* a time, not really."

The shape of the scalp, the smoothest, feathered strokes.

"But I can't be alone, can I? Of course not; I'm not that special. Anomalies like me exist all around the world. So when does an anomaly quit being an anomaly and start being just the way things happen to be? What if you and I are not the last of our kinds, but one of the first? The first of better creatures in a better world? We can hope, can't we? That we're not of the past, but the future?"

Giles holds the drawing at arm's length. For a character sketch, it's not bad. And what are character sketches for? Practice for a grander work. Giles chuckles again. Is that what he's planning? My, he hasn't felt this precocious in decades.

He takes a breath and turns the paper toward the tub. The creature cocks his head until his second eye crests from the water. He stares at the sketch, then tilts his head to compare it to his own submerged body. Occam types might insist self-awareness in the creature was impossible, but Giles would tell them different. The creature knows he's being depicted, and that it's different from a reflection in a river. This is, in short, the magic of art. To concede the possibility of being captured in this way is to actively collaborate with the artist. By God, Giles thinks, it's true: They are not so different from each other. Giles might still, under the right light, bathed in the right water, be beautiful, too.

5

THE TWO-WHEELED GROCERY cart is more agile than Elisa's janitorial equivalent, but Baltimore's sidewalks present a more robust challenge than polished laboratory floors. It's late afternoon, forever since she's slept, but she still isn't tired; cradling the creature in the van seems to have injected her with the opposite of whatever had filled Hoffstetler's syringe. She is electrified. She got off the bus several stops early so that she could take a scenic walk home, burn off this nervous energy. As badly as she wants to see the creature again, the brine odor of the Patapsco lures her forward, like a child to fresh-baked cookies.

She wrangles the cart past an off-limits pier and working wharf. There she finds a thin pedestrian jetty. Is it legal to walk it? The last thing she needs is police. But there is nothing suggesting a ban. She walks out onto the river, the shadow of city buildings sliding off her back like a nightgown. There is no fence, no protective posts, nothing but a sign reading No Swimming! No Fishing! Opens to the Sea at 30 ft! The idea of fishing has always revolted her, and no one at Home ever taught her to swim, but she understands the sign well enough. Once the water level reaches the 30 ft mark painted on a concrete stanchion—assuming it ever rains again—the canal will provide access to the bay, as well as the ocean.

Elisa parks her cart and toes the edge of the jetty, closing her eyes against a spluttering salt spray that suggests the day is not as halcyon as she has perceived it. This explains why people on the bus had their collars upturned and their postures locked so as not to feel the chill of their own clothes. It also helped explain why the woman who'd sat across the aisle from Elisa hadn't noticed her sunny smile until the third attempt.

The woman had been pretty, everything that Elisa, until the events of the past day, had ever dreamed of being, just how she'd always imagined Julia of Julia's Fine Shoes. Slim, but with curves enough to fill out a striped flannel dress, the ensemble accented with rhinestone buckles, a matching pin, bracelets, earrings, and wedding ring. Only the blond beehive felt out of date, and that Elisa attributed to the fact that, well, this was a working woman, and working women, as Elisa well knew, were busy.

When she'd finally caught the woman's eyes, the woman had hesitated before smiling back; like everyone else, she'd seemed taken aback by Elisa's gaiety. She'd glanced down at Elisa's hand, seeming to take note of the absence of a ring. To Elisa's surprise, the woman showed not scorn but relief; the smile became less performative, more genuine. Elisa got the sense that, as much as she admired this beautiful, professional woman, the woman admired her even more. Even crazier, Elisa felt she could hear the woman's primary thought: *Do what your heart tells you. At all costs, follow your heart.*

At last, Elisa is doing just that. But here, at the edge of the world, the temperature dropping by the second, Elisa finds herself troubled by the woman's pinched expression. If a woman who has it all can be so unhappy, what hope has a graveyard-shift janitor, one who can barely make rent, one whose inability to speak cuts her off from most of society, one who happens to have a highly classified amphibious man lying in her bathtub?

Elisa opens her eyes, turns around, squints north. There is no more doubting it: It is a gray, foreboding day. The proof is in the distant marquee lights of the Arcade, which Mr. Arzounian doesn't switch on unless it's dark enough to warrant the expense. Elisa's stomach seesaws. She can see the Arcade from here, which means the creature is that close to this river. The proximity upsets her. She grabs her cart, wheels it around, heads home as quickly as she can.

She finds Giles asleep, upright on top of the toilet lid, snoring lightly, his hands caked in charcoal. Quietly, so as not to wake him, she lowers herself to the ratty rug, folds her arms on the tub rim, and nestles her chin into them. She gazes into the creature's eyes, still bright underwater, and listens to the soft bubbling of his breath. He blinks, a greeting. She unfolds an arm and fins her index finger through the water until it touches the back of his hand. Unexpectedly, he rolls the hand over so that she is touching his palm, her finger the single stamen of a huge, dewy, unfolding flower. Now she listens for her own breath, but hears nothing. Hands are how the two of them talk, but this? This is a *touch*. Elisa pictures the woman on the bus, how rigidly she sat, touching no one. An absence of fear, Elisa realizes, can be mistaken for happiness, but it isn't the same thing. Not even close.

6

WATCH THE WORLD in rewind. It's faster, scoured of soul, a knife grated over fish scales until all iridescence is gone. Stop. Enjoy the fleshy slap of magnetic tape stretched thin. Play. Infinite hallways, all identical, white-coat clones gliding through like platelets. Isolate a person of interest. Toggle, toggle. Dissect the tape into seconds, half-seconds, quarter-seconds. Men are no longer men. They are abstract shapes you can study like an eremite studies scripture. That shadow in that scientist's pocket could be the secret to all life. The muddy grin of his freeze-framed face might be the devil's skull. Sixteen cameras. Infinite clues. Rewind, stop, toggle. This hallway, that. There's no way out. All routes lead right back here, to his office. No closer to the truth. No further. He's trapped.

Strickland's eyes feel like spoiled sausages about to rupture. All that green candy he brought back from the jungle, when he should have brought back vials of buchité. A couple of drops and he'd see everything these tapes were hiding. Hour after hour after hour he's been at this. Took only one hour to master the playback console. M1 Garand rifle, Cadillac Coupe de Ville, VTR deck—it's all got the same guts. You put your hands to it, make it part of you. He quit feeling the buttons and dials around noon. Now it feels like he can direct the tapes with his mind. *That's the secret*, he thinks. Let the footage flow by like water, dip your hands into it, and catch yourself a fish.

And there it is. Just like that. Camera 7. Loading dock. The first few seconds of the final tape before the blackout. The camera, does it bump upward? A couple of critical inches? Strickland toggles. Before, after, before, after.

He gets up out of his chair. The hallways, he swears, have gotten brighter. He shades his eyes with a hand, who cares if the MPs think he's nuts, and travels past F-1 to the loading dock, the same route as the stolen creature. He pushes through the double doors and drops his hand. There is no sun. It is night. He's lost track of time yet again. The ramp is empty but for puddles of oil. He whirls around. Looks up at Camera 7. Then looks straight under it.

Four people stand there, faces rubbery with shock. Each holds a cigarette. They have uniforms, lousy postures, different shades of skin. What they share is laziness. The time since the asset's theft he's spent slaving in his office, and they can't endure five minutes without a break, and down here, where it's against regulations? But Strickland needs information. He tries on a hard, waxy smile.

"Y'all taking a smoke break, huh?"

Does Fleming hire mutes exclusively? No, he decides. They're just terrified.

"Don't worry, you're not in trouble." He extends the smile, feels his wax lips start to crack. "Heck, I ought to join you. I'm not supposed to smoke inside, either, but darn it if I don't do it anyway." The janitors steal glances at their untapped, elongating ashes. "Tell me something, though. How do you lift the camera so you don't get caught?"

Names are sewn to their uniforms, just like tags on a dog.

"Yo-lan-da," he reads. "You can tell me, honey. Just curious is all."

Dark brown hair. Light brown skin. Black eyes. The kind of thin lips that like to mouth off. Not in front of him, though. She knows her place. Strickland lets his wax grin melt a little. It works. He can smell her sweat through her perfume of bleach. She drops her eyes from the shit-scrubber cohorts she must think she's betraying and gestures at an object behind them. It's no sophisticated gadget like the one that blew the fuses. It's a broom. A motherfucking broom.

Strickland's mind is the VTR. It forwards, stops, plays, rewinds, toggles. He's closing in on the critical frame.

"Say." He means to sound convivial, and doesn't, and doesn't give a shit. "Any of you folks ever see Dr. Hoffstetler back here?"

7

ZELDA'S FIRST STEPS off the bus in front of Occam are unsteady, her neck sore from glancing for a wave of helmeted Empties coming to take her away, her ankles wobbly in preparation for being slung to the ground and handcuffed. All day she considered it. Come to work? Call in sick? Ride into the sunset? She'd even broken down and told Brewster, with certain facts massaged for believability, a half-lie regarding Elisa's theft of an undefined valuable to which Zelda, unwittingly, had become party. Brewster had been firm of opinion: turn her in. Because if it comes out any other way, you're the one who's going to take the hit.

She spots Elisa ahead of her on the sidewalk and feels a shiver of relief. This is a good sign. Elisa might have taken off, left the city, abandoned Zelda to whatever questions might come. But no: She's right here, right on time, striding on pretty shoes down the moonlit walkway into the front lobby. Zelda trails her at a short distance, watching for the clues Brewster warned about, attempts by Elisa to get a supervisor's attention, that sort of thing. Again, nothing of the sort. Elisa goes into the locker room. Zelda has no choice now but to follow and sit alongside her on the bench. For a time, they don't look at each other, but Zelda can feel the cart, the one with the squeaky wheel, between them, heavy with its otherworldly load.

Dressed, Elisa goes into the storeroom and begins loading her cart. Zelda follows her, does the same. She watches Elisa's hand extract a roll of trash bags. Zelda does likewise. Zelda, then, lifts a jug of glass cleaner, and the second she sets it back, Elisa picks it up. They move on two separate pulses but are inching closer to synchronicity. When Zelda puts her hand on a new foxtail brush to replace one she's abused into paddle flatness, Elisa's hand lashes out and grips the same handle.

Zelda knows Elisa's cart as well as she knows her own. The girl never uses her foxtail brush and certainly doesn't need another. Elisa's fingers spill over Zelda's in a pile. Some fingers brown, some white, but in all other ways of equal experience: calloused by scrubbing, grimed under the nails, pinked by corrosive cleaners, and emerging from dingy Occam cuffs. Zelda sobs once, but holds it inside, no matter the toxicity of the room's chemical cloud.

It is a quiet and invisible forgiveness. There are other people in the locker room. Beyond, there is Fleming and Strickland. Everywhere else, cameras and Empties. The only hug Zelda dares is the infinitesimal squeeze of Elisa's fingers inside hers. Knuckle presses to knuckle, before Elisa's hand cedes the foxtail brush and pushes her cart from the room. Zelda remains, closes her eyes, breathes in the fumes. The tiny finger-squeeze is the full-body embrace she's waited on for weeks; it's the hot tears onto a comforter's neck; it's acknowledgment, appreciation, apology, admiration. *We will survive this*, the squeeze says. *Together, you and I will make it through.*

8

WE RISE /// SUN is gone still gone only fake suns here fake suns are all we have felt for many cycles we do not like fake suns fake suns make us tired but the woman is blind without fake suns and so we try to like them for her for her for her the water in this cave is small but we begin to heal and it is better water than the last water no water should bring pain water should not be flat water should not be smooth water should not be empty water should not have a shape there is no shape of water /// in this cave there is only woman and man and food but it is good to have hunger we have not had strong hunger since river since grass since mud since trees since sun since moon since rain hunger is life and so we rise and the fake suns come closer the man did not hide the fake suns when he went away we miss the man the man is good he sits by the small water and uses black rock to make small twins of us long ago the river people made small twins of twig and leaf and flowers and twins are good twins make us eternal and now the river people are gone and we are sad but the man is good and makes twins all day and this brings us more strength more hunger /// the woman has planted trees in this cave and light from real suns comes from the outer caves and now we touch the planted trees and they touch us and they are happy and we love the trees and the woman has planted other trees on the walls small flat trees they do not smell like trees and they are not happy not alive but the woman planted them and we will love these small unhappy trees for her for her for her /// moving free no metal vines holding us it has been many cycles since we moved free and this small cave becomes a bigger cave and there is the man he holds the twins he makes of us his eyes are closed but he breathes in life patterns and makes sleep sounds and that is good and we are hungry but we will not eat the man because the man is good /// we smell the woman the smell is strong and there is another cave her cave and we go inside and the woman is not there but her smells are alive her skin her hair her liquids her air the strongest smell are her flippers on the wall so many colorful flippers we love her flippers and we worry she has lost her flippers but there is no blood smell no pain smell no fear smell and we are confused /// hunger and we go past the man to the place of smells it is flat and tall and white and we try to lift but it is heavy we try to crack but find no seam and we push and pull and it opens and the smells the smells the smells it is a very small cave of smells a cave with its own fake suns and we take a rock but it is not a rock we squeeze and it cracks it is milk and milk is falling and we hold it high and drink and it is good and we chew on the rock and it is not good we reject it and we take a new rock and it opens and it is eggs so many eggs and we are happy we eat the eggs and they are not the solid eggs the woman gives us they are liquid eggs but they are good and the shells are good to chew /// we forage good foods many good foods and the man makes happy sleep sounds and we are happy and there is another flat and tall and white thing and we think it holds more food and we push and pull the same and it opens but there is no food there is a passage and from the passage come different smells outside smells and bird sounds and insect sounds and we do not want to miss the woman when she returns but we are explorers it is our nature to explore and we are fed we are stronger and it has been so many cycles since we have explored and so we go

9

THE RED PHONE. It won't stop ringing. He won't answer it. He can't. Not until he's got the situation by the short, scaly tail. For five minutes it will ring. Thirty minutes will pass, if he's lucky, an hour. Then it will ring again. He's got to focus. Hoffstetler. This Trotskyite pinko. Glancing at the phone like he's never seen the color red before, like it isn't the same red as his homeland flag. Strickland shuffles the papers Hoffstetler handed him. An act, just to let the white coat sweat. He didn't read more than the opening sentence. Can't feel the papers with his dead fingers. Doesn't care, not anymore. Paper is for men, not Jungle-gods.

"Do you need to answer that?" Hoffstetler asks. "If you'd like me to come back . . ."

"Don't you go anywhere, Bob."

The phone keeps ringing. The monkeys have dug their way into that sound, too, howling their instructions. Strickland squares the paper and grins. Hoffstetler avoids his eyes, looks around, nods at the monitors. Half are live, half are paused since yesterday. Strickland feels the same, half alive, half dead, desperate to find Deus Brânquia even as his veins are being threaded with thick lianas vines.

"How is the investigation?" Hoffstetler asks.

"Good. Very good. We have a lead, a very promising lead."

"Well, that's . . ." Hoffstetler adjusts his glasses. "That's wonderful."

"You sick, Bob? You look a little gray."

"No. Not at all. It's this gray weather, perhaps."

"Is that right? Coming from Russia, I figured weather like this would be like being home."

The phone, the monkeys, keeps ringing.

"I don't know. I haven't been there since I was a boy, of course."

"You came to us from where again?"

"Wisconsin."

"And before that?"

"Boston. Harvard."

"And before that?"

"Are you sure you don't want to answer the—"

"Ithaca, wasn't it? And Durham. I've got a good memory, Bob."

"Yes. That's right."

"Impressive. I mean that. Another thing I remember from your file is you had a tenured position. People work hard for that, don't they?"

"I suppose they do, yes."

"And you gave it all up for us."

"I did, yes."

"That's remarkable, Bob. Makes a man in my position feel good."

Strickland snaps the paper he holds. Hoffstetler jumps in his seat.

"I guess that's why this caught me by surprise," Strickland says. "All those honors you gave up just to join our little project. And now you're leaving?"

The red phone stops ringing. The bell's vibration continues for twelve more seconds. Strickland counts them off while watching Hoffstetler's reaction. The scientist does look sick. But so does everyone at Occam these days. He's got to have better proof. If he pins shit this serious on their star scientist and he's wrong, that red phone will only ring louder. He breathes through his nose, feels it scorch with Sertão heat. Energized, he studies Hoffstetler's eyes. Dodgy, but they've always been dodgy. Sweaty, too, but half of these eggheads faint at the sight of an MP.

"I do wish to return to my studies."

"Oh yeah? What kind?"

"I haven't decided. There is always more to learn. I suppose I've been thinking about multicellularity in the taxonomic tree. I might also follow my interest in random and volitional nondeterministic happenings. And I don't believe I'll ever tire of astrobiology."

"Big words, Bob. Hey, how about you teach me something? That last one. Astro-whatchamacallit."

"Well . . . what would you like to know?"

"You're the professor. First day of class, they're all staring at you. What do you tell them?"

"I . . . used to teach them a song. If you want to know the truth."

"I do. I do want to know the truth. I never took you for a crooner, Bob."

"It's just a little—it's a children's song—"

"If you think I'm letting you out of here without singing this little ditty, you're crazy."

Now Hoffstetler is really sweating. And Strickland is really grinning. He places a hand over his mouth to ensure that delirious monkey screams don't begin hooting up from his throat. Hoffstetler tries to laugh it off, but Strickland won't budge. Hoffstetler winces, stares at his hands in his lap. The seconds ticking by only make it more painful. They both know it. Hoffstetler clears his throat and, to Strickland's joy, begins to sing.

"The color of a star, you can be sure, is mostly due to its temp-era-ture."

It's an off-key warble that betrays, more than is typical, the man's Russian accent. Hoffstetler knows it, too, sure as shit, and he swallows hard. Strickland claps his hands, his dead fingers flopping like plastic.

"Beautiful, Bob. If you don't mind me asking, though, what's the point of it?"

Hoffstetler lurches forward, quick enough to kill. Strickland startles, rocks back in his chair, grabs for the machete, if that's what it is, stashed under his desk. He curses himself. Never, ever underestimate cornered prey. The weapon, though, isn't needed. Not yet. Hoffstetler perches on the edge of his chair, but not beyond it. His voice still shakes, but not from fear. Humiliation has produced anger, and it's as sharp as cliff-side rocks.

"The point is that it's true," Hoffstetler snaps. "We're all made of stardust, Mr. Strickland. Oxygen, hydrogen, carbon, nitrogen, and calcium. If some of us get our way and our countries fire off their warheads, then we shall return to stardust. All of us. And what color will our stars be then? That is the question. A question you might ask yourself."

Friendly palaver is over. The two men glare.

"Your last week," Strickland says slowly. "Gonna miss you, Bob."

Hoffstetler stands. His knees are knocking. At least there's that.

"Should there be a development, of course, I'll return right away."

"You figure there will be? A development?"

"I am sure I don't know. You said you had a lead."

Strickland smiles. "I do."

Hoffstetler's not even out of sight when the red phone starts ringing again. Monkey screams, accusatory this time. Strickland slams his right fist to his desk hard enough to make the receiver tremble. It hurts. But it's also satisfying, like squashing longhorn beetles, bullet ants, tarantulas, all those Amazon pests. When he does it again he chooses the left fist. Fewer fingers to hurt over there. Hardly feels it at all. He slams, and slams, and slams, and believes he feels a pop in one of the fingers, another of the black stitches ripping free. Like the sutures in Deus Brânquia. Who is falling apart faster? Who will outlast the other?

He picks up the phone, not the red one, and dials Fleming's extension. Fleming might be General Hoyt's errand boy, but he's under Strickland's command, too. He picks up on the first ring. Strickland hears the clatter of a dropped clipboard.

"When Dr. Hoffstetler leaves today," Strickland says, "I want you to follow him."

10

LIGHT LEAPS FROM between the wood underfoot like playful animals many good colors bird color snake color roach color bee color dolphin color and we try to catch it but it is just light and sound too the woman calls it music it is different from our music but we love it and we glow our love and we follow it the light and the music down the passage until we see another object flat and tall and white and we push and pull and go inside and it is a cave that smells of the good man his skin his hair his liquids his breath his sickness there is sickness it is faint the man cannot yet feel it or smell it and it makes us sad but there are good smells too the black rock the man uses to make our small twins we can see the small twins all over the cave so many twins and we touch our twins and our claws smear the black and we lick the black and the black does not taste good and there is a man skull and on top of it is hair as fake as the fake suns and this makes us lonely in our river there are many skulls death is all over and it is good it is good to know death so that you can know life /// here is a better smell the smell of food the best food living food and we feel the animals in the cave all animals are our friends and they come out of hiding with pointy ears and whiskers and long tails and their eyes shine like ours they bow to us they offer themselves they are beautiful we love them we accept the sacrifice and we take one and we squeeze so there is no pain and we eat our friend and it is good it is blood fur sinew muscle bone heart love and we eat and we are stronger and we feel the river again all the gods the feather god the scale god the shell god the fang god the claw god the pincher god the tree god all of us part of the knot there is no you there is no me there is only we we we we we /// a noise a bad noise a crack like the bad man and his pain stick the lightning stick and we hiss and we turn and we attack and the bad man makes a pain sound but we have done wrong it is not the bad man it is the good man the good man has come back to his cave found us eating his pointy ear whiskers long tail friend and we are sorry we change to sorry color to sorry scent to sorry liquids to sorry stance we did not mean to attack we are not foe we are friend friend friend and good man smiles at us but his smell goes bad and the good man lifts his arm and looks at his arm and blood comes a lot of blood and the blood falls like rain

11

A PROJECT LEAD enjoys access to every room at Occam but one, and it is here Hoffstetler finds himself: the ladies' locker room. There are, Slava Bogu, no cameras here; he has come to consider cameras to be gargoyles flapping their wings in the high reaches to report his every move. Hovering at the locker-room door would get him branded as a pervert—acceptable in these final days except for how it would spur further interrogation—so he'd slunk inside, nosed out a bygone shower room filled with supplies, and hidden behind a keep of industrial cleaner.

A harsh bell marks the close of the overnight shift. He hears the drudging entry of the graveyard shift's quartet of women. He feels dizzy. It must be the stench of ammonia. Unless it's panic. The rest of the week, he repeats to himself, is all he needs to last. His first and, he hopes, last lie to Mihalkov was that the syringe had worked and the Devonian was dead, and Mihalkov had rewarded him with details: On Friday, Hoffstetler's phone will ring twice, and he is to proceed to the usual spot, where the Bison will take him to a ship, and the ship will sail him home, to Minsk, to his waiting parents. Mihalkov had even lavished praise on Hoffstetler for his dauntless years of service. He'd called him Dmitri.

Hoffstetler tears off his glasses, rubs eyeballs aflame from chemical vapors. Is he going to faint? He focuses on locker-room sounds. He is a cataloger by nature and trade but has done little study in the classification of feminine noises. Silken rustles. Pert snaps. Delicate jingles. Evidence of life that he has never known, but still might, if he can just survive until Friday.

"Hey, Esposito." The woman's voice is of Latin accent and is as harsh as the shift siren. "Did you tell that man we were out there smoking?" A pause for Elisa's signed or gestured reply. "You know what man. The one that gives you the looks." Pause. "Well, someone told him that we move the camera. And the only one of us that doesn't smoke is you." Pause. "You act all innocent. But you're not. You watch your back, Esposito. Or I'll watch it for you, entiendes?"

Footsteps march away, followed by sympathetic murmurs—Hoffstetler believes they come from the one named Zelda. He holds his breath against fumes, waits for sounds of Zelda leaving Elisa's side. Instead he hears a rumble from upstairs, the lobby, the day shift beginning to arrive. There is no time. Hoffstetler makes his move, scrambling on all fours across the dank tiles. He peers around a corner. Elisa is sitting on the bench. Zelda stands beside her, combing her hair in a locker mirror. He has to take the chance. He waves a hand to get Elisa's attention.

Her head whips in his direction. She is clothed but covers herself reflexively, a leg cocking back, ready to kick. She's wearing shoes of startling flair—bright sequined green—and the heels crack loud against the tile and Zelda whirls and sees Hoffstetler and her chest expands to scream, but Elisa snatches Zelda's blouse and springs from the bench, dragging Zelda behind her into the dim aqua glow of the shower, her free hand signing as wildly, no doubt a litany of questions. Hoffstetler lifts his own hands, begging for a moment.

"Where is it?" he whispers.

"They've got us," Zelda gasps. "Elisa, they've got—"

Elisa signs curtly to Zelda, something that shuts her up, and then signs to Hoffstetler, gesturing for Zelda to translate.

Zelda eyes Hoffstetler with misgiving before stating, simply, "Home."

"You've got to get rid of it. Right away."

Elisa signs. Zelda translates: "Why?"

"It's Strickland. He's close. I can't promise what I'll tell him if he uses—he's got that *baton*—"

He doesn't need to know sign language to understand Elisa's panic.

"Listen to me," he hisses. "Do you have means to get it to the river?"

Elisa's face drains of emotion. Her head drops down until she stares at her bejeweled shoes, or perhaps the mold of the tiles showing between them. After a moment, her hands rise, torpidly as if attached to weights, and she signs with a mournful reluctance. Zelda translates each fragment as it comes.

"The dock. Opens to the sea. At thirty feet."

Zelda looks at Hoffstetler pleadingly; she doesn't know the significance of these words but Hoffstetler does. This fragile-looking janitor of incalculable ingenuity must live near enough to the river to get the Devonian to some kind of pier. But that's not good enough. If the spring drought persists, the creature will be beached there, a flopping fish no better off than being chained to one of Strickland's posts.

"Is there anything, anything at all?" he pleads. "That van—you took it away in a van—could you make it to the ocean—"

She's shaking her head in childish refusal, eyelashes thick with tears, cheeks and neck splotched red except for two keloid scars that hold a smooth, gentle pink. Hoffstetler wants to grab her by the dress and shake her, rattle that brain inside her skull until the selfishness is knocked clean out of her. But he has no chance: A phone is ringing, it is answered, and the angry woman with the Latin accent is shouting, her voice reverberating from the locker room's surfaces.

"Phone call for Elisa? If that isn't the stupidest thing I've ever heard. How the hell's she supposed to take a phone call?"

"*Who is it, Yolanda?*"

The boom is loud enough to pull Hoffstetler from his tarn of consternation. It comes from Zelda, discounted by Hoffstetler as dumbstruck by fear of losing her job or worse. With the situation for the three of them as dire as it has ever been, this woman's leaping, lioness defense of Elisa hands to Hoffstetler a tiny, precious gift, thinner than cellular membrane, smaller than a subatomic particle: hope.

Zelda's brown eyes boil with a warning for Hoffstetler, and then it is she, this time, who takes Elisa by the arm and drags her away. Hoffstetler has no choice but to recede, though not far, knowing he'll need to escape the locker room before the dayshifters begin filing inside, knowing he's got three more days of this pressure, knowing he won't sleep tonight with Elisa uncommitted to the only sensible course of action. It is entirely possible that he'll never sleep again. He ducks behind the bottles of cleaning fluid while Yolanda's last few grouses echo.

"I'm a custodian, Zelda, not AT&T. Jerry? Jeremy? Giles? How am I supposed to remember?"

12

EACH OF THE thousands of times Elisa has seen Giles's apartment, it has been a world of tweed browns and pewter grays. Now it is bright red. Blood on the floor. On the wall. A bloody handprint on the refrigerator. Elisa entered too speedily to sidestep and now helplessly watches her green shoes track red across rug and linoleum. She grabs Giles's drafting desk for support, sending two cats bounding. She forces herself to study the blood, tries to determine which direction it leads. But it leads every direction.

Including back out the door. She lopes that way and sees a thin stripe of blood connecting Giles's door to hers. She bursts into her apartment and there he is, collapsed on the sofa. She rushes to his side, her knees landing on black charcoal sketches accented with red blood. Giles's face is pale; he blinks in slow motion; he is shivering. His left arm is wrapped, very poorly, in a blue bath towel soaked purple. Elisa looks at the bathroom.

"He's not here," Giles croaks.

Elisa holds his face in her hands. He is warm, not cold. She questions him with her eyes, and he responds with a weak smile.

"He was hungry. I startled him. He's a wild creature. We can't expect him to act any other way."

If she's going to do it, she tells herself, do it fast. She grabs the towel, unravels the sticky fabric from his arm. Running from wrist to elbow is a slash so spiderweb thin that nothing but the creature's cusped claw could have carved it. It is deep, still bleeding, but not gushing, and Elisa dashes into the bedroom, rips a clean sheet from a shelf, dashes back, and begins winding it. It's like a cloth whirlpool enveloping the arm in sea foam—even here, even now, she can't stop seeing water. Giles winces, but his smile hangs on like a cheap mask. He puts a clammy palm to her cheek.

"Don't fret over me, dear. Go find him. He can't be far."

Elisa doesn't know what else to do. She bolts to the outer hallway, closing the door behind her. It is difficult to see anything but the most garish streaks of blood, but she forces herself and finds a spackle of red tracking a separate path toward the fire-escape stairs. Impossible, she thinks. The creature would be too frightened. Then fanfare blares from the theater below, and it's not so different, is it, from the records she played in F-1? She runs, crashing down metal steps so fast she feels the vertigo of a plunging elevator, and then she's tripping through the alley and down the Arcade's sidewalk, snared by a velvet rope, dazed in the signboard's brilliance.

In such light, the spots of blood, only a few now, stand out like scattered jewelry. They lead into the theater. Elisa throws a glance at the box office. Mr. Arzounian mans the booth, but he's yawning, fighting sleep, and Elisa doesn't falter. She looks at her feet, those emerald green, thick-buckled, Cuban-heeled Mary Janes, not bad for dancing, and tells herself that she is Bojangles with the TV volume turned down, and she dances past Arzounian as she's danced past so many woolgathering Occam men.

The chafed carpet beneath her shoes gives way to Navajo-motif terrazzo flooring. Elisa cranes her neck to the dusty, muraled dome that, according to Mr. Arzounian, greeted celebrities, politicians, and giants of industry in the forties and fifties, back when the Arcade mattered, back before the upper offices were sacrificed to build a couple of rat-trap apartments. Age and disregard don't mean something isn't beautiful; Elisa has come to believe this with all of her heart. The lobby, though, is too bright, and Elisa knows the creature will seek darkness.

Even awash in the film's coruscating light, Elisa can't find the back of a single head in any of the theater's twelve hundred seats. It doesn't matter: the screen, balcony, and constellations of ceiling lights lend the theater the majesty of a basilica. And hadn't she worshipped here as a girl? It was here she'd found the raw materials to build a beautiful fantasy life, and it is here where, if she is lucky, she might salvage what is left of it.

It's with a pious stoop that she slinks down the aisle. These are the final days of *The Story of Ruth*, the biblical epic about which she knows nothing except its loudest dialogue and every single music cue. Between peering left and right down shadowy ranks of seats, she passes her eyes over the screen, where a sweaty mob of enslaved men pound rock in a quarry under the bug-eyed glower of a giant pagan statue. So this is Chemosh, the name she's so often heard rumbling up through the floor. If her creature, too, is a god, then he is one far less frightening.

She's hatching nightmares of him wandering downtown Baltimore when she sees a dark shape floundering between the first and second row. She ducks beneath the projector rays. There he is, knees pulled to heaving chest, arms wrapped around his head. Elisa scurries into the row, stealth abandoned, heels clacking, and the creature hisses, a harsh warning she hasn't heard since her first approach with the egg. It's a feral noise, and she stops, fear icing her body, no braver than the countless beasts that once showed their bellies to this superior thing.

Cries of pain caw out, and like the jungle field recordings they blast from speakers, the sound effects of men's backs whipped while trying to move the stone idol. The creature envelops his head in his hands as if trying to crush his own skull. Elisa lowers herself to her knees and crawls across the gummy floor. The cascading colors of light make kaleidoscopes of the creature's eyes, and he scuttles back, stumbling to his knees, short on breath.

A deafening crash and Elisa can't help but look: Chemosh toppled, pinning a screaming slave. The creature responds with a piteous dog-squeak and dog-shiver. Perhaps afraid that he has caused this onscreen pain, he stops retreating and instead reaches out to Elisa. She slides across the floor and wraps him in her arms. He is cold. He is dry. His gills flutter against her neck, coarse as sandpaper. Thirty minutes, Hoffstetler had warned, that's as long as he's got. There's an emergency exit. It feeds right into the alley. She'll get him out, upstairs, back to safety. She just wants a few more seconds of embracing this beautiful, sad creature who, in this world, can never be safe.

13

HER HAND ACHES from signing "hospital." But Giles won't go, and she understands why. Doctors know claw wounds when they see them, and there are protocols regarding animal control: visits to Mr. Arzounian, searches of the Arcade Apartments to make sure a tenant isn't harboring a dangerous beast. She is, though, and both she and Giles know what the local government does with dangerous beasts: They are taken from their unfit masters and put to sleep.

So she'd capitulated to Giles's request and provided him with a guesswork treatment of iodine and bandages. He'd made jokes at every step, his way of making it clear that he wasn't upset, but it had done little to soothe her. One of his cats, eaten. A wound that will sprout who knows what sort of infection. Giles is old and not especially robust. If something happens to him, it'll be her fault—her and the heart she can't contain. Her heart, then, is a wild animal, too, a second living thing to be locked up should animal control arrive at the door.

Elisa is monitoring Giles, making sure he ingests both the soup and water she poured, when they both hear water dribbling into the bathtub. They stare at each other. One thing they have come to learn is that the creature can move into, out of, and through water without a sound, which means he is warning them, on purpose, that he has stood up. Giles's hand tightens around his spoon like a shiv, and it breaks Elisa's heart. Everyone is changing, and none for the better.

It takes a full minute for the creature to exit the bathroom. He plods slowly, face tilted to the floor, gills flat and submissive, lethal claws tucked out of sight behind his thighs. His finned back is curled in a submissive hunch, and he keeps one shoulder to the wall as if he's chained himself to one of Strickland's concrete posts. Elisa is confident that not once in his ageless life has the creature known the misery of regret, and she stands, holding out her arms, as eager to accept his apology as she is reticent to accept her own.

The creature, afraid to look at her, slouches past her open arms, trembling so badly that scales ping off and land on the floorboards, where they twinkle as brightly as the constellation of lights on the theater's ceiling. He shuffles across the room like one of Chemosh's whipped slaves, his head dipping lower until it matches the height of Giles, seated at the table. Giles shakes his head, holds up his hands.

"Please," he says. "You've done no wrong, my boy."

The creature releases his hands from their hiding place and raises them, so gradually that it's imperceptible, until all ten of his claws, half-retracted into his fingers, snag at Giles's bandaged arm. Giles looks at Elisa; she stares back, sharing his confusion and hope. They watch as the creature lifts Giles's arm from the table, as tenderly as if it were an infant, and positions it beneath his downturned face. Despite the creature's meekness, the pose is disquieting: It looks as if he is about to eat Giles's arm, like a scolded child forced to finish his dinner.

What happens is less violent and far stranger. He licks it. The creature's tongue, longer and flatter than a man's, extends past his double-jaws and laps at the bandage. Giles's mouth moves, but he looks too startled to manage actual words. Elisa is no better prepared; not a single letter forms from her dangling hands. The creature rotates Giles's arm as he licks, wetting the entirety of the bandage until it is soaked to Giles's skin, until the dried blood is liquid again and the creature is licking it clean. He lowers the glistening arm to Giles's lap, slowly leans over, and then, like some parting kiss, licks the top of Giles's head.

The ritual, abruptly, is finished. Giles blinks up at the creature.

"Thank you?"

The creature doesn't react. It looks to Elisa that he is too ashamed to move. But it has been a long day for a being whose only true comfort is inside water: His gills and chest begin to expand and shake. Elisa wants to wash Giles's arm, reapply iodine, rewrap it in sterilized bandages, but she can't bear the idea of insulting the creature. She steps close and settles a hand upon his bowed back, gently pushing him toward the bathroom. He allows it, but only in a backward stumble that doesn't impede his genuflection to Giles. It is the least graceful she's seen the creature, and she has to tug his arm to get him through the bathroom doorway, a whack from his shoulder joggling the air-freshener trees.

She folds him into the tub. The lights are off and his face slides underwater, and yet his eyeshine is undiluted. Elisa breaks his gaze to pour salt into the water, but feels him watching. Throughout her life, she has felt men on the street or bus trace her movements. This is different. This is exciting. When she reaches into the tub to swirl the salt, their eyes meet, only for a second, but in that second she reads both gratitude and amazement. The idea is outlandish. *She amazes him.* How is that possible, when he is the most amazing thing that ever lived?

Elisa finishes stirring. Her hand is beside his face. Such a small thing to move it, so she does, cupping her palm to his cheek. It is smooth. She bets the scientists never noted this in all their data.

They only registered teeth, claws, spines. She caresses him now, her hand gliding down his neck and shoulder. The water has turned him the same temperature as the air, and maybe this is why she doesn't feel his hand sliding up her arm until he is at the soft, bluish flesh of her inner elbow. His palm's scales are Lilliputian daggers, nicking playfully at her skin, while his claws poke, never enough to puncture, as they travel her biceps, leaving white scratches in their wake.

After dressing Giles's wound, Elisa had changed into a gauze-thin shirt dating back to Home, and when the creature's hand shifts from her arm to her chest, the cotton soaks instantly, as if by magic. First one breast, then the other, is heavied by the grip of the shirt slicked to her skin. She feels naked beneath his hand, can feel every shiver of her hitching chest, breathless but not because there is anything illicit here. He is always naked before her, and it feels overdue that she join him in this natural state.

The room incandesces from below. *The Story of Ruth*, she thinks, the projector cranking up for another screening. But there is no music. It is the creature, his body lights suffusing the water with pink, like flamingos, like petunias, like untold other fauna and flora from a world she knows only from field recordings: reek-reek, chuk-a-kuk, curu-curu, zeee-eee-eee. She arches her back, leaning her full weight into a palm wide enough to cradle her entire chest.

Somewhere far away, Giles hisses in pain. Elisa realizes her eyes are closed; she opens them. She finds that her whole body has moved. She is bent over the tub so far that her hair dangles into the water. She wants to keep going, tip forward until she drowns as she has drowned so many times in dreams, but Giles is hurt, and it's her doing, and she needs to treat that wound again, especially after it was licked. With great effort she straightens her spine. The creature's hand trails down her belly and reenters the water without splash or sound.

Elisa covers her wet shirt with a bathrobe before moving into the main room. She does not, however, go to Giles. She walks past him, across the apartment's length, to the kitchen window. She leans her forehead onto it. She presses her hand against it. Her vision blurs, but not because she's crying. There is water on the window, hanging in small globs on the pane, slugging in wet streaks down the glass. Yes, she might be crying after all.

It is raining.

14

HE TURNS THE dial with his good hand. The images are thin, discolored. Goddamn hunk of junk. Shelled out for it at a place called Kosciuszko Electronics. Is it the cord? The wiring? Did one of his kids spill a glass of juice on it? He has half a mind to bust off the back of the television just to be able to finger the guilty party. He's stopped by the irrational fear that the TV's innards will look like the gadget that blew Occam's circuits, a scorched tangle. He hadn't been able to identify that. What makes him think he'll be able to diagnose this?

Or it's the weather screwing with the signal. All this time in Baltimore and he swears this is the first rain he's seen. It's been pelting all day. There's an antenna on the roof, an arachnid thing like one of the space-capsule transceivers he's glimpsed at Occam. It's tempting to climb onto the roof to tinker with it, right there in the rain. Watch the storm thicken and roll. Laugh at lightning. Be in the sort of danger a man can understand.

Instead, there's this. Living-room ruins. A family struck by lightning, provided you know where to check for burn marks. Tammy's droning on about a puppy. Timmy wants to watch *Bonanza*. Lainie's twaddling about gelatin parfait, some orange glop she's proud of despite having dumped it from a box. All their meals come from boxes these days. Why is that? Strickland knows why. Because she's gone most of the day, doing who knows what. He shouldn't have come home. He should have slept another night at the office. After all, General Hoyt had called Occam only four hours ago. Worse—he'd called Fleming. And the message relayed had been clear as glass.

Strickland had twenty-four hours to find the asset before his career was over.

What does *over* mean? Court-martial? Military prison? Worse? Anything was possible. Strickland got scared. So he'd climbed into his busted-up Caddy, the one people at Occam, he swears, are starting to whisper and laugh about, and driven it home. Soon as he'd arrived here, Fleming had called. He'd done what Strickland asked and trailed Hoffstetler like a pro. Shouldn't have surprised Strickland. Fleming is a dog, after all, and a dog has a nose for shit. Fleming says he's got photographs of Hoffstetler in an unfurnished house packing up belongings. He's got Hoffstetler linked to a Russian attaché called Mihalkov. Deus Brânquia might still be in the country, even the city. Strickland needs to be out there, right now, in the night, in the rain, finding the creature, ending all of this, fulfilling his destiny.

Instead, he keeps cranking the dial. Where the hell is *Bonanza*?

"*Bonanza*'s for adults," Lainie says. "Let's keep it on *Dobie Gillis*."

Strickland flinches. He must have muttered it aloud. He glances at Lainie. He can barely stand the sight of her. Yesterday, she came home with new hair. The beehive gone as if chopped by an Amazon machete and replaced by a smoother style, an S-wave curled girlishly at the neck. But she's not a girl, is she? She's the mother of his children. She's his goddamn wife.

"But Dad said we could watch *Bonanza*!" Timmy cries.

"If Timmy gets to watch *Bonanza*," Tammy reasons, "then I should get a puppy."

Dr. Kildare. Perry Mason. The Flintstones. Same three shows, a couple of dead channels. It's all he sees. He feels a tremor of thunder. He looks to the window. Nothing to see but rain, exploding against the glass like bugs on a windshield. Except the guts keep being washed away. His guts, too. His career, his life. This lampoon of American bliss. Gelatin fucking parfait, imaginary puppies, a Western program that's nowhere on the dial.

"Nobody's getting a puppy," he says. "You know what happens to puppies? They become dogs."

Doctor, lawyer, caveman. He's getting the characters on the channels confused with his own reflection in the screen. He's the doctor, he's the lawyer, he's the caveman. He's the one regressing, devolving. He can feel it in the crumbling away of his civility, the rise of primitive bloodlust. Scalpel, gavel, club.

"Richard," Lainie says, "I thought we said we'd at least—"

"Dog's a wild animal. You can try to domesticate it. You can sure as hell try. But one day, that dog's going to show its true nature. And it's going to bite. Is that what you want?"

He wonders. Is Deus Brânquia the dog? Or is he?

"Dad!" Timmy's flapping his arms. "You just passed it!"

"What did I say, Timmy?" Lainie scolds. "That show's too violent."

People dying on the surgical slab, people dying in jail, an entire species dying out. The three channels spin faster. Ghost channels, too, phantom signals, purgatories of unclaimed static. He can't quit turning the dial.

"*Bonanza*'s not violent," he snarls. "The *world's* violent. You ask me, it's the right thing to watch. The only thing. You want to learn to be a man, Tim? Then you need to learn how to look a problem in the eye and solve it. Shoot it in the face if you have to."

"Richard!" Lainie gasps.

The dial breaks. Snaps off right in his hand. Strickland stares at it, dumbfounded. There's no putting it back. The plastic is broken. He lets it drop to the carpet. It doesn't make a sound. The kids don't make a sound, either. Neither does Lainie. They're mute. Finally mute. Just the way he wants them. The only noise is the crinkle from the static channel on which the dial is stuck. It sounds like rain. He stands up. Yes, rain. The rain forest. It's where he belongs. He'd been a coward to run here, when his real home is out there.

He walks to the front door, opens it. The patter becomes a roar. Good, good. If he listens close, he can hear the monkeys, messengers of Hoyt, swinging through the wet trees, hooting their blasted redactions, instructing him what to do. It's like Strickland's back in the Yeongdong gold mine under all those bodies. Yes, sir. He'll rip through flesh and dislocate bone until he finds breathable air. It doesn't matter anymore who gets torn apart.

A moment later, he's outside. In the seconds it takes to get to the Cadillac Coupe de Ville, he's sopping. Rain slams to the steel surface, the mad drumming of jungle cannibals. He runs his fingers over the hood ornament, some primitive idol. Through the grille teeth, dripping with what feels like blood. Along fins so sharp they cut beads of rain in half. What had the dealer said, that grinning, razor-burned Mephistopheles? Just plain power.

He runs his hand over the fractured paint. His wet bandages unravel and drop away. Both of his reattached fingers are as black as the night. He frowns. He can't even see his wedding ring. With his other hand, he presses on one of the noxious fingers. He can't feel it. He presses harder. Yellow liquid squirts from under the fingernail, hits the back of the car, is erased by rain. Strickland blinks water from his eyes. Did he really see that?

Lainie is suddenly beside him, hunched under an umbrella.

"Richard! Get back inside! You're scaring the—"

Strickland grabs Lainie's blouse with both hands. Pain is sucked from his fingers into his arm. He slams her down to the car's crushed back end. A gust snatches her umbrella, tosses it into the night. The Caddy barely reacts to the impact of Lainie's body. That's craftsmanship. Top-notch suspension. Perfectly calibrated shock absorbers. Lainie stares straight into the driving rain. It muddies her makeup into clown blotches. Flattens the teenage haircut she's so smug about. He adjusts his grip, holds her by her skinny little neck. He has to lean down to be heard over the thunder and rain.

"You think you're smarter than me?"

"No—Richard, please—"

"You think I don't know how you go downtown every day? How you go behind our backs?"

She's trying to peel his fingers from her neck. Her fingernails dig into his black fingers. More liquid seeps from them, drops of rancid yellow spattering her cheeks and chin, aglow under the streetlight. Her mouth is wide open, filling with rain. If he does nothing else at all, just holds her here, she'll drown.

"I didn't—mean to—it's just a—"

"You think people won't find out? Small shit-hole city like this? They'll see, Lainie. Just like they see this crashed car. And what will they think? They'll think I don't deserve to be here. That I can't control my own. And I have enough problems already. Do you understand?"

"Yes—Rich—I can't—I can't—"

"It's you who's ruining this family. Not me. *Not me!*"

Strickland almost believes his own accusation. He tightens both hands around her neck, tries to solidify the belief. Vessels fatten in her eyeballs like red ink dropped onto paper. She coughs up what looks like a tongue of blood. The whole thing's revolting. He pitches her body behind him, easy as hiking a football. Hears her body thump against the garage door. A soft sound compared to the monkey screams. The rain has turned his clothes into a second skin. Naked again, just like the Amazon. He can feel his keys in his pocket, sharp as broken bone. He extracts them. Walks the long, satisfying length of the Caddy, the length of a whole life, still salvageable.

He opens the door, drops behind the wheel. It's dry inside. Tidy. Still smells new. He fires the ignition. Sure, the car moans when he puts it in gear. But it'll get him where he needs to go. He pictures the locked drawer of his desk. Inside, his Model 70 Beretta, the same one he used to shoot the pink river dolphin. He'll miss the Howdy-do. Men grow attached to their tools and it was a good one. But it's time to advance. He stomps the gas, pictures the spray of mud from the back wheels. All over the garage door, over Lainie's blouse. The suburbs turned ugly, though that shouldn't surprise anyone with a brain. Everything's ugly underneath.

15

IT'S MORNING, BUT there is no light. Overflowing drainage ditches are teethed with traffic cones. Side roads are cordoned by sawhorses. The bus she's riding slices through a foot of standing water that buffets the tires. All of it, the earth's gush, the sprawling darkness, reflects her anguish. She has checked the river levels twice a day since the downpour began, an act equivalent to carving out her heart ounce by ounce. Tomorrow, Dr. Hoffstetler will get his way. She and Giles will load the creature back into the Pug, drive to the foot of the jetty, lead the creature to the water's edge. Today, then, is her last day and night with the being who, more than anyone ever, sees her as more than she is. And isn't that love?

She looks at her feet. Even in the lightless murk of the bus floor she can see the shoes. *The* shoes; she still can't believe it. Yesterday, before managing a few anxious hours of sleep before going to work, she'd lived out a dream. She'd gone inside Julia's Fine Shoes, and though stunned by the spicy scent of leather, made a quick turn to the window display, nabbed the low-slung, square-toed, silver-encrusted lamé pair from its ivory column, and marched them to the checkout counter.

As it turned out, the Julia of her long-held imagination, that for-midable beauty with a brain for business, didn't exist. She'd asked about it, and the woman at the register had told her. It was just a nice-sounding name. This had soothed Elisa as she'd gone home and snugged the glittering shoes around the sides of her feet. If Julia didn't exist, why, she'd be Julia. Providing for the creature had drained her funds, and this extravagant purchase left her flat broke. She didn't care. She still doesn't. The shoes are hooves and just this once, over this final day, she wants to be a beautiful creature, too.

Elisa gets off the bus and expands her umbrella, but it feels wrong, a cumbersome human contrivance. She tosses it into the

265

gutter, turns her face to the sky, and loses herself in water, tries to breathe inside it. She never wants to be dry again, she decides. She's drenched when she gets home and glad of it; rain patters from her clothes as she heads down the hall, forming puddles she hopes won't ever evaporate. Before the creature's trip to the theater, she'd never locked her front door. Now she feels for the key she's ferreted inside a defunct lamp and fits it into the lock.

Giles isn't at his usual spot. He told her before she left for Occam that he'd check in, but that he'd wanted to complete the full painting for which he'd been training with his charcoal sketches. He was on fire, he'd told her. He hadn't felt so inspired since he was a young man. Elisa didn't doubt it, but she also wasn't stupid. Giles, too, knew the end was at hand and he wanted to give her space to say her farewell.

He'd left the radio on for her, of course. Elisa dawdles by the table to listen. She has come to depend upon the radio: politics, sports scores, dull listings of local events that provide sane counterpoints to the untamed fantasy she is living. She has kept it playing nonstop. Yesterday the creature, wrapped in sodden towels, had sat at her table with her, his first time on a chair—a tricky thing with his spine fins and his short, plated tail. He'd looked like a woman fresh out of the shower and she'd laughed, and though he couldn't possibly have understood, he'd lit up, his version of a laugh, golden light pulsing about his chest while his gills wiggled.

She stirs Scrabble tiles with her fingers. She's been trying to teach him printed words. The day prior, she'd brought home magazines from work to show him things he'd never otherwise get to see: a 727 airplane, the New York Philharmonic Orchestra, Sonny Liston punching Floyd Patterson, a spectacular movie still of Elizabeth Taylor in *Cleopatra*. He'd learned with such fervor. With the delicate movements of one accustomed to tearing things with his claws, he extended a long index finger and thumb, picked up the still of Elizabeth Taylor, and placed it atop the 727, which he then set atop the New York Philharmonic. Then, like a child playing airplane, he pushed the 727 across the breadth of the table until it landed at another photo of *Cleopatra*'s Egypt.

The meaning was clear: *For Elizabeth Taylor to get from New York to Egypt, she'd have to take a 727.*

It was information, of course, he didn't need. He did all of it, she was certain, just to see her smile, hear her laugh.

None of that means that he is well. A grayness has settled over him like grit from a factory. His brilliant scales have lost luster and turned teal like an old penny on the sidewalk. He seems, in short, to be growing older, and this, she fears, is her most unforgivable crime. For how many decades, if not centuries, had the creature lived without losing a notch of vitality? At least Occam had filters, thermometers, processions of learned biologists. Here there is nothing to sustain him but love. In the end, it isn't enough. The creature is dying, and she is his murderer.

"Heavy rains expected to deluge the upper Eastern Seaboard today," the radio buzzes. "Baltimore will continue to get the worst of it, expecting anywhere between five and seven additional inches by midnight. This storm isn't going anywhere, folks."

She picks up a black marker left on the table from language lessons. A desk calendar sits there, too, each day devoted to a cornball inspirational quote that she can no longer read without tearing up. She uncaps the marker. If she doesn't write it, if she doesn't make it real and see it for herself, she doesn't know if she can carry through with it. Moving the marker across paper is like moving a knife across her own skin.

MIDNIGHT—THE DOCKS

Tonight, she will call in sick for the first time in years. Even if Fleming registers it as unusual behavior, it will be too late. Will she return to Occam on Monday? The issue feels trite. Probably not—she doubts she could stomach it. What she will do for money, she has no idea. That, too, feels like the banal concern of a stagnated realm she has left behind. Giles had a certain look the day he came to her saying that he would help break out the creature. She thinks she must have this look now, too. After bidding good-bye, there will be nothing left to lose that matters.

This is a joy she will miss above all others: The creature coming into view after a period she has spent away. This is the last time she'll feel this delirious thrill, so she does it slowly, entering the bathroom as she might cold water, inch by inch. He sparkles like chromatic coral beneath the surface of a virgin sea. She is powerless to resist his call.

Elisa closes the door behind her and comes forward, chest hitching enough to make her dizzy with what first feels like tearful sadness before she feels the stronger, guttural pull and identifies the emotion as passion. There is, all at once, no question of what she will do, nor any surprise. It was always going to end like this, she realizes, from the first moment that she looked into the tank in F-1 and was pulled inside, not physically but in every other possible way, by the star clusters of his scales and supernovas of his eyes.

The plastic shower curtain is bunched against the wall. Elisa yanks it. A metal ring pops free. She does it eleven more times, rings tinging off the walls and getting lost in foliage, each tear of the curtain an astonishing, irreversible act of destruction no graveyard-shift janitor on the planet would have dared. She spreads the curtain across the floor like a quilt onto a bed, tucking it into the wainscoting and stretching it over the gap under the door. When the plastic is as taut as she can make it, she stands. She can't command water like the creature, but she has the next best thing: modern plumbing.

Elisa plugs the sink and cranks the knobs. Water fires out. She leans over the tub and does the same. Running both faucets at full-blast is another thing no poor person would ever do, but she's not poor, not today. Today she is the richest woman in the world; she has everything she could want; she loves and is loved, and as such is as infinite as the creature, not human nor animal but *feeling*, a force shared between everything good that has ever been and ever will be.

She removes her uniform; it is the unburdening of quarry rock from Chemosh's toilers. She unsnaps her bra and peels off her slip; it is the unshackling of any creature trapped by another. Each item of dropped clothing makes no sound: the water has overflowed both sink and tub and is filling the spread curtain, lapping at her ankles, sliding up her calves like a warm hand. Only her silver shoes remain; she props a foot on the edge of the tub so the creature can see it, a flipper more fantastic than any he has ogled on her bedroom wall, the only thing she has that is as bright and beautiful as him. It is the most brazenly sensual posture she's ever struck, and she hears the Matron calling her worthless, stupid, ugly, a whore, until the creature rises from the flooded tub, a thousand silent waterfalls cascading from his body, and steps over the edge into her waiting arms.

They curl to the floor together, her parts finding reciprocal space in his parts, and his into hers. Her head sinks underwater, a wonderful feeling, and then they roll, and she is on top, gasping, water pouring from her hair, and he is under the sloshing surface, and to kiss him she must dip her face under, which she does, and ecstatically, the tedious lines of her rigid world softening, the sink, toilet, doorknob, mirror, even the walls themselves relinquishing their shapes.

The kiss reverberates underwater, not the fussy wet *tsk*s of human lips, but a rumbling thunderstorm that pours into her ears and runs down her throat. She takes his scaled face into her hand, his gills throbbing against her palms, and kisses him forcefully, hoping to stir the storm they've started into a tsunami so as to force a flood; perhaps her kisses, not the rain, can be what saves him. She exhales into his mouth, feels the bubbles tickle past her cheeks. *Breathe*, she prays. *Learn to breathe my air so we can be together forever.*

But he can't. He uses his strong hands to force her above water so she won't drown. She's panting, for all sorts of reasons, her hands planted to her chest to help it rediscover oxygen. Her hands, she discovers, are covered with the creature's twinkling scales. The sight enthralls her, and she runs her hands over her breasts and belly, spreading the scales, wishing this was how she really looked. From the theater below she hears a passage of dialogue, one she's heard a hundred times: *Trouble your heart no more. Be strong through this time.*

For from the widow of your son will issue children, and children's children. Yes, why not? Each bead of water on her eyelashes is its own entire world—she's read such things in science articles. Couldn't one of them be theirs to populate with a new, better species?

No bathtub fantasy she's ever had can compare. She searches out his every crest and pocket. He has a sex organ, right where it should be, and she has hers, too, right where she left them, and she pulls him inside her; within so much rocking water, it happens easily, the tectonic shift of two subsea plates. The effulgence of the theater lights eking through the floorboards and plastic are overwhelmed by the creature's own rhythms of crystalline color, as if the sun itself is beneath them, and it is, it has to be, for they are in heaven, in God's canals, in Chemosh's slag, every holy and unholy thing at once, beyond sex into the seeding of understanding, the creature implanting within her the ancient history of pain and pleasure that connects not only the two of them but every living thing. It is not just him inside her. It is the whole world, and she, in turn, is inside it.

This is how life changes, mutates, emerges, survives, how one being absolves the sins of its species by becoming another species altogether. Perhaps Dr. Hoffstetler would understand. Elisa can only perceive the edges it, glimpse the foothills of the mountain, the horn of the glacier. She feels so small, so gloriously tiny in such a huge, wondrous universe, and she opens her eyes underwater to remind herself of reality. Plant leaves swim by like tadpoles. The curtain has ripped and flaps at them like worshipful jellyfish.

The storm outside, in the real world, doubles with the storm from *The Story of Ruth*, the end of the biblical drought. Her body convulses with sensations, each like the unclenching of a fist. Yes, the drought is over. It is over, it is over, it is over. She smiles, her mouth filling with water. Finally, she is dancing, truly dancing, across a submerged ballroom and fearing no misstep, for her partner has got her tight and will lead her anyplace she needs to go.

16

HE FLITS THE brush through the paint. Bernie likes green? Too bad he'll never see this. It's a green the likes of which Giles never dreamed possible. How did he mix it? He recalls a base of Caribbean blue, a touch of grape, dapples of harvest orange, streaks of straw yellow, daubs of gloaming indigo, his signature cotton-clay red—what else? He doesn't know and doesn't care. He's coasting on impulse here. It's rousing, and yet there's a peace to it as well. His brain doesn't smart from focus; it rambles and stretches, tying disparate threads together in shiny, department-store bows.

Bernie. Good old Bernie Clay. Giles thinks of the last time he saw him. In hindsight, he can see signs of stress all over the guy. The yellowed collar no volume of bleach can scrub, the gut bulging the shirt—Bernie had always been an anxious eater. Giles forgives him. He's never felt more forgiving. For too long, ill will has clogged his arteries like cholesterol, an ominous substance he just read about in the news. Today, the cholesterol is flushed and only love remains. It flows into his every long-dug trench. The cops who arrested him at the bar in Mount Vernon. The executive cabal that got him fired. Brad—or John—of Dixie Doug's. Everyone struggles against the qualms and uncertainties that life twines about them.

How had it taken him sixty-three years to recognize the futility of anger? When Mrs. Elaine Strickland, a woman half his age, knew it on instinct? Giles doesn't believe a dawn will rise that he won't privately thank her. Just this morning he'd tried calling her at Klein & Saunders to express what her candor had meant to him, how it'd forced open storehouses of courage he'd never suspected he had, but the voice that answered didn't belong to Elaine, and couldn't say why Elaine hadn't shown up to work.

Quite all right with Giles: He has a lifetime's backlog of patience upon which to draw. Mrs. Strickland is, after all, one of two beings to whom he credits his renaissance. The other is the creature. Giles chuckles in wonder. Elisa's bathtub has become a portal into the impossible. The work Giles has done alongside it, from atop a toilet seat of all places—he is so thankful to know the sort of divine inspiration typically reserved, he is certain, for only the greatest of masters.

While the creature belongs to no one, no place, and no time, his heart belongs to Elisa, and Giles has left the two of them to share these final hours. Besides, Giles needs to complete his painting. It is, without question, his life's finest work, and what existential relief there is in knowing you have managed, at last, to live up to your potential. The fulfillment of his hopes is to show the finished piece to the creature before the creature is gone, and that requires working on it day and night.

Working, however, hasn't been a problem. Twenty hours he's been at it now and he feels tip-top, as unflagging as a teenager, powered as if by a fabulous drug that has the sole side effect of suffusing him with confidence as powerful as the storm outside. He makes the boldest brushes of color without pause. He paints the finest slivers of detail without arthritic tremor. He hasn't broken for a bathroom break in half a day, and when was the last time he made it two hours without peeing?

He laughs, and his eye catches a fluttering cloth. It's the bandage Elisa coiled around his arm. He's working so briskly that it has come loose. Strange that he hasn't noticed. More strange, he thinks, is that he hasn't needed to take aspirin for pain since before bed. Perhaps the cut wasn't so deep after all. Still, the bandage will trail across wet paint and that won't do. He sighs, sets down his brush. A quick, fresh dressing—maybe brush his teeth while he's at it—and then it's back to the easel! He can hardly wait.

Giles doesn't realize that he's whistling a show tune until the jaunty song cuts off. He blames the misperception on his speed: He's unwrapping the bandage as if reeling in a catfish. He quits unwinding and carefully pushes the rest of the bandage into the sink. There's no blood. Is he so exhausted that he's looking at the wrong side of his own arm? He rotates it, finds nothing. Not even a wound, which, last time he checked, was pink and puckered.

He makes a fist, watches the cords of his wrist thicken. The shock of it settles slowly, rescuing him from full impact. The wound isn't the only thing gone. There used to be liver spots on his arm. There used to be a scar from a youthful collision with a cotton loom. These, too, have been replaced by smooth, perfect skin. Giles checks his other arm. It is as old and wrinkled as ever.

Giles sputters in disbelief. It sounds rather like a laugh. Is that an appropriate reaction to the supernatural? He looks up into the mirror and, sure enough, the deep lines of his face are curved in jubilance. He looks good, he thinks, and notes that he hasn't held this opinion of himself in more years than he can remember. His eyes flick upward. Ah, there's the reason. He hadn't noticed until now.

He has a head full of hair. Giles reaches for it, but slowly, as if it might be scared away. He pats it. It does not scatter like dandelion puffs. It is short and thick, a rich brown with familiar traces of blond and orange. More than that, it's springy; he'd forgotten the resilience of young hair, how it resists being constrained. He pets it, stunned by the satin texture. It's erotic. This, he thinks, is why young people are so lustful: Their own bodies are aphrodisiacs. Only after he thinks this does he notice a pressure against the sink. He looks down. His pajama bottoms are tented outward. He has an erection. No, that's too clinical a word for this adolescent response to the slightest sexual thought. It's a boner, a hard-on. He can feel youth swell his every molecule with lightness, quickness, pliancy, bravado.

There is a knocking at his door. A pounding, really, a sure sign of emergency next door. Giles knows himself well enough to anticipate a sick, sinking sensation, but whatever has affected his body has also affected his spirit: The alarm he feels is at the end of an upsurge, a tilting toward challenge rather than edging away. He lurches toward the door, mindful enough of the silly pendulum of his erect penis to grab a pillow to hold in front of him. Elisa can't see him like this! He chuckles, despite everything.

He whips open the door and finds the perspiring, red face of Mr. Arzounian.

"Mr. Gunderson!" he cries.

"Ah, the rent," Giles sighs. "Tardy, it's true, but have I ever—"

"It is raining, Mr. Gunderson!"

Giles pauses, allowing the drumroll of rain on the fire escape to interject.

"Well, yes. I can't argue with you there."

"No! In my theater! There is rain in my theater!"

"Are you asking me to witness a miracle? Or do you mean a leak?"

"Yes, a leak! From Elisa's apartment! She leaves the water on! Or else a pipe is broke! She will not answer the door! It comes through the ceiling, right onto paying customers! I will find my keys, Mr. Gunderson, and I will open her door myself if it doesn't stop! I must go downstairs! Make it stop, Mr. Gunderson, or the both of you will live at the Arcade no more!"

He's gone then, careening down the stairs. Giles doesn't need the pillow anymore; he backhands it onto his sofa and jogs, in socked feet, the distance between apartment doors. He swipes the key from its lamp haven, inserts it with a dexterity that delights him, and barges in. He doesn't know what he expects. More blood? Destruction from some fit of rage? Nothing is amiss until he divines that the floorboards near the bathroom have not been recently mopped. They are, instead, covered in a half-inch of water. He charges, socks soaking as he splashes through the thin pool. This isn't a situation for knocking; he hurls open the bathroom door.

Water bursts outward, drenching Giles from the knees downward. A day ago, the force of the tide, not to mention the plain shock of it, would have toppled him; today, though, his legs are roots, planted firm even as standing lamps and end tables behind him topple to the floor in the rushing tide and its sloppy cargo of unpotted plants. The edge of a shower curtain, which must have held back

274

the flood, flops like snakeskin onto his socks, revealing Elisa and the creature lying in the center of the floor.

They should be carved in marble in this exact position, Giles thinks, and by someone who knows how—Rodin, Donatello. Elisa is glistening wet, freckled with muddied soil, sparkling with scales, naked. The creature is, too: Though always unclothed, there's a reckless need to his pose that makes him *naked*. His arms and legs are interlocked with hers, his face nuzzled into her neck. Her left hand strokes his scalp and cups the back of his head where his ridge of fins begins. He does not look good, and hasn't in a while; he does, however, look content, as if he has chosen his fate, and does not, even upon pain of death, plan to regret it.

Giles expands his view, and along with it expands the spectacular. The room is a bathroom no more. It has become a jungle. He squints before realizing his vision is perfect, even without glasses. Did their lovemaking, whatever form it took, arouse household mold spores to blossom into rain-forest verdure? No, that's not it. The plants that withstood the flood are languid, even voluptuous, with moisture, but it's the hundreds of tree-shaped cardboard air fresheners that have turned the room into an unimaginable wilderness of ravishing color. Shamrock green, lipstick red, sequin gold. Where did Elisa find so many? They are layered over every single inch of wall. Pumpkin orange, coffee brown, butter yellow. The low-budget ingenuity behind the cardboard jungle makes it all the more breathtaking. Amethyst purple, ballet-slipper pink, ocean blue. It is a home not quite Elisa's and not quite the creature's; it is one of a kind, a strange heaven built for two.

It takes a while for Elisa to register Giles. Her eyes are half-closed, dreamy. She absently pinches the shower curtain and pulls it over them as she might a bedsheet. Giles's role, he supposes, is that of the fellow who didn't knock, and he waits to feel disgusted by the vile, unnatural act he has uncovered. How many times, though, have these same adjectives been applied to people like himself? Today, nothing is wrong; nothing is taboo. Perhaps Mr. Arzounian will kick them out.

Giles can't force himself to care. Just as likely, in this world, Mr. Arzounian doesn't exist at all.

Giles kneels, tucks the shower curtain around them. New neighbors, he tells himself, happy young lovers who he, newly young himself, will find to be true, long-lasting friends. Elisa blinks up at Giles and extends an arm shimmering with scales. She runs her fingers through his brand-new hair and smiles gently, as if to ask, *What did I tell you?*

"Can we keep him?" Giles sighs. "Just a little bit longer?"

Elisa laughs, and Giles laughs, too, loudly so that it might echo in the confined chamber and keep the silence of an uncertain future at bay, so that they might go on pretending that this happiness will last forever and that miracles, once found, can be bottled and kept.

17

TWO RINGS: IT'S the signal Hoffstetler has been waiting on since midnight, as there was no telling how technical Mihalkov would be in defining *Friday.* Nevertheless, when the phone rings in early afternoon, it's like being pounced upon by a panther. Hoffstetler's arms and legs spring upward to protect himself, and a hysterical scream rises to the top of his throat. The first ring draws to a ludicrous length, long enough for Hoffstetler to think that it's Mr. Fleming calling, suspicious of Hoffstetler's failure to show up for his last day at work, or Strickland wishing to tell him that he's figured the whole thing out.

The second ring, though, is terse, severed by the caller, and it gongs off the bare walls, empty cabinets, steel cot frame, and dishes. The last moans, he hopes, of a lonely life. He should be giddy. Instead, he is paralyzed. He can't swallow. He has to force himself to breathe. Everything is going as planned. Every detail is in place. The loose floorboard, glued shut. His passport and cash, bulging the inside pocket of his jacket. His single suitcase, packed and impatient by the door.

He dials a taxi with memorized numbers and returns to the kitchen chair upon which he's spent the past fourteen hours. Another fourteen hours after that, he tells himself, and he'll be in Minsk, where he can get started on his new profession: the business of forgetting. Did the janitor get the Devonian to the river? Or had it died in her possession? In the tall white snowbanks of Minsk, he can bury such questions forever and attempt to get beyond the dismal hunch that, if a being like the Devonian can be allowed to die, then the whole of planet Earth is doomed.

A taxi honks. Hoffstetler takes a deep breath, stands, and waits for his wobbling knees to lock. The moment is heavy; it is also inevitable. Warm tears fill his eyes. *I've kept myself out of reach of all of you*, he thinks, *and I'm so sorry*. The students for whom he'd felt affection, the friends he'd almost had, the women who might have made him happy. Their ellipses had touched—but nothing had happened. In all of time and space, there is nothing sadder.

Hoffstetler picks up his suitcase and umbrella and steps outside. The cab awaits, a yellow smear beneath a silver scud of pouring rain. An ugly day, by all accounts, yet Hoffstetler is struck by beauty everywhere he looks. This is America: He bids his adieus. Good-bye to the green buds yawning awake from the skeletons of bony trees. Good-bye to the bright plastic children's toys waiting in front lawns to be renewed with springtime vigor. Good-bye to the cats and dogs blinking from windows, proof of interspecies symbiosis. Good-bye to households of strong brick, cozy television light, comfortable laughter. Hoffstetler lifts his elbow to wipe the tears, but they have mixed with rain.

He's had this cabbie before, a violation of his own rules of conduct, but it's his final trip, what could it matter? He tells the man where to go, then peers out the window, wiping fog from the glass, unwilling to miss a single sight. American automobiles, he'll miss them, too, their preposterous shapes, brash spirits, and gregarious pigments. Good-bye, too, to that big green Cadillac Coupe de Ville idling across the street, a gorgeous machine, even if its back end is smashed.

18

IT IS A good day for disappearing. Lainie can't help but think it. She parts the pleated mustard drapes of which she was once so proud and gazes into a barrage of rain that bounces like marbles to the street. Baltimore, land of dirt and concrete, is now of water, pouring not only from sky but also from everything else. Rain torrents from roof gutters, dumps from trees, cascades from railings, whirlpools behind passing cars. It falls so hard that it seems to shoot upward from tripped booby traps. In such a downpour, you can't see far. You could step into it, be lost in seconds, and that is precisely the idea.

Timmy's backpack is so crammed with toys it takes both of his arms to hold it, leaving his tears unwiped. Tammy's bag, too, is bursting, but she doesn't leak a tear. Lainie wonders if it's because she's a girl and has learned that the masculine maxim of never running away from trouble is *bullshit*. (Lainie finds herself cursing in her thoughts lately, another exciting development.) Tammy looks up at her mother, eyes dry and perceptive. The girl has always paid heed to the lessons of picture books. Running is why animals have feet, why birds have wings, why fish have fins.

Lainie became aware of her own feet, their full potential, only this morning. Richard was shambling through the house, eyes swollen, shoulders cracking banisters, tearing free the black tie his dead fingers refused to knot and letting it slop to the floor. She was in her standard position, the patch of carpet permanently dented from the ironing board, skimming the Westinghouse Spray 'N Steam over one of Richard's dress shirts. He'd gotten home late; she'd felt his half of the bed sink and she'd clung to her side of the mattress so as not to roll into his bottomless hole. This morning, he'd wakened at full boil, slithering his greasy body from bed and dressing without a rinse, his hand constantly dipping into a coat pocket that sagged with the weight of an object as heavy as her iron.

She'd kept beaming into the shifting textures of the TV. The news was no better or worse than any other day. Sportsmen excelling. World leaders orating. Blacks marching. Troops amassing. Women linking arms. Nothing connected one story to the next except forward progress, each spotlighted individual advancing, improving, evolving. At some point, Richard left, the slam of the front door his farewell peck, and the floor had trembled, and that tremble had shaken the ironing board, and her thumb had slipped from the setting dial, and she was just *standing there*, all at once certain that she was the only one in the world not moving.

The iron was too heavy to set upright. She'd had no choice but to let it settle onto Richard's shirt. For ten seconds, normalcy was rescuable with a twitch of her wrist. Then smoke began to seep. The Westinghouse sank into the Dacron blend the same way an idea soaks into a mind. Lainie let the smoke coarsen. She let the toxic fumes thistle her sinuses. She'd only pulled the iron from the melted smutch of the board when the children had rushed downstairs, sniffing the smoke, at which point she'd turned, and smiled, and told them, "We're going on a trip. Pack all of your favorite things."

Now she has three heavy bags biting down on her shoulders. One of her arms has gone numb; she doesn't mind. Numbness: It's how she has survived life with Richard. The woman known as Mrs. Strickland is a corseted, aproned, lipsticked shield from the sting of discarded potential, and to use that shield to advance her own purposes, just this once, is thrilling. She adjusts the straps, her fingertips brushing the furrows in her neck from Richard's choking. Everyone will see the bruises. Everyone will know. She takes a deep breath. All you have to be, she tells herself, is honest. Truth will begin to pour, and freedom will begin to rise.

A cab pulls up in front of the house, its tires sizzling through standing water. Lainie waves at it through the screen door.

"Come on, kids, let's hustle."

"I don't want to," Timmy pouts. "I want to wait for Dad."

"It's too wet," Tammy says. "The rain's high as my dress!"

Lainie has regrets. She regrets that she'll have to quit her job over the telephone from Florida or Texas or California or wherever they land, and that doesn't strike her as very professional. But she'll explain to Bernie the reason she had to leave, and Bernie will forgive her, probably even agree to serve as a reference. There's another regret: not jotting down Mr. Gunderson's address, so that at some point in her deliriously undefined future she could write him, let him know that the instant he'd handed over his leather portfolio bag, she'd understood that it was never too late to exchange the things you believed defined you for something better. His bag, in fact, is one of the three strapped over her shoulder right now. Turns out, it can carry quite the load.

Mostly, she regrets that it took her so long to arrive at this front-porch launchpad. Her sloth has had real costs. The children have seen and heard things that have shaped them in unkind ways. Timmy's dissection of the skink remains a troubling, unresolved thing. Thankfully, both children are young yet; Lainie's no Occam Aerospace Research Center scientist, but she knows that maturation is no straight line and that her influence upon her kids has a long path still to run. She lifts the bag from her right shoulder so that all three hang from her left, and kneels, wrapping an arm around Tammy while leaning into Timmy.

"Run," she whispers to him. "Right through the puddles. Make the biggest mess you can make."

He frowns down at his clean pants and shoes. "Really?"

She nods and grins, and he begins to grin, too, and then he bolts down the steps with a hoot, marauding through the yard, dousing himself from both directions. Tammy panics, of course, but that's why Lainie's got her arm around her. She lifts her daughter, propping the girl on her hip, opens the door with a foot, and stands beneath the awning that had once represented so much promise but is now laden with enough disappointment that she worries it might collapse and she, trapped beneath it, might crumple.

But Timmy is at the cab, soaking wet and laughing, and hopping in place for her to hurry up, and Lainie laughs, too, and realizes that no, she won't crumple, she won't crumple ever again. She runs into the waterworld. She likes how the rain cracks crisply on her short haircut, how it slides off the curled back. The cabbie takes her bags, and she crashes into the backseat, yelping as raindrops run down her back. She brushes water from Timmy's cap and wrings the ends of Tammy's hair as both of them howl and giggle. She hears the trunk door slam, and then the cabbie lurches into the front seat, shaking his head like a wet dog.

"We're all going to float to Timbuktu if this doesn't let up," he chuckles. "You going far, ma'am?"

He looks at her in the rearview mirror. His eyes skip downward to her bruised neck. Lainie doesn't flinch: let truth pour, let freedom rise.

"Somewhere I can rent a car. You know a place?"

"The one by the airport is the biggest." His voice is softer now. "If you're aiming to get a car without a reservation, I mean. If you're aiming to leave quick."

Lainie consults his identification card: Robert Nathaniel De Castro.

"Yes, Mr. De Castro. Thank you."

The cab pulls from the depths of the curb and starts down the middle of the road.

"Apologies for the crawl. Little tricky on the roads today. But don't you worry. I'll get you where you're going, safe and sound."

"It's all right. I don't mind."

"You look happy. The three of you. That's good. Some people, a little rain falls, they get a little wet, it ruins their whole day. Earlier on, dispatch sent me to pick up this joe, take him to this industrial park over by Bethlehem Steel. Second time I've took this joe there. There's not a thing over there—not a thing. I circled around to check on him. I was kind of worried, you know? And there he was, sitting on a concrete block in the rain. Now *there's* a joe who doesn't look happy. There's a joe who could use a rental car, you know? Looked like he was waiting for the world to end. From the look on his face, I half believed it would, too."

Lainie smiles. The cabbie keeps talking, a pleasant distraction. The children have their faces pressed to the windows, and she rests her chin on Tammy's sweet-smelling scalp. Outside, it's as if the cab has run off a cliff and is sinking into the sea. To survive under so much water, she thinks, she'll have to learn to breathe inside it, to adapt into a different kind of creature. Strangely enough, she's confident that she can. The world is rampant with creeks, streams, rivers, ponds, lakes. She'll swim through as many as it takes to find the right ocean for them, even if it takes so long she has to grow flippers.

19

RAIN DROPS LIKE wet cement. Hoffstetler's umbrella carves out a small, dry column eddying with his own breath. It looks like smoke, feels like he's being burned at the stake. Anything beyond the umbrella is difficult to see: gray breath, gray rain, gray concrete, gray gravel, gray sky. But he knows where to look, and after an anxious eternity, exhaust fumes, one more layer of gray, rise along the path. The black Chrysler sharks through the water.

Hoffstetler wants to dive into the heated leather backseat, but even the fruition of an eighteen-year mission doesn't mean the riddance of asinine protocol. He picks up his suitcase, stands from the concrete block, and bounces upon the balls of his feet, woozy with excitement. He's so close now, so close to shaking the trembling hand of Papa, to wrapping both arms around Mamochka, to making amends for the life he's lived by starting to live a better one.

The driver's door, as usual, is thrown open with a clack. The Bison, as usual, steps from the running car, his black suit complemented by a black umbrella. Then, something unusual: The passenger door, too, opens, and a second man exits beneath the spreading wings of his own umbrella. He shivers in the cold, shrugs himself more snugly into a scarf that threatens to flatten his boutonniere. Hoffstetler feels a dropping sensation, as if he'd slid off his concrete block to find no ground at all beneath.

"Zdravstvujtye," Leo Mihalkov says. "Bob."

The rain against Hoffstetler's umbrella is deafening; he tells himself sounds cannot be relied upon. *Zdravstvujtye* is a cold greeting, and *Bob*, instead of *Dmitri*? Something has gone wrong.

"Leo? Are you here to—"

"We have questions," Mihalkov says.

"A debriefing? In the rain?"

"One question, really. It will not take long. When you injected the asset with the solution, how did it react before it died?"

Hoffstetler is still pinwheeling through a vortex. He wants to reach out for his concrete block, the Chrysler's grille, anything to save himself, but if he lets go of the umbrella, he'll drown in all the water. He tries to think. The silver solution, what might it have been? He should know; this is his field. Surely one ingredient was arsenic. Was another hydrogen chloride? Could there have been a scintilla of mercury? And what ruin would such a cocktail wreak upon the Devonian's anatomy? If only the thrum of rain weren't so disorienting, he might be able to figure it out. Instead, there is no time. All he can do is blurt and pray.

"It was instant. The asset bled. Profusely. Died right away."

Rain falls. Mihalkov stares. The ground bubbles like lava.

"That is correct." Mihalkov's voice is gentler now, pitched for a booth at the back of the Black Sea Restaurant, soft in the storm's kettledrums. "You have made your country proud. You always have. You will be remembered. Very few can say that. Not even I will be able to say it when my own time comes. In that way, I envy you."

A KGB man like Mihalkov would have detected the slow-motion closing of this mousetrap a decade earlier, but Hoffstetler only sees it now. Hadn't he insisted to the Devonian that he didn't possess true intelligence? He's spent too much time in America for Moscow to be comfortable with him back on Soviet soil. All that has ever mattered is that his mission reach completion. To believe anything else was reveling in fantasy. His mama and papa are likely alive as promised, but only as collateral. Now, they will be eliminated, shot through the skull, their bodies weighed with rocks to sink into the Moskva River. Hoffstetler says good-bye to them, quickly, and that he's sorry, frantically, and that he loves them, desperately, all in the second before the Bison lifts from his hip a revolver.

Hoffstetler cries out and, on instinct, hurls his umbrella in the direction of the Bison, and before he hears the shot, the umbrella blacks out the world, a singularity swallowing the man, the gun, the rain, all of it. These are trained killers, though, and he a bungling academic, and what feels like an iron fist whacks his jaw and what feel like hot stones explode from his face. Teeth, he thinks. He's spinning now, cheeks ballooned with blood, tongue sludgy with splattered flesh.

Now he's on the ground. Blood gushes from his mouth in a single splash, the upending of a bowl of tomato soup. Cold air lances through his face from left to right, an odd feeling. He's been shot through the cheek. Mama would be so upset, her little boy disfigured, his nice straight teeth turned to rubble. He tries to raise himself to his knees, thinking that if he shows Mihalkov the damage done, he might leave it at that, but his head weight is all off, and his knees slip in the mud, and he is on his back, the rain coming at his eyes like silver spears.

The Bison's black form, still holding his umbrella, occludes all light. He looks down with the same void of personality as ever, and aims the revolver at Hoffstetler's head. The bang, Hoffstetler thinks, is oddly muffled for being the shot that kills him. Stranger yet is how it's the Bison who recoils. There is a second bang, and the umbrella falls from the Bison's hand, on top of Hoffstetler, like soil being pitched into an open grave, and it takes a moment for Hoffstetler to dig his way out and prop himself on his elbows, the rain sluicing a hot mix of blood and saliva down his chest.

What he sees is the Bison's still, fallen body, the red puddle about him being thrashed into pink by the clobbering rain. Hoffstetler's eyes won't focus, but he can see shapes, Mihalkov's slender ovoid shuffling with a haste incongruous with his usual demeanor. He's pulling his own gun, that's clear even in abstract, but perhaps spoiled on lobster and caviar, he holds on to vanity too long, choosing not to drop his umbrella, and in those crucial few seconds, Hoffstetler's savior, whoever he is, rushes forward, his own weapon still smoking from the Bison's murder, and he's no amateur, either. The pistol is held with two hands, steady in the storm, and a single shot is all it takes.

Mihalkov is thrown against the car. Now he drops his umbrella. His gun, too. A circle of red blooms on his shirt, a second boutonniere. He dies instantly and is instantly forgotten, just as he predicted he would be. Hoffstetler squints through the cloudburst to watch the gunman kneel beside the body to make sure it's dead, then bolt upright and move, with spiderlike speed, toward Hoffstetler. It is the rain that obscures the man's identity until he looms over Hoffstetler. It is also, Hoffstetler supposes, disbelief.

"Strickland?" His voice is mushy, lispy. "Oh, thank you, thank you."

Richard Strickland reaches down, loops the thumb of his free hand into the hole in Hoffstetler's cheek, and pulls. Pulls so hard Hoffstetler's whole body is dragged through the mud. Pain arrives belatedly, full-fleshed and muscular from under a blanket of shock, and Hoffstetler screams, feeling the jagged rip of his cheek, and screams again, and keeps screaming, until the mud being plowed by his shoulder fills his eyes and his mouth and he is blind, and mute, and then nothing at all.

20

RECLAIMING WAKEFULNESS IS leaping into a nightmare. A thunderous roar subsumes everything. Hoffstetler's eyes whirl upward, expecting needles of rain, but there is a tin roof, hence the roar. He's on a concrete porch, some sort of outbuilding. He sees thick plaits of rain pound crumbled brick and oxidized steel. He's still in the industrial park. A shadow lurches across his vision. He blinks liquid from his eyes—rain, blood? It's Strickland, pacing the length of concrete. He's gripping something small, a medicine bottle. He upends it over an open mouth, but it's empty. He curses, whips the bottle into the rain, stares down at Hoffstetler.

"You're awake," Strickland grunts. "Good. I've got things to do."

He squats down. Instead of that orange cattle prod Strickland brings everywhere, he's got a gun, and he pulls the slide and noses it into Hoffstetler's right palm. The barrel is cold and wet, a puppy's nose, Hoffstetler thinks.

"Strickland." As soon as Hoffstetler says it, his mangled cheek, all those severed nerves, scream to life. "*Richard*. It hurts. The hospital, please—"

"What's your name?"

He's been lying for two decades, it's instinct: "Bob Hoffstetler. You *know* me."

The gun discharges. A bullet into cement sounds surprisingly rubbery, a resounding *thwap*. Hoffstetler's hand feels swatted. He lifts it. There is a tidy, singed hole through the center of the palm. His instinct is to contract the fingers to see if they still work, for there are thousands of book pages still to flip, scores of analyses yet to write, but instead he revolves it. The exit wound is a ragged starburst serrated by flaps of skin. Blood vessels drape from the hole. He knows it is about to bleed; he presses it against his chest.

Strickland pins Hoffstetler's other palm with the gun.

"Your real name, Bob."

"Dmitri. Dmitri Hoffstetler. Please, Richard, please."

"All right, Dmitri. Now give me the name and ranks of the strike team."

"The strike team? I don't know what—"

The gun blasts again, and Hoffstetler screams. He brings his left hand into his chest without looking at it, though he can't ignore the puff of smoke exhaling from the burnt flesh. His hands, what are left of them, clasp on to each other, while actions Hoffstetler might never again make race through his head: feed himself, bathe himself, clean himself after using the toilet. He's sobbing now, his tears funneling into the hole in his cheek and gathering salty on his tongue.

"Now look, Dmitri," Strickland says. "Those guys who came to pick you up, someone's going to notice they're gone. Things are moving fast now. There's nothing I can do about that. So I'm going to ask again."

Hoffstetler feels the hard barrel of the gun screw into his kneecap.

"No, no, please, no, Richard, please, please."

"Names and ranks. Of the strike team that took the asset."

Through the red eruptions of pain, Hoffstetler understands. Strickland believes the Soviets stole the Devonian. Not a single infiltrator like Dr. Hoffstetler, either, but some penetration unit toting high-tech tools as they wriggled through air ducts to collar their quarry. A strange sound escapes Hoffstetler's throat. It must be a bleat of pain, he thinks, but then another one escapes and he recognizes it as a laugh. It's *funny* what Strickland thinks. And here, as the wick of his life burns toward bottom, he can't think of any more surprising, and welcome, sound on which to end. He drops his jaw and lets the laughter peal, bubbling out blood, slushing out pebbles of tooth.

Strickland's face goes red. He shoots, and Hoffstetler screams, and he can see from the bottom of his vision the bottom half of his leg sliding across concrete, but his scream mutates right back into laughter, and he's so proud, and Strickland's lips peel back and more gunshots follow, his other knee, both elbows, his shoulders, pain detonating until it is not pain at all, just a pure, raw state of being that amplifies the fermata he's chosen as his final one: laughter. The jolly sound rings from his mouth, the hole in his cheek, the new holes all over his body. Strickland has stood up, is unloading his clip into Hoffstetler's stomach.

"Names! Ranks! Names! Ranks!"

"Ranks?" Hoffstetler laughs. "Janitors."

Hoffstetler feels a shot of regret like one more bullet—perhaps he shouldn't have said that—but he's too light-headed to think. The stew of his guts runs down the sides of his torso, steam rising from his entrails to curl before Strickland, little fists of protest. He is twirling backward and downward, moving rapidly after a lifetime rooted behind lecterns and desks, and still, stubbornly, he's a scholar till the end, the words of his favorite philosopher, Pierre Teilhard de Chardin—who but a career academic has a favorite philosopher?— bleeding through the haze. *We are one, after all, you and I. Together we suffer, together exist, and forever will recreate each other.* Yes, that's it! A lifetime spent alone doesn't matter, for he's not alone here at the end. He is with you, and you, and you, and he wouldn't have noticed any of it if not for the Devonian. Here is the ultimate emergence, quickened by sacrifice: finding God, that mischievous imp, hiding where we least expected, not in a church, not on a slab, but inside us, right there next to our hearts.

21

WHAT WAS ZELDA doing in the seconds before her front door was kicked in? Before the wood securing the dead bolt disintegrated into daggers and left the chain lock dangling like a mugger-torn necklace? She thinks she was cooking. She often does before heading to work, stocking Brewster with a day's worth of food. She sniffs bacon, butter, brussels sprouts. There's music, too, a deep-throated crooner. She must have been listening to it. She wonders if she'd been enjoying herself, if she'd been happy. It seems vital to remember these details, for she's certain they will be her last.

Until now, the most surreal sight of Zelda's life was the asset from F-1 staring back at her from Elisa's laundry cart. It had been so incongruous, that fearsome, brilliant beast situated inside a gray, driveling bed of soiled rags. Even that vision, though, pales against this: Richard Strickland, that horrid man from work, bug-eyed, drenched with rain, spattered with blood, and holding a gun in her living room.

Brewster where he always is when work is scarce, in the Barcalounger at full recline, socked feet propped on the leg rest, a can of beer in one loose fist. Strickland blocks the TV, and Brewster scrutinizes him in mild perturbation, as if the ghoul had appeared behind Walter Cronkite's news desk instead of inside their duplex. Strickland snorts and spits a flume of spit and rain and blood. He steps over it, smirching the clean carpet with the flat pancakes of mud adhered to the bottom of his shoes.

Zelda doesn't need to ask why any of this is happening. She lifts her hands before her. She finds she is holding a spatula.

"Nice home you have here." Strickland's voice is garbled.

"Mr. Strickland," she pleads, "we didn't mean any harm, I swear."

He frowns at the walls, and for an instant Zelda can see her cheerful decorations through the man's ferocious red eyes: mendacious trifles, mawkish mementos, idiotic knickknacks commemorating a happy life that could have never been all that happy. Strickland flicks his wrist lazily. The gun barrel smashes the glass of a framed photograph, a lightning-shaped crack splitting the face of her mother.

"Where'd you put it?" He staggers drunkenly. "Basement?"

"We don't have a basement, Mr. Strickland. I swear."

He slides the gun along a shelf of porcelain figurines. One at a time they drop, shattering on the floor. Zelda flinches with each one: the little accordion boy, the big-eyed deer, the Happy New Year angel, the Persian cat. Just baubles, she tells herself, without real significance, except it's a lie, they *are* significant, they are three decades of evidence that she has, on occasion, saved enough money to purchase herself something frivolous, something that simply looked nice, exceptions to the hard rules of knotty steaks, generic cereal, government cheese.

Strickland swivels, his muddy heel grinding porcelain, and points the pistol at her like an accusing finger.

"*Sir*, Mrs. Brewster. You got a real problem with names."

"Brewster," says Brewster. Hearing his name stirs him. "That's me."

Strickland doesn't look at him but waggles his head. "Oh. Right. Zelda Fuller. Zelda D. Fuller. Old Delilah." He lopes from the wall, halving the distance to Zelda so quickly she drops the spatula. "You never let me finish the story." He swings his gun arm, obliterating a ceramic vase once belonging to Zelda's grandmother. "Samson, as I remember it, betrayed by Delilah, blinded and tortured by the Philistines, at the very last second is saved. God saves him." He punches the gun through cabinet glass, pulverizing her mother's good china. "Why's he saved? Because he's a good man, Delilah. A man of principle. A man who, down to his last little fucking ounce of energy, is trying to do the right thing."

He backhands the stovetop beside Zelda, flipping a pan and shooting bacon grease atop Zelda's sign language handbook. The grease sizzles and burns holes through the pages. Zelda feels a blast of indignation. She darts her eyes over her spoiled home, the path of crude destruction doing its best to destroy the memories of every struggle she has overcome. Strickland's a couple of feet away. The gun might swipe her face next. It doesn't matter: She lifts her chin as high as she can. She will not be frightened. She will not give up her friend.

Strickland leers at her. A white froth that looks like upchucked aspirin has gathered in the corners of his lips. Slowly, he displays his left hand. Despite the stupefying terror, Zelda recoils from the repellent sight. She hasn't seen these fingers since she and Elisa had found them on the lab floor. Now the bandage is gone and the operation is exposed as a failure. The fingers are the glossy black of rotten bananas, inflated to the point of rupture.

"God gives Samson back all his strength," Strickland says. "Gives him back all his power. So that Samson can bring ruin raining down on all the Philistines. He takes hold of the columns of the temple. Like so."

Strickland stashes the gun in his armpit so that he can pinch the two dead fingers.

"And then? He breaks them."

Strickland tears off the fingers. They detach as if perforated, with a series of light pops—just like snapping beans, Zelda thinks before screaming. She hears a thud, Brewster dropping his beer, and a zing, the Barcalounger springing to starting position. Strickland's eyebrows lift in surprise at the brown fluid that geysers two inches from the finger holes before dribbling down his hand like slopped gravy. He considers the two black sausages he's still holding, and drops them on the kitchen floor. From one of the fingers pops a wedding band.

"It's Elisa," Brewster blurts. "Elisa what's-her-name. The mute. She's the one that has it."

The only sounds are the rustle of rain coming through the open door, the yammer of the television, and the soft glug of beer emptying onto the carpet. Strickland turns. Zelda reaches for the stove to keep herself upright, then shakes her head at her husband.

"Brewster, don't—"

"She lives over a movie theater," he continues. "That's what Zelda says. The Arcade. Just a few blocks north of the river. Easy trip from here. Five minutes, I bet."

The weight of the gun appears to double. Zelda watches it hitch downward until it points at the floor.

"Elisa?" Strickland whispers. "Elisa did this?"

He stares at Zelda, face drawn in shocked betrayal, arms shaking slightly as if in search of a hug to keep him aloft. Zelda doesn't know what to say or do, and so makes no sound or move. Strickland's face falls. He pouts at the finger smudged across the linoleum, as if longing to have it back. He breathes for a minute, shallow at first, then more deeply, before raising his head and squaring his shoulders. Military bearing, Zelda guesses, is all this wrecked man has left.

He plods across the carpet, shoes dragging through the mud. He lifts the telephone as if it, too, is of cinder block weight, and dials as if through clay. Zelda stares at Brewster. Brewster stares at Strickland. Zelda hears the pip-squeak report of a man picking up on the other end.

"Fleming." Strickland's voice is so lifeless that Zelda shudders. "I was . . . I was wrong. It's the other one. Elisa Esposito. She's got the asset above the Arcade. Yes, the movie theater. Reroute the containment unit. I'll meet it there."

Strickland gingerly replaces the receiver into its cradle and turns around. He surveys the glass, the porcelain, the ceramic, the china, the paper, the flesh—so much detritus generated so quickly. His comatose manner suggests to Zelda that he'll never leave this spot, will become a fixture in her home that she'll have to glue back together along with the rest of the ruin. But Strickland is a wound watch. Cogs inside of him turn and he moves, shuffling between Brewster and the television and out the open door.

One more lurch and he's gone, melted into the rain.

Zelda bursts forward and reaches for the phone. Brewster, though, is out of his chair at last, and moves more rapidly than she's ever seen. The Barcalounger rocks and yowls, abruptly empty, and Zelda finds her husband's arm held crosswise over the phone.

"Brewster. Please move."

"You can't get involved. *We* can't get involved."

"He's going to her home. Because of you, Brewster! I need to warn her. He has a gun!"

"Because of me we saved our skins. They don't get your friend, who do you think they blame next? You think they're just going to forget? Forget the black folks who stuck their noses in? We're going to repair that door and we're going to pick up those . . . things he left on the floor, and we're going to sit down and watch TV. Just like normal people."

"I never should've told you. I never should've said a word—"

"You finish dinner; I'll find some seltzer to scrub the rug—"

"They love each other. Don't you remember? Don't you remember what that was like?"

Brewster's arm sags. But he does not abdicate the phone.

"I do remember," he says. "That's why I can't let you make that call."

His brown eyes, so often half-shut and glazed by television strobes, are wide and clear, and in them she can see the reflection of debris left behind by Strickland. In truth, she can see a lot more than that. She can see Brewster's own history of battling and losing, always losing but never quite quitting, not even when Zelda spins her risky fantasies of quitting Occam and starting her own business. In that way, Brewster is brave. He has survived. He's still here, surviving. He's a good man.

But she's a good woman, or wants to be, and that particular achievement is measured by the distance between the change bowl, where Brewster's car keys rest, and the gaping front door, and beyond that, the distance between the front door and Brewster's Ford snoozing in the rain. She knows she can make it; Brewster will be too stunned to follow. She knows she can make it to Elisa's, too, even in this Old Testament tempest. What she doesn't know is what good she can do once she gets there, or what will be the aftermath. But such things are always unknowable, aren't they? The world changes, or doesn't. You fight for the right things and be glad you did. That, at least, is the plan, the best one Zelda D. Fuller's got.

22

ELISA KNOWS EVERY leaf of her jungle, every vine, every stone, and detects no malice in the shadow that slides over her. She opens her warm, wet eyes, enjoying the playful resistance of droplets trying to keep individual eyelashes mated. They peel apart, one by one, reluctant and languorous. It is Giles, backlit by living-room light, standing over the tub, smiling gently, and she wonders if the hothouse mugginess of the room is to blame for the tears filling his eyes.

"It's time, dear," he says.

She winds her drowsy arms around the dozing creature, unwilling to recall, but unable to stop herself, either, how several hours ago, possibly several millennia, she'd knocked on Giles's door to beg of him the greatest, most terrible favor. She'd signed her request briskly so that the grief wouldn't prolong: unlock her apartment before midnight, rouse her from the tub, and ignore any protests she might make. The bathwater she lies in, she notices, has gone cold, yet she has no desire to leave it. It can't be that late already. It can't be. She's had all day, all night to say good-bye to him and she hasn't even begun.

Giles plants his hands to his knees in order to hunker down, but halts halfway. He's holding a long, thin paintbrush, fine-tipped for detail, and seems to have forgotten it. Now there's green paint all over one knee of his trousers. He chuckles, stows the brush into his breast pocket.

"I finished." He can't keep the pride from his voice, and Elisa is glad he doesn't. "It won't be the same thing as having him. Not even close. But I believe it's the closest anyone could ever come. And it's for you, Elisa. You'll have it to remember him by. Let me show it to you on our way out—show it to both of you. Now, please, sweetheart. It's late. Won't you take my hand?"

Elisa smiles, lost in awe over her friend's head of hair, his face's boyish brio, his skin's healthful hue. His aspect is tender, but resolute. She looks at his outstretched hand, the knuckle hair clotted with paint, the fingernails swathed in paint, the cuff of his sweater ringed in paint. She raises a hand from the water. The instant it leaves the creature's back, he bristles, holds her more tightly. Elisa hesitates, her hand occupying the midworld between her watery wedding bed and Giles's solid ground, and she doesn't know if she can bridge the gap.

There is a crash. Down on the street. It's close, against the building itself. And loud. Metal, glass, plastic, steam. Elisa feels the brunt in her body, a concussion in her lungs, and she knows, she *knows* she has lingered too long. Giles knows it, too: He reaches across worlds and snatches her wrist. Even the creature knows it: His claws protrude, scratching like a lover's fingernails across her naked back. They move in concert. Water sloshes over the tub rim. Plants topple from the sink. Cardboard trees swing from the walls. They have been found.

23

It's the rain's fault. Must be two inches deep, suctioning him toward the gutter. Lashing the windshield with dizzying ecliptics that make him misjudge the turn. The movie theater springs into view, its thousands of lights smudged like drizzled yellow paint. He cranks the wheel at the adjacent alley, relying on the ballyhooed power steering, but too late. The bashed-in back end muffs the simplest maneuvers, and his Caddy—his beloved teal Cadillac Coupe de Ville, two-point-three tons and eighteen and a half feet of palatial leisure, zero to sixty in ten-point-seven seconds, AM/FM stereo sound, crisp as a fresh dollar bill—rams into the side of the theater.

Strickland shoves his way out. He tries to shut the door, force of habit, but he's not used to missing two fingers. He misses the door entirely, his hand slicing through rain. He takes stock of the disaster. Front end smashed, back end smashed. The American dream demolished from both ends. It doesn't matter. He's the Jungle-god now, the monkeys ripping apart his stupid human skull. He stomps through ankle-deep puddles. A man with a name tag rushes at him from the box office, gesturing in dismay at the broken bricks strewn across the sidewalk.

In the jungle, this man is just a buzzing carapanã. Strickland lashes out with the Beretta, strikes him in the nose. A pennant of blood flaps before the rain splatters it to the sidewalk. Strickland stalks past the writhing body, hunts beneath the waterlogged glitz of the marquee bulbs. Finally, back in the alley, he spots it. An alcove, a door to the overhead apartments. Elisa, his voiceless vision, his hope of the future, his betrayer, his prey. The Caddy blocks the whole alley. He has to climb over the indented hood. The bifurcated engine spews steam, and Strickland pauses inside it. The heat of the Amazon, the leprous thrill, the warm viper squirm, the sweltering swirl of piranha, all of it picking him down to the hard, clean, sharp, efficient bone.

What's that he sees at the other end of the alley beneath a moth-flickered light? A white van missing its front bumper, painted with the words MILICENT LAUNDRY. Strickland pushes from the scorching steam and grins, feeling a million hard darts of rain bouncing off his skull.

24

THEY SWAY AT the top of the fire escape, overweight with the creature between them. Elisa wears the quickest of coverings, her ratty pink bathrobe and the first shoes she saw, Julia's silver-encrusted specials, which she grabbed like talismans, and sure enough she slips, her top half pitching over the guardrail. The creature, draped in a blanket that barely hides him, pulls her from the brink. Below, Elisa sees the Pug. Also below, a car wreck, a goliath green machine wedged between alley walls, blocking the Pug's only exit path. Directly beneath them, out of view, she hears the knob of the Arcade Apartments being throttled, then the loud whacks of a shoe kicking the door, then a blast so loud all the raindrops freeze in place for one second, red light from the gunpowder flash transforming each drop into the blood of an expiring world.

The man's footsteps race upstairs. Giles, in turn, pulls Elisa down the fire-escape stairs. Their descent is the opposite of their inchworm climb with the creature a week ago, a madcap scramble, feet slipping and bodies colliding. Elisa can only tuck her head into the creature's neck and hold on to Giles's sopping sweater. He leads them onward, fast, undaunted. His new hair is slicked to his head and the paintbrush in his breast pocket bleeds green through his shirt. Her heart, if punctured, would bleed green, too, she thinks.

They reach the alley with broken hearts, but not one broken bone.

"We'll have to go on foot!" Giles cries over the downpour. "Just a few blocks! We can make it! No discussion! Go, go!"

The alley is its usual minefield of potholes. Elisa has never cared until now, when every other step plunges one of them shin-deep into oily water. There's no time to unbuckle the silver heels. They progress like damaged pistons, one up, one down. It's taking them far too long. Finally, they are at the crashed car, blinded by its headlights. Elisa crawls over the scrunched hood, then helps Giles hoist the creature. Giles is last, gathering the fallen blanket, wrapping it back around the creature, and shoving them onward. Elisa throws a look back at Mr. Arzounian, who gawks from the sidewalk, a hand pressed to his broken nose, perhaps believing that the strangest film he ever screened has come to life.

25

STRICKLAND SMELLS DEUS Brânquia. The memory floods back from the Amazon. The Gill-god's scent of brine and fruit and silt. In Occam's labs, antiseptic cleaners had blotted it out, and that had been a mistake. How stupid are humans to rob themselves of their most critical defensive sense? He knows who's to blame. The janitors. Their soap, bleach, and ammonia weren't wiping away the crud of this world. It was hiding a second world, an ascendant one, unless Strickland moves fast and puts an end to it.

Two apartment doors. He picks the first one. Doesn't bother with hands or feet. He points the Beretta, fires at the knob. The door is of lousier quality than Delilah Brewster's. The middle third of it disintegrates into sawdust. Strickland boots away the sharp-edged clingers and shoulders inside, gun raised, as prepared as he was at the bottom of the pile in Yeongdong to murder anything that breathes.

Deus Brânquia, colossal, beatific, resplendent, lords from the center of the cramped, dusty apartment. Strickland was wrong that he was ready. He isn't. He screams, and falls to his knees, and fires, and screams, and fires, and screams. Bullets pass right through Deus Brânquia. The Gill-god doesn't react. The gun goes hot in Strickland's hands. His arms tremble from the discharges. He throws himself back against the wall and covers his face. Deus Brânquia gazes down at him, patient and unchanged.

Strickland wipes rain from his eyes, begins to understand. This Deus Brânquia isn't real. Not in the sense of a thing that he can kill. It's a painting. Bigger than life, disorienting in detail. It *is* Deus Brânquia, somehow, as if painted with Deus Brânquia's blood and scales upon a rock dredged from Deus Brânquia's grotto. Strickland angles his head and the picture of the Gill-god seems to lift its arms, offering embrace. Some kind of visual trick. Strickland rejects the memory. It barges in anyway. His chasing of Deus Brânquia to the fateful bayou. His cornering of it in a cave. How it had reached out to Strickland, accepting his violence, anger, and confusion, understanding the obligation Strickland felt to the god he called General Hoyt. Strickland, in reply, had harpooned Deus Brânquia. Until now, he'd never noticed that he'd impaled himself on the harpoon's other end, binding the two of them forever, wound to wound.

26

ELISA CAN'T DENY that it is a form of miracle. The night she has no choice but to walk in public with the creature at her side is a night so brutally beset by sheeting rain that the streets are empty. Rogue automobiles idle in parking lots, drivers hoping to wait out a storm that they must suspect won't ever end. Woeful loners huddle under bus-station carapaces or store awnings watching the water rise ever higher over their shoes. The sidewalks are impassable, so Elisa and Giles walk along the highest available ground, the center of the road, the creature supported between them, his gills opened to the rain.

She can barely walk under the soaked housecoat. Giles, though revived in spirit, is still old. They are not going quickly enough. The man in the Arcade Apartments will catch them. Elisa throws a look behind her, waiting to hear the crunch of the ruined Cadillac rolling after them like a tank or see Richard Strickland part curtains of rain, grinning lazily, saying to her, once again: *I bet I could make you squawk. Just a little?*

If not Strickland, some good citizen will approach to help, and all will be lost just the same. Elisa looks about frantically, hair spitting rain. One more miracle is all they need. An abandoned car with the keys in the ignition, a maniac bus driver still running his route. Elisa starts signing to Giles: "Too slow." He isn't looking. She reaches past the creature, drags the sign across Giles's arm. He pats her hand, but it's not a response. He's trying to get her attention. He pulls to a sudden halt. The creature pitches, and Elisa nearly topples in her silver heels. Stopping is a terrible idea; she glares at Giles. But he is staring at the curb, eyes wide open against the downpour.

To their right, a dark mass gathers in the gutter. Mud, Elisa thinks, coughed up by inundated sewers. But the mass is moving. Swimming through cascades of rain. Scrabbling over wet pavement. Elisa identifies the creatures with a dull shock. Rats, pouring out of the flooded sewers. Far off, a horrified observer screams. The rats tussle past one another, pink tails twitching, spreading across the road like tar, wet pelts winking in the streetlights. Elisa looks left and it's the same, a black ripple of rodents. She feels Giles clutch at her hand and she holds her breath as the rats encircle them. The madness intensifies: The rats stop en masse, holding a five-foot distance, black eyes staring, noses twitching. Hundreds now, waiting for a signal.

"I confess, my dear," Giles says, "I do not know what to do."

Elisa feels the creature stir from beneath the soaked blanket. A single huge, taloned hand emerges, and though his body heaves in a struggle for breath, the hand is steady. It makes a smooth, curling gesture, a benediction, the rain gathering in his scaled palm. The field of soaked rats undulate in a collective shiver, one small body to the next, and a strange scritching noise rises to compete with the beat of rain. It is the scrape, Elisa realizes, of a thousand minuscule legs backpedaling across pavement. She wipes rain from her eyes, but there is no mistaking it.

The rats are parting, creating a path to let them pass.

The creature drops his hand and slumps so heavily that Elisa and Giles have to snap together to keep him from collapsing.

"'It ain't a fit night out for man or beast,'" Giles quotes, his voice trembling. "W. C. Fields." He swallows, nods at the road ahead. "Together, then, we go. Into the fray."

27

Molten tears blaze down Strickland's face, already burned from the Caddy's steam. He will not become a human again. Changing would be crawling back into the womb, voiding his whole history, confessing to a purposeless life. Impossible, no matter how badly he might want it. The monkeys shriek and he does what they say, forcing himself to look at Deus Brânquia. Mere paint, mere canvas. He stands, finds equilibrium. Yes, that's right. If he has to, he'll yank off another two fingers, a whole arm, his own head, anything to see the blood flow and prove which one of them is real.

Strickland passes through the splintered door into a hallway uproarious with rain, and faces the second apartment. Best to save bullets. Six or seven kicks and he's inside. It's worse than Lainie's unpacked boxes. It's a slovenly hole fit for vermin. That's all Elisa Esposito is. The second the Negro told him how Elisa had been raised in an orphanage, he should have known. No one has ever, will ever, or should ever want her.

He follows her smell into a cluttered bedroom. The wall over the bed is covered with shoes, many of which, to his shame, he recognizes. His cock responds, and he wants to rip it off the same as he did his fingers. Maybe later, when he comes back to watch the whole building burn. Deus Brânquia's smell is thick here, too. He hurries to the bathroom, finds a tub varnished in luminous scales. Little air-freshener trees cover every inch of wall. What in the holy hell happened here? The idea he's beginning to form disgusts him.

Strickland teeters into the main room. His vision spirals. They're not here. Somehow the asset got away. The Beretta grows heavy in his hand. It pulls him to the right, to the right, in one circle, then another. He's spinning. The detritus of Elisa's world, the world he once wanted, swirls into an ugly brown. He glimpses something, has just enough sense left to notice it. He has to jam the gun against a rattletrap table to halt the nauseating rotations.

A day-by-day calendar. Inked across today's date are the words *MIDNIGHT—THE DOCKS*. Strickland checks the clock above the table. Not quite twelve. There's still time. Still time if he can stop spinning, if he can run in a straight line. He snatches a phone from its cradle on the table, dials with a finger that looks long and insectile next to its missing brethren. Fleming picks up. Strickland tries to tell him to divert the containment crew, coming all the way from Occam, to the docks just down the street. He can't tell if his instruction succeeds. His voice no longer sounds like his own.

███████████████████████████████████████

████████████████

28

THE RATS WERE all she noted at first because they so outnumbered the rest. By the time she sets her foot on the jetty, her dazed eyes have accepted other subterrestrial dwellers among the palpitating legion, predators and prey alongside one another in a cross-species peace that imitates that of Elisa and the creature. Matted squirrels, red-eyed rabbits, ponderous raccoons, sewage-stained foxes, bounding frogs, scampering lizards, glissading snakes, and, squirming beneath them all, a layer of worms, centipedes, and slugs. Insects churn above the rolling rodentia, a black stripe that persists even through the driving rain. On the periphery, overland animals have begun to arrive, too. Dogs, cats, ducks, a single mysterious pig, drawn forth as if to bow before a god that they, in their beastly hearts, had always awaited.

The animals peel from the jetty to let the trio pass. The pier is as short as Elisa remembers, maybe forty feet, though that is plenty. The thirty-foot depth mark has been far surpassed; only the top of the stanchion is visible. The river level is mere inches below the jetty and it bucks in the storm, spilling across the planks. Here it is, then. All elements are aligned. Yet Elisa stands still, rain drilling into her flesh. Her breaths come in scraping jags; she realizes that they resemble the creature's labored pull of air through his flapping gills. She feels a hand on her wet back.

"Hurry," Giles whispers.

She cries, but so does the sky; the whole universe sobs, the people and animals and land and water, all weeping for a unity nearly sealed between two divergent worlds, but that could not, in the end, be sustained. Elisa's arms dangle at her sides and she feels the cool, damp scales of the creature's hand slide against hers. They are holding hands. For one final time, they are joined. Elisa looks at his beautiful face through the prison bars of rain. Great onyx eyes gaze back, betraying no inclination to take to water, despite how the absence will kill him. He will stand here forever if that's what she wants.

So she walks. To save his life, she walks. One step, two steps, wading through the sloshing water. Over the storm's blast, she can make out the chattering retreat of the beasts, as well as the splashing footsteps of Giles, her sole follower. Forty feet doesn't take long. Elisa finds herself at the end, the very end. The square toes of her silver shoes align to the edge of the jetty. The creature's feet line up as well, his toe claws jutting over the perimeter. Inches below, black water spumes. Elisa takes a deep, salty breath and turns to him. Gusts of apocalyptic wind catch her pink bathrobe and rip free the belt, and the coat flutters about her naked body like butterfly wings.

He glows green. His light lanterns through the rain, pulsing like a lighthouse. Even now, Elisa's breath is stolen away. She tries to smile. She nods at the water. The creature surveys the depths; his green glows brighter and she sees his gills yawn in yearning. He looks back at her, liquid coursing from his face. Can he cry? She believes he can, though his sobs do not come from his chest. Thunder rumbles from above: That is his cry. He releases her hand, slowly, gingerly. He signs her name, his favorite word, E-L-I-S-A, then folds his own webbed hand so that he can gesture the index finger from his chest to the water. He then turns the finger in a counterclockwise circle.

The signs, though clumsy, read: "Go alone?"

The broken parts of Elisa's heart break further. For how long has the creature been the last of his kind? How long has he swum alone? She can't let herself be deterred. She nods, points at the water. He signs again, a pinching gesture: "No." She flings her arms downward in frustration. He keeps signing, faster now, he's learned so much: "I need"—but she doesn't let him finish, she can't bear it, she needs, too, but their needs can't matter, and she pushes him, and his body twists toward the water, nearly falling. His blue eyeshine swirls with green. His shoulders curl inward. He stares down at the water. He turns to face it. She is glad, for she doesn't want him to see her fingers, which, though kept at her side, act on their own, signing, "Stay, stay, stay, stay, stay."

"Elisa," Giles cries. "Elisa!"

29

THE VERÃO, THE dry season, is over. The wet season, with its secret name, its secret purpose, has returned. There is no mistaking it. Rats, lizards, snakes, flies, a world made wholly of living, breathing things. They glint evil eyes, open fanged mouths. They come at him. The monkeys in his head shriek their orders, each of them just as secret. He's a loyal solider. He is the asset, *their* asset. He roars and runs, kicking and thrashing against rabid squirrels clinging to his pants, manic rats biting into his calves. They can't stop him. He, Jungle-god, delivers punishment, cracking brittle skulls beneath his heels, throttling tiny, squealing necks with his hands.

Then he's on the jetty, tearing off a last rat along with a chunk of his thigh. Waves smash into the walkway, walls of water rising on either side, a military saber arch. The black tunnel focuses him upon its end. There stands Elisa Esposito and Deus Brânquia, their backs to him, gazing down at the river's vortex. Strickland covers the distance in seconds, his feet sure despite the river's spray. There's an old man, too, off to the side. Strickland recognizes him. It's the driver of the laundry van. It's all coming together now. Oh, what a pleasure this will be.

The old man sees Strickland and cries, *Elisa!* But Strickland is coming too fast. The old man does the last thing Strickland expects, rushing him. Strickland has to stop, his foot slipping across the slick planks, the whorling torrent. He's off-balance. All he can do is swing the Beretta. It cracks the side of the old man's head. He goes down hard and lands badly, his torso rolling off the side of the jetty and into the raging waters. There is a suspenseful second, the old man trying to grip the wet wood. He can't do it. He drops headfirst into the barbed waves.

Now Elisa sees him. Strickland rights himself, aims the gun at Deus Brânquia, ten feet away. But his eyes flick toward Elisa. She's wearing next to nothing, an untied housecoat. And shoes. Of course, shoes. Sparkling silver heels meant to torture him. This temptress, this jezebel, this deceiver. She was the true Delilah all along, distracting him from her scheme. Instead, he'll make her serve as witness to Deus Brânquia's end. Starting now, the Gill-god is of the past. And he, Richard Strickland? It's like the Cadillac salesman said: *The future. You look like a man who's headed there.*

He's satisfied to be right about one thing. He does, at the end, make the mute girl squawk. It's her only way to warn Deus Brânquia of the bullet about to be fired. She gulps a water-swirled breath and, her neck veins drawing taut, screams. Strickland is certain it's the first to ever expel from her weakling throat. It's a little sound, the breaking of whatever is left of her voice box, the same croak the vulture chained to the *Josefina* made when it choked on Henríquez's logbook.

The noise is unique enough to pierce the howling squall. Deus Brânquia turns. Lightning strikes, slashing white through the Gill-god's blue-green glow. But it is too late. Strickland, man of the future, wields a weapon of the future. He squeezes the trigger, once, twice. In gale winds and pelting showers, it sounds tidy. Pop, pop. Two holes appear in Deus Brânquia's chest. The creature wobbles. Drops to its knees on the jetty's edge. Blood spouts outward, mixes with rain.

After such an epic hunt, across two continents, against so formidable a foe, it's disappointing. It is, however, the nature of the hunt. Sometimes, your prey rages in death, becomes legend. Other times, it winks away, becomes nothing stronger than a fairy tale. Strickland shakes the rain from his face, aims at Deus Brânquia's bowed head, and pulls the trigger.

30

IN THAT INSTANT, Elisa knows the frenzy that makes a man cover a grenade for his fellow soldiers, that makes mothers sacrifice their lives for their children, that makes anyone in love impatient to lose everything so that their loved one can carry on. But there is no opportunity. She raises an arm, as if she could ward off the bullet by gesture alone. It is as far as she gets. Everything happens at once.

Strickland's body wrenches to the left at the moment of firing. The thin, sharp end of a paintbrush has been impaled through his left foot. Just behind him is Giles, resurfaced and clinging to the edge of the jetty. It is the person who dragged Giles free of the current who has taken the paintbrush from his pocket and stabbed. It is Zelda, incredibly Zelda, materialized here at world's end, sprawled across the walkway, drenched and muddy, her fist still clenched around the brush, her hand gone green from the drizzling paint.

Strickland reaches for his foot, stumbling to a kneel. Hope punches Elisa in the chest. Then, she realizes, it isn't hope at all. She falls to her own knees, mirroring Strickland. Her thighs quake and she clenches them with both hands, not wishing to fall any farther. It's no good. She pitches forward, bracing herself in a push-up pose. River water splashes across her face, over her fingers. The water is black, it is blue, it is purple, it is red. She looks sharply down at her chest. There is a neat bullet hole directly between her breasts. Blood spurts out, onto the planks, and is instantly washed away.

Her elbows are paper. She wilts. Her vision rolls over. She sees an upside-down world: charcoal clouds with lightning-bolt capillaries, a shower of racing rain, police lights flashing against nearby boats, Strickland scrabbling for his gun, Zelda pounding her fists on his back, Giles back on the dock and reaching for Strickland's ankle. Elisa sees green, and blue, and yellow; then faster, violet, and crimson, and umber; then faster, peach, and olive, and canary; and faster, every color known and unknown, outshining the storm. It is the creature, the magnificent grooves of his body phosphorescent, and he has caught her in his arms, his blood pouring into hers, hers spattering into his, both of them connected by the liquid of life even as both of them are dying.

31

A WAVE NUDGES the Beretta toward the depths, but Strickland is quicker. He crawls for it, seizes it, joins both hands to hold it tight. Now to rid himself of the twin rats nipping at him. He rolls onto his back, kicks the old man in the face. He shoves Delilah Brewster several feet down the jetty. Strickland is bitten all over, spurting blood from his foot, blinded by the downpour. Still he props himself on an elbow, opens his mouth to the rain. It is his rain now. He brings himself to a sitting position, gasping water into his lungs, and cranes his neck.

Deus Brânquia fountains with color. It stares at Strickland through blades of rain, past Elisa, who is cradled in its arms. Slowly, it lowers her to the walkway, where waves lick against her. The Gill-god stands. Strickland blinks, attempts to comprehend. It's been shot twice in the chest. And yet it stands? And yet it walks? Deus Brânquia continues down the jetty, its body a torch in the night, an infinite thing that Strickland, stupid man, believed he could make finite.

Strickland tries anyway. He fumbles the gun upward, fires. Into Deus Brânquia's chest. Into its neck. Into its gut. Deus Brânquia wipes a hand across the bullet holes. The wounds dribble away along with the rain. Strickland shakes his head hard enough to spatter water. Is it the freshly filled river that gives it such strength? Is it the gathered beasts supplying their master with life force? He'll never know. He isn't meant to know. He's crying. The same big, ragged sobs he told Timmy he wasn't ever allowed to cry. He lowers his face to the jetty, ashamed to meet the Gill-god's everlasting eyes.

Deus Brânquia kneels before him. With a single claw, it hooks the trigger guard of the gun, gently removing it from Strickland's grip and lowering it to the dock. A spate of black water explodes across the jetty, steals the gun, swallows it down. With the same claw, Deus Brânquia tilts Strickland's face upward by the tender underside of his chin. Strickland sniffles, tries to keep his eyes closed, but he can't. Their faces are inches apart. Tears stream down his cheeks, across the bridge of Deus Brânquia's claw, down the brilliant scales. Strickland opens his mouth and he is glad, here at the end, to hear that his own voice has returned.

"You *are* a god," Strickland whispers. "I'm sorry."

Deus Brânquia cocks its head to the side, as if considering the plea. Then, with a single, casual motion, it moves its claw from Strickland's chin, touches it to Strickland's neck, and draws the claw across his throat.

Strickland feels opened. It isn't a bad feeling. He has been closed to too much, he thinks, and for too long. There is a lightness to his head. He looks down. Blood is jetting from his slit throat, spilling down his chest. It empties him of everything. The monkeys. General Hoyt. Lainie. The children. His sins. What remains is Richard Strickland, the way he began, the way he was born, a vessel containing nothing but potential. He is falling backward. No, it is Deus Brânquia, guiding him down, tucking him into water as soft and warm as blankets. He is happy. His eye sockets fill with rain. Water is all he can see. It is the end. But he laughs as he dies. Because it is also the beginning.

32

GILES SEES CIVILIZATION reassert itself from nature's wilds. Vehicles with histrionic lights and infant bawls. Men in uniforms and rain gear, sprinting for the docks, hands steadying the jounce of equipment belts. They skid to a halt before the beasts massed at the foot of the jetty, not as many as before, but enough to impress. Civilians have also begun to gather, people who wouldn't brave a storm like this except to seek out the incredible colors they saw radiating from the docks, some madman, maybe, launching fireworks in the downpour.

He coughs water from his lungs. He ought to be dead. He recalls striking the river bottom and paddling furiously to resurface, only to be clenched by a riptide and tugged toward the bay. A hand had grasped his wrist, though, pulling him back to the jetty. Their palms should have slipped from each other's, but this hand had a good texture for gripping, calloused by scouring pads and perpetual pushes of brooms and mops, a hand rather like Elisa's.

It had been the black woman Giles had glimpsed at the Occam loading dock, their clandestine colluder. How she was here he couldn't begin to guess, but then again, nothing about the woman added up: round, middle-aged, given to appearing at momentous junctures, driven by some unlimited cache of courage. The second he had a hold on the jetty, she'd unsheathed the paintbrush from his pocket and attacked the man with the gun. Now that man is dead, his throat pumping so much blood even the whipping waves can't disperse all of it.

Giles struggles to an elbow. The woman pulls his shivering body close to hers. Their heaving breaths equalize as they squint through the spray to watch the creature stand, flick the man's blood from his claw, and walk on webbed feet to Elisa's collapsed body, his glorious lights dimming with every step.

"Is she . . . ?" Giles croaks.

"I don't know," the woman says.

"Put your hands up!" men shout. The creature takes no heed. He lifts Elisa from the jetty. The shouts change to *"Put the woman down!"* but these have no better effect. The creature stands in place for a moment, black against the river foam and sterling rain, a tall, strong shape at the edge of America. Giles is too exhausted, too heavied by grief to cry out, but he mouths the word *good-bye*, both to the creature whose healing touch gave him the strength to resist drowning

tonight, and to his best friend, who gave him the strength to resist drowning for the past twenty years.

Without a sound, without a splash, the creature, holding Elisa, dives into water.

Men come at last, their shoes splashing up the jetty. The ones with firearms go all the way to the end, pinning their hats to their heads in the gusty winds while trying to follow the flashlight beams being shone at the waves. The ones with medical kits drop down first beside the dead man, and second beside Giles and the woman. A medic runs his hands over Giles's head and neck, along his torso.

"Are you hurt?"

"Of course he's hurt," snaps the woman holding Giles. "We're all hurt."

Giles surprises himself by chuckling. He will miss Elisa. Oh, how he'll miss her, every night as if it's morning, every morning as if it's afternoon, every time his stomach rumbles because he has forgotten to eat. He loved her. No, that isn't right. He *loves* her. Somehow he knows that she isn't gone, nor will she ever be. And this woman? His savior? He might already love her, too.

"You must be Giles," she says as the medic examines her.

"And you," he says, "must be Zelda."

The absurdity of formal introduction under such apocalyptic settings makes both of them smile. Giles thinks of Elaine Strickland, who disappeared before he could tell her everything she had meant to him. He will not make that mistake again. He reaches out, takes Zelda's hand. Salt water slides between their palms and seals them together. She leans her head against his shoulder as the rain drums against them, melting them, or so it feels, into one being.

"Do you think . . ." Zelda begins.

Giles tries to help. "That they're . . ."

"Down there, I mean," she offers. "That they might . . . ?"

Neither can finish. That is all right; they both know the question as well as they know that, for them, there will be no definitive answer. Giles squeezes Zelda's hand and sighs, watching his plume of breath—still strong, he observes—dissipate beneath a shower that he believes might, at long last, be waning. He waits until after they are swaddled in hospital blankets, after they are in the back of the ambulance they insisted upon sharing, after he suspects Zelda has forgotten the question, before he offers his best guess at the answer.

33

ELISA SINKS. POSEIDON'S fist grabs her, rolls her back and forth like a crocodile rolls its prey. Twice she has pushed herself to the surface only to see Baltimore, her homeland, diminish to a piddling twinkle. She is shot, and can't kick, and slides under for the final time. Down here, it is dark. There is no air. There is only pressure, like dozens of hands pressing her flesh as if to staunch her wounds. Blood escapes anyway, spreading through the water, a scarlet gown to replace the natty bathrobe that has floated away.

Elisa parts her lips, lets cold water pour in.

From blackness he comes. She believes he is a school of glittering fish until each of the million points of light is revealed as one of his scales. He brings his own underwater sun, and by its radiance she watches him move in unimaginable ways. He is not inside the water, but rather part of it, walking straight through it as if down a side-walk, quite the trick, only to then rebel against gravity, pirouette like a flower caught in the wind. With perfect precision he meets her with a kiss to her head; he wraps his arms around her, enveloping her in his sea-sun. His wide palms slide up her back, crest her naked shoulders, and dive between her breasts. He then wiggles away to hold her by the sides, like she's a child on a bicycle she's only starting to learn.

Elisa blinks, her eyelids oaring aside pounds of water. The hole in her chest has been erased. The surprise is that she feels no surprise, only an easy, pleasant approval. She looks up to find the creature has swum off to her right, holding only to her hand. Elisa becomes aware that he is preparing to let go. She shakes her head, her hair aswirl like seaweed. She's not ready. She brings her free hand close to sign her apprehension, but human appendages are lousy at cutting through water. His hand unleashes hers, and she is falling, falling, falling, though it is tricky to say for sure in so black a void. Perhaps, in fact, she is rising, rising, rising. She kicks her legs. Julia's beautiful silver shoes tumble past her like exotic fish. She no longer needs them.

He emerges again from the deep. They stand before each other on nothing but water, new and naked, the ocean their Eden. His gills expand and contract. Elisa, too, breathes. She does not understand how, and doesn't care, for the water-air is wonderful! It tastes like sugar and strawberries, fills her with an energy she's never felt. She can't help it: She laughs. Bubbles rollick from her mouth and the creature playfully swats them. She reaches out, caresses his soft gills. She believes she could look at him forever.

And she might. Something inside her is beginning to expand. These are the parts, she realizes, that made the Matron, maybe the only person to know the truth, call her a monster. Elisa feels no hate for the woman; she realizes that, down here, hate has no purpose. Down here, you embrace your foes until they become your friends. Down here, you seek not to be one being, but all beings, and all at once, God and Chemosh and everything in between. The change in her isn't only mental. It's physical, of skin and muscle. Yes, she has arrived. She is full. She is perfect.

She reaches out to him. To herself. There is no difference. She understands now. She holds him, he holds her, they hold each other, and all is dark, all is light, all is ugliness, all is beauty, all is pain, all is grief, all is never, all is forever.

34

WE WAIT WE watch we listen we feel we are patient we are always patient but it is difficult the woman we love it takes her a long time it takes her so long to know to see to feel to remember and it is not happy to see her struggle it is not happy to see her with pain but we struggled too we all struggled and the pain and struggle are important the pain and struggle must happen if she is to heal as we all have healed as we have helped heal her and now it is happening it is happening there is understanding and it is beautiful she is beautiful we are beautiful and it is a good sight a happy sight the lines on her neck the lines she thought were scars but are not scars it is a good sight to see those lines split open for the gills to open for the gills to spread wide it is a happy sight and now she knows who she is who she has always been she is us and we speak together now we feel together now and we swim into the distance into the end into the beginning and we welcome all who are willing to follow we welcome the fish we welcome the birds we welcome the insects we welcome the four-legs we welcome the two-legs we welcome you ///

come with us

ACKNOWLEDGMENTS

Thanks to Richard Abate, Amanda Kraus, Ricardo Rosa, Grant Rosenberg, Natalia Smirnov, Julia Smith, and Christian Trimmer.